D0551330

the legacy

Caroline Bond was born in Scarborough and studied English at Oxford University before working as a market researcher. She has an MA in Creative Writing from Leeds Trinity University, and lives in Leeds with her husband and three children.

Also by Caroline Bond

The Forgotten Sister
The Second Child
One Split Second

the legacy

caroline bond

Published in hardback in Great Britain in 2021 by Corvus,
an imprint of Atlantic Books Ltd.

10 9 8 7 6 5 4 3 2 1

A CIP catalogue record for this book is available from the British Library.

Hardback ISBN: 978 1 83895 282 2
Trade paperback ISBN: 978 1 78649 928 8
E-book ISBN: 978 1 78649 927 1

Printed in Great Britain by TJ Books Limited, Padstow, Cornwall

Corvus
An imprint of Atlantic Books Ltd
Ormond House
26–27 Boswell Street
London
WC1N 3JZ

www.corvus-books.co.uk

To Alex, Rachel and Geena.

We promise not to include too many surprises in the will.

Chapter 1

Rachel Hewson was nervous – which was unlike her. In her twenty-six years as a solicitor she'd drafted innumerable wills and overseen the distribution of hundreds of thousands of pounds of assets: property, investments, jewellery, boats, shares in race horses and, in one memorable case, three fields of rare-breed pigs. During that time she'd witnessed all manner of behaviour by the family and friends of the deceased, from the truly appalling to the impressively magnanimous. She'd seen greed and generosity, meanness and big-heartedness, connivance and cooperation. A death tended to bring out the best, and the worst, in humanity – although, in her experience, most people didn't so much change as become more exaggerated versions of their true selves. But in all her years spent administering the last wishes of the dead, she'd never before been asked to put together a will like Jonathan Coulter's.

He'd phoned the firm, out of the blue, one morning in early June and asked *to be put through to a senior partner*. Rachel – who was the *only* senior partner at the firm, now Charles had finally retired – had taken the call. It was a short conversation, focused mainly on her availability to oversee the drafting of a new will, *as soon as practicably possible*. Mr Coulter had been adamant that she must personally conduct the whole process, *from beginning to end*, including working with the executors after his death. Rachel had reassured him on all counts, though she'd pointed out that it was difficult to commit to being available to assist the executors in their responsibilities, given that the date of 'implementation' was impossible to predict. His final question had been a surprisingly practical one. 'I presume you have a downstairs office we can meet in.' Rachel was able to confirm that wouldn't be a problem.

When Jonathan Coulter arrived at the offices of Greenwood Solicitors four days later, Rachel understood his ground-floor office request. Her new client was obviously seriously ill. He clattered into the reception area leaning heavily on a walking frame – the type with wheels, much favoured by old ladies who strung their shopping bags between the handles – but Jonathan Coulter was no old lady. He was a smartly dressed man in his late fifties/early sixties. He must, Rachel guessed, have been over six foot tall, though it was hard to tell, given his pronounced stoop – the result of him having to lean forward and steer the walker. It looked a very uncomfortable way of getting around. His movements as he headed towards Rachel were rapid, but unstable. The woman accompanying him, who was not introduced, stayed close behind, presumably ready to steady him, should she need to. He stuttered to an abrupt stop, raised himself nearly upright and extended his hand. As Rachel took it, she had to swiftly recalibrate, because Mr Coulter had no strength in his fingers. The resulting handshake was a light touch of palms and fingertips. It felt oddly intimate.

He grimaced. 'Sorry. It's the best I can do.'

'Hello, Mr Coulter.'

'Jonathan, please.'

Rachel smiled her acknowledgement. 'It's very nice to meet you. Please, come through.' She turned and led the way. The clatter of the walking aid against the hardwood floor was loud – an erratic syncopation of frame and dragged footsteps. She slowed her pace.

Once inside the room, Jonathan collapsed into the proffered chair, with evident relief, and shoved the frame away. 'Do me a favour, Lisa. Take this damn thing out with you, will you?'

'Lisa' grabbed hold of the contraption and backed out of the room, banging it against the paintwork on her way out. It was a small office, unsuited to cumbersome disability aids. As Lisa awkwardly pulled the door closed she said, 'Of course.' There was a beat. 'But, please, shout me when you're ready to leave.'

Jonathan bristled. 'Message received and understood. No dancing out under my own steam, I promise.'

With Lisa gone, he shifted his body around awkwardly, obviously trying to get comfortable. He lifted his right hand with his left and positioned it on the arm of the chair. Rachel waited, respectfully trying to avoid watching as he reassembled himself. The end result was surprising. Once seated and settled, Jonathan Coulter seemed to lose ten years in age and gain five inches in stature. His face grew smoother, the tension dropped away and he smiled. He really was quite a good-looking man, with a strong jaw and intelligent eyes. His voice, though breathless, was deep, his accent hard to pin down.

'Thank you for agreeing to our meeting today. I appreciate you fitting me in at such short notice. But, as you can see, getting my will sorted is something of a priority.'

Struggling to think of an appropriate response, Rachel pulled her notepad towards her and uncapped her pen. 'I'm listening.'

Which is what she'd done as Jonathan coolly and calmly laid out the plans for his estate after his demise. He was concise, reflective and, above all, rational. Rachel heard him out without interrupting – the same as she would any client – making a record of his wishes as he spoke. When he'd finished, she read back through her notes, buying time. Then she fulfilled her legal responsibilities by highlighting the difficulties inherent in his proposal and pointing out the potential consequences, intended and otherwise, of his approach. He listened politely – but respectfully, and very firmly, refused to change a thing or elaborate on his decisions.

By the end of their half-hour together, Rachel was in no doubt as to Jonathan's mental capacity, despite his very evident physical frailties. There was nothing left for her to do but fulfil his instructions.

That had been five months ago.

Now Jonathan was dead.

And within the hour his family would be arriving to hear his last will and testament.

Chapter 2

MEGAN PULLED the front door closed behind her, carefully. She didn't want Chloe to hear her leaving; she needed a little time to compose herself before the meeting at the solicitor's. It still felt wrong living in The View with Jonathan's youngest daughter. When Chloe had moved back home, just before Christmas – after Jonathan's symptoms had taken yet another turn for the worse – it had been positioned as a temporary arrangement. One designed to support Jonathan, help Megan and give Chloe some time to sort herself out – again. And although she couldn't deny that Jonathan had liked having his daughter around, Megan had not. For her, Chloe's presence had proved more of a strain than a help. Living under the same roof had certainly not brought the two of them any closer together. And now, in the wake of Jonathan's death, their very personal sorrow was only making that tension worse.

Hence Megan's need for half an hour on her own.

She walked up the driveway, glad to have escaped the claustrophobic confines of the house. The wind was a welcome shock. Cold, unforgiving. It roused Megan. When she reached the top of the drive she stopped and looked back.

The View. An almost-grand, late-Victorian villa, built – according to Jonathan – by one of the town's mayors for his son and family, in the days when nepotism was flaunted, and respected. The View epitomised solid, small-town wealth and ambition. It was a lovely house, with big rooms, high ceilings and ornate cornices. But it was the view out, as much as the space inside, that made the house special. From its vantage point, perched on the edge of the South Cliff, the views out across the bay were glorious. Megan had given up her life in Darlington, her friends, her job and her independence, to come and live with Jonathan in this large, looming house on the edge of a cliff, in a small seaside town, at the end of the line.

Five years.

So much happiness.

So much pain.

Had it been the right decision?

She was no longer sure.

The realisation that Jonathan was gone for ever thumped into her all over again, like a fist hitting a bruise, but she made herself keep moving. She turned onto Belvedere Avenue, leaving the house behind. Even buckled with grief, she knew that the sight and sound of the sea would be good for her soul. And her soul was sorely in need of something to soothe it.

When she reached The Esplanade she sat down on the first empty bench and looked out across the bay.

Jonathan was the first man to ever truly love Megan. He had made her feel simultaneously vulnerable and powerful; utterly confused and, at the same time, sure. She had known as soon as she met him, at a teachers' conference in a faceless business centre in Newcastle, that there was something between them and that, if she pursued it, it would lead somewhere exciting, but scary. He was, of course, totally wrong for her. A married man. Much older than her. A respected professional colleague. He was exactly what she did not want – and yet she had.

And he had wanted her.

That had been both the problem and the joy.

An attraction that led to a flirtation. Texts and emails that blossomed into deep, interesting conversations. A craving that led to sex. Sex that deepened and strengthened their connection. The emergence of a deep and abiding affection – which turned into love.

Megan took three deep, lung-filling breaths, trying to draw some of the calmness of the view inside herself. As much as she wanted to, she knew she couldn't stay where she was, clinging on to her memories of Jonathan. The clock was ticking. She had an appointment to keep.

The trouble was, she knew she was walking towards, not away from, more upset.

Jonathan's children, en masse. Her 'stepchildren' – in theory, but not in practice.

There were many reasons why Megan had never fulfilled the role of stepmother, not least because they already had a living, breathing and presumably loving mother. It had also been made painfully clear – by all three of them, in their own very different ways – that the last thing they wanted was the woman who had wrecked their parents' marriage 'playing Mum'.

Chloe, Noah and Liv.

Youngest to eldest.

Twenty-six, thirty-four, thirty-seven.

A Performing Arts graduate turned shop assistant. A travel rep turned hotel inspector. A star student turned A&E consultant.

'Underdog' to 'top dog'.

Shambles to success.

Jonathan's children.

There were so many different hierarchies at play. So much intertwined sibling history that she hadn't been around to witness or shape. Even if they had been less hostile, Megan knew she would still have struggled. They were like a knot that was too tightly entangled to be unravelled, at least by her. The thought of having to face them at the solicitor's, without Jonathan at her side, filled Megan with – she tried to identify the feeling pressing down on her – dread was probably the most honest answer.

She 'got' why they had never accepted her, and she understood why they would never forgive her. But surely, after all that had happened, there had to be a chance they might find it in their hearts to let old resentments go. They were all hurting. All grieving Jonathan's loss. This surely was the moment for them to come together – share what they had in common, rather than dwell on what divided them.

The tide was beginning to retreat, leaving behind an arc of pristine wet sand. It was a beautiful blowy November day, fresh, clean. It gave Megan's flattened spirits a nudge.

Perhaps the meeting would go okay.

Perhaps it would give her a chance to prove to them that she'd only ever wanted Jonathan – not what came with him, or after him.

Perhaps they would embrace and let old enmities die.

Perhaps.

Chapter 3

RACHEL HEWSON decided to take a stroll away from her desk. She had all the paperwork for the Coulter meeting in order. She'd mentally rehearsed what she was going to say and had speculated as to the questions they were likely to ask. She was ready. There was nothing more she could do.

She headed down the corridor into the small room next to the kitchen. The room was little more than a cupboard really. It was home to the Hoover, the reams of paper that they still went through and – the real motivation for Rachel's visit – the three video monitors. They'd had the security cameras fitted in the summer after an incident with an estranged, enraged husband who had felt the need to vent his frustrations on Greenwood's, having been explicitly prohibited from doing so on his long-suffering partner. The cameras covered the pavement in front of the offices, the conference room and reception area. Death and divorce were all good for business, but less so for tempers. Rachel hoped this wouldn't be the case with Jonathan Coulter's family – though given his idiosyncratic instructions, it was highly likely that the meeting was not going to be straightforward.

Rachel scanned the monitors. By the look of it, the first member of the Coulter family had already arrived. She was fairly confident that the woman pecking at her mobile with slim fingers and glancing repeatedly out through the big plate-glass windows at the high street was Olivia, the eldest daughter. From the telephone conversations they'd had, and the follow-up confirmatory emails, it was obvious that Olivia had nominated herself 'head of the family', now that her father had passed. It was always useful to know who was the key decision-maker in inheritance cases. If you had a grasp of the dynamics within families and knew who had the most influence, who the least, it was sometimes possible to reduce the degree of conflict. Reduce, but not avoid it altogether. On the phone Olivia had been polite, organised, but she'd sounded hassled. All their exchanges had been about the practical arrangements, as if her priority was the speedy resolution of the matter rather than the substance of it. Rachel suspected that Olivia's perspective might well be about to change.

In the flesh, or at least in the grainy black-and-white image on the small screen, Olivia gave off the same sense of impatience as she had on the phone. A trait she'd inherited from her father, possibly? Even with the tremors caused by his illness, it had been obvious that Jonathan Coulter was a restless, energetic person. Children inherited so much from their parents – not just their money. People tended to focus on the similarities in appearance, but Rachel had worked with families where the link between the 'parent' and the 'child' was much more deep-seated; mannerisms, temperaments, values, indeed whole personalities were passed on through the genes.

A change in Olivia's posture alerted Rachel to the arrival of another member of the Coulter clan. Recognition bloomed on Olivia's face as the door to the offices opened. She rose from her seat and greeted the woman with a brief hug. This must be the younger sister, Chloe. They exchanged a few words that Rachel couldn't hear. The new arrival carried her grief more obviously than Olivia. It was evident in her posture and the way she shrugged off her coat as if the pockets were filled with bricks. Underneath she was wearing a plain shift dress that, through the unforgiving lens of the camera, looked very creased. The contrast between the two women was marked. Olivia – smartly dressed, poised, present. Chloe – dishevelled and curiously absent. Greetings over, the women chose their seats and looked away from each other.

Ten minutes later the door opened again and another young woman entered – in a flap – all scarves and apologetic gestures. Again there was a short dance of welcome, with brief hugs and limited words.

And then there were three.

The new arrival sat next to Olivia and struggled out of her jacket. Then, for a second, both women looked up and stared directly at Rachel through the camera lens. Two very different dress styles and manner, but the same eyes and shape of face. That's when Rachel realised her mistake.

There were not three relatives in reception, but two. The second woman to arrive had been Megan, Jonathan's partner, not his daughter.

Rachel's error brought a flush of embarrassment to her face, which she was thankful there was no one around to witness. She knew, of course, that Jonathan Coulter had been divorced and that his new partner was his junior by quite a few years, but seeing the three woman together brought home how close in age the offspring and the new partner were. It was yet another ingredient that was bound to make the coming meeting fraught. As she watched them sitting there, not speaking, Rachel wondered if she was reading too much into the fact that the daughters had chosen to sit together – opposite, rather than next to, Jonathan's partner, Megan. The poor woman! It was unprofessional to take sides, of course, and Rachel knew she would be scrupulously professional in her dealings with the Coulter family, but she couldn't help but feel some sympathy for her.

God, she wished they could just crack on with the meeting.

But as the clock inched round to 10 a.m., they were still not 'good to go' because they remained one family member down.

The son.

Noah.

Chapter 4

LIV WONDERED how many hours of her life she'd spent waiting for Noah – and apologising for him. The solicitor, Ms Hewson, was polite, but her appearance in the reception area and her mention of *another client meeting at midday* was obviously a gentle reminder that their needs were no different from, or more important than, anyone else's. Damn Noah! He'd promised he'd be on time and for once she'd believed him, because who – other than a complete embarrassment of a human being – would turn up late for the 'reading' of their own father's will?

She should've known better.

She did know better.

Olivia couldn't think of a single occasion when her brother had been on time. Lateness was 'his thing'. Over the years the whole family had learnt to accept it – though that didn't stop them resenting it. Eight-year-old Liv sitting in the car every morning before school, fretting about missing registration. Teenage Liv pacing the departure lounge at airports with their parents, waiting for Noah to come back from the shops, the toilet, the games arcade – wherever – so that they could board just before they closed the gate, under the baleful gaze of all the already-seated passengers. Liv's childhood felt like one long wait for Noah. Even now as adults, with full-time jobs and families of their own, it was the same. Every Christmas Day for the past few years had been spiked with a huge dose of non-festive frustration – Freddie and Arthur building themselves up into a frenzy of anticipation – having to wait for 'Uncle No' to appear, so that they could open their presents with Grandpa or Grandma, depending on whose year it was to host. He did it every single time they got together, and it drove Liv mad. Today was no different, though even by Noah's standards, this was a new low.

As they waited, Liv sneaked a glance at Megan, wondering what was going on behind her blank expression. Liv didn't know where to start with that one. What to say that didn't sound contrived and insincere. If Noah had been on time, this awkward hiatus could have been avoided. They would all be in the room by now, being briefed by Ms Hewson. And once they'd been briefed, they could all flee back to their own lives, free to negotiate the shock and awkwardness of their father's sudden, though expected death in private – which was where Liv preferred to experience any emotion.

Megan coughed, quietly, surprising them all. Her hand flew to her mouth as if she was embarrassed to have made a sound. She looked shattered, but then she would be. Liv knew how difficult the past couple of years had been for Megan. Though Liv found her a hard person to warm to, there was no doubting how dedicated she'd been to their father. Had it not been for Megan, Liv's own life would have been much more complicated by her father's illness. He would have needed far more support and that burden would, inevitably, have fallen to her. Chloe? Not really her wheelhouse. Noah? He would have promised a lot, then delivered very little, if past and present performance was anything to go by. Where the hell was he? Liv wondered what Megan would do now. No partner, no kids, no real roots in Scarborough, no home... unless their father really had done something unthinkable in his will – which she was ninety-nine per cent certain he wouldn't have. Not their family home!

Liv got up and paced.

She wanted this meeting over and done with. Her job left very little over by way of energy and thinking time – factor in two small children and a husband she saw only briefly, and Liv's plate was already full. The idea that it could be about to get even fuller made her feel anxious. She turned away from the thought. It was too stressful. She had, of course, known her father was dying, they all had, but she had not expected him to die so suddenly. She'd been confident they would have one more Christmas together. The arrival of a book on John Coltrane from Amazon the day before, one of his gifts, had only served to remind her how misplaced that confidence had been. She was a doctor – she should have known better. But predicting the end of a life, especially one ravaged by disease, was always extremely difficult. Standing in the outer office of the solicitor's waiting for the meeting to begin, Liv felt uncharacteristically panicked by the weight of responsibility pressing down on her.

The thought that they might have to reschedule the meeting made her want to punch something – very hard. When Noah finally appeared, twenty excruciating minutes later, it was only the presence of the receptionist that stopped it being her brother.

Chapter 5

BY THE time they were finally settled in the meeting room, Rachel's nerves had been sharpened by a touch of irritation. She tried not to let it show.

She began briskly. 'What I'm going to do today is explain the provisions that Jonathan has put in place for the dispersal of his assets. I'll also take a few minutes at the end to talk you through the rights and responsibilities of executors. It helps if everyone is on the same page. Each executor will be given a copy of the will to take away with them today. We retain the original for safe-keeping.'

Nobody said anything. They all waited, trying hard not to look too eager, or too interested, or on edge, or any of the things that they were, no doubt, actually feeling.

Rachel went on, taking care to make sure she scanned the room as she spoke – inclusivity was important. 'Alongside his will, Jonathan also put together a Statement of Wishes. It's because of the stipulations in this statement that I wanted to get you all together, in person. I do appreciate you making the effort to come into the office today.' The glance Liv gave her brother at this point was not friendly. Rachel forced herself to concentrate. 'I have received apologies from Ms Eloise Coulter. I assume one of you will update her on our meeting.'

They all nodded, with the exception of Megan.

'Rather unusually, Jonathan asked me to read out his Statement of Wishes before I distribute his will.' She slid the statement out of her file. 'If we're all ready?' They gave their assent. She felt a red flush begin to creep up her neck above the collar of her shirt. 'Just to clarify, a Statement of Wishes is quite common nowadays. Many people write one in order to express their views with regard to the details of their funeral, any specific bequests or gifts, and so on.' She picked up the sheet. 'Jonathan's statement is a little more particular.' She looked down, then paused again. 'I should make it clear that a Statement of Wishes is the expression of an individual's desires, but it isn't a legally binding document. I thought you should know that – in the circumstances.'

The prevarication was obviously infuriating them. The atmosphere in the room teetered on the edge of exasperation.

Rachel pushed her glasses up her nose and began. Jonathan's words, accented by her faint Welsh lilt, filled the room:

'Dear Liv, Noah and Chloe,

If you're listening to this being read out at the solicitor's, then I'm sorry, it has obviously beaten me. That's okay, I suppose. Something gets us all eventually. It's just bad luck that my end has come much sooner than I would have liked.

Knowing that you are dying is remarkably helpful in making you focus on what really matters. The problem is, it doesn't, unfortunately, endow you with any profound insights into how to deal with the consequences of your death. Indeed, I've found the opposite. Knowing that my time is limited has led me to reflect more on the mistakes I've made in my life, especially as a husband and a father, rather than on the successes. I'm hoping that I managed the grandpa bit okay? Or at least I did until I became so sodding useless.'

At this point Rachel paused and took a sip of water.

'I used to think of myself as a fair man and not a selfish one, but I've come to realise that neither of those descriptions is true. On reflection, I realise I've chosen a route through life that has been in my own best interest. Some of those decisions have been at the cost of others – especially, ironically, the people I love most. For that, I am truly sorry.

I am determined not to make the same mistake in death. Hence my will.

I hope you understand, respect and execute my wishes.

I have every faith you will.

I ask that you do your best.

I hope your best is better than mine.

Dad

P.S. Knowing how long it takes you three to agree on anything, I've added a small incentive to the situation. I FORBID YOU TO HOLD MY FUNERAL UNTIL EVERYTHING IS SETTLED.'

Having got through the statement, Rachel leant back in her chair and waited for the implications to sink in. At her elbow sat a small stack of snow-white envelopes – Jonathan's will. The siblings had all studiously avoided looking at them while she was talking. Perhaps they thought such attention would appear too nakedly eager. Now they stared. Only Jonathan's partner, Megan, didn't shift her gaze. She continued to focus on the small window over Rachel's left shoulder – the window that faced out onto a brick wall. Randomly Rachel remembered her old ballet teacher telling the class that if they kept their eyes on a fixed spot, it would stop them wobbling as they did their spins. Maybe Megan was practising the same discipline.

Rachel acquiesced to their silent request. 'I think it best if you read the will itself.' She picked up the envelopes, stood and walked around the table. She placed a copy in front of each of the siblings.

There was no envelope for Megan.

No one moved for a beat of one, two, three; on beat four, Noah reached out his hand, prompting Liv to snatch up her copy. Chloe followed suit.

Rachel watched Megan flinch as they tore open their envelopes, but she kept her chin held high. Rachel felt a flush of admiration and pity for her. For a minute the only movement was the blinking of their eyelids as each of the siblings read the enclosed document.

Noah was the first to register his response – 'What the fuck!' – said with energy, shock and, to Rachel's ears, a note of amusement.

The older sister, Olivia, hadn't finished reading. She held up her hand, warding off his pre-emptive reaction. The younger sister, Chloe, was alternating between reading and looking up in bewilderment. 'I don't understand. Hasn't he left any other instructions?'

Noah answered her, somewhat sharply. 'Chloe, it's not complicated. Dad's left it to us to decide.'

Liv turned the page, obviously looking for more than the scant six paragraphs. There was no more.

Rachel had put the will together for Jonathan. She'd even sourced the witnesses to sign it, when Jonathan explained that he wanted its contents to remain confidential until his death. He had been very explicit about that. She knew exactly what the will said. It was succinct. Short on words, but not on implications.

Liv had reached the end of the document – her second read-through. She laid the papers down on the table. 'Well, this is going to take some sorting out.'

'You can say that again, Sis.' Noah seemed to be enjoying the confusion in the room. It was insensitive, especially with Megan sitting there silently and stoically at the end of the table.

'Was there another will? Before this one?'

Rachel had wondered how soon they'd get round to that. Liv was the quickest off the mark. 'There was an original will, written and amended in the 1980s, when you were young children. Then changes were made after your parents got divorced in...' she checked her well-prepared notes; she'd known this wasn't going to be a straightforward meeting, '2015.'

'And when was this version written?' The older sister again.

'Jonathan approached the firm in early June to get the ball rolling. It was signed off, as you can see by the date, on the twenty-eighth of the same month.'

As if choreographed, all three siblings sat back in their chairs simultaneously, absorbing the information that the will was only five months old.

The pause was broken by Megan, who asked in a quiet voice, 'What does it say?'

Megan had not been given a copy of the document, as was

correct. She had not been named as an executor and, therefore, had no legal right to know what instructions the will contained. Jonathan's insistence on this had puzzled and troubled Rachel, but she had been in no position to query it. It was none of her business. A client's wishes were to be recorded and executed, not challenged.

A silent exchange of glances between the siblings landed the problem of Megan firmly at Liv's door. She picked up her copy, hesitated, then – instead of passing it over to Megan – began reading its contents aloud, her voice steady and even-paced:

'The Last Will and Testament of Jonathan Avery Coulter,
28 June 2019

- *I appoint my children, Olivia Louise Redpath, Noah Avery Coulter and Chloe Emma Coulter, as joint executors of my estate.*
  - *There is only one specific bequest to be made:*
  - *A cash lump sum of £5,000 to Lisa Joanne Browne, who currently resides at 12 Prospect Close, Scarborough, YO12 6EN.*
- *I leave the remainder of my estate, in its entirety – including all my remaining financial assets (after any debts are paid), including the house at 67 Belvedere Avenue, Scarborough, YO11 2UU, and all its contents, etc. – to my executors.*
- *My executors must agree unanimously on the fair and appropriate division and distribution of the estate.*
- *Should my executors be unable to reach such an agreement, the proceeds of my estate will go – in its entirety – to the Motor Neurone Disease Association, Francis Crick House, 6 Summerhouse Road, Moulton Park, Northampton, NN3 6BJ, tel. no. 01604 250505.*

- *I appoint Rachel Hewson of Greenwood Solicitors to fulfil the instructions of my executors.'*

While Liv read out the stark paragraphs, Rachel studied Megan. She sat remarkably still, her expression guarded. The only discernible sign of stress was the way she kept pressing down on the nail of her little finger with her thumb. When Liv finished, Rachel felt compelled to offer Megan something other than words. 'Ms Brooke, would you like a glass of water?' But Megan shook her head.

The awkwardness was just as Rachel had feared. She began to fill the silence with well-intentioned waffle.

'I appreciate that it's going take you some time to talk this through and reach your conclusions. I want to stress that your father's "conditions" are not legally enforceable. I would strongly advise you *not* to rush into any decisions regarding the estate, despite your father's injunction. And, as his surviving family, the nature of his funeral service is entirely up to you.'

They made no move.

It was Megan who stirred. She pushed her chair away from the table and stood up. 'I'll leave you to it.' Her voice broke the impasse. They all shifted in their seats. Rachel admired Megan's calmness, or at least her pretence of it. Megan made for the door. Rachel stood up, intending to follow her out. She had a duty of care to the whole family, not only the executors.

'Before you go.' Noah stopped her departure.

Rachel turned in the doorway. 'Yes?' She wished he would just spit it out. She didn't want Megan to leave before she had a chance to speak to her.

'I've got a question.' He paused. 'Who the hell is Lisa Browne?'

Chapter 6

WITH MEGAN and the solicitor out of the room, the brakes came off.

'Did you know about this?' Noah was first on the offensive.

'No, of course not!' Liv responded. 'You?'

'No!' Noah replied. They stared at each other.

'Neither did I, if either of you is interested.' Chloe's jibe went unnoticed.

'So who did you think was his executor?' Noah asked.

'Well, me, as the eldest. He asked me ages ago.' Liv picked up the will again and scanned the totally unhelpful instructions. She really could do without this. The panicky, sick feeling in her stomach increased.

'And of course you assumed it was just you he wanted.' Noah's sarcasm was sharp and squarely directed at Liv.

She was not in the mood for it. 'Oh, don't start getting snippy. I thought it was going to be a straightforward, but not inconsiderable, admin job. He gave me the impression that everything was sorted out. That he'd left clear instructions for me

– or whoever – to execute. I had no idea about this.' She waved the will around. 'He did mention that he was going to update his will, but he didn't go into any details.'

'And you didn't ask?' Noah didn't look convinced.

'It didn't seem appropriate, in the circumstances. I didn't want him thinking I was prying… or questioning his capacity. You know what he was like about stuff like that, especially as he got sicker.'

'Don't you think it's weird there's no mention of Mum? Nothing at all? Or Megan?' Chloe said.

'Yet there's five thousand pounds for this Lisa Browne character.' It was obviously still niggling Noah that such a large sum had been set aside for someone who didn't even register on his radar.

'She's not "a character"!' Liv made air quotes. 'She's the carer who has been helping to look after Dad.'

'Which one?'

'Oh, for God's sake, Noah. The one who's been virtually living in the house for the past few months. Since his last fall,' Chloe said. 'You must have met her.'

Noah nudged the indignation back a notch. 'Oh, yeah.' He made a show of looking like he was remembering. 'Now I come to think about, I did meet her once or twice at the house.'

'On one of your rare visits.'

Noah didn't react to Liv's dig. He was still worrying away at the bequest to Ms Browne. 'It's a lot of cash, for someone who was only doing her job.'

'Noah! Don't you think the money for the carer is less of an issue than the conditions of the will itself? Why has Dad left it to us to decide?' Liv asked. 'And Chloe's right. Why hasn't he made any specific provision for Mum, or for Megan? What the hell is that about?'

'How should I know? He never really talked about money with me.' Noah had a habit of taking personally questions about his relationship with his father.

Liv was trying to think logically rather than emotionally. Their father had liked to be in the driving seat. Being in control had always been important to him – sometimes more important than was good for him, or for those close to him. The will, and the bizarre accompanying statement, was completely out of character.

Unless...

Liv's brain ticked.

Unless the will was their father's reaction to the decline in his mental and physical powers. A rational, if atypical, recognition that he was no longer able to make clear, coherent decisions. Intelligence and confusion were uncomfortable bedfellows. The thought saddened Liv profoundly. 'Maybe he was worse than we realised. Maybe he was worried that he wasn't well enough to apportion his legacy appropriately.' She began to warm to her explanation. The more she thought about it, the more it made sense. 'Maybe he came to the realisation that it was better to let us decide.' It was possible. His health had been deteriorating. The will could be his solution. Perhaps their father's last act of self-determination had been to allow them to negotiate their own inheritance.

'So he left it up to us,' Noah stated.

'Looks like it,' Liv agreed.

'You're not suggesting we do it *now*?' Chloe asked, shocked and scrambling to keep up.

'No, of course not,' Liv snapped. She regretted her tone when she saw Chloe wince. She made a real effort to keep her voice level and soft. 'But we are going to have to start getting our heads round it – and sooner rather than later. There's a lot to think through. We'll need to get together again.' The thought of that made Liv feel claustrophobic, but there was no avoiding it. Her mind started clicking through her schedule, working out what could be moved, what covered by Angus, what would have to be sacrificed. Family logistics: yet another of her areas of expertise and responsibility. She was so focused on her thoughts that she didn't hear Noah's comment, only Chloe's response.

'Noah! Don't! I can't bear to think about him like that.'

'Like what?' Liv asked, forcing her attention back into the room.

Chloe had her hands up to her face, as if shielding herself from Noah's words. 'Lying somewhere on his own, waiting for us to make a decision.'

Liv shot Noah a look – he really should know better than to bring up their dad's ghoulish edict not to bury him until they had divided the estate, especially not in front of Chloe. She steered the conversation back to practicalities. 'What about getting together Thursday this week? I'm not working. We could meet somewhere halfway, a hotel or somewhere.'

'Thursday's not good for me,' Noah said.

'Or me,' Chloe added.

Liv had to bite her tongue. It couldn't be that hard for a part-time sales assistant to swop a shift, surely. 'Well, the rest of the week is impossible for me,' she countered. 'What if you two came over to ours one evening?'

'I can't. I'm already away two nights next week, as it is. A last-minute job in Malaga. Josie will have a dicky fit if I say I'm coming to yours for a night, on top of that.'

And on it went.

After fifteen minutes of fractious discussion about which date would fit into everyone's schedule, and the best venue for their meeting, the only issue that was clear was that Jonathan had been absolutely right about one thing: getting the three of them to agree on anything was virtually impossible.

Chapter 7

MEGAN DIDN'T wait to say her goodbyes. She turned down Ms Hewson's offer of tea and sympathy, wanting to put as much distance between herself and Jonathan's offspring as possible.

In the taxi she caught her breath.

She wondered what was going on back at the solicitor's. She imagined their surprise, and delight. Jonathan had cut her out of his will and given them free rein. She wondered what they would do with it.

She looked out of the window and watched the world pass by. The rootless feeling that had haunted her since his death intensified. She was heading back to a home that was effectively no longer hers, to a life with no purpose, to a future that was hard to imagine.

The taxi turned onto Ramshill and headed along The Esplanade. The tide was fully out now, revealing a wide band of gleaming smooth sand. On a whim, she asked the driver to pull over and drop her off. His concerned, *Are you sure, love? It's blowing a gale out there* was appreciated, but ignored. She paid and watched him swing the car around and head back into town, hunting for another fare. He was right, the wind was still strong. Her cheeks hurt as if they'd been slapped. But it was better than the oppressive heat at the solicitor's. She started walking, relishing the fight against the elements. It was perfect weather for her grief, and anger. She walked until she was warm, her eyes watering, her lungs full of cold air. Blood pumped through her system, expanding her sore heart. Just before the clock tower she took the path down to the Italian Gardens, out of the worst of the wind. She couldn't face going back to the house and the clamour of mounting questions that couldn't be answered by the empty rooms.

At this time of year the gardens were bleak, a pattern of neat circles of heavy clay soil, empty of plants. Everything was sodden. At the heart of the gardens was a shallow pond choked with dead bulrushes. In the centre, Eros balanced precariously on his weather-beaten globe, his arm reaching out into thin air. At either end of the gardens stood two ornately painted wooden shelters, now faded and in need of repair. They dated back to the glory days of Scarborough, when the great and the good used to the promenade along the South Cliff – looking down on the poor unwashed below. Megan chose the shelter on the left. Inside, the sound of the waves was muffled, the force of the wind diminished. *D loves G 4ever* was scrawled in marker pen on the chalky wall. The place was scruffy, but at least it was peaceful.

She was not.

What she felt – what had begun coursing through her in that claustrophobic room as the solicitor had spoken so smoothly and professionally – was rage. It was a fury not directed at Ms Hewson, with her smart suit and kind face, or at Liv, or Chloe; not even at Noah, with his rudeness and insensitivity; but at Jonathan. For everything. Her emotions crackled. She had thought she couldn't feel any worse than she already did, but she'd been wrong. She was incensed with him.

For sneaking off to the solicitor's without telling her.

For spending weeks, if not months, secretly planning the whole charade.

For letting her walk into that meeting unprepared.

For thinking the whole thing was some sort of game that he could control from beyond his as-yet-unfilled grave.

For handing everything over to his kids.

For bowing to their resentment and cutting her out, just as they, she suspected, had wanted him to.

For abandoning her to face this on her own.

And on top of all that – as if that wasn't enough – she was blindingly, roaringly furious at him for dying.

She had stayed with him through it all, and yet he had not stayed with her. And for that she was livid.

He had left her.

He had given up.

She had so many things she wanted to say that she would now never be able to. There was so much pent-up emotion inside her that had no possible outlet.

His dying was *selfish.*

He had been *selfish.*

There, she had finally admitted it to herself.

Megan banged her fists down on the bench. Once, twice, three, four, five times – harder and harder – trying to release some of the fury that had been building up since his death. No, that wasn't true. The rage had been brewing inside her for far longer. It had been bubbling under the surface throughout the seemingly endless, stressful months of being trapped in the house with Jonathan. It had fermented silently inside her with every long, slow hour that she'd dedicated to loving and caring for him. Her secret rage had, it now felt, always been there, the dark underside to all that incessant positivity and hope.

Throughout his illness she had put his needs first, subsumed her own. Her sole objective had been to make his life as good as possible. She had changed shape around him. Reinvented herself to become the carer that his illness demanded, rather than the lover and partner she had once been.

She had been selfless.

And yet, all that time, he'd been planning and plotting behind her back, drafting this elaborate ending to their story.

Damn him.

Damn him.

Damn him!

Her tantrum raged and she indulged it. She let her grief flood out, feeling the scorch in her nose and throat. On and on it burnt – until there was no more fuel left.

The gardens came back into focus. Eros hadn't moved. The wind was still blowing off the sea, and Jonathan was still dead. There was still today, and tomorrow, and all the other days after that to be got through. There was still the house – for a while at least – and his family to endure. And there were still Jonathan's last wishes to be observed, before his soul could be put to rest.

Chapter 8

THE COUNTDOWN to their weekend get-together seemed interminable. Who knew a week could feel like a lifetime? Living in The View with Megan, but without her dad, was more uncomfortable than ever for Chloe. The meeting at the solicitor's had obviously not helped. How could it? She and Megan were even more wary of each other than they were before. As the days dragged by, they rotated stiffly through the house like characters on a cuckoo clock. Despite their habit of polite avoidance, Chloe was still hyper-aware of Megan's presence. Listening out for somebody all the time, feeling their sadness in the soft closing of a door or the clink of a solitary mug being lifted from a cupboard, was stressful and tiring. The longer it went on, the more Chloe was reminded of how much of the soul and energy of the house had come from her father.

Flowers were delivered to the house almost daily. Every time Chloe came home from work there seemed to be a new bouquet. Megan shoved them haphazardly into vases, still wrapped in their layers of unnecessary cellophane and tissue. She put the accompanying notes on the kitchen windowsill, where they got wet, the carefully composed messages of condolence becoming illegible blurs. Megan exhibited the same disinterest in the barrage of sympathy cards that arrived. She left them unopened on the side, piling up, a small mountain of cream and pale-purple envelopes.

By the Thursday evening Chloe had had enough. She simply couldn't tolerate the lack of respect for her father's memory any longer. She opened and put up the cards, reading each one as she did so. They were from colleagues, family friends, distant relatives – a parade of familiar and unrecognised names. Many of them had taken the time to write lovely things about her dad: what an honour it had been to know him, work with him, learn from him. There was much praise for his contribution to teaching, the inspiration he provided, the rigour and commitment he brought to the profession. There were also plenty of funny, more personal recollections, most relating to his cricketing days and his penchant for expensive Scotch. The messages conjured up a man who had been respected and liked. The cards made Chloe feel both proud – they deserved to be on display – and sad, because the man captured in the messages was very different from the one who had been her father at the end.

There was a grand total of two cards from Megan's family. Chloe had no qualms about opening those as well. Why should she? Megan plainly was not bothered. The one from Megan's father was succinct to the point of impersonality: *Sorry for your loss. Love, Dad x.* Megan's sister, Sarah, had written a much more heartfelt note about love and bereavement – she seemed to have some personal experience of it. Chloe couldn't remember her father ever mentioning Megan having a sister.

Not that he was prone to discussing anything that touched on the seismic shift that his affair, and subsequent choice of Megan over their mother, had occasioned. Chloe and Noah had often speculated about Megan's family's attitude to her relationship with Jonathan. Having your daughter or sister 'run off' with a married man nearly twice her age couldn't have gone down well. Chloe wondered if they would attend the funeral – a funeral for which there was, as yet, no date and no organisation. She felt a flutter of panic.

It was out of her hands. She could do what she could do, nothing more, so she focused on the job in hand.

Cards sorted, Chloe gathered together the bouquets, unwrapped them and set about arranging the myriad flower stems properly. There were so many that she had to use a random assortment of jars, jugs and mugs from the back of the kitchen cupboards to hold them all. Pleased with her efforts, she put a flower arrangement in each of the rooms, even the bathroom.

The act of sorting the flowers and the cards, as much as it was a solitary task, brought Chloe some comfort. When she'd finished she sat on the stairs. The whole house was filled with the scent of lilies and roses. It finally looked, and smelt, as it should do: a house of mourning. Not that she knew what one of those should look like. Her father was the first person she had loved who had died. A sob rose in her throat. The sombre atmosphere and the silence settled on her, bringing her loneliness to the surface. She pulled her phone out of her pocket and tried her mother again. It went straight to voicemail. She didn't leave another message – it felt too needy – but as she sat on the step and listened to the quiet, Chloe admitted that was exactly what she was.

Her mother had been frustratingly unforthcoming all week. It was almost as if, having drawn close to her children in the first few shock-filled days after Jonathan's death, Eloise had once again taken a step backwards, retreating, as she so often did, into her work and her routines and her life far away from Scarborough.

Their mother's withdrawal had forced Chloe to rely on her siblings. And, as always, that experience had been a bumpy and curiously unsatisfying one.

Liv had been in contact daily. In fact it had felt more like hourly. She'd sent a steady stream of precisely composed emails, often with attachments, that provided very little in the way of comfort. Indeed, they brought more pressure than peace into Chloe's solitary existence. Liv's lengthy missives usually contained requests for very specific pieces of information from Megan. Information that was *essential.* Liv wanted everything *available* and *in order*, in advance of their planned get-together at the weekend. Chloe deeply resented her own designated role as go-between. Discussing anything personal with Megan was difficult at the best of times; and this, most definitely, was not the best of times.

Chloe had tried, but Megan's responses to the many and varied requests were always vague. When Chloe asked for some specific pension paperwork that Liv wanted, Megan mumbled something about sorting it out *when she had time*; and when Chloe prompted her, again, about speaking to the bank, all she got, by way of response, was an incline of the head that could easily have indicated 'no' as much as 'yes'. As the days passed and there were no files forthcoming and no calls made, it became clear that Megan had no intention of doing anything Chloe asked of her.

Liv was not happy, as she made abundantly clear when she called. Her 'You have to be more direct with Megan' was no help whatsoever. And when Chloe, in a fit of exasperation brought on by the stress of it all, had yelled at Megan's retreating back that they really needed access to her father's files, and that they had every right to see them, as executors of the will – another useful 'Liv observation' – Megan had stopped, turned and stared, dark-eyed, at Chloe, before saying, slowly and very deliberately, 'It's all in the files on the bookcase by the desk in his room. Be my guest.' And she'd actually stepped aside, as if ushering Chloe towards her father's room. That had been cruel. Megan knew Chloe hadn't been able to set foot inside the room since the night he died.

The only person who had any sympathy was Noah. He phoned most evenings and although he was very little practical help, he was at least a welcome distraction. His witty riders in response to Liv's big-sister bossiness were funny. As always, Chloe felt slightly guilty about their childish sniggering behind Liv's back, but it didn't stop her texting Noah regularly to update him on the latest in the saga of *Liv vs Megan*. No matter where he was or what he was doing, Noah always made time for her, even when it was obviously inconvenient – like at Malaga airport. Chloe cherished her relationship with Noah, puerile as it was. There was no judgement – at least not of her – and that was a relief.

If it hadn't been for Noah and her job, she really thought she might have lost it.

She'd gone back to work a couple of days after her father's death, despite her supervisor telling her to take as much time off as she needed. But being busy was better than the alternative, and the kindness of her colleagues and customers had been preferable to Megan's sealed-off, flinty sadness. As Chloe sat at her till in Marks & Spencer, exchanging chit-chat about the weather and the erratic bus service with a steady stream of shoppers, at least her hands were occupied, if not her brain. At work she was useful, competent and appreciated, especially by the regulars. Her favourite was an old gent called Harold, who came into the store most days. He made a point of coming to her till. He always wore a shirt and tie with a proper coat and a hat – a fedora in the winter, a straw boater in the summer. His basket normally contained a small white sliced loaf, a pack of ham or a piece of mature Cheddar and a single-serve ready meal, most often a shepherd's pie. Chloe wanted to tell him it would be much cheaper to shop at Tesco, but that would have been disrespectful. Instead she smiled and scanned his paltry selection of groceries. He always tipped his hat to her as he walked away.

Since her father's death that one small gesture had taken on a whole new meaning and significance.

At long last Friday finally came round.

As Chloe finished her shift her mood was better than it had been all week. Liv and Angus and the boys were due to arrive at 6 p.m. Noah had been less specific, but Chloe wasn't too worried; she knew he wouldn't let her down. The thought of the house being full made her happy. All of them back together. It would shift the balance.

Instead of heading straight home, she went back down onto the shop floor. She picked out three bottles of decent wine, along with a couple of bags of sweets for the kids and some posh chocolate for the adults. A basketful of treats. Just like the old days, when Friday night was 'eat as many sweets as you like' night. Eloise had been strict about their schoolwork and their bedtimes, and surprisingly lax about everything else.

Megan walked into the kitchen as Chloe was unpacking. The way she glanced at the shopping, but didn't say anything, irritated Chloe.

'It's only some extra bits for tonight.'

Megan blinked. 'Thank you.' It was, as always, an odd response. The treats were not for her.

Chloe opened the fridge, intending to chill the wine, only to be confronted by shelves groaning with food. The door compartments were already fully stocked with wine, milk, fresh juices. On petty principle, Chloe extracted one of the existing bottles and replaced it with one of her own. Despite her back being turned, she could sense Megan watching her. The fridge started to beep. Chloe kept it open, on purpose.

'Have you heard from Noah?' Megan asked.

The beep was truly irritating. Chloe shut the door. 'Yeah.'

'Has he said what time they'll be here?'

'Not for definite.'

Chloe heard the puff of Megan's breath. 'It would help to know, so I can decide what to do about the meal. I don't suppose you know whether he wants Lily to eat with us or not? I think Liv's planning to feed the boys earlier and get them up to bed before we sit down.'

Chloe turned round to face her. 'You know Noah. They'll be here when they're here.'

She looked past Megan and saw the collection of pans on the hob and a covered tray on the side. It was like being on a Martha Stewart set. Megan must have been cooking all day. She was such an odd contradiction of a woman. Chloe softened, slightly. 'You could always plate them something up, if they're really late.'

Megan nodded. She picked up a tea towel and pointlessly rehung it. Once again they had exhausted their conversational reserves. Chloe left Megan to her martyred preparations, desperate for the arrival of her siblings.

Chapter 9

LIV AND her brood arrived, as promised, at 6.05 p.m., in a flurry of noise. The boys, Arthur and Freddie, shot into the house and proceeded to run around like animals released from captivity. It was remarkable how different they were. It was as if Liv and Angus's genes had taken it in turns to make a child. Freddie, at six, was the eldest, though he was not much taller than his younger sibling. He was unequivocally Liv's offspring. Slim, fair-haired, with delicate features that looked set for life to be just a little too feminine to be handsome. In contrast, Arthur, at three and a half, was a mini-Angus. Ruddy-faced, solid, scabby-kneed, quintessentially a boy.

Angus enveloped Chloe in a hug and she immediately felt better. Liv's embrace lacked the same power, but it was equally welcome. Megan stood back, letting them bond. Her offer to make some coffee enabled them to swerve any awkwardness in terms of greetings. Now they were past the initial shock of Jonathan's death, physical contact with Megan was once again something to be avoided.

'How are you holding up, Chloe?' Angus hauled a selection of bags and coats into the hall – they had brought a lot with them.

'Not bad, though it's good to have you here. It's been a really odd week.'

'Only to be expected, I suppose.' He started sorting through their mound of stuff.

'Things no better?' Liv took off her coat and hung it up, neatly.

'No. Not really.' Liv and Chloe glanced simultaneously towards the kitchen, where the subject of their frustration was quietly, and helpfully, preparing drinks for the new arrivals.

Armed with their overnight bags, and immune, or indifferent, to the undercurrents of the conversation, Angus asked, 'Which room?'

'Megan has put you in the rooms at the back, I think.'

Angus nodded his thanks and headed upstairs.

Instinctively the sisters drew closer together. Chloe dropped her voice to a whisper. 'We've been avoiding each other most of the time. She keeps going out. I don't know where. She never tells me what's she's doing. And, like I said, whenever I ask her anything she's really evasive.' Chloe could tell by Liv's expression that the rigour of her attempts to get information from Megan were being doubted, and judged. That was the problem with Liv; her relentless efficiency didn't leave any space for other people's efforts, especially if those efforts failed. Chloe tried to defend herself. It was okay for Liv to fire off endless emails and texts about what she wanted sorting, but it wasn't as straightforward as that. Dealing with Megan necessitated navigating a minefield of sensitivities, past and present. 'She's not exactly been in the mood for doing anything to help us.' Then, for good measure, Chloe added, 'I can't say I blame her.'

'Have you at least got the files I asked for?'

'No.' Chloe's resentment at Liv's irritated tone grew. 'I tried. She said they're on the bookcase in Dad's room.' She didn't add that she'd been too anxious to go in and fetch them herself. It was silly, she knew that, but the thought of opening the door and stepping inside the room actually frightened her. She knew her sister would have no patience with such 'hysteria'.

Liv glanced across the hall at the closed door. 'I'll get them tonight, after we've eaten.'

Chloe was offended and, at the same time, relieved to have the responsibility taken away from her. Let Liv wade in. That's what she did best.

The boys reappeared in the hall, skidding across the polished floor in their socks. Liv sent them upstairs to bother their dad. The thunder of their feet was shockingly loud after the past week of monastic quiet. Liv rolled her shoulders and swung her arms back and forth, presumably to loosen the stiffness from driving. The stretching seemed to improve her mood. She was more conciliatory when she next spoke. 'If it makes you feel any better, she's been equally unforthcoming with me. I must have asked her three times for the passcodes for Dad's bank accounts, but she's still not sent them to me.'

Chloe briefly, and irrelevantly, had a mental image of the inside of Liv's brain as one huge spreadsheet, with endless columns of tasks and deadlines.

'And what about the plans for the funeral?' Liv's neck made a cracking noise as she circled her head left to right.

Chloe's column obviously had a lot of 'pending' categories. She wished her nephews were back downstairs – anything to deflect Liv from her lengthy inventory of tasks. 'The brochures arrived.' They had.

'And?'

'I looked at them.'

'And?' Liv waited, but Chloe had nothing more to add. 'So have you chased up the funeral directors about possible dates for the crematorium?'

'Not yet.'

At that, Liv did give vent to her frustration. 'Aw, come on, Chloe! You're here – you've got far more time than I have. I've spent most of the week speaking to the solicitor, chasing the pension company and I've been at work. Surely you could have got *something* sorted on the funeral. Time's ticking. We can't leave him indefinitely at the undertaker's.'

Chloe couldn't bear to think about it. She turned away and walked into the lounge, forcing Liv to follow her. She pulled the door closed. 'It's not that simple.' Liv looked at her expectantly. Chloe pushed down her qualms about blaming Megan for her avoidance of the issue. 'I don't think Megan's ready to start talking about it yet.'

'It's been nearly a fortnight. Besides, we need to get some dates booked in or we'll start running into the Christmas period, and then it'll be nigh-on impossible to get a slot.'

Chloe felt hot, and cold. 'I know. But... well, wait and see what you think. I'm not sure about her mental state at the moment.'

Liv's body language did not exude sympathy. 'So you're saying that nothing's been done?'

'Not as such.'

Liv reached for the door handle, and Chloe knew that Liv would sweep in and start calling the shots. The thought was enough to galvanise her to speak.

'It's not just Megan. Liv, what about what Dad wanted?'

'Meaning?'

'Well, should we ignore what he said in his will? He was quite clear about not wanting to be... laid to rest until we've sorted everything out.'

For a split second Liv looked uncomfortable, but she didn't let it show in her voice. 'As the solicitor said, the Statement of Wishes isn't legally enforceable. And besides, I'm hoping we'll have agreed what we're going to do by the end of this weekend – so there's no reason to hold off planning the funeral.' Her unshakeable confidence was hard to argue with. Course of action decreed, Liv opened the door and headed in the direction of the kitchen.

Chloe let her go, feeling a shiver of sympathy for Megan.

Chapter 10

TO EVERYONE'S surprise, Noah arrived while they were having coffee and cake. Freddie was the one to hear the front door open. He scrambled up from the floor and ran into the hall, followed by his brother. 'Uncle No!'

Liv didn't move from her position on the sofa. She glanced at her watch, pointedly. 'Well, well, pigs can fly when they try.'

In the hallway the chorus began. 'Uncle No!'

'Yes.'

'Uncle No!'

'Yes.'

'No.'

'Yes.'

The panto 'call and response' routine had started when Freddie first learnt to talk. It was now a feature of every family gathering, made all the more manic by the wait the boys normally had to endure before their uncle's late arrivals.

Noah came into the lounge, bedecked by the shouting, excited boys. He peeled Arthur off his leg and threw him, squealing, onto the sofa. Freddie released his grip voluntarily, thereby avoiding the rugby antics.

'Hi.'

The men shook hands. The siblings exchanged kisses. Megan disappeared, without being asked, presumably to fetch Noah a coffee. There was a beat.

'Where are Josie and Lily?' Liv asked.

'They're not coming.' Noah flopped down on the sofa next to Arthur.

'Oh. Why?' Liv was disappointed. She approved of Noah's partner. Josie was the yin to his yang – grounded and sensible, in direct contrast to Noah's impulsiveness. Liv had been imagining Josie's presence as a steadying influence on the weekend's proceedings. Besides, it was nice for the boys to spend time with their cousin, Lily. It happened far too infrequently.

'Josie's having to work tonight. One of her staff cried off at short notice, so she's standing in.' Josie was the manager of a unit for teenagers with behavioural problems. A tough job that she was very good at.

Noah started tickling Arthur, which set off a chorus of 'No, no. I'm gonna wee-wee!'

'Who's looking after Lily?'

Noah threw Liv a warning glance. 'What is this: twenty questions? Josie's mum. And Lily has a dance competition on Saturday that I'd forgotten about, so it makes more sense for them to stay at home. Is that okay with you?'

Liv switched her attention to Arthur. 'That's enough. If you need a wee, go to the toilet. Noah, leave him be. I don't want them cranking up to a frenzy right before they go to bed.'

Freddie, ever alert to his mother's instructions, chipped

in with, 'Mummy. Please. Not bed yet. Uncle No has only just arrived and I'm not tired.'

'I didn't mean you're going to bed now. Megan is getting you some tea. After that you'll go up and have a bath and story before bed.'

'Can Uncle Noah read to us?'

Liv was bemused by Freddie's fascination with her brother, but it was undeniable that from birth he'd wanted to be around Noah. He seemed drawn to the wildness and mayhem. Somewhat irritatingly, Arthur loved Noah as well, but in a much healthier, take-it-or-leave-it kind of way.

'Will you, Uncle No, please?' Freddie pleaded. There it was, that desperation for attention. Liv felt for her eldest son, whilst wishing that he was more robust.

Noah deferred to Liv. 'If that's okay with your mum, I'd love to. But first Uncle No needs a proper drink. Red or white?' he asked the room, just as Megan returned, bearing a fresh pot of coffee.

Chapter 11

THE SIMPLE act of holding the cigarette between her fingers brought Chloe some comfort. She savoured the moment, delaying lighting up. It was the ritual as much as the nicotine that mattered. Vaping just didn't hit the spot in the same way. She looked around the garage. It was crammed with the detritus of family life. Megan's cleansing touch hadn't reached this far. Chloe was glad. In fact, if anything the garage was even fuller than before, because now there was more space available. Her dad had eventually sold his car, after it became obvious he would never drive again. She pushed the thought away, as she always did whenever her brain filled up with a memory that was too bulky to accommodate.

She lit up, inhaled, exhaled, watched the smoke drift. She pushed the door to the house shut with her foot, sealing herself off. Another drag. She felt like a teenager, smoking in secret. In truth, she would never have smoked in the house – it was, after all, a filthy habit – but she still preferred to blame her exile on Megan's fussiness rather than her own fastidiousness. The *one* benefit of having Megan around was that there was always a scapegoat to hand.

Chloe's eyes ranged over the boxes, cluttered shelves and piles of unidentifiable stuff that spilled from all four corners of the garage. As a teenager she'd been press-ganged into a number of failed attempts to impose order on the chaos. Eloise had tried to position these infrequent purges as 'fun.' They had been anything but. They had been hard work, overseen by an increasingly impatient, dirt- and heavy-lifting-averse mother. The wall of big plastic boxes at the far end of the garage were a testament to Chloe's efforts. They contained a miscellany of school reports, trampolining certificates, football trophies, Best-in-Year chemistry-prize textbooks, newspaper clippings, Brownie badges and even a few of Noah's old judo outfits. Liv had, needless to say, contributed the most bricks in the wall. Was it sentimentality that had led their parents to keep all these mementoes of their childhood achievements? Perhaps, but from memory, it was more that Eloise had simply wanted rid of their stuff.

Chloe heard the door from the house to the garage scrape open. Instinctively she hid her cigarette. A wholly futile gesture, given the unmistakeable smell of fag smoke.

She was relieved it was Noah. 'I thought I'd find you in here.' He eyed her cigarette. 'You said you'd given up.'

'I have,' Chloe said, as she took another drag, 'just not consistently.'

Noah shook his head in mock disapproval. 'You'd better not let Liv catch you. You'll get the lecture, again.'

'She's not gonna know, is she? Not unless somebody goes blabbing to her.'

Noah pushed a pile of their dad's old magazines out of the way – Jonathan had been a regular subscriber to all sorts of worthy publications. He boosted himself up onto the ledge. His legs no longer dangled.

Chloe offered him a puff on her cigarette, but he declined. 'You sure? It's taking the edge off the proceedings nicely.'

Noah held up his smeary glass. 'I'll stick to one toxin at a time, thank you very much.' He glanced around. 'Nice spot you've got here. Though it's fucking freezing.'

Chloe smiled. 'I like it. It's quiet, and Megan never comes in here. And I came prepared.' She had – an old fleece that she left hanging on the hook by the door. 'What's going on?'

Noah put down his drink and tried to hug away the chill. 'Angus is bathing the boys, and Liv is helping Megan.'

Their shared skirting of domestic responsibilities had a familiar, warm camaraderie to it.

Noah's eyes flitted around the garage. He picked up a *National Geographic*. 'Did Dad ever leave magazines on your bed, folded open on articles he thought you should be interested in?'

'Sometimes.'

'He was quite old-school, wasn't he?'

'Yeah.'

'I don't think he could get his head around how he'd managed to raise such a philistine. He hated that I don't read.'

'He never gave up, though, did he?' Chloe smiled.

'No. He was an eternal optimist, and stubborn as sin.' Noah laughed. 'A book every birthday and Christmas! Did you ever read any of yours?'

'Some of the novels – the shorter ones! But there's a mountain of untouched non-fiction on the floor in my bedroom.'

'He couldn't stop being a teacher, could he, even at home?'

'No. It's just a pity we were such bad students.'

'At least he had Liv.'

'That he did.' They didn't need to say any more. Chloe pinched out the end of her cigarette and dropped it in the bin, disposing of the evidence.

Noah threw aside the magazine. 'Have you thought about how you want this weekend to go?'

Chloe wandered around the garage as she considered her response. Her fingers trailed across a pile of bike locks, an old rust-bloomed Breville toastie-maker and the huge toolbox with the vicious snapping lid, which only ever appeared in the house when there was an emergency – by which point Eloise would already be on the phone, booking a professional, in the full knowledge that their father's bodged repair wouldn't last. DIY had not been his strong suit. 'I just can't face the thought of any aggro, when everything is still so raw.'

'There doesn't have to be "aggro" – if we agree.'

'Noah, I don't want to think about the will tonight. Please.'

'Okay, okay.' He held up his hands, left it a beat, then went on, 'Would it help if I told you my take on things?'

'If you must.' When Noah was in full flood there was no stopping him.

'The way I see it, Megan is our biggest problem.' He never could whisper.

Chloe hissed, 'For God's sake, Noah, keep your voice down.'

He climbed down from his perch and came to stand near her. 'I don't want us to falling into the trap of feeling sorry for her, and ending up doling out cash to her that was intended for us.'

'I don't understand why Dad didn't simply name his beneficiaries,' Chloe said.

'I don't know. And I guess we never will.' Noah ran his hand through his hair, adding a vein of dust to his dark curls. 'All I'm saying is… we have to remember who's family and who isn't.'

Chloe nodded, but the knot in her stomach didn't loosen. 'I wish Mum was here.'

Noah made a non-committal noise. 'I'm not sure that would make things any easier. Can you imagine it: her and Megan under the same roof? That would be interesting.' He chuckled. Chloe didn't. 'Hey.' He touched her chin with his dusty fingers, raising her face to meet his. 'It's going to be okay. I've got your back, I promise.'

Chloe moved away from his touch, unwilling to let the grubby practicalities of money mix with her feelings of grief.

'And I suppose, when you think about it, it's a nice problem to have.'

'How is any of this "nice"?'

'At least there is a legacy.'

'Noah!'

He shrugged. 'Ah, come on, Chloe. Don't tell me you haven't thought about it. Whatever we decide, we each stand to inherit a decent amount of money. The house alone has to be worth half a million – more probably.' She wouldn't be drawn on the subject, but he seemed unwilling to let it go. 'If we divide the bulk of the estate between the three of us, that's a life-changing amount. Well, it is to you and me. I'm not sure it'll make much difference to Liv. She and Angus are already fairly well set up, as it is. And Mum. Well, Mum got her settlement after the divorce, didn't she? I can't see her expecting much.'

Chloe tried to ignore the unpleasant sensation that her brother was attempting to influence her in order to mask his own greed. She reminded herself that Noah's financial situation was more pressing than her own or Liv's. He had a mortgage, a child and a partner whose part-time job presumably didn't bring in much. His own job as a hotel inspector, though glamorous, was not in reality well paid or predictable. They'd all expected him to look for something more permanent and closer to home, once Lily arrived. How Josie tolerated his extended trips away in luxury hotels she didn't know.

'Noah! Chloe!' They both jumped guiltily at the sound of their names.

Noah saluted. 'We best go. *Mein Führer* is calling.' He jostled her towards the door and, despite her reservations, Chloe felt a rush of affection for her brother. Pratting about with Noah, it felt like old times.

Chapter 12

IT WAS sensory overload. An invasion of sights, sounds and smells. Her once-calm, lovely sitting room was buried beneath the shrapnel of Jonathan's sprawling family. There were greasy wine glasses on every surface, pistachio shells scattered on the carpet, dessert plates on the side-tables, complete with half-eaten slices of tart drying out in the heat of the fire. From her position on the window seat, Megan could see a knife caught between the sofa cushions. It needed moving before one of the boys got their hands on it. Megan knew it was the normal mess generated by a family, but it still bothered her. The urge to sweep it all up was intense, but that would be rude and would reveal her true emotions – her desire to scream and shout, and drive them all out of her house.

It was going to be a long weekend.

She turned away and stared out into the night, seeking solace in the view. Across the bay the castle glowed orange, lit for prettiness now, rather than as a defence against the Vikings. Scarborough had a long and proud history of having to repel unwanted guests.

The thought would have made her smile in the past, when she had humour and resilience – and Jonathan to share the joke with. The castle ruin looked like it was floating in mid-air, the wooded headland beneath it indistinct in the darkness.

Behind her there was the unmistakeable sound of another bottle being opened. The wine had been flowing ever since Noah arrived, loosening tongues and lowering barriers. Was Liv ever going to take the boys up to bed? The alcohol in Megan's stomach was certainly increasing her bitterness. She heard Angus distractedly tell Arthur to stop running around for the fourth time, his tone carrying no weight or threat. Chloe – who seemed to be speaking to no one in particular – was talking about how different it was going to be at Christmas. Nasty as it was, Megan couldn't shake the belief that the conversation was a performance for her benefit. Every time they mentioned Jonathan, it felt like someone was flicking playing cards at her, the sharp edges cutting her thin skin. She knew she was being over-sensitive.

There was a clatter and she turned to see the bowl Arthur had been clutching to his little round belly fall and bounce across the floor, spraying crisps everywhere. He then proceeded to walk through the crisps, smashing them deeper into the carpet. Angus hauled himself off the sofa and did his best to tidy up, with a 'Sorry, Meg', but it made little difference. Crumbs in the carpet, it was hardly a crime. At least the mishap finally prompted bedtime. Angus swept both boys up and carried them out, ignoring Freddie's protests – something about a promise Noah had made. She really needed to try and relax.

For most of the evening the voice dominating the conversation had been Noah's. He was an anecdote machine. A litany of happy tales of high jinks with his father flowed from his wine-stained lips: the time they bumped into Freddie Flintoff in town and got invited to the cricket, for free; the driving lesson that ended with the Volvo – 'you remember, the second-hand red one that always smelt of dog, no matter how often Mum had it valeted' – in the ditch; the time Jonathan hired a full-sized panda costume for the New Year's Eve party. On and on his voice went: *the time we were happy, the time we were a proper family – the time before you.*

It was purgatory.

It was too much.

Megan stood up suddenly, causing Noah to pause, mid-flow. With their attention on her, she picked her way through the debris littering the room, stepping over Noah's legs – why couldn't he sit on a chair like a normal adult? – and walked out of the room, leaving them to it.

Sadly, the hallway was little better than the sitting room. There was a huge jumble of boots and shoes by the front door, and far too many coats were loaded on the hooks. One of the coats had slipped off the hunchback of garments and was lying on the floor. With its outstretched arms, it looked like the victim of a nasty accident.

Megan left the abandoned coat where it was and crossed over to the kitchen. One glance at the cooking pots spread across the work surfaces made her hesitate. The dishwasher swish-swished as it laboured through its first load of the evening. She swerved away from the equally soiled dining-room. That left 'the study' – the place that had come to be Jonathan's bedroom when the stairs had become too much of a challenge. Her decision on whether to seek sanctuary in there was made by Noah appearing in the hallway. His face was flushed from the fire and the wine.

'You all right there, Megan? You look lost.' As always, there was a sarcastic edge to his tone. Why wouldn't she be all right in her own home? He leant against the wall, as if waiting to see what her next move was going to be. She refused to oblige, and stood her ground. Noah shrugged and set off up the stairs. 'I promised to read to the boys.' She nodded at his retreating back. 'I'll be back down in a jiffy.'

At the turn in the stairs she heard him stumble.

Only when he'd gone did she push down the handle and step inside Jonathan's room.

Chapter 13

'AND WITH a snort the dragon made crumpets for all three of them. They ate them sitting on top of the world, watching the clouds playing tag above the mountains.' Noah closed the book and put it on the floor. Arthur was already asleep, mouth open, his breathing congested. The boy was a snot factory. Freddie was wide awake, sitting up in bed, hugging his knees with his hands.

'One more? Please, Uncle No.'

'No, Buster. It's late. You heard your dad, you need to get some sleep. You've got a busy day tomorrow.'

Like the obedient child he was, Freddie didn't push it. He lay down and pulled the duvet up under his chin, then curled up on his side like a dormouse. 'Will you come down to the beach with us tomorrow?'

'Maybe.' Noah knew it was best to be honest with Freddie. 'But not in the morning. Me, your mum and Auntie Chloe have some things we need to sort out.'

'About what to do with Grandpa?'

'Sort of.' Noah wondered what Freddie had overheard.

'Maybe we could go in the afternoon?'

You couldn't fault the kid for trying. And it was, Noah sentimentally and possibly a little emotionally recognised, nice to be wanted – by somebody. He stroked Freddie's hair. 'We'll see. But I'm not promising.' Getting Lily to bed was never this straightforward. Noah patted Freddie's head one more time. 'Light on or off, Fredster?'

'On, please. Just till I get to sleep.'

'Right you are. Goodnight, mate.' Lulled by the wine and the calm mood in the bedroom, Noah bent down and dropped a kiss on Freddie's cheek.

'Uncle No?'

'What?'

'Grandpa isn't still here, is he?' Freddie asked.

Noah was caught off-guard. 'Here?'

Freddie lay still and serious under the covers. 'In the house.'

'No, Freddie. He's not still here.' Noah didn't elaborate on where precisely Grandpa was. That was a conversation best left to Liv.

'Okay.' It seemed enough to reassure Freddie. Noah was relieved. Trust was a lovely thing. His nephew closed his eyes. 'Night-night, Uncle No. See you in the morning.'

'Night-night. Sleep tight. Mind the bedbugs don't bite.'

On the landing Noah stopped to regroup. His conversation with Freddie had lowered his guard, allowing a softness to creep in that he knew was dangerous. He could hear his sisters' voices down in the lounge, an uneven see-saw of words, more weight on Liv's side than on Chloe's. Megan had said very little all evening, which was understandable, but unnerving. Her silent, submissive presence was like a reproach. She was probably still standing in the hall, waiting to be called upon to make more coffee or fetch another duvet – a martyr to the bitter end. He thought about his half-finished glass of wine on the mantelpiece, being warmed by the fire. The View was a big house with old windows. No matter how hard the radiators laboured away, there were always pockets of chilliness and untraceable draughts. But instead of heading downstairs back into the bosom of his family, Noah went into his room.

Except it wasn't really 'his' bedroom.

It pissed Noah off that Megan had put him in the worst room in the house. It was a decent size, but it was dark, featureless and, most depressing of all – in a house called The View – it was view-less. No, that wasn't quite true; should you bother to stick your head out of the window, you were rewarded with a glimpse of the garage roof, the bins and the property next door. Noah sat on the bed, a small double, and took in the anonymity of the room. On the floor under the window, Megan had set up a bed for Lily – a single inflatable mattress, which was possibly one of the surviving relics from their family camping trips. She had bothered to pick out some pretty bed linen and, from somewhere, had found an old doll, one of Chloe's perhaps, which was propped on the pillow. Thoughtful touches that his daughter wouldn't get to see. Another chink briefly opened up in Noah's barricades. But the thought of Freddie and Arthur settled in their proper beds, in their own room – his old room – next door to Liv and Angus, who had been given the big bedroom at the back overlooking the sea, helped to shore up his defences.

Liv always seemed to come out on top, by design and by right. Her two kids trumped his one. Her big, present husband of ten years obviously outweighed his small, absent, live-in lover of five. Her noble profession, administering to the sick, made his freelance gig as a hotel assessor seem more like self-indulgence than work. (Sometimes, when he looked at his income per month, he had to agree.) The family pecking order was still being observed, even without his father to impose it.

Noah pulled out his phone and contemplated trying to call Josie, but her text had been unequivocal.

> It's been a long day. We're going to have an early night.
> Speak tomorrow.

In other words... *leave us alone*! And why press 'return' and leave *speak tomorrow* hanging there, like a threat? Noah badly wanted to reach out to them, but the thought of stoking Josie's anger stopped him even texting, Goodnight, sleep tight, as he always did when he was away. How fucked up was that? He couldn't even say 'goodnight' to his own child. His stony exchange with Josie before he'd set off for Scarborough had been full of repressed anger. It was going to take time and a huge effort to dig those splinters out. Josie had been clear: their daughter was her priority, not him. The added implication that one child was more than enough to be dealing with at any given time had stung – though it was, of course, justified. Immaturity: it was a tag Noah was sick and tired of.

The depressing room only added to his creeping self-pity. The patterned curtains, the balding carpet with its indentations from furniture past, the precarious pile of old games on the top of the wardrobe – it all smacked of neglect. But there was no avoiding it: this was his 'home' for the next couple of days, and a crap room without a view was a small inconvenience in the grand scale of things. He stood up and grabbed his bag, intending to unpack, but when he went to put his few bits of clothing away in the wardrobe, he was confronted by a row of bulky winter coats and waterproof jackets. It looked like a full ski-lift. He yanked open a drawer. It was full of sheets. In the end he stuffed his clothes back into his bag.

This room had always been the one least used in the whole house – it had never been a family bedroom. For a brief period his mother had designated it their playroom, but he and Liv had avoided spending much time in it even back in the day, preferring the garden, irrespective of the weather. In hindsight, it struck Noah how often their mother used to come up with plans for them to take themselves off, out from under her feet. At the time it had seemed like encouragement to explore and play, but as an adult he wondered whether her gift of freedom was rooted more in her own need for time to herself than in her desire for them to have adventures. After the failure of the 'playroom' scheme, the room had briefly become a study for his dad, but again it was rarely used for the same reasons: the lack of light and a view. Latterly it had been billed as a guest room – though how many guests ever visited the house after the break-up of his parents' marriage, Noah didn't know. Very few, he guessed. Many of his dad's friends never set foot in The View again after they heard about Jonathan's choice of his mistress over his wife, proving that loyalty was alive and well, at least outside the confines of the Coulter family.

The sound of a door opening and closing downstairs pulled Noah back to the present and the task in hand.

Their inheritance.

There was no point being squeamish about it. Over the next forty-eight hours he and his sisters got to play God, deciding not only their own futures, but also those of Megan and his mother.

He straightened up.

Let battle commence.

Chapter 14

EVEN WITH the door shut, Megan could still hear their voices, but at least they were muffled, pushed into the background – where they belonged. She pressed her back against the wood, shutting them out and her in. She left the light off. Moonlight flooded in from the garden. A monochrome wash. It seemed appropriate that everything appeared colourless.

The room was exactly as it had been the night Jonathan died. No one, except her, had set foot inside it since the undertakers had removed his body. And that was the way she wanted it. Lisa had offered to come in and clear up, but Megan had stopped her, saying it could wait. And wait it had, frozen in time, there for her whenever she chose to step backwards.

Tonight was one of those times, when she needed the past, not the present. When she needed him, not them.

But she was worried, because she was aware that even her ownership of this confined, sad space, this last piece of Jonathan, was going to be wrested from her over the coming days – just like everything else.

They were here to take their father back.

She took the desk key from her pocket, unlocked the top drawer and lifted out the box. The simple act of holding it in her hands brought her some comfort. She climbed onto the bed and pulled the duvet up around her. Wrapped in solitude, she travelled back to the morning after Jonathan's passing.

It was pitch-black outside, death and darkness made sense, but as the clock on the cooker ticked over to 6.07 a.m., Megan was forced to accept that although Jonathan was gone, life went on – even for her. The dawning of another day demanded some sort of response, but what, she couldn't fathom. She found herself sitting at the kitchen table, in her dressing gown, her stomach full of cold tea and adrenaline – though when Lisa offered to make her another brew, she still said 'yes'. It was something to do. She watched Lisa moving around the kitchen, completely at home. Before long there was yet another mug of tea in front of Megan, along with a plate of toast. Mechanically she picked up a slice and took a bite. Salty butter and warmth. She took another bite, washed it down with hot tea, forced herself to say something.

'Do you know where Chloe is?' Chloe had refused to come and say goodbye to her father – perhaps *refused* was too harsh; been *unable to*. Megan dimly thought she should go and check on her. His family, they were her responsibility now.

Lisa was leaning against the kitchen cabinets, nursing her own tea. 'I think she's still in her room.'

Megan didn't shift. She couldn't summon up the momentum to move on to the next stage – which she assumed was telling other people Jonathan was gone. 'What do I need to do?' She had no one else to ask, no experience of what had to be done after someone died. Lisa did.

'Nothing. Not straight away. Eat your toast.'

So Megan found herself doing just that: taking small bites, chewing, swallowing, sipping her tea, while Lisa stood guard. Before long the plate was clear. Lisa seemed to take that as a sign. 'May I?' She pointed at a chair.

'Sorry, yes. Of course.' How rude to leave Lisa standing there. She must be tired as well – it had been a long night. She should have gone home hours ago, yet here she was, making herself useful, as always.

Lisa sat down opposite Megan and placed her mug carefully on the table. 'I know it's little comfort, but it's good that the doctor has already issued the death certificate. It simplifies things. You'll have take it to the Register Office to register Jonathan's death. It's quite straightforward. You have to do it within five days of the certificate being issued, so you have time.'

'I meant more that I need to start ringing people. Noah and Liv. I have to tell them their father has died.'

'Yes, you do.' Lisa paused and Megan wondered if she was speculating on how difficult those conversations were going to be, given the state of her relationship with Jonathan's children. Lisa had been around long enough to see how strained things were, and not just with Chloe. 'I know it sounds hard, but once it's done, it's done. And they can contact the wider family. It's better to share the load with these things.'

Megan nodded. The thought of it swamped her. Their grief and shock, their resentment that it was her making the call. She wasn't sure she could face it, but she was going to have to. He was – he had been – their father. Lisa was still talking. 'People always start rushing around after someone dies, but there's really no need. The funeral can't happen for a while anyway.' Christ, the funeral! She'd have to plan it with them. Lisa moved her mug but didn't take a drink. 'The one thing you probably *should* do, sooner rather than later, is ring the solicitor.'

Megan nodded, but it was a reluctant nod. Once she started doing things like registering his death and calling lawyers, she was admitting he was gone – which couldn't be true. The toast floated queasily on top of the sea of tea in her stomach. She looked up and met Lisa's eye. Something in her gaze changed, became more insistent. 'Yes. Okay. The death certificate. And I need to ring the solicitor.'

Lisa continued to stare at her. 'The details are in the front of the big lever-arch file, which is on the bottom shelf of the bookcase in his room. All his paperwork is in there. It should help when you get round to sorting things out. And his laptop is on the top of his desk. The passwords are on the notepad.'

Christ, she really was efficient. Somewhere in the back of her brain Megan wondered why Lisa knew all this, but she didn't raise it. What was the point? Lisa knew so much about them. Megan felt a flare of shame. This is what came from sticking your head in the sand – the paid 'help' knew more than she did.

There were a few moments of quiet. Megan drifted. When she looked up she was surprised to see that Lisa had disappeared. She stared at the empty chair. It was better than thinking.

Then Lisa was back. 'Megan?'

'Yes.' She forced herself to concentrate.

'There's something I need to give you. It's from Jonathan. He asked me to make sure you got it, and opened it, as soon as possible after his death.' Without fanfare, Lisa put a bulky

A5 envelope on the table. Megan stared at the parcel, but didn't reach out to take it. The insistence was back again. 'Megan? Are you listening to me? This is the key to Jonathan's desk. I think you should keep the contents of this envelope safely locked up, in the desk, after you've looked at it.'

Megan was having trouble following what Lisa was saying, but her face looked so serious that she felt she had to say something. She managed a clear 'yes'.

'You must promise me that you'll open it. This morning. Before you do anything else. Before you go and check on Chloe. Before you start ringing people. You won't forget, will you?'

Megan moved her head to indicate she had got the message. That finally seemed to placate Lisa, because she stood up.

'Good.' She paused. When she spoke again her tone was gentle. 'You will get through this, Megan. People think they won't, but they do. There isn't really any choice. I am sorry. I know how much of a shock this is, but he is free of it now. No more pain or struggling. We have to be grateful for that – for him.' She hesitated, seemed to weigh up whether to say anything more. She obviously decided she wanted to. 'He was an interesting man. It was a genuine pleasure getting to know him, however briefly. It has been a privilege to care for him.' Megan realised with a jolt that she was listening to Jonathan's first eulogy. Still Lisa seemed reluctant to leave. 'Before I go, do you want me to clear up in there?'

They both knew where.

'No!' Megan snapped. It came out rudely, but the thought of Lisa being in Jonathan's room suddenly infuriated her. So many barriers had been breached over the past few months, but the thought of Lisa touching his things, throwing stuff away, stripping the sheets off his bed was too much. Lisa had done more than enough. This last awful closing down of Jonathan's life, of their life together, was her job. His things were Megan's things. Lisa had no reason to go into his room ever again. No one did. 'No. Don't. I'll sort it out – later.' Only as an afterthought did Megan remember to add, 'But thank you for offering.'

'I'll be off then.' Lisa gave no hint of being offended. 'Unless there's anything else I can usefully do?'

Megan shook her head.

Lisa walked around the table. She slowed as she passed, but wisely refrained from reaching out. Megan couldn't have abided a hug from her. There was only one person she wanted to touch her, and that was never going to happen – ever again. At the door Lisa stopped. 'I'll keep in touch, Megan. If I can help, with anything, let me know. And I mean anything.' She paused, composing her last words. 'Though I'm sure it's no comfort at present, I know he loved you very much. Take care of yourself. And don't forget.' She pointed at the envelope. 'Don't leave it. Open it now.' And with that, she finally left Megan alone with her loss.

The parcel sat on the table in front of her. Megan's name was written on the front, not in Jonathan's handwriting but in Lisa's. She stared at it, wondering whether she could faint, but the tea and toast in her system wouldn't let her. She heard the front door close. Lisa leaving. She pulled the package towards her, picked up the butter knife, wiped it on the sleeve of her dressing gown and slit the envelope open.

Whatever was inside was stuck fast.

She had to rip the envelope apart to get the contents out. A letter, a thick formal-looking document and a small box fell onto the table. She was drawn to the box. It looked old. A proper antique, beautifully made out of some sort of dark wood, with a lighter-wood pattern inlaid on the lid. Megan ran her fingers across the top, imagining Jonathan's fingers doing the same. It was an object that invited touch. She picked it up. Whatever was inside slid around. She lifted the lid.

Inside the box was a set of keys. Megan recognised them instantly by the enamel rainbow fob. They were the keys to her old house in Darlington. She looked at them, confused.

She'd been given the key ring by a pupil at her first school when she was a newly qualified teacher. Her first-ever gift from a student – she'd been touched.

When she'd clipped the keys to her own home onto it, she'd felt proud.

When she'd had to hand those keys over, when she'd sold her house to move in with Jonathan, she'd felt sad.

Somehow, they were back in her possession.

Megan rested her head back and closed her eyes, feeling the cool weight of the house keys against her palm. The wine-loosened voices of Jonathan's children leaked through the closed door and stained the peace.

She had a decision to make, one she'd been wrestling with all week.

How much to tell them?

How much they deserved to know?

Deserved. That was the word that was causing her problems. She owed Jonathan's children nothing. Or did she? Did she owe them honesty? Or was Jonathan's gift to her hers alone to cherish? On this and so much else, she was confused and conflicted.

She could – in theory – walk upstairs, right this minute, pack a bag and just walk out. Leave them to their wrangling and self-interest. Was that what Jonathan intended her to do? For her to take the escape route he'd prepared for her? Had that been his plan all along? She was tempted.

But what right had they to drive her out of her own home? Why should she give them free rein as they picked over his legacy, his belongings, his memory – like noisy vultures? Why should they be able to act is if she didn't exist; no, worse, as if she'd never existed – as if her relationship with Jonathan was little more than a blip, an aberration? If she left them to it, wasn't that tantamount to admitting she should never have been in his life in the first place?

There was also a slim, hard thread of curiosity running through Megan that wanted to see how they would treat her, now that she was truly alone. They would, of course, find out about the house in Darlington eventually, but until they did, her fate appeared to rest totally in their hands. What would they do with such power? Just how badly, or well, would they behave without their father's influence? This weekend she would get to see them in their true colours.

And on top of all that, there was the problem of Jonathan's macabre instruction not to hold his funeral until everything was decided. The thought of him lying on a mortuary slab – eyes closed for ever, heart still for ever – waiting for his last rites haunted her. His will had consigned both of them to purgatory; a purgatory whose duration and outcome were dependent on the whims of his children. What had he been playing it?

Another wave of rage pulsed through her. 'Why, Jonathan, why?'

The sound of her own voice startled her.

The answer came in the unmistakeable sound of something breaking. Megan jumped. As she scrambled upright, the box slid off the bedcovers and fell down the gap between the bed and the wall – she would have to retrieve it later. She dropped the key ring into the top drawer of the desk, locked it and hurried across the room.

She pulled open the door.

Chloe was standing, barefoot, in the middle of the hall surrounded by a fan of smashed crockery. Behind her the doorway was filled with Noah and Liv and Angus. Their attention immediately swung from Chloe to Megan.

'You klutz!' Noah's unhelpful contribution lit Chloe's short fuse.

'At least I was trying to clear up! Don't just stand there gawping at me. Help!' As always with Chloe, there was a shimmer of self-pity beneath her words.

Liv and Angus stepped forward, carefully, and started picking up the biggest pieces. Noah made no such move.

With a pang Megan realised that the broken pots were the bowls Sarah had made for her and Jonathan as a *new life together* present when she'd moved in, the only such present they'd received. 'I'll get the dustpan.'

'No, it's okay.' Liv didn't look up, but continued to retrieve chunks of pottery. 'Tell me where it is and I'll fetch it.'

'I don't mind.' Megan made a move towards the kitchen.

Liv looked up. 'I said, we'll do it!' Her voice was as sharp as the broken shards.

Defeated, Megan, left them to it.

Chapter 15

CHLOE SNAPPED awake. She lay in the glare of the moonlight, her heart thumping in her chest, simultaneously glad to have woken up and upset that she was now even more conscious of being alone in the small, dark hours of the night. Her phone told her it was 1.08 a.m.

She'd been having different versions of the same nightmare over and over again ever since her father died. In her dreams she would always be doing something ordinary: drying her hair, sitting at her till at work, shopping, looking at her phone or in a bar with her friends. Gradually she'd become aware of the sound of a baby crying. No one else in her dreams ever heard the child and they would carry on as normal, but she would grow increasingly distressed and would start searching for the baby. The weirdness was that she would look in totally illogical places: in handbags, underneath floorboards, behind mirrors, inside people's mouths. The crying would grow louder, then fainter, then stop – only to start up again the minute she ceased searching.

She always woke mid-dream.

She never found the child.

That her brain was tormenting her was disturbing, and tiring, but it made sense to Chloe. It was her punishment for not being there when her father died and for failing him ever since.

The night of his death she'd slept soundly and dreamlessly while he lay suffering in a room directly beneath her. It had taken the weight of Megan sitting on her bed, and the pressure of her hand on Chloe's shoulder, to wake her. Groggy as she'd been, she'd known immediately that something was wrong. Megan *never* came into her room. 'Is it Dad?' She'd pushed herself upright.

Megan hadn't answered her – not at first – but patted her shoulder awkwardly. Her touch through the thin material of Chloe's T-shirt had felt shockingly intimate. 'Yes. I'm sorry.' Another ineffectual, invasive pat of sympathy. 'He's gone.'

She'd believed Megan – why wouldn't she? – but automatically she'd been difficult. 'What do you mean, "gone"?'

'Chloe. He's died.'

'No.'

'Yes.'

Megan had reached out and touched Chloe again. This time it was quite an aggressive motion, both hands on her shoulders, pushing her back against the pillows. 'I'm sorry, but he has!' The image of her dad lying dead downstairs tumbled like the fragments of a kaleidoscope through Chloe's mind, gaining and losing coherence. Megan spoke slowly and firmly. 'He just stopped breathing.' The shaky image sharpened and settled. Megan took her hands away from Chloe's shoulders, as if finally convinced that her news had got through.

'Was it bad?' Chloe finally asked. There was a pause.

'No. It was quick at the end. He's at peace now,' Megan said. 'No more pain. No more frustration.' It was a logical thing to say after all the distress of the past few years, but it sounded trite. How was Chloe supposed to be thankful that her dad – who was laughing and being sarcastic not eight hours ago – was now dead? Gone. For ever. Megan leant forward and Chloe tensed, expecting another awkward physical exchange, but Megan was not reaching out for a hug, she was reaching for the light switch.

She clicked on the bedside lamp. For a few seconds Chloe was blinded. Once her eyes had adjusted, she found herself face-to-face with her father's... partner, lover or, Noah's favourite, mistress. They had never settled on an accurate description of what precisely Megan was. His death wasn't going to make that any easier. No label seemed to fit accurately, or comfortably. But at that point, in the middle of the night, in a big, dark house on the edge of the cliff, perhaps it didn't matter. Because in the light of the lamp, Chloe saw the face of a woman who had been robbed of the one person she loved more than anyone else in the world.

'What now?' Chloe forced herself to speak.

Megan pulled a hank of her hair over her shoulder and unconsciously stroked her own neck with the end of it. Her eyes strayed from Chloe's face to a point on the wall above her head. 'We obviously need to call your brother and sister to tell them.'

'And we need to call Mum.' Chloe suddenly, desperately, wanted it to be Eloise sitting in her bedroom, not Megan.

'Yes.' Another self-calming stroke – comfort dredged up from wherever it could be found. 'But not yet. There's no point ringing any of them at this time of night. It won't change anything. We'll call them in the morning.' She seemed to lose momentum. She stared at the wall for a few seconds, saying nothing. The only sound was the soft rasp of her hair against her skin. 'The thing we need to do now, apparently, is call a doctor to come and certify the death.'

The kaleidoscope shook again and Chloe 'saw' her father, lying on his back in the empty room downstairs, eyes open, robbed of movement and speech, looking like death but still alive, trapped inside a body that had gone from malfunctioning to collapsing. 'Christ, he is definitely dead, isn't he?'

Chloe's sharp tone brought Megan back into the present. 'Of course!'

But Chloe was already pushing aside the covers, and Megan. She scrambled out of bed, preparing to come to her father's aid.

'Chloe. Stop. He's dead. Lisa checked.'

'Lisa?' Chloe paused, confused.

'Yes. She's downstairs with him.'

'What's Lisa doing here?'

'Helping.' The vagueness was back.

'Since when has she been staying overnight?'

'Not now, Chloe.' They faced each other. 'I'll see you downstairs, when you're ready.' And with that, Megan walked out of the room slowly, closing the door with great care as she left.

And that's when Chloe really failed her father.

Because although she forced herself down the stairs and to the doorway of his room, she didn't go in. She couldn't. She stood in the hall, trying to slow her breathing as a way of controlling the scrabbling fear, but it didn't work. The room on the other side of the door was silent, and it was that lack of noise that truly terrified her. Her dad had never been a quiet man. He was a talker, a holder of opinions, a benign but articulate dictator when it came to family matters. Then, with the onset of MND, he had become noisy in a different way. His clattering walk, his breathing, his laboured speech, even the way he swallowed – it had all had a new cadence and volume. It had been impossible to live with her father and not be aware of his presence. But now, standing outside his room, Chloe could feel his absence, and she couldn't face it.

Plus, she had never seen a dead body before.

The sound of movement inside the room jolted her. She took a few steps backwards. The door brushed the carpet as it opened. Lisa came out. She stopped when she saw Chloe.

'Ah, Chloe. There you are.' It was said kindly. 'You can come in.' Her voice was shockingly normal. There was no whispering or reverence in her tone. When Chloe didn't move, Lisa gave a slight nod. 'It's okay.' But it wasn't – Chloe could feel the panic inside her, expanding. 'Megan is sitting with him while we wait for the doctor. I have rung, but it may be a while. You won't be in there on your own.'

But Chloe knew she couldn't.

Lisa put whatever she was holding down on the side and came over to Chloe. Very gently she placed her hand on Chloe's upper arm. 'There's nothing to be frightened of. It's just a body.' She studied Chloe's face, reading her distress in it. 'But there's no rule that says you have to "go and say goodbye", either. Not if you don't want to. It's an odd idea, when you think about it. After all, they've already gone. You do what you think is right for you. I was going to make us a cuppa. Do you want to come into the kitchen instead?' She picked up her stuff and walked away.

Chloe looked at the open door to her father's room, took a deep breath and followed Lisa.

She had been pathetic. She'd taken her sweet tea up to her room and crawled like a scared child back into bed, where she'd waited, feeling abandoned and bereft, aching to call her mother, but failing to do even that. At some point the doorbell had rung and there was a male voice in the hall, presumably the doctor. She listened to Lisa welcoming him, in her chirpy everyday pitch, taking responsibility for it all, while Chloe herself sat hunched up in bed, barely able to breathe and totally unable to go downstairs and help. After what felt like for ever, there were more voices – the undertakers?

Without so much as the whisper of footsteps, Megan was suddenly in Chloe's room again. 'They are about to take him away, Chloe. Are you sure you don't want to come down and say goodbye?' Chloe dumbly shook her head. Megan didn't push her. 'Okay. I thought I'd better check.' She turned and left.

A little while later, despite being huddled underneath her duvet, Chloe heard the muffled sounds of something heavy being removed from the house and knew it was her father's body.

And ever since the memory of that night had plagued her.

Which was why, when she'd come into the hall earlier in the evening and heard a voice saying his name on the other side of the door, she'd freaked out. Of course it had been Megan speaking. Who else could it have been? No one else went into her father's room. But it had shaken her badly.

1.25 a.m.

Night hours passed achingly slowly.

Chloe started scrolling through her messages, seeking comfort in the glow of her newsfeed. There was a world outside the house: people getting on with their lives, people having nights out, getting happily drunk with their friends or their lovers, people not trapped in a house full of the ghosts of regret. She longed for a reality that was as normal and thoughtless as that. After a while the images of everyone else's 'best lives' began to depress her. There were so many happy families and loved-up couples, so much concerted enjoyment. She switched to her messages. Nothing new. Out of desperation, she caved in and decided to call her mother, knowing full well it would go straight to voicemail. Even as she scrolled through for her number, Chloe imagined Liv's judgement on, and Noah's mockery of, her pathetic dependency. The baby of the family, still acting like a baby. The thought made her flush with embarrassment, but it didn't stop her leaving a message. Perhaps the timing of the voicemail might help to summon the maternal in Eloise. Perhaps?

Options exhausted, Chloe had no choice but to lie down and wait for morning.

Chapter 16

THEY'D AGREED to meet at 10 a.m. Angus had taken the kids to the park to give them some peace, free from the interruptions of pee requests and the half-hourly demands for snacks. Before the boys left, Liv supervised the allocation of hats and gloves, bodywarmers and scarves. How many of the items would make it back to the house was in the lap of the gods. The boys were like snakes, endlessly shedding their skins or, in their case, their sensible warm accessories. Liv watched them head off through the lounge window, envying Angus. With them gone, the house was quieter, sadder.

She waited until they were out of sight before reluctantly turning back to the task in hand. Someone – Megan? – had thoughtfully, or perhaps pointedly (given how much booze some of them had got through the previous night), put a jug of water and some glasses on the dining-room table. Liv took a sip of her green tea. Chloe sat at the table with her third coffee of the day. Noah's beverage of choice was not known, as he was yet to make an appearance. He was so predictable.

'Shall I go and get him?' Chloe asked at ten past.

'Yes.' Liv heard the crackle of irritation in her own voice. It was not a good start.

Chloe went out into the hall and shouted up the stairs, 'Noah! Get your arse down here. Now!'

Liv winced and a wave of queasiness rippled through her. She put her tea down and poured herself a glass of water. It was cold. Sipping small, chilly mouthfuls helped to settle her stomach a little.

Noah eventually appeared, looking sheepish, scruffy and empty-handed. Not so much as a notepad or a pen. He was about to head over to the window, but on seeing Liv's face he thought better of it. He pulled out a chair and deposited himself at the table. They were finally ready – as ready as they'd ever be – to discuss what they were going to do in response to their father's bizarre will. Noah rasped his hand across his stubbly chin. 'It's like a scene out of *The Sopranos*. I'm not in any immediate danger, am I?'

'Only if you carry on in that vein,' Liv snapped.

'Sorry.' He didn't look it.

Liv popped the button on the blue folder and withdrew the financial breakdown that she'd put together from the information the solicitor had provided, and from what she'd managed to find in her father's files. The files that Megan had finally given up, after being asked firmly and directly for them. Chloe really needed to work on her communication skills. The breakdown was an incomplete picture; quite a number of the headings had question marks against them, and a lot of the figures were very rough estimates, but they were thought-through guesses. It had taken her a lot of time and effort to put it together, working in the quiet kitchen while everyone else slept. Everyone except Megan, that is. She'd appeared downstairs at 7 a.m., dressed in the same, or possibly a different, shapeless dress-and-sad-cardigan combo. She'd been surprised to find the kitchen occupied, looked aggrieved and made a silent, overly polite performance of withdrawing.

'Shit, you have been busy, haven't you?' Noah eyed the documents.

Liv ignored him. 'Well, I thought it was important that we had at least a rough idea of the value of Dad's financial assets before we got into it.' She saw that both of her siblings had turned to the last page of her notes, zeroing in on the estimated total.

Simultaneously Chloe said, 'Wow' and Noah said, 'Um.'

Liv felt defensive. 'I've put in an educated guess for the house, and I'm waiting to get access to his current and savings accounts.' Megan had yet to give her the key card and the passcodes, despite promising that she would. 'The big unknown is the size of Dad's pension pot. He had a couple of different policies. I've chased them, but there's a lot of money-laundering checks to go through before they'll release any information.'

'You think we should sell the house straight away?' said Chloe.

'Of course we'll sell it. What else would we do with it?' Noah responded.

'Hang on. Can we all just take a breath,' Liv said. They looked at her, Chloe concertedly, Noah sporadically – his eyes kept returning to the breakdown of assets. Liv needed them both to focus. They only had two days to devise a plan, and time was ticking, but they had to be logical. Whatever they agreed this weekend, she needed it to stick. She couldn't face going round after round on this, not in her current state. 'Maybe it's best if we talk about what's in the will, before we get down to looking at the finances.' She stopped and waited for one of them to take up the conversation. Neither did. Again the responsibility of it all pressed down on her. She took her copy of Jonathan's will out of the green file. Colour-coding helped to keep her thoughts organised and her stress levels manageable – and green was a calming colour. 'What did you guys think when the solicitor explained what Dad had said?'

Chloe took a swig of her coffee before answering. 'I suppose I was a bit surprised. But there again, I don't know what I was expecting. It wasn't something I'd given much thought to.'

'Really?' Noah asked.

Chloe looked rattled to be challenged by Noah. 'No.'

'Even with his diagnosis?'

'No!' She said it more firmly. 'Day-to-day he seemed to be coping. And in the last couple of months he seemed on better form. Not well, obviously, but happier in himself, less frustrated. He was relatively stable, healthwise. So no, what he'd written in his will, as you very well know, wasn't a top priority for me. I wasn't thinking about Dad dying, I was helping him to live.'

Liv wondered what the two of them had been talking about together, in the garage, without her.

'Hey. Lighten up. It wasn't a priority for me, either.' Noah poured himself a glass of water and glugged half of it down. 'I'm just saying that I knew he thought about what would happen after he died, quite a lot.'

'How?' It was Liv's turn.

Noah finished his drink. 'Cos he mentioned it every now and again.'

'What did he say?'

'Well, only that he was putting everything in order for us.'

'Us?'

'Yes. Us. Me. Whatever. The implication was that it was sorted.'

'Well, it isn't, is it?' Liv said.

Noah pulled a face, somewhere between a smile and a frown. 'Well, it doesn't have to be complicated. He had three children. He explicitly left the division of the estate to us. That would imply, to me anyway, that his priority was to see that we were all okay.'

'Meaning?'

'Well, if you want me to get straight to it... a three-way spilt between us of the bulk of the estate, with something for Mum and something for Megan, maybe.' The bald statement of his opinion didn't surprise Liv. Noah liked to keep things simple, even when they weren't. But it was interesting that Chloe wasn't disagreeing with him, and even Liv herself didn't really know what to say by way of a valid argument. 'Am I wrong?' Noah asked.

'What do you mean by "something for Megan... maybe"? She was his partner, whether we like that or not. She was the one who cared for Dad when he got sick. Was there for him at the end. And this is her home. We have a responsibility to think about what's going to happen to her,' Liv said.

'It's her home – for now.' Noah was the king of reductive thinking.

'Jeez, Noah. He's only been dead twelve days and you're already talking about throwing her out on the street.'

'Stop being so melodramatic. You know full well that I don't mean right this minute.' Noah tipped his chair back and balanced it precariously on its rear legs, like he used to when he was a teenager. 'But that's the whole point of this bloody weekend, isn't it? To get everything agreed, so that we can all go back to our lives.'

Chloe suddenly spoke up. 'You both seem to be forgetting that this is my home as well. Where am I supposed to live?' The red rash creeping up her neck confirmed her rising agitation.

'Look. I'm not saying sell it immediately.' Noah banged his chair back down on its legs. 'But it's the biggest asset. It's been too big for Dad for years. Five bedrooms, the grounds. It should have a family living in it.'

'It has. Or at least it used to!'

As always, Noah chose to ignore the signs that Chloe was teetering on the edge. He ploughed on regardless. 'Hey, don't shoot the messenger. I'm just saying what other people are thinking. Liv, surely you agree?'

Liv spun her mug through 360 degrees, buying time. As she did so, she noticed the old stain on the tabletop – caused by paint seeping through her art homework onto the veneer. Noah was right. The house needed to be sold; it was too full of the past. It was probably worth in the region of £600,000 to £700,000, which made it by far the biggest asset. But the complications of a newly bereaved and disinherited Megan and a currently homeless, partner-less, rootless Chloe did complicate the matter slightly. Never mind what their mother would say. To date, Eloise had said surprisingly little, which was puzzling Liv. Their mother was not normally one to keep her own counsel. Liv pushed that thought to one side for the time being. They needed to agree an outline of what they were going to do, before they said anything to their mother. If they presented anything other than a united front, it was going to get messy.

'Can we take a few steps back. If I'm being be honest, the will shocked me. Not so much the contents, though even they seem odd to me, but more the cloak-and-dagger approach of the whole thing. Whenever Dad talked to me about his affairs, I thought, like you said, Noah' – olive branch waved – 'that he was on top of it all. When he got the diagnosis, I know that ramped up his desire to put his house in order. From the way he spoke about it, I got the impression that he'd broken down everything in detail. Made everything clear, in terms of who was to get what. And when I looked through his paperwork, it was very organised. But the will... and that bizarre Statement of Wishes. Well, it's just so out of character.'

Chloe nodded. 'And the fact that it's a new will. When did the solicitor say he changed it?'

Liv started looking for the exact date. The revision bothered her as well. She had read though the file Ms Hewson had given her. The original will had been written back in 1982, soon after Liv was born. It was revised, but only marginally, in 1985 after Noah's birth, and then again in 1993 after Chloe arrived on the scene. At which point it had been simple. Everything to Eloise, apart from a series of bequests to close friends and local charities. Then there was a gap of more than twenty years. At the end of which he'd had his midlife crisis, lost his head, fallen for Megan, abandoned his marriage, driven their mother away and, far too quickly, installed his young lover in their home. Liv had been shocked and distressed to see how, immediately after the decree nisi came through, their father had rewritten the original will to reflect that seismic shift. He had cut out their mother, brutally and efficiently, as if she was something cancerous.

They were all aware of the financial wrangling around the time of the divorce – it had been impossible not to be. It had been heartbreaking to see their parents descending into the mire. They had sided with their mother, of course. How could they not? It had been a huge relief when the pair of them finally agreed a financial settlement and something that vaguely resembled a truce.

What the actual divorce settlement had been, they'd never found out – which was a reflection of their parents' old-fashioned reticence to discuss money and, very possibly, an indication that their mother had taken their dad to the cleaner's. Whatever the settlement was, it had plainly been enough for Eloise to start a new life, in her own home – a very nice two-bedroomed town house in York – and set up a new business. It was something to do with professional development. Liv still didn't fully understand what their mother actually did, for the extortionate daily rate she claimed to charge.

After the hatchet job of cutting their mother out of the original will and reapportioning his estate with percentage legacies for each of them, and any subsequent grandchildren, plus a slightly revised list of bequests to specific charities and close friends, there had been no further changes. Until the last revision five months before his death. When he had filleted the will of every detail, and had made them executors instead. An action that seemed totally out of character, and pointless.

And here was an even stranger thing. Having gone to the effort of rewriting his will – not once, but twice – at neither point had their father so much as mentioned Megan. If Megan really was the love of his life, the woman for whom it had been worth ripping his marriage apart, why was she not a beneficiary? It made no sense, especially after her years of caring for him through his illness. Liv was struggling to find a rational reason for his behaviour. Had his awareness of his own mortality made him reassess? Had he weighed up his life and reflected on his decisions? Perhaps this new, final will was a sign of his regret at being so blinded by his passion for Megan? Perhaps it was his way of trying to compensate for breaking up the family?

But that left Megan as their problem – which was hardly fair. She must be feeling so abandoned by their father, served up to their mercy, or their spite. And there was spite. Liv didn't like to admit it, but there was. How could there not be?

Liv realised that Noah and Chloe were both looking at her, waiting. She glanced down at her notes. 'He called the solicitor's in June, and the will was signed by the twenty-eighth. It was witnessed by two people who are members of staff at the solicitor's.'

'Why not one of us?' Noah asked.

'Because if you witness a will, you can't be a beneficiary of it.'

Noah raised an ironic eyebrow, impressed by Liv's legal knowledge, but programmed to mock it.

'Ms Hewson told me. I thought it was strange as well.'

Noah stood up and started walking around the table. 'This just gets weirder. Do you believe Dad was thinking straight?'

Liv and Chloe objected at the same time. 'Noah!'

He held on to one of the chairs and stretched. 'Again, can we all stop being so over-sensitive. He was ill, in pain, dying, very probably depressed; do you not think that might, conceivably, have affected his judgement?'

'Ms Hewson said he was of sound mind. If he hadn't been, she wouldn't have been able to draw up the new will.'

'And that's down to her to decide, is it?'

'Yes, it is actually.'

'So it stands. Even if Megan decides to challenge it?' Noah queried.

'Yes.' Liv felt swamped by the lack of clarity and all the questions. They needed to move on and get down to deciding something.

'I think she might,' Chloe said.

'What makes you say that?' Noah seemed surprised when Chloe spoke, as if he'd forgotten she was in the room.

'Just the way she's been since he died.' She stopped.

'So you keep saying. What precisely do you mean by "the way she's been"?' Liv prompted.

'Well, you've seen her. She's all over the place. It's like she's here, but she's not. She's been drifting round the house like a ghost ever since he passed. Then she has these bursts when she goes manic – cleaning and shopping and cooking. Even on the night he died, she was strange. She *seemed* calm, but she was really quite aggressive with me. Like she was struggling to keep control.'

Liv found herself imagining how dreadful that night must have been, and having some sympathy for Megan. Chloe was not good in a crisis; not that good most of the time, if the truth be told.

Her sister went on, 'And in the meeting at the solicitor's, when you read out the details of the will – well, that was hardly a normal reaction, was it? She acted like a zombie, but inside I think she's screaming.'

Liv didn't want Chloe and Noah to go off on one of their 'slag off Megan' jaunts. It would waste time and oxygen. Besides, Ms Hewson had been very clear that the will was valid. 'I don't think laying into Megan is going to get us anywhere. She's had a tough time. I'd be surprised if she wasn't struggling at the moment. And this…' she indicated all the paperwork spread across the tabletop, 'can't be helping. This mess is on Dad.'

Noah stopped prowling. 'Hang on there, Liv. What do you mean: this is *on* Dad? In my book, he hasn't done *anything* wrong. Unless I'm missing something.' He paused.

Liv said nothing. There was no point, when Noah was in one of his self-important moods.

'All he's done is leave his legacy to us to decide, which I think is a good thing. Better than him leaving the lot to Megan.'

There was another long pause, during which neither Liv nor Chloe disagreed with him.

Chapter 17

MEGAN RETREATED upstairs, hurt that Angus hadn't thought to invite her along on the trip out with the children. Even big, bluff, kind Angus excluded her – schooled, no doubt, by Liv.

She looked around the bedroom – *their* room, which had become *hers*. The stripping down of their marriage had been a series of tiny cuts and discreet incisions, but Jonathan's move downstairs had been a stab-wound. It made sense, of course, especially after his fall. It was the only safe thing to do. And, as Lisa pointed out, it meant that Jonathan was closer to the action during the day – less isolated, more part of the household, which was good for his mood – but for Megan it had been a watershed moment, not just of losing more of Jonathan to the disease, but of losing another big chunk of him to Lisa.

Lisa.

A bit-part player in the grand scheme of things, but the person without whom she and Jonathan would never have got through the last seven months.

Was it really only seven months?

It felt like a lifetime.

Megan's arms had been buried up to her elbows in the washing machine when the doorbell rang. Another candidate for the role of Jonathan's PA. The washing load plopped wetly into the basket. She reached inside and peeled free a pair of pyjama bottoms that were stuck to the drum, but she had to leave the lone sock, because the bell rang again, more insistently this time.

This one was early.

Megan dried her hands hastily on a tea towel and straightened her jumper – there was no time for lipstick, her go-to 'armour'. The bell rang a third time just as she reached for the door handle. *All right, all right. I'm coming.*

The woman standing on the doorstep smiled. 'Hello. I'm Lisa, Lisa Browne.' She was middle-aged, with short hair, average height, average weight, average-looking. She extended her hand. She had a firm, confident handshake.

'Come through.' Megan fixed on her welcome-smile. 'I was about to make a coffee. Would you like one?'

'No, thank you.' So brisk efficiency it was going to be then.

Once they were settled, Megan asked the usual questions, using the CV that the agency had emailed over as her starting point. Lisa Browne had spent twenty-three years in the care sector, working in a mixture of nursing homes and in-home settings. Her résumé listed a series of employers, spread across the country. She had moved around quite a lot. Megan made a mental note to ask her about that later on in their chat. Lisa had good references, attesting to her professionalism and her 'lovely manner with service users, especially those with mental impairment.' On the downside, she had only the most basic qualifications; she had no physical therapy experience and no direct experience with MND sufferers. But she answered all Megan's questions in a calm voice. There was no fidgeting or fudging of her answers. She was happy with the proposed hours. She nodded with understanding when Megan explained about wanting to hold on to her three days at work at the local comprehensive school, at least for the time being. To all intents and purposes, Lisa Browne seemed *fine*. An acceptable, flexible candidate – Megan had interviewed far worse.

But the problem with a formal interview was that it didn't allow for the real questions. Which were... What are you like as a person? What will it feel like to have you around for long periods of time? Can I share a kitchen with you without feeling uncomfortable? Can I bear to have you see me first thing in the morning in my dressing gown, with my face creased and vulnerable? Will I be able to relax, knowing you are under my roof listening and learning about our lives?

And the biggest question of all: How will you get on with Jonathan?

How will you cope with his resentment at having to rely on someone *like you*? How will you respond to his black humour? His moods? His challenging views, on a wide range of topics. His impatience? His refusal to take advice? His need to control what is happening to him? Jonathan was not a passive old person, grateful for the help, happy to chat on mindlessly, accepting of his lot.

Lisa was looking at her, waiting. She had her own questions about 'the patient'.

Megan described Jonathan's symptoms, detailing the hard facts clearly and succinctly. She described the rampant progress of the disease in recent months and the increasing degree of his physical impairment, using the familiar terms common to all motor neurone sufferers. She went into the level of assistance required. Jonathan's medication. Sleep patterns. Exercise routine. She was very informative.

None of it really described Jonathan. The man who, as she spoke, was sitting in his study, waiting to be introduced to this next *indignity.* Megan contemplated forewarning Lisa about his resistance to being helped, his stubbornness, but bottled it. 'Perhaps it would be best if you met Jonathan in person.' Throwing her in at the deep end – it was mean, but it was as good a test as any.

Lisa nodded, unfazed, and stood up.

She was keen.

She was going to need to be.

Forty minutes passed, and still Lisa did not re-emerge from the study. Megan filled the time with small, mindless tasks and repeated trips across the hall, which yielded no clues as to how their conversation was going. She was staring into the fridge, thinking about what to put together for lunch, when Lisa surprised her by appearing in the doorway and announcing, 'We're all done.'

Megan felt flustered and stumbled over her words. 'Good. Fine. I'll show you out then.' Listening to herself struggling to string together a coherent sentence, she felt a slight bristle of resentment. Surely it was down to her to decide when the interview was at a close. She still hadn't asked Lisa about her habit of not staying in any job or location for very long – but the opportunity had gone. At the front door Megan said she would be in touch with the agency *after she and Jonathan had had time to reflect on the other applicants.*

Lisa smiled, said, 'Fine' and set off up the drive with a spring in her step.

It was a short reflection.

Jonathan was adamant that Lisa was the best candidate they'd seen. Her limited qualifications didn't seem to trouble him, which surprised Megan. With every other applicant he'd been unbelievably picky.

'She doesn't have any direct experience of MND.' Megan was surprised at herself for raising it. She was the one who was desperate for them to appoint somebody.

Jonathan waved Megan's concerns away, saying, 'I don't know, Meg. There was just something about her I liked.'

Relieved that he was finally accepting having someone else around to help, Megan phoned the agency that afternoon to secure Lisa's services.

She started work the following week, and their lives were never the same again.

Because Lisa proved to be exactly what they needed. Competent, unobtrusive, helpful. Megan was able to go off to work without worrying – at least not as much as before. And when she got home, it was to a clean, orderly house, sometimes with a meal prepared, and to a Jonathan who was less agitated and resentful, and far more alert than he had been for months.

As the weeks went by, and Lisa took over a lot of the physical work and some of the mental strain, life stabilised. And although Jonathan's symptoms continued their destructive march through his body, his mood definitely improved, so much so that Megan was able to carve out thin slivers of time for herself. Lisa was forever encouraging her to have a bath or go for a run, or to go out for a drink with a friend. These little gasps of freedom, after holding her breath for such a sustained period, were good for Megan. Very quickly she grew to rely on Lisa, trusting her with some of the administration of Jonathan's illness – of which there was a lot – with his prescriptions and his physical therapy.

It was a huge relief to share the load with someone. His family was very little help. Liv called regularly for updates, to offer advice, suggest alternative approaches and question what the doctors had said, and she did come to visit as often as work and family would allow, but her involvement was not without its tensions. Every call and visit made Megan feel inadequate and defensive. Noah was far less involved – turning up at the house unexpectedly, then dropping off the radar for weeks on end, but at least his contact seemed to bring Jonathan some pleasure. If nothing else, Noah seemed to be able to make his father laugh. And then there was Chloe, whose presence in the house was no help whatsoever. She obviously loved her father, but in terms of making a positive contribution to his care or even to the general running of the house, she was as good as useless.

No, the person who made the real difference was Lisa, and for that Megan was grateful.

Until that gratitude was tainted.

Megan had been out for a run. She'd been reluctant to go at first as Jonathan had had a bad day, but Lisa had encouraged her, saying it would do her good. She'd been right. After ten minutes of wheezy, breathless effort Megan had got into her stride. The sun on her face, the fresh air in her lungs, her arms and legs pumping: it all reminded her that she was still young and fit. For a glorious hour she'd enjoyed the blankness of her mind and the simplicity of putting one foot in front of another. By the time she'd returned home, sweaty and tired, she'd felt lighter, more positive. As she came in through the back of the house she'd been pleased, and surprised, to hear laughter coming from Jonathan's room. He must have continued to pick up. She pulled off her trainers and padded into the hall in her socks. The door to his room was ajar. There was another chortle, a noise that, though distorted by his condition, still contained joy. Instinctively Megan drew herself up onto her toes and crept the last few steps across the hall to his room. She wanted to hear him laugh again. She missed his laughter.

'Show me another one?' Jonathan's voice.

'Would you like to go modern chic, eco-friendly or tasteless bling?'

'Oh, eco, I think... In death as in life, et cetera. But not wicker, that always strikes me as a bit girly.'

'Okay.' There was a pause. 'How about this... the Diamant Fourteen: *A wooden coffin with fourteen facets. Available in silk matt-black or white, with six painted solid-birch handles. Constructed from Nordic birch.* Apparently' – there was laughter in Lisa's voice as well – '*the Diamant series marks a break from the traditional use of valuable hardwoods and offers a more sustainable approach. The coffin interiors are upholstered with a modest butterfly-patterned organic cotton, inspired by the wild surrounds of the Jacob Jensen Design studio in Hejlskov. Price –* ooh, very reasonable,' Lisa added sarcastically, '*nine hundred and ninety-nine pounds, including VAT.*'

'It looks like something you'd pick up flatpack, from Ikea.'

'You said you wanted something environmentally friendly.'

'Why not a cardboard box?'

'You might as well. It'd certainly be cheaper.'

'But where would we find one big enough to accommodate all this brawn?' There it was again – the sardonic humour he used to share with Megan.

'Oh, trust me, you can find anything you want on comparethecoffin.com.'

'You're making that up!' There was another spluttery chuckle, more of a cough than a laugh.

'I am not. Look!' Lisa's voice, in contrast to Jonathan's, was strong. 'Let me see if they do a cardboard range for the truly stingy.'

Megan was frozen by the tone as much as the content of their conversation, the fun they were having – discussing Jonathan's death. The elation from her run drained away, replaced by an uneasy mix of shock and jealousy. She crept away, leaving them to continue their 'jolly' conversation.

When she raised it with Jonathan later that evening, after Lisa had left for the day, he paused and put his glasses on his lap. 'We were just having a laugh.'

'About coffins!'

He took a breath, coughed. 'Yes. About coffins.' Though his hands were shaking, his voice was steady.

'It upset me.'

'You weren't meant to hear.' He studied her. 'I'm sorry if we upset you.' He wiped his mouth. 'But it helps.'

'What helps?'

'Being able to talk to Lisa about stuff like that.'

That hurt. The admission, and the use of 'we' – there wasn't supposed to be a 'we' that involved the paid carer. 'You can talk to me.' But even as the words left Megan's mouth, they both knew they weren't true.

Jonathan's expression softened and he reached out his hand – asking her forgiveness but also her permission. 'We were messing about. Lisa has the same black sense of humour that a lot of doctors and nurses have. Not Liv, obviously.' Megan knew that the jibe at his daughter was designed to placate her. It did not. 'I suppose being around illness and death full-time toughens you up. That's one of the reasons Lisa and I get on. Nothing fazes her.'

Megan knew it was unreasonable to be jealous of Jonathan's relationship with Lisa, but that didn't stop her feeling excluded. 'Do you not see how upsetting it is that you find it easier to talk to her than to me?'

He looked concerned. 'Megan, I'm sorry. I love you. I truly don't want to cause you any more pain than I already am.' He lifted his chin, with difficulty. 'But Lisa is a person with some very specific, very relevant experience, and she has a way of looking at life, and death, that is... helpful to me in the current circumstances. The way she is. The way we talk. It relieves the pressure, and I think, in the long run, it's good for both of us.'

Megan couldn't argue with the fact that Lisa had made a positive difference to both their lives, but that still didn't mean her presence wasn't a mixed blessing. But because she loved Jonathan and because what he was saying was true, she said no more. Instead she went and sat on the arm of the chair, taking his hand in hers. In this position, touching, but unable to look into each other's eyes, they made their peace – and admitted yet another breach into their relationship.

As if summoned by the memory, a message from Lisa pinged into Megan's in-box. It was uncanny how she was always – *just there.*

Megan read the text. It was another offer of help. More kind, unsentimental words. In her current vulnerable state, she felt pathetically grateful, and conflicted. It should not be Lisa who was there for her. She should be sharing Jonathan's death with her family – with *his* family.

But none of *them* understood.

None of *them* had been there at the end.

None of *them* comprehended the full extent of the impact of MND on Jonathan.

None of *them* knew what had been going through his mind in the last few months of his life.

None of *them* could answer any of her questions.

But Lisa could.

Chapter 18

THEY RECONVENED after a comfort break, which had been prompted by Noah's urgent need to pee and to get away from Liv, if only for a few minutes. She was relentless. As soon as they were all gathered around the table she got straight back to business. 'I have an idea that might help us decide what to give Mum and Megan.' She paused and Noah could have sworn his big sister looked uncertain for a second. 'Bear with me on this. My idea is that we work out what their share should be on the basis of time.'

'What?' Noah's head was banging. Dehydration and Liv's voice were making it worse.

'I'm suggesting we work out what to give them on a pro-rata basis.'

'Fuck me, Sis. I thought you were a doctor, not a sodding accountant.' She really was something when she got going.

Chloe winced. 'Noah. Shush. Hear her out.'

Liv ploughed on. 'I think it might be a fair way of deciding things, and it has the benefit of taking the emotion out of it. Megan is entitled to something, there's no point arguing about that – we just have to work out what.' She pulled a piece of paper towards her. 'Mum and Dad were together how long?'

Noah shrugged, genuinely at a loss. It was Chloe who came to their rescue. 'They were married in the summer of 1979.'

'Do we know when they actually first got together?' Liv asked.

Once again Chloe proved to be the reliable family archivist. '1977. Mum said they met when she was in her second year at uni, so we could check precisely, but they must have been together for the best part of forty years.'

On her piece of paper Liv wrote: *Mum x 40 yrs and Megan x 5 yrs.* 'So if we used the time they each spent with Dad as the basis of our calculation, that would mean Megan would get roughly one-eighth of whatever we give to Mum, out of whatever lump sum we decide to set aside for them.'

Noah, whose head felt like it might crack in half, said, 'You are kidding, aren't you?'

Liv bristled. 'I know it seems a bit simplistic, but we weren't getting anywhere earlier; we were just going round in circles, trying to second-guess what proportion of the estate Dad intended to go to Megan and Mum.'

'Oh, and this is your big idea?'

'Noah. Don't.' Liv's voice went up a notch.

'Don't... *don't* me! Are you seriously equating Mum and Megan? A marriage and a midlife crisis.'

'I'm only trying to come up with a workable solution.'

'Okay.' He stood up, suddenly agitated. 'Let's give your *solution* a whirl. In fact if we're going do it, we might as well go the whole hog.' He grabbed the piece of a paper and the pen and scored through the number five, hard. 'Best start by being accurate. We "found out" about Megan the Christmas of 2014, but that's not when it started.

He'd been shagging her for more than a year by then, so, if you want to be wholly accurate, we owe Megan another few per cent.'

Chloe cleared her throat as if she was about to say something, but then seemed to think better of it.

Noah ignored her. 'And, dear Sis, you've missed us off your list. If this is going to come down to the numbers, then you need to factor us into your equations.' He bent over the piece of paper and scribbled their names down, then added a number beside each. 'That gives Liv – thirty-seven; me – thirty-four; and I'm sorry, Chloe, that puts you on twenty-six, though given that your birthday is next month, Liv might be kind and let you have twenty-seven.' He shoved the paper back across the table at Liv. 'There! You can crunch the numbers on that for us, and we'll see where we end up. It's interesting to note that this impartial system of yours means you come out on top. Who knew?' He gave a cartoon shrug.

Chloe finally spoke up, but so quietly that neither Liv nor Noah heard her.

'What?' Noah snapped.

She had to repeat herself. 'How do you know how long he'd been seeing Megan for? You just said Dad had been sleeping with Megan for more than a year before we found out. How do you know?'

Liv joined in. 'Yes, Noah, how the hell do you know that?'

Noah cursed himself for his slip. Now it would become a whole other thing. God, families were sometimes more trouble than they were worth. There was a clatter in the hall. Then another. The noise scraped across his already frayed nerves. His sisters were both staring at him. He was left with no choice. 'Dad told me.'

'When?' Liv and Chloe chimed together.

'I don't remember exactly. One evening.'

'Recently?'

His attempt at a nonchalant shrug didn't quite work. 'Does it matter when he told me?'

They both stared at him. Liv answered. 'Yes, it does. You're saying that you've known details about his affair for ages, and yet you never said anything to either of us.'

'I didn't think it was something Dad wanted broadcasting.'

'So why did he tell you?'

Noah took offence at that. 'Perhaps because he wanted to talk to somebody he knew would listen, not judge him.' This comment was met with a hostile silence.

'Does Mum know he spoke to you?' Chloe asked.

'What do you think?'

'So... no!'

'Correct, Chloe! I did not have a heart-to-heart with our mother about our father's illicit affair with a woman half his age.'

'What did Dad actually say?' Liv wanted the details. She obviously couldn't bear the thought of Noah knowing more than her.

Noah rubbed his hand over his face. 'Not much.'

'Go on.'

'Look, we were having a drink together one night, around the time things were really rocky with Mum. She was out, so it was just the two of us in an empty house, with a bottle of Scotch. He was in a bit of a state. Not like his usual self at all. We drank... a lot. We talked.'

'And?'

'And he told me what had been going on.' Noah regretted getting into this, but it was too late now. Liv and Chloe both looked appalled.

'So, go on. What did he say?' Liv pushed.

Noah felt no desire to share the details of his father's single-malt-laced, self-pitying monologue with his sisters – not least because he didn't want them to feel the same disappointment he had, at the realisation that their dad was no different from the next guy. Nor did Noah want to dwell too much on the sympathetic ear that Jonathan had automatically assumed would be forthcoming, when he confessed to his relationship with Megan. In choosing to unburden himself to Noah, his father had seemed to be including him in a club that Noah had no desire to be identified as a member of. So instead what he said was, 'He obviously felt guilty. Wanted to explain his actions.'

'That was it? He felt guilty?' Liv was like a woodpecker stabbing away at a tree.

'More or less.' Their silence forced him to elaborate. 'He talked about how he'd really fallen for Megan. How it had surprised him that he was still capable of falling in love, at his age.'

'He never talked about any of this to me.' Chloe sounded aggrieved. There it was again, their desperate jockeying to be the chosen one. It was pathetic really.

'And what did you say in response?' Liv pecked on and on – it was amazing that her beak didn't snap clean off.

Noah felt his headache pulse. 'I don't really remember.' Liv snorted. 'I didn't excuse him, if that's what you're implying. I was shocked and mad with him. But at the end of the day, it was his life.' He wanted to get off the topic of his father's infidelity and the sticky subject of secrets. 'What can I say? It was one booze-soaked conversation, a long time ago. I didn't think there was any point mentioning it.'

The noise in the hallway was back, adding yet another layer of irritation to what was turning into a fairly exasperating morning.

'But if you'd told us, we might have been able to do something!' Liv just wouldn't accept that shit happened. You couldn't always fix things.

'So their divorce is my fault now, is it?' He heard the anger in his voice.

'I'm not saying that,' she snapped back.

'It sounds to me like you are.' They were like kids again, bickering and scoring points. 'I didn't think it was my place to go wading into our parents' marriage, pointing fingers and blaming Dad for fucking it all up. Besides, if you want someone to blame, how about Megan? If she'd walked away at the first sign of something between her and Dad, then he would very probably have stuck with Mum and we could have stayed one big happy family!'

There was a beat while they all took a moment to contemplate how far away from a big happy family they were at that precise moment.

Liv held back for all of two seconds before opening her mouth again. 'Is this why you're so set against Megan getting a decent share? You want to punish her for seducing Dad?'

Noah sighed. He felt exhausted and it was only 11.15 a.m. 'Do I need a rational, reasoned argument for why I don't feel predisposed to give away my inheritance to the woman who wrecked our parents' marriage?'

'No.' Liv and Chloe together, this time.

'Good!' Finally something they agreed on.

'So...' Noah rubbed his forehead, trying to scrub away his headache, 'given that we now have Liv's patented algorithm to settle this, why don't we let her do her stuff with the maths? You give us a shout when you've got the final *score on the doors* worked out, and we can reconvene and start arguing again.'

Chloe's plaintive 'We're not arguing' went unheard, or at least uncommented on.

Noah stood up. He simply couldn't stand being in the room any longer. 'If we've nothing else to discuss, I'm off for a shower and something to eat.' He walked over to the door.

He was behaving like a bit of tosser and he knew it, but he felt no inclination to stop. He blamed his banging head and the not sleeping; and the twenty unanswered calls to Josie; and bloody Liv with her stupid idea about divvying up the estate according to time served! And that damn noise. He couldn't believe Liv and Chloe hadn't noticed it. An erratic clatter followed by quick thudding footsteps, then another clatter, then another. It sounded like something being dropped or thrown, repeatedly. It was irritating, and very distracting.

He stood up, walked over to the door. And then, for old times' sake, Noah found himself unable to resist having the last word. 'Cheer up, Liv, at this rate we'll be through by lunchtime.' He yanked open the door and stepped out into the hallway – where the mystery of the noise was finally solved.

Arthur was posed, halfway up the stairs, his arm raised, mid-throw. Noah tried to moderate his tone to be child-friendly. It wasn't the little guy's fault that his mother was an uptight, anal control-freak. You can't pick your family.

'What are you up to, Buddy?'

'Just playing?' Arthur lowered his arm and held his hand behind his back. He looked guilty.

'Playing what?'

'Flying races… like in the dragon book.'

'Races, eh?'

Arthur nodded, seriously. 'I'm seeing which one the flies the best.'

It was only then that Noah noticed the scatter of chess pieces across the hallway floor. The frustration of the past twenty-four hours boiled over. 'Whatever you've got in your hand, I want you to give it to me!' Arthur blinked in shock at Noah's raised voice. 'Now!'

Arthur held out his fist and uncurled his fingers. And there, resting on his sweaty, chubby palm, was the white queen. Noah lunged up the stairs and snatched it from him. Then returned to the hall and started collecting up the other pieces, checking each one for damage as he did so.

'These aren't toys, Arthur. Anyway, you shouldn't be throwing things around, especially things that *do not* belong to you! You could have broken them.' Noah was too focused on his task to see Arthur's lip wobble, and the appearance of an audience for their altercation.

Angus had emerged from the kitchen, mug of coffee in his huge paw of a hand. 'What's going on?' Mild-mannered Angus. A man so laid-back that the desire to smack him in the face was occasionally overwhelming.

Liv appeared in the dining-room doorway. This was turning into an unfunny farce.

On seeing his mother, Arthur decided that he was, on reflection, really upset and promptly burst into tears.

His sobbing only served to wind Noah up further. 'He was chucking these around the hall. Where did you get them from?' He knew he was barking at his nephew and he should stop, but he couldn't. He was mad; why not direct some of that anger at a child, especially one who had no respect for other people's property?

Arthur, who was by now wailing as if mortally injured, ran over to his mother and buried his face in her stomach. Liv immediately went into full-blown Mommy Bear mode. 'Noah! He didn't mean any harm. You need to calm down.'

Noah got up from the floor, his hand full of chess pieces, not knowing who to shout at next.

Angus instinctively, and gallantly, padded across the hall and slid in front of his wife and child. Deflect-and-distract tactics. 'It's my fault, Noah. We found them in the chest upstairs. We were playing with them in bed this morning. Arthur liked the shapes. He must have gone upstairs and taken a handful when we got back from the park. Sorry, mate. I didn't realise they had any sentimental value.'

God, he really did need a punch. That would wipe the placatory easy-going smile off his stupid face. *Sentimental!* How dare he? It was such a reductive word, so at odds with the emotions careering around Noah's body. They were all staring at him – none of them kindly. 'Well, I'd appreciate it if you didn't let the boys have every sodding thing they ask for. It wouldn't hurt them to hear "No" every now and again.' Ignoring his crying nephew, Noah swept – as imperiously as he could manage, for someone who had just bawled out a three-year-old – up the stairs, leaving them free to talk about him behind his back.

The biscuit tin containing the other chess pieces was, as Angus had said, lying open on the floor of his old bedroom. Noah retrieved it, and the board. He took everything into his room and closed the door. He wiped the board with his sleeve and put it on the chest of drawers, then carefully laid out the pieces, polishing each one on the hem of his jumper before putting them in place. Black first, then white, as family tradition dictated. He was relieved to discover that none of the pieces had been lost.

It had taken him until he was seventeen to beat his dad. That's how much of a purist his father had been. There was no throwing a game to build his son's confidence, no matter how often their early games ended in strops and lengthy sulks. Yet another life lesson meted out in accordance with Jonathan's principle that children were not a protected species. As he was very fond of saying, repeatedly, chess was a game of skill and strategy – to get good at it took time and patience; to win, you had to be better than your opponent. Hence Jonathan had merely ignored his son's angst and his wife's pleas for a little humility, and had been merciless. At the time Noah had seethed with teenage frustration. They'd go months between games, with Noah refusing to give his dad the satisfaction of trouncing him, again, but eventually he'd always come back, desperate to try and best his dad. He'd secretly spent hours watching online tutorials, and even – though it damaged his street-cred no end – sought opponents at school, and later at sixth-form college, in order to improve his game. Indeed it was probably down to Mr Watson, his history teacher, who was always happy to play a few moves over lunchtime, that Noah eventually beat his dad. The realisation he'd *done* him, and that Jonathan would have to forfeit the game, was one of the best moments of Noah's life. The fact that his dad hadn't been gracious in defeat – he'd actually been really pissed off about it – had only served to make the victory even sweeter.

Noah stood back and looked at the chess set, taking pleasure in the memory. His sisters wanted their recollections of their father to be rose-tinted. Noah was glad his came to him in black and white. It was far more honest. Even aside from the infidelity, Noah knew his dad had been flawed. He'd competed at everything. Aggressively. He'd been a royal pain in the arse a lot of the time. He was unforgiving and opinionated. Argumentative. Often impatient. A tough-love sort of dad.

And Noah missed him more than he wanted to admit.

Chapter 19

LUNCH WAS eaten in relays in the kitchen, no one feeling inclined to accommodate anyone else's tastes or timings. Having laid everything out ready for them, Megan had disappeared, again. She was like a shoemaker's elf, silently and, Liv suspected, grudgingly catering for their needs. After they'd eaten, they drifted off into separate rooms. Liv and Angus remained in the kitchen with the washing-up. They couldn't leave it all to Megan. As they cleared away the plates, Liv became aware of how quiet the house was. 'Where are the boys?'

'Noah offered to take them out to run off some energy. His way of saying "sorry", I guess. Freddie was delighted.'

'And Arthur?'

'Oh, you'd have been proud of him. Still holding a grudge. He's switched allegiance to Chloe. She offered him a game of Snakes and Ladders. I'm not sure he even knows it's a board game, so I suspect that odd hissing noise you can hear is him pretending to be a python.'

'Where's Noah taken Freddie?' Liv liked to know where her children were at all times.

'Down to the sea front. Noah said Freddie could spend his pocket money in the arcades.'

'Where was I when all this was agreed?'

Angus picked another mug out of the dishwasher. 'You were on the phone.'

Was there a touch of reproach in his comment? Liv suspected there was. She'd been calling work – following up on the staff rota for the coming week. Life didn't grind to a halt just because they were caught up in some weird Gordian knot of her father's making. Her irritation with Angus, with Noah, with the whole stressful situation came out in her voice. 'Oh, great. Life lessons with Uncle Noah, just what Freddie needs.'

Angus stopped drying the mug in his hands and looked at her, his face expressive, and not of agreement.

Liv rowed back on the sarcasm. 'Sorry.' She was. It wasn't Angus's fault that she had a hundred and fifty things winging around inside her head, instead of the usual one hundred and one. 'Too sour, even for me?'

The tea towel squeaked in the mug again. 'A tad. And maybe it's just what Freddie needs.'

Suitably chastised, Liv pulled out a stool, conceded Angus's point, but kept the focus of the conversation on her brother. 'Don't you think Noah's behaviour is a bit erratic at the moment? One minute it's like he's competing for some Best Uncle award – all the roughhousing and reading them bedtime stories – and the next he's too hungover to be bothered, or he's yelling at the kids like a total dick. He's wired.'

Angus smiled. 'Stop worrying. If Noah's happy to keep Freddie out of our hair for a few hours, and Freddie's happy to be with his favourite uncle—'

'His only uncle,' Liv chipped in.

Angus finished his sentence, unperturbed, 'Then I, for one, am not going to complain.' He fished a handful of cutlery out of the dishwasher and walked over to the drawer. Each knife and fork was individually dried and polished before being put away. A marriage of opposites. Angus deliberate, unhurried, placid. Liv, well… Liv knew that she was none of the above.

She stretched and laid her hands on the counter, relishing the cool granite against her palms. Angus continued with his task, methodically. It felt odd to Liv to have so much to do and yet be sitting around doing nothing, but there was nothing she *could* do until Noah deigned to re-engage with the small matter of their father's will. She was stuck – because, for the first time in many, many years, she was dependent on the cooperation of her siblings. What the hell had her dad been thinking?

In place of being able to move forward, she went back to nibbling away at her suspicions about Noah. 'Has he said anything to you about why Josie's not here?'

'You mean, man-to-man?' Angus raised his eyebrows, mocking. 'Since when did your brother confide in me?'

Liv acknowledged with a shrug the unlikeliness of such a heart-to-heart taking place. Noah and Angus weren't close. They were too different – in personality and tastes and morals, and football fandom and, well, in everything really. Liv also recognised that her husband's view of her brother had, very probably, been badly skewed by her own fraught relationship with him.

She picked an apple out of the fruit bowl and rolled it from hand to hand. She had no intention of eating it. Her stomach was already fighting with the sandwich she'd forced down at lunch. 'You'd think Josie would want to be here – be involved in the decisions, I mean, even if it is just being in Noah's ear, calming him down.'

Angus had moved on to the glassware. 'Text her, if you're that bothered.'

'And say what?'

It was Angus's turn to shrug. 'No idea.'

Liv's gaze flicked around the kitchen. The units, lighting and decoration were new, but it was the same layout as in her childhood. The fridge still opened awkwardly; it was positioned too close to the back door, and the floorboard that ran down the middle of the room still didn't lie flush, thereby creating a tiny but very real trip-hazard. And much of the crockery was the same. Last night's meal had been eaten off the same plates they'd had their teas off as kids; only the lumpen bowls were new. And there were fewer of those now – after Chloe's little accident.

Her eyes snagged on a bundle of letters wedged in the rack on the countertop near the microwave. Death generated a lot of correspondence. Angus's presence prevented her from standing up, fetching the stack and flicking through it. She had no intention of reading the contents of any of the letters addressed to Megan – obviously – but it would be helpful to know which of the banks and financial institutions were represented in the pile, just to double-check that the solicitor's list was complete.

'Liv?'

'Sorry – what?'

'Are you all right? I know how difficult all this is for you, on top of grieving for your dad. You can talk to me: offload some of it, if you want to. It is what a husband is for, you know – apart from the other thing.' Angus grinned, amused by his own joke.

She smiled at him. 'Thank you, but I'm fine.'

'You sure?'

'Yes, honestly,' she lied.

Angus's smile faded and he looked serious for a change. 'You look tired,' he persisted.

'Gee, thanks,' she countered.

'You know what I mean. I worry about you. About the stress of it all.' Did he? Liv wasn't too sure. Angus was an optimist by nature. He truly believed that most things worked themselves out in the end, and that worrying was wasted energy. It was an attitude that Liv envied. He came and put his arms around her. 'Okay. I'll take you at your word.' She was glad he couldn't see her face. 'But how about some fresh air before you get stuck into round three? Why don't we walk down to the front? We can take Arthur. Maybe meet up with Noah and Freddie? Have a romp on the beach? Do something nice together for a change? It might help.'

Liv nodded. Perhaps it would.

Chapter 20

THE AMUSEMENT arcades never seemed to change, and that's why Noah loved them. The mad syncopation of a thousand jewel-bright bulbs. The cloying sweetness of candyfloss cut with the mineral smell of coins. The carpet – the less said about the mash-up of colours and stains, the better. And the sounds! The mechanisation of fun: clicks, clunks, whirrs overlaid with cheap pop music and the regular evocation of joy and despair. They were good places to lose yourself for an hour or so.

Noah always closed his eyes for a few seconds when he first stepped inside. It was an involuntary reaction, a reboot back to his factory setting – child mode. It felt good.

Simple actions and reactions. Risk and reward. You anticipated winning. You won. Then you lost. It was so gloriously, addictively straightforward.

Freddie poked him in the thigh, bringing him back to the moment. 'What first, Uncle No?' His eyes were bright, reflecting the glare.

'First, young man, we need to get you loaded up. This way.' Like a sensei guiding his pupil, Noah led Freddie over to the big yellow change machines. 'Now, how much have you got on you?'

Freddie put his hand in his pocket and produced two one-pound coins. Jesus, Liv was such a tight-ass!

Noah smiled. 'That's a good start.' He took out his wallet and extracted a tenner. Freddie's eyes widened. 'So if I give you this, how much will you have to spend then?'

Freddie did the maths in his head, then grinned. 'Twelve pounds.'

'Correct. All you have to do is decide how many ten-pence, two-pence and pound coins you want. Take a pot – that's for your change.' Freddie grabbed one of the branded plastic tubs and Noah showed him how to feed the machine. Freddie's delight as the cascade of ten-pence coins crashed down the shoot into his pot was infectious.

The next half-hour was filled with the delight of a hundred small decisions: which game to play, which horse to back, which motorbike to race on. They made three trips back to the change machine, replenishing their pots. Freddie was cautious at first, feeding his two and ten pences – and the occasional *big spender* pound – into the slots slowly, taking his time choosing which machine looked ready to pay out. But under Noah's tutelage, he quickly lost his caution and began to play instinctively, happily. His favourite game turned out to be the classic coin drop. A good choice, in Noah's estimation. The illusion of skill, the tantalising piles of ten pences just ready to fall into your clutches, with the judicious insertion of the right coin into the right slot at precisely the right time. The series of small wins, the coins cascading into the metal-lipped pocket with a satisfyingly loud, soul-pleasing clatter. The smell of arcade money on your fingertips. Noah was so enthralled himself that he didn't realise Freddie's luck had taken the inevitable turn for the worse and his pot was nearly empty, again.

'These are my last two, Uncle No.'

'You'd better make them count then, Buddy. There's no more when they're gone.'

Freddie held his penultimate coin to the slot and waited, his eyes focused on the slide, then he committed and pushed it in. The ten pence dropped, rolled into the space, wobbled, fell on its side – way too far to the left to make any difference. His mouth pinched into a frown. He took his last coin and lined it up with the slot, waited, breathing through his pursed lips. He waited for three moves before sending his final lonesome offering on its way. It dropped, rolled, fell and landed perfectly on the ledge, slap-bang in the middle. It had to be a win. The shelf moved forward, Freddie's coin joined the others, pushed against the pile, edging at least a quid's worth of winnings towards the lip, then withdrew. Noah and Freddie waited, but nothing dropped. Game over.

'That's not fair,' Freddie wailed.

'That's how it goes, Bud.'

'No!' Freddie's face flushed red. He raised his fist and thumped the glass, leaving a small smudge of rage.

'Whoa, there, Freddie. You can't go round lamping the machines. You'll set the alarm off, and the police will come and take you away.' Freddie's expression immediately switched from anger to anxiety and, before Noah could take back his flippant comment, his nephew burst into tears. Not again? His track record with his nephews was beginning to follow a depressingly familiar pattern. Noah was mortified, but also slightly irritated by Freddie's display of histrionics. Learning to lose gracefully, to be told 'No', to have things not always go your way were all essential life skills that Arthur, and Freddie, were going to have to master sooner or later.

A jolt of recognition that he sounded like his father softened Noah.

The bribe of an ice cream got Freddie out of the arcade, and the addition of sauce, a flake *and* sprinkles stopped the sniffling. Armed with their 99s, Noah led Freddie across the road. They climbed through the railings and settled, side-by-side, on their backsides on the cold concrete of the sea front, their feet dangling above the damp sand. It was only when Noah passed Freddie his ice cream that he realised his nephew was still clutching his empty change pot. They made their exchange in silence. The ice cream and the stiff North Sea breeze seemed to revive Freddie's spirits.

'Are you going to tell Mummy I was naughty?' he asked.

Noah jiggled Freddie's arm, pushing his nose into his cone. 'Course not. What do you take me for? A snitch?'

Unity restored, Freddie impressively licked the ice cream off the tip of his nose. He grinned when Noah tried to mimic him and failed. They had a happy few minutes comparing tongue lengths, and listening to the seagulls screaming above their heads, before Noah decided to do his bit for his eldest nephew's moral education.

'It's normal to get a bit ticked off when you don't win, Fredster – I get that.' The nickname was designed to soften the lecture. He didn't want to sound *too* much like his father. 'But you're going to lose sometimes. It happens to us all. And it's good to get used to the feeling and to know how to handle it.'

Freddie squinted at him, serious. 'Why?'

'Well, because...' Noah didn't really have a good answer for that, so he went for an honest one, 'people will like you more if you're a good loser.' Freddie carried on licking his ice cream, and Noah felt the pressure to reclaim some street-cred with his nephew. 'Besides, you aren't ever going walk out of an amusement arcade with more money than you went in with. It's not the way it works.'

Freddie stopped slurping his ice cream and asked, 'Then why try?'

The boy was just one long series of awkward questions.

Noah decided it was time they headed home.

Chapter 21

THERE WERE good reasons why no one in their right mind did any gardening in December. The ground was unyielding and every plant seemed to be armed with spines or thorns. But to Megan, crouching in the big flower bed, her fingers turning blue, it was still preferable to being inside the house. With each handful of dead foliage she ripped out, she felt both better and worse. She was aware that she was casting herself as the victim and that her prostration, alone in the bleak garden, with the wind off the North Sea scouring her skin, verged on attention-seeking behaviour. But as there was no one watching, it was a performance that was doing her very little good. The thought of them pecking over the details of Jonathan's legacy, as they had picked their way mindlessly through the lunch she'd prepared, made her angry. She grabbed another handful of dead peony leaves and yanked. She should have cleared the garden in the autumn, but that had been impossible. Her every waking hour, or so it seemed, had been dedicated to caring for Jonathan by that point. As a result, the garden had run wild. Her desire to tame it now was illogical.

The way things were going, it seemed highly unlikely that she would be around to see the fruits of her labours.

The sound of a car engine broke into her thoughts. A dark-red BMW turned off the main road into the drive. Megan leant back on her heels and watched as it drove down the slope and stopped in front of the house. What now? Or, more accurately, who?

Another adversary?

The driver's side door opened and a pair of elegant female legs clad in smart black boots appeared. Then, like a character out of a TV ad for something upmarket and expensive, Jonathan's ex-wife Eloise emerged from the car.

She stood and looked up at the house.

Megan knelt on the frozen earth and watched her. She wanted to laugh at the contrast between the two of them. Eloise – smart, stylish, feminine, 'dressed for the occasion', but an occasion that was far more glamorous than the one she was gatecrashing; and Megan – bundled up in Jonathan's waterproofs, an asexual lump of green and brown, crouched in the mud like a character in a Bruegel painting.

Eloise didn't move. The drizzle dusting her dark hair gave it a silvery shimmer.

What was she waiting for?

Eloise had walked out of The View for the last time five years ago. A departure that Megan had not been present to witness. At the time she'd been glad to be as far away from the drama as possible, but there was escaping the fact that it had been her actions that had driven Eloise out of The View: the place she'd no doubt been carried over the threshold by a young, virile, vibrant Jonathan; the house she'd returned to after the births of three children; and the home where she'd raised those children and watched them grow. The View was where Eloise had lived with Jonathan, where she'd loved him and where she'd discovered he had betrayed her. And it was the place, according to Jonathan, that Eloise had vehemently sworn she would never return to, ever again – *not over Megan and Jonathan's dead bodies.*

Maybe it was the memory of that curse that was causing Eloise to hesitate now.

One out of two. She hadn't quite got her wish.

After what felt like for ever, Eloise finally headed up the steps and, to Megan's shock, walked straight through the front door into the house.

Chapter 22

ELOISE HAD had absolutely no intention of coming to Scarborough.

And yet here she was.

Back home.

To her relief, no one appeared to welcome her when she stepped inside the house, which gave her a few moments to acclimatise. She examined her emotions and found, to her surprise, that she felt totally calm. She would need to be, judging by the increasingly strained pitch of the communications she'd been having with all three of her children. Of course they'd expressed their turmoil very differently. Liv had been cool and contained, her messages informative, detailed – almost as if theirs was a professional rather than a personal relationship. Chloe had been far more straightforward – *she was upset, she was lonely, she needed her mum.* But it was Noah who was concerning Eloise the most. He'd been in touch far more frequently than usual and, when they'd spoken, he'd been solicitous and affectionate. Eloise couldn't shake the feeling that he was play-acting, using hackneyed, sentimental phrases that were not his normal way of speaking, or feeling. And woven through his somewhat rambling soliloquies had been a clear message: *There's nothing for you to worry about. Leave it to me – and the girls. We'll get everything sorted.* In other words, *stay out of it.*

Which was precisely why she'd come.

She put her handbag on the side and glanced at herself in the mirror. She'd made an effort with her hair and make-up, and her clothes. Those efforts had paid off. Though she said it herself, she looked good – far better than the last time she'd passed this mirror.

Then she'd been in no mood for appraising herself; she'd been too side-swiped. Her exit from The View – with her bags packed and her passport in her hand – had been a grand gesture. To this day she was glad she'd topped off their weeks of exhausting soul-searching with *a scene.* There had been shouting on both sides. They'd let words and emotions erupt that had been smothered for years. The result had been awful and painful and loud, and very undignified. But surely that's what the end of a long marriage, the end of a love affair, should be! Going out with a bang not a whimper proved you cared, that you still had feelings – despite everything – for the person who had betrayed you. Not good feelings, of course; not a love strong enough to repel the threat of a younger, prettier, no doubt more biddable, adoring *life partner,* but passion nonetheless.

In reality, what came after Eloise and Jonathan's showdown had been far harder to deal with: the knowledge that their connection as a couple was broken, irrevocably, that they no longer shared a life. For while it was incontrovertibly true that it had been Jonathan who smashed their marriage, it was she who had stomped on the fragments, ensuring nothing survived. She'd been very thorough: refusing mediation, fighting him tooth and nail over the divorce settlement, extracting her pounds of flesh, chunk by bloody chunk, until there was only the stripped-down carcass left. The last act, expunging him from her life, had been the hardest of all. It had taken discipline and a rigid adherence to her pride, but she had managed it. To weaken and call a truce, maybe even to have found a way back to some sort of diluted, polluted friendship, would have been to let Megan win – and Eloise would not do that.

So effective had she been in erasing Jonathan from her heart that even when he'd fallen ill, she'd held firm. She'd heard about it all, of course, through the children. How hard the diagnosis had hit him, and how aggressive and unrelenting the progress of his condition was. And she'd felt for him, as you would for anyone who'd been dealt such a cruel blow, but she didn't contact him directly. Didn't send a letter or a card, or offer to visit. Nor did his diagnosis change how often she allowed herself to imagine how he was coping, how *they* were coping – well, not much.

Her face stared back at her in the mirror. She touched her mouth with a fingertip, checking her lipstick hadn't bled into the corner. She looked composed. She would remain composed. She was here for the children. That was all. It was not the time for reopening old wounds.

'Mum!' Chloe appeared on the stairs. She bounded down the last few steps and came to embrace her mother. A tight, long, hungry hug, which Eloise returned, but was the one to end. 'You came.' Chloe looked rumpled, her clothes and cheek creased, as if she'd just woken from a nap. A nap in the middle of the afternoon at the age of twenty-six. Eloise tried to suppress the familiar disappointment with her youngest child.

'Of course I did.'

'Oh, I'm so glad you're here. It's been so upsetting, and difficult. We don't seem to be getting anywhere and—'

Eloise cut Chloe off before she could get properly started. 'Do you mind if we talk in the kitchen, darling? It's been quite a long drive and I could really do with a drink.'

Chloe looked a little crestfallen. 'Sorry, yes. Of course.' To Eloise's discomfort, her daughter took her hand to lead her through into the kitchen. 'I've got so much to catch you up on.'

Chapter 23

As they were heading back along the sea front, Freddie slowed to a stop. 'Who's that?' He pointed at Zoltar – still there, stranded in front of the Coney Island Arcade, locked in his weatherproof box, his pale-gold turban askew on his head.

'That, young Freddie, is a sultan from the Far East.'

'What does he do?'

'He tells fortunes.'

'What's a "fortune"?'

Noah hesitated. 'Well, a "fortune" usually means a lot of money. But what Zoltar does is tell you what's going to happen – in the future.'

'Like after Christmas.'

'Yeah. That kind of thing.'

They wandered over and stared at Zoltar. He stared right back at them, as he had done at generations of day-trippers, his hand poised, ready, on his plastic crystal ball.

'How does he work?'

'You cross his palm with silver and he tells you what's going to happen.'

'Can we ask him to tell us our *fortunes*?' Freddie liked new words.

'Only if we pay him.'

Freddie's expression grew serious. 'But I haven't got any pennies left.'

Noah relented. 'Well, it's a good job I've still got a bit of shrapnel on me.' He extracted a pound coin from his wallet and gave it to Freddie. 'It goes in that slot there.'

Freddie pulled out the slide, fitted in his coin and pushed it back in. The boy had learnt how to 'feed the machine'. Noah felt amused that he'd passed on at least something to his nephew in the past hour. There was clunk and a whirr, and the lights in the box began to flash. Noah watched Freddie's delight as Zoltar's deep, rumbling voice boomed out across the sea front. His piercing blue eyes flicked back and forth and his hand jerked up and down. There was another whirr and the fortune card slid out of the slot. That was always the bit that had fascinated Noah as a child. The slow glide of the patterned ticket out of the churning bowels of the machine. The lights and movement stopped as abruptly as they'd begun, and Zoltar fell silent again. Freddie glanced at Noah, seeking permission.

'Go on. Take it. It's your fortune.'

Freddie wiped his ice-cream-and-syrup-sticky hand down the front of his coat before he took his ticket. Noah watched as he studied the fairground-inspired design on the front, before turning it over. Noah had forgotten what was actually written on the cards and, like Freddie, was surprised at the amount of closely packed text. Freddie looked to Noah for help – the writing was well beyond his reading age.

Noah scanned the ticket with its cod, old-fashioned phrases about *challenges and triumphs*, and opted for a child-friendly paraphrase. 'It says, "*You are a fine young man and you will grow up to be*"' – Noah quickly thought about what his nephew wanted or, more precisely, what he thought he lacked – '"*strong and quick. You will be lucky in your life and make many, many friends, who will be loyal to you. And you will travel to lots of interesting and exciting places, and learn secrets other people cannot begin to imagine.*"' Then, overcome with another of the sudden emotional waves that seemed to have been hitting him since his father's death, he added, '"*And you will be loved and will be happy and healthy.*"'

Freddie beamed. Noah passed him his fortune card and watched as he unzipped the 'secret' pocket on the sleeve of his jacket and carefully put the ticket inside. Time for home. But Freddie had other ideas. 'What about you, Uncle No? Don't you want Zoltar to tell you your fortune?'

The answer to which was 'No', but Freddie was hopping from foot to foot, itching for another go. Not above a little manipulation – a trait that Noah couldn't help but be impressed by – Freddie defaulted to charm. 'Go on, Uncle No. I bet he'll say something really good about you.'

In reality Zoltar 'said' exactly the same thing, which was no great surprise to Noah, but was a disappointment to Freddie, although at least the ticket that emerged was different. Noah skim-read it and gave Freddie a made-up rendition that focused on his *cat-like agility, his sporting prowess and his future as a leader of men.* Fortunes foretold, they walked on. They passed numerous litter bins, but Noah kept hold of his ticket. A fake future was better than an uncertain one.

Chapter 24

IT WAS his bright-blue coat that made Freddie easy to spot. He was hunched down in a squat by the shoreline, his head nearly touching Noah's. They seemed engrossed. Angus and Arthur waved. It took a couple of attempts to attract their attention. When they finally registered Angus, Liv and Arthur's presence, they raced up the beach – Noah outstripping Freddie easily, until the last few metres, when he pretended to trip. He sprawled headlong onto the sand, letting a red-cheeked Freddie win.

'Have you had fun?' Liv asked, though she knew the answer. Freddie had syrup all down the front of his coat and a grin on his dirty face. 'I see you've already had an ice cream.'

'Yes. Uncle No got me one, with a flake and strawberry sauce *and* sprinkles.'

'I hope you said "thank you".'

'Of course he did.' Noah looked relaxed, happy even.

'We spent ages in the arcade, then we had our ice creams and then we had our fortunes told, and we were going to come back to Grandpa's, but then you rang, and Uncle No said we could go and look for popping seaweed while we waited for you.' Freddie was breathless with excitement and sugar.

Up on Angus's shoulders, Arthur had obviously had enough of being left out. 'I want popping seaweed.' He started throwing his weight around.

Angus lifted him over his head and deposited him on the pavement. 'Whoa there! Will you show your brother how to spot this special seaweed, Freddie?' Freddie nodded and puffed out his chest, happy to play the marine biologist. 'Come on, then.' Angus led Arthur down the ramp to join his brother. 'We'll see you back at the house.' He actually inclined his head towards Noah before they departed, reminding Liv of her promise to invest in a little sibling bonding of her own.

With her boys on their way back down to the sea, Liv looked at Noah, both of them at something of a loose end.

'Shall we go back via the Spa?' Liv suggested. Maybe Angus was right; perhaps what they needed was a bit of R&R.

'A trip down memory lane?' Noah asked.

'Yeah, why not.'

Chapter 25

THE SPA was a glorious old structure nestled in the far corner of the South Bay. The layers of rust and peeling paint only added to its melancholic charm, like a trim of grubby lace on a faded but still elegant gown. The complex was a pleasure palace built in 1879 to attract the great and the good to the seaside, to take the restorative spa waters and spend their hard-earnt cash. Day-trippers and locals still made the trek around the bay from the noisy modern amusement arcades to peer through the windows of the silent outdoor ballroom, imagining it in its heyday, when the tiled floor would have been full of twirling couples falling in love to the strains of a live orchestra.

For Liv and Noah, the nostalgia was far more personal. The underbelly of the ballroom was where they used to play as kids.

Liv had forgotten how deafening it was beneath the Spa at high tide. The salt-rimed arches amplified the noise of the waves, creating a surround-sound effect. It was as if the sea was simultaneously behind and in front of you. It was disorientating, and strangely threatening. At least that was how Liv felt now, as a chilly adult picking her way around the deep puddles of sea water in her duck-down coat and all-terrain footwear.

As a child she used to find the furious howl of the waves against the sea wall exhilarating. Liv and Noah had had what might be viewed as an idyllic childhood, at least from the elevated, anxious promontory of modern parenting, with its focus on every potential threat and hazard, real and imagined. Not for Eloise such protective paranoia. From a young age, Liv and Noah had been allowed to roam free, as long as they stayed together. In hindsight, Liv found their mother's misplaced confidence in the two of them 'not to do anything too stupid' quite shocking. The thought of letting Arthur and Freddie go anywhere on their own until they were teenagers seemed ludicrous and irresponsible. But for Noah and Liv, it had been their norm.

They used to explore the cliffs below the house as if they were an extension of their garden, mindless of the hazards. The winding, broken paths down to the sea, the derelict shelters covered in graffiti that smelt of piss, and the hidden pockets of Victorian landscaping: it was all their territory. They'd spend hours looking for rabbits, picking primroses, building dens and, if Noah had managed to filch any matches, trying to light fires – all far from adult supervision or sanction.

By unspoken agreement, they would always keep an eye on the sea, waiting for the incoming tide before venturing down to the passages underneath the Spa's old outdoor ballroom. Its position, jutting out into the South Bay, made it the best place to play their own unique version of Chicken. This involved taking it in turns to creep down the barnacle- and seaweed-encrusted steps, being very careful where they put their feet, flirting with the incoming tide. They would dare each other to go lower and lower, timing the waves. Legend had it that the seventh one was always the biggest and, therefore, the most likely to sweep you off your feet and out to a watery grave.

How they had made it to adulthood unscathed was a mystery. Yet at the time Liv hadn't questioned it. They lived near the sea. They played near the sea. Their mother trusted them to be sensible and to look after each other. That was the way it was.

Being back on the crumbly paths beneath the Spa with Noah after all these years was an experience soaked in nostalgia and sea spray. The sound of the waves was the same – loud and booming. It was like being inside a headache. The tide was smashing against the sea wall, sending sheets of spray up onto the path. Noah walked near the edge, tempting fate. Liv stayed back, fully aware of the metaphor. It was far too noisy to have a conversation, which was fine with her.

Suddenly Noah stopped walking and stepped up to the edge. He dramatically threw his head back and his arms wide, as if embracing the onslaught. Jesus, he was such a poser! Liv walked past him, refusing to be an audience for his histrionics. But after fifty metres or so she couldn't stop herself looking round. Noah hadn't moved. He was still standing right on the lip of the walkway. Just as she was about to shout at him to *stop pratting about*, the seventh wave hit. For a split second he disappeared in an arc of water, and she was sure he'd been swept off his feet into the sea. She froze. The wave crashed, broke apart and spread a sheet of white foam across the concrete, then retreated, leaving Noah standing, covered in spray. Her anxiety switched to anger. 'You dickhead!'

He turned and grinned at her, sea water dripping off his cap. 'Oh, lighten up. Don't you remembering us doing it as kids?'

'Yeah, I do, and you were an idiot then.'

Noah seemed about to make one of his usual sarcastic comebacks, but the look on her face stopped him. He took off his cap, shook it, replaced it – then smiled at her, looking for a second so like his eight-year-old self that Liv felt a bubble of affection rise to the surface of her irritation. Having had their fill of wave-dodging, they climbed the pebble-dash stairs back up to the promenade level, side-by-side.

Despite the late hour and the scarcity of visitors on a wild winter afternoon, the little gift shop on the arcade was open – an act of defiance and optimism that Liv found touching. The shop front looked exactly the same as it had when they were kids: the carousels of buckets and spades, the fishing nets, the board smothered in fridge magnets, the tubs of beach balls. Without saying anything, Noah made a beeline for the shop. Liv groaned inwardly. All she wanted was to sit down and have a hot drink. The shaky feeling that had swept over her down by the sea had lessened, but hadn't lifted completely. She was certainly not in the mood for rooting through tat. Noah, however, obviously was. He went inside and she was forced to follow him.

The inside of the shop was as rammed as the outside: shelf upon shelf of tacky ornaments, snow globes, plaster crabs and – for some reason – money boxes in the shape of Rasta men smoking spliffs, leaning on lighthouses. It was a 1970s memorabilia-collector's wet dream. It wasn't too much of a stretch to imagine that some of the stock had been there since their childhood.

'I want to pick something up for Lily,' Noah finally explained. 'She'll be sorry to have missed going to the beach and playing with Freddie and Arthur.' He began searching. Liv leant against the door frame. She hoped he would be quick.

Surprisingly they weren't the only customers. A young family was also shopping or, more accurately, mooching around the shelves, bickering. A couple, poorly dressed for the weather in thin jackets and sneakers, with three cold offspring in tow. Liv felt sympathy – a day-trip in the rain, with young children, on a budget, was nobody's idea of fun. From her vantage point, she worked out that there was some type of altercation brewing between the eldest and the middle child about the price of each other's chosen gift. She closed her eyes for a few seconds, enjoying the blasts of hot air from the overhead heater hitting the top of her head. It made her feel pleasantly swimmy.

The next thing she knew, there were raised voices. Both male. One of them Noah's. 'There's no need for that. He didn't do it deliberately.'

The father and Noah were facing off. The floor of the shop was littered with hundreds of fluorescent bouncy balls, some of them still bouncing. The young girl behind the till looked like a startled rabbit. 'And what the fuck has it got to do with you?' The man jutted his chin forward.

Noah didn't back down an inch. In fact, to Liv's dismay, he took a step closer. 'I'm just saying you should calm down, pal.' It was the 'pal' that did it.

'Oh, I should, should I? And I think you should keep your nose out of other people's business.'

The kids had fallen silent. They watched, open-mouthed, as the ruck developed.

Simultaneously the young mum and Liv spoke. 'Leave it, Danny!'... 'Noah, what the hell?'

Both women were ignored. The tension ramped up.

'Is this how you get rid of all the frustration in your life? By smacking people half your size?' What, in Christ's name, was Noah playing at? He was asking to be punched and, by the look of it, the man was about to oblige.

Liv took matters into her own hands. She navigated her way down the narrow aisle, avoiding the Day-Glo rubber balls as best she could, grabbed Noah's arm and pulled him out of the shop. The bell above the door tinkled merrily on their way out. Noah resisted, but not enough to stop her bundling him back onto the pavement.

Outside, they faced each other. Noah was breathing heavily, still wrestling with his anger.

'Come away, Noah. You don't want to give him time to decide he really would quite like to smack you in your smug, interfering face.'

Noah glanced back into the shop one more time, obviously tempted, but, thankfully, followed Liv as she walked away.

They went into the café-bar a few doors along the promenade. Liv checked that the coast was clear before pulling the door shut behind them. 'What do you want?' What she wanted was to sit down.

Noah's expression had morphed from furious to sulky. 'A pint.'

Needing to keep control of the situation, she told him to go and find somewhere to sit while she ordered their drinks. He chose a table at the rear of the bar and sat with his back to the room, effectively putting himself in the naughty corner. As Liv waited for their order she watched him, wondering what the hell had got into her brother. Even from across the room she could see the tension in his posture.

When she placed the tray on the table in front of him, he looked at the drinks, then at her, and huffed. Liv had ordered a pot of tea. Beer was the last thing he needed. 'Noah, please. For the next half-hour can we just be civil with each other? I really can't be doing with any more aggro.'

He looked at her, still holding on to his grievances, whatever they were, then suddenly his gaze cleared and he grinned. It was like spending time with a storm: bright sunshine one minute, dark clouds the next. 'Oh, please, Liv. Let's argue. It's one of the few things about this weekend I'm enjoying!' That broke the tension.

Liv rewarded him with a thump on the arm. She shrugged off her coat, set out their cups, added milk, waited for a count of ten, then poured. The tea streamed out, hot and strong. They obviously didn't skimp on teabags in the Farrer's Bar. Despite her drink being way too hot, Liv added half a sachet of sugar and took a sip. The rattled feeling subsided. They drank their tea, Noah out-slurping her in an attempt to make her laugh – like a naughty child playing to an audience to erase past misdemeanours. It worked. It was good to be warm and calm. Equilibrium restored.

Liv gave it a good five minutes before tackling the elephant in the café. 'Are you going to tell me what that was all about?'

Noah put down his cup. 'He was bang out of order.'

'Very possibly. But it had nothing to do with you. What on earth possessed you to go wading in?'

'He walloped his kid for knocking over a box of bouncy balls. The kid was terrified. What sort of prick lamps his kid for an accident?'

'Still, nothing to do with you.'

'It just got to me, all right?'

Small things taking on way too much significance – because

the big things were too hard to deal with? Liv understood. Grief fucked things up, especially if they were fucked up already. The lull between them was comfortable, for a change. It was Liv who eventually attempted to resuscitate their conversation. 'It's weird being back home, isn't it? I mean all of us, together, in the house.' She immediately regretted the comment. They were hardly 'all together', given the yawning, ill-explained absence of Josie and Lily. But Noah simply shrugged.

She decided on a different approach: kindness. 'Are you all right?' She couldn't help but think they were echoing her own exchange with Angus. Different people, different roles – the same avoidance of the truth.

'Yep. Fine and dandy. The sea air agrees with me.'

'Noah! Please?'

'I'm fine.'

'There's something up. I can tell.' He always did find it hard talking about feelings, an inheritance from their father.

Noah's smile disappeared. And the storm clouds gathered again. 'What, you mean apart from the fact that our dad's just died of a horrible illness?'

Liv refused to react. 'Yes, apart from that.'

Noah looked away again. 'Nothing.'

'That's not true.'

'Leave it, Liv. I'm not one of your patients.'

She reached out and put her hand over his and held it there, reminding him that she was his big sister and she cared. 'I'm worried about you. Is everything okay with you and Josie?'

He pulled his hand away. 'None of your business, Sis. You know better than to go interfering in other people's relationships. Or you should do. We're fine.'

Okay, so that was a dead end. Liv took another sip of tea – it really was too strong. She watched a couple a few tables away share a slice of chocolate cake, each taking a forkful in turn. A scrupulous division of pleasure. Maybe some mea culpa would help. 'We're not getting very far, are we?'

Noah wiped his mouth with the back of his hand, as if trying to rid himself of the taste of the over-stewed tea. 'Oh, I don't know. We've established that I'm a heartless, money-grubbing, selfish bastard; Chloe is clueless; and your application for the Institute of Chartered Accountants stands a very good chance of being accepted.' He smiled, but this time his joke had teeth.

'Noah! Please. This is serious. We need to find a way of agreeing something. I don't know about you, but I don't fancy coming back for another round to get this resolved. We need to sort it out this weekend.'

'On that, my dear Sis, we agree. Are you saying you've given up on the patented Redpath time-served algorithm?' Liv's expression must have conveyed her fatigue. He relented. 'Okay. You know my main issues.'

'Go on.'

'I think it's ridiculous that the carer is walking away with five grand.'

Liv let slip a puff of exasperation. 'Noah, that's the only stipulated bequest. There is nothing you can do about that. Forget about it. In the grand scheme of things, it's an irrelevance. We need to focus on the division of the estate.'

Noah obviously did not view £5,000 as irrelevant. 'But don't you think it odd that he left her so much? She was only employed for a few months.'

'You're getting distracted.'

'If you say so. But there's something fishy about it.'

'The estate, Noah. We need to focus on the division of the proceeds of the house and Dad's savings. That's the big picture.' Liv wanted to lay her head down on the table and leave it there. It was like *Groundhog Day*, and she was Bill Murray, the only one desperate to move forward. 'Noah, I need you to focus! What do we do about Megan? That's the big issue.'

'How about we cut the bitch out!'

'We can't do that.'

'But that's where you're wrong, Liv. We can. Dad explicitly left it to us to decide. He must have had his reasons for that.'

'And you think cutting Megan out is fair?'

'Think about it. If he'd wanted her to have something, he would have put it in his will. It's a new will, after all. He had the golden opportunity to allocate whatever he saw fit to her – and yet he didn't. That tells me that, for some reason we don't know about, he decided she wasn't entitled to anything.'

It was uncomfortable hearing Noah voice her own suspicions. 'But she looked after him. Was there for him.' In ways they had not been. 'She nursed him at the end.'

'Did she, though?' Noah's eyes were glittery, almost as if he was excited or high. 'It sounds like she used a lot of his money to pay for carers. How much of it she actually did herself, we'll never really know.'

Liv couldn't let that stand. She'd been over to spend more time with their dad than Noah. She's seen the toll Jonathan's MND had taken on Megan. She might not like the woman, but she did respect the way she'd coped with their father's illness – with their father. 'Noah. That's not fair. She was here all the time, apart from when she was at work. She had virtually no life.

His illness had more of an impact on her than on anyone.'

'Not more than on Dad.'

There was nothing to say to that.

Noah suddenly leant forward, conspiratorial. 'I think she's holding out on us. You said yourself she's not been very forthcoming with the information you've asked for. The silent treatment works well if you're hiding something.'

'Oh, for God's sake, Noah. Now you're being ridiculous. She's in shock. Grieving. She's lost her... partner, and she's about to lose her home.'

'*Her* home! You mean our home! Jeez, Liv. Why are you being so... hair shirt about this? It's our inheritance. That's the way it works. A five-, pardon me, six-year affair doesn't give you the right to inherit anything, in my book. Megan should leave with what she arrived with. Nothing.'

'Since when did you become so heartless?'

'Since Dad died and left us with a decision that will affect my family. I'm a husband and a father now, Liv. I'm not going to be ashamed of putting Josie and Lily first.'

'So this is all about them, is it?'

'Yes. It is.'

Which made it all the more strange that Josie and Lily hadn't come with him. But for the first time ever in her relationship with her brother, Liv found herself not saying what was really on her mind – whether that was down to her current weakness or Noah's repressed anger, she couldn't say. Instead she changed tack, moving on to what she thought was safer ground. 'Okay. Just for the time being, let's put the issue of Megan to one side. What about Mum?'

Noah picked up his cup and took another drink, put it down, scanned the room – his body language leaking awkwardness. 'I've spoken to Mum, and I don't think she's expecting much.' Even his language struck a false note.

'When was this?'

'This past week.'

'Really?'

'Yes.'

'And you're saying she's passing on her share?'

'Not passing exactly, but she's sorted now. The divorce settlement saw to that. I honestly think her priority is us.'

'That doesn't sound like Mum to me.'

'Ask her yourself. She's moved on, Liv. I think it's time we all did.'

Liv was shocked to catch her brother in so blatant a lie. 'Indifference' was not the impression she'd got from her mother's messages. Though, on reflection, Eloise had given very little away in her communications with Liv. But still, a self-sacrificing obsession with her offspring did not sound like their mother, not at all.

Without warning, Noah stood up. 'Don't you think we should be getting back?'

She did, but she couldn't escape the sense that Noah wanted to leave more to avoid further conversation than to get back to the house and their negotiations.

He shoved his arms down the sleeves of his jacket impatiently. 'I think we'd get a lot further, next time we all sit down, if you'd own up to what you really want to happen, instead of trotting out all this scrupulous impartiality crap. It's time you said what you really think, Liv.' With that, he walked away.

As Liv watched him weave his way out through the tables without waiting for her to catch up, she admitted to herself that his advice deserved serious thought.

Chapter 26

God, Liv was irritating. She never did or said anything honestly – from her heart, or her gut. She was much too concerned with how she looked, how she came across, even when no one was watching. Being such a control-freak, it must be so sodding tiring.

And his sister did look tired.

Noah's phone was ringing. He dug it out of his pocket. Caller ID: Josie. At last. Contrarily he let it ring, watching the sea arc and fizz across the promenade. The lights were coming on around the bay; 4 p.m. and it was already drawing in dark. The call went to his voicemail. He imagined Josie nursing a mug of decent tea, warm and snug in their kitchen, with Lily clattering around with her Baby Annabell buggy – her new favourite plaything. She'd started to ask about having a baby sister; other mums in Josie's group were onto their second child, so Lily was familiar with swollen bellies and dolly-sized siblings. It was not a conversation he and Josie had had. Nor were they likely to, given the way things were. The thought of his small, beautiful family being so many miles away, physically and emotionally, made the cold worse. The

North Sea battered against the old defences and Noah stood and watched.

He knew he was confusing Josie. Loving her, but forever leaving. Making promises, then breaking them. Swearing to be more honest with her, whilst never telling her the truth. Hounding her, then ignoring her calls. He understood her frustration. And Lily, he was fucking up that relationship as well. You had to be there, to be a good dad, he knew that. There was no compensation for not being present. He'd learnt that from his own father, the hard way.

Noah looked at his phone. Josie had not left a message. He couldn't blame her.

There was an abrasive scraping sound, metal on concrete. The young girl was dragging the merchandise back into the gift shop. She disappeared inside, lugging a basket of beach balls, then came back out and started to edge the big carousel with all the fishing stuff towards the doorway. In the wind it was a quite a tussle.

'Do you need a hand?' Noah jogged over. She eyed him warily. He smiled, his most endearing smile. 'By way of an apology. I was out of order earlier. I didn't mean to cause trouble. Sorry. But he was a bit of a bully.' She relented. Together they brought the last of the stuff inside. There was a lot.

'Thank you.' She held the big bunch of keys in front of her, a clear signal for him to be off.

Noah smiled again. 'I know it's completely cheeky, but I couldn't grab a quick something for my daughter, could I?' Her expression said 'No'. Noah wasn't that easily dissuaded. 'She's three.' Nope, he was still not hacking through her defences. 'She's just lost her grandad. My dad – he died last week. I'm here to sort out his funeral.' That did it.

Five minutes later the girl locked up the darkened shop behind them.

'I'm this way.' Noah indicated the steps that ran up the side of the building. She looked relieved. They parted ways. Noah set off climbing. There was no sign of Liv.

As a kid he'd known exactly how many steps there were back up to The Esplanade, depending on which route you took. He knew the paths and the shortcuts. The best vantage points and the hardest-to-find hiding places. This time he chose the best-lit route.

Before long he was out of breath. The weight of the tiger didn't help. It had been the biggest soft toy in the shop. It looked like something out of Siegfried & Roy. White fur with grey stripes, big floppy paws, a huge head and long, very realistic whiskers. Perfect for Lily. Noah shifted the furry synthetic beast from one shoulder onto the other, flexing his back. The ache in his muscle was deep, with a jagged edge on the left-hand side.

Another big, stupid gesture. It was all he seemed capable of at present.

He stopped four times on the way up, trying to shift the pain, and the weight of the tiger. It seemed to grow heavier and more cumbersome with each set of steps. By the time he reached the top he was sweating, and deeply regretting his choice of gift. But, heroically, he finally made it. As he walked the last ten minutes back to the house, he passed an elderly couple. The woman did a double-take.

Noah slowed down to let them gawp. 'It's for my daughter. She's obsessed with animals, especially big cats.'

The woman smiled indulgently. 'I'm sure she'll love it. What child wouldn't? She's a lucky little girl.'

Noah was grateful for her comment, but he knew it wasn't true.

Chapter 27

SHE WAS not as Eloise remembered, though Eloise's memory of Megan had – even she would have to admit – been quite seriously affected by the corrosive distortions of bitterness and jealousy. For a start, Megan was much shorter in the flesh; perhaps the perpetual addition of slutty high heels, in Eloise's imagination, had skewed her height perceptions. She also looked much older and 'flatter' – far more nondescript – than the Cadbury's Caramel Bunny that had been burrowing away in a dark corner of Eloise's heart for the past five years. But there again, watching the man you 'loved' die slowly was liable to knock the sheen off most people. Eloise waited to wince at her own viciousness, but didn't.

'Oh.' Pause. 'Hello.' Megan's voice, likewise, lacked the ooze and drip that Eloise heard whenever she let her get a word in edgeways inside her head. To her credit, Megan didn't scream at the sight of her lover's ex-wife standing in 'her' kitchen.

'Hi. I hope this is okay. The kids asked me to come over. I thought it would be good for us to be together, at this difficult time.' Megan could hardly argue with that, could she?

'Mum, do you want topping up?' Eloise waved away Chloe's offer of more coffee, though it was good to hear 'Mum' being used once again in the kitchen. From the brief glimpses of the hall and her perusal of the kitchen, it seemed a lot had changed since she'd been ousted. She'd expected that. What new partner wouldn't want to erase all evidence of her predecessor? Eloise couldn't wait to have a good poke around and see what Megan had got past Jonathan, and what he'd dug in his heels about. He'd obviously lost the argument about the crockery on the dresser – it was hideous. Eloise had to stop the smile in her head transferring to her face. The opportunity to judge Megan, and her choice of home furnishings – and find her lacking – might yet prove to be a compensation of the visit.

The crushing awkwardness of their tête-à-tête was interrupted by the arrival of Arthur and Freddie. They ran into the kitchen, screeched to a stop when they spotted their grandma, then ran over to greet her. From her position crouched down, being hugged and covered in sandy, sticky kisses, Eloise glanced up at Megan. She was rewarded by the sight of Megan's face flickering with distress. Eloise's qualms about coming over to Scarborough were lessening by the minute. Angus looked briefly startled to see his mother-in-law, but he covered it up well with a hug. She was back in the bosom of her family. All she needed now was Liv, and Noah's little gang, and they would all be together. A united front. *Poor* Megan.

Eloise wasn't surprised that her eldest daughter hadn't put in an appearance yet. She imagined Liv with her head down in Jonathan's study, surrounded by every available piece of paperwork, leaving Angus to entertain the boys, as per usual. 'Where's Liv?'

'She's walking back with Noah.' Angus started collecting up Freddie and Arthur's joyously and carelessly discarded shoes and coats. 'Boys. Go and wash your hands. Now! You both pong of seaweed.' They thundered out. Angus followed them, presumably to ensure that his instructions were followed. He was an attentive father.

Noah and Liv having a powwow, without Chloe – Eloise filed that snippet away. Christ, what had Jonathan been thinking? Three siblings always created a difficult dynamic, and their family had been no different. Liv, Noah and Chloe's childhood had been one long sequence of overlapping grievances: who ate the last bag of crisps, who broke the swing, who got the best bedroom, who got the most attention, who was Dad's favourite? (They never seemed to care who was hers.) They fought about anything and everything.

It had been Jonathan who found their relentless jockeying an issue. He'd seen it as a problem to be fixed. To her, it was an irritant to be ignored. Eloise believed that sibling rivalry was natural. Her approach had been to starve it – and them – of the oxygen of attention; unlike Jonathan, who had always insisted on wading in, adjudicating, explaining, trying to get them to act like mature adults when in reality they were feral children. Had he forgotten those seemingly endless years of strife? Or had he remembered them all too well? Hence this last, contrived attempt to force some sort of unity onto the three of them. They would never know – but Eloise was coming round to the view that it was worth being around to find out.

While she'd been reflecting on family dynamics, Megan had picked up a dishcloth and begun wiping down the draining board, her back to the room. Eloise watched her, trying to guess what was going on inside *her* head. She failed. Perhaps it was only polite to actually ask. 'How have you been coping?' There was a pause during which Chloe glanced at her mother, her expression pinched. She was obviously worried about where Eloise was taking the conversation and, no doubt, puzzled as to why she was including Megan in it. Megan didn't reply – assuming the question wasn't aimed at her, or not wanting to answer it. Both were equally possible. For some perverse and wholly unkind reason, Eloise realised she truly wanted to know how Megan was feeling. 'Megan?' She raised her voice. 'I asked how you've been.'

Megan slowly wrung out the cloth and draped it over the tap before turning round. 'I've been... okay.'

Eloise nodded. 'It was sudden, though, wasn't it?'

Megan reached out a hand and gripped the countertop. 'It was.'

So that's the way she was going to go. Rationing. 'And the funeral. Has there been any further news on a possible date?'

'No.'

'Really? I would have thought you'd have got something booked in by now.'

'It's complicated.'

'How so?'

Megan swallowed as if her throat was full of gravel. 'Because of the conditions in Jonathan's will.'

Eloise knew exactly what she was talking about. Liv had emailed her copies of the will and the Statement of Wishes. 'Oh, that.' Something sparked in Megan's eyes. Game on. Eloise pushed. 'Surely you're not paying any credence to that nonsense?'

Megan looked down at the floor, took a breath. 'It was what he wanted.'

It was too good an opportunity to pass up. 'And Jonathan always gets what he wants, does he?'

'Excuse me.' Megan dashed out.

'Mum!' Chloe sounded shocked, but the look on her face was one of sneaking admiration.

'What? I was only making conversation. Has she been like this the whole time?' Eloise walked over to the sink.

'Yes. More or less. She never said much before – well, not to me – but since Dad died she's been virtually silent.'

'In shock?' Eloise took hold of the dishcloth between her finger and thumb and pulled it off the tap into the sink.

'Yeah. Probably. I mean, it was a shock. It was awful. But...' Chloe fiddled with one of her ear studs.

'But what?'

'Nothing.'

'Chloe. You're the one who's been here through it all. You can talk to me. I know how hard it's been.'

'Really, Mum, it's nothing.'

Eloise defaulted to the tactic that had always worked when Chloe was young – silence.

As predicted, a few moments later Chloe blurted out, 'We think there might be something she's not telling us.'

Eloise made herself hold back. 'What do you mean?'

Chloe's fidgeting migrated from her earring to the chain around her neck. 'Last week, when I was trying to get things sorted, she was... well, she seemed reluctant to help. We needed some information digging out. Stuff Liv wanted. Megan said she would get it for us, then she didn't.'

'Financial information?'

'Mainly. There were some medical notes Liv wanted to see as well.'

Eloise left another gap for Chloe to fill.

She obliged. 'Megan gave Liv the files, in the end. I'm sure it's nothing. More a case of her being forgetful than wilfully obstructive.' Eloise nodded, not necessarily in agreement, but rather to encourage Chloe to say more. It worked. 'Let's just say it's been really awkward, and she's not made it any easier.'

They both left it at that – for the time being.

Eloise's return to the bosom of her family was getting more interesting by the minute.

Chapter 28

CHLOE WAS upset when she discovered their mother had chosen to book a room at The Crown. She'd assumed, wrongly, that they would have a shuffle round and make space for her at The View. She'd offered Eloise her own bed without hesitation, imagining how reassuring it would be to share a room with someone after all this time – perhaps the rhythm of another person's breathing might chase away the dreams. The look of horror on Eloise's face at the suggestion had hurt, deeply. The awareness that she was the only one trying to hang on to their home, and with it their sense of themselves as a family, was depressing. In Chloe's fragile state, her mother's indifference felt like yet another abandonment, and she'd endured enough of those.

Perhaps she was too sentimental, but at least she cared about something other than the money.

The Crown prided itself on being the nicest hotel in Scarborough. It sat in the bend of The Esplanade, a long vanilla-ice-cream-coloured building, with an edging of black wrought-iron railings. It was elegant – much like their mother. Chloe watched Eloise check in and was struck by how at home she looked, with her smart clothes and soft leather overnight bag. Expensive luggage, just one of the many new tastes that her mother had acquired since leaving Scarborough, and her family. Chloe heard the male receptionist say he'd upgraded Eloise. Of course he had.

They travelled up to her room in silence. It was large, with three long drop-windows – a sea-view triptych. Her mother moved fluidly around the room, perfectly at home. She unpacked her cosmetics and toiletries in the bathroom, and hung a dress of muted blues and greens, a pair of smart black trousers and a silk shirt up in the wardrobe. Then she opened one of the windows a crack to let the cold air freshen the somewhat stuffy atmosphere. Chloe watched. 'You could've stayed. At the house,' she clarified.

Her mother sat down and unzipped her boots. Took them off – unhurried. 'I don't think that would've been such a good idea.'

'But it feels wrong that you can't stay with us.'

Eloise flexed her toes. 'It's not my home any more, Chloe.'

'But...'

'No. There are no "buts". I used to live there. Now I don't. And I'm fine with that.'

'But it must hurt seeing Megan... in your place.'

Eloise planted her feet firmly on the carpet. 'Chloe. Look at me. It's ancient history. I've moved on. My life no longer revolves around that house.'

'But it's still our family home.'

'Not for much longer,' Eloise retorted.

Sometimes, just occasionally, Chloe could see why her father might have felt the need to seek out kinder company. She flopped backwards onto the bed.

A minute passed.

She heard her mother sigh and stand up. Eloise went into the en suite, shut and then locked the door, leaving Chloe on her own.

The seagulls wheeled and racketed around outside the window. Chloe wished she could scream along with them, but she knew that would not be tolerated. Instead she lay, stranded on the bed, staring up at the ceiling.

Sadly, the ceiling – despite its ornate central cornice and crystal-teardrop chandelier – failed to provide any answers.

Chapter 29

ELOISE TOOK longer than strictly necessary freshening up, conscious all the time of the dark cloud on the other side of the door. As she brushed her hair and reapplied her lipstick she wondered, not for the first time, where she and Jonathan had gone wrong with their youngest daughter. Chloe was so aimless and dependent, compared to Liv. So diffident and downbeat, compared to Noah.

Was it the divorce?

It had been a mess, and Chloe had been around to witness more of it than the other two, but she'd been twenty-two at the time – an adult – so surely it couldn't have been that much of a formative experience? Eloise didn't like to think about that period of their lives too much. There was still some residual shame. More shame for Jonathan of course, but she hadn't been without fault. Seeing your parents lose all respect for each other – it must have been hard.

But in truth Chloe's tendency to be easily knocked off-course, indeed never to find her true course, had been evident, way before Eloise and Jonathan's marriage had imploded. She had always been unsure of herself.

Could it be that, as the baby of the family, they had spoiled Chloe, stunted her emotional development by expecting too little of her? Eloise tried to think back to Chloe's childhood, but it was difficult. To be brutally honest – and Eloise found that since her divorce she favoured the unvarnished truth over polite dishonesty – she had only vague memories of Chloe as a child. By the time she came along, the novelty of being a parent had well and truly worn off. Chloe had been loved as much as her brother and sister – Eloise was sure of that – but her childhood milestones were less celebrated, less noticeable... fewer? She just seemed to ride along in Liv and Noah's slipstream. By rights, Chloe should have been the most robust of the children, helped along by having older, confident siblings to learn from and mimic, but it hadn't worked out that way.

The raw truth was that Chloe was insipid.

The unkindness of the thought gave Eloise pause. Her youngest daughter was grieving. Still lying prone on the bed in the adjoining room, waiting for someone to comfort and reassure her.

Eloise gave herself one last check in the mirror. An attractive but rather forbidding face looked back at her. She softened her expression and vowed to do better as a mother.

'Darling.' The endearment at least pulled Chloe upright. 'I know these past few weeks have been hard on you. Being around your dad and seeing him so ill must have been awful. Truly awful. And I'm sure you were a great help and comfort to him. But we must look for small mercies in all this. He's free of the pain now. You said yourself how much he hated being so... different, so limited in what he could do. And he wasn't going to get any better, was he? Perhaps it's a kindness it didn't go on any longer.'

Eloise crossed the carpet and sat next to Chloe on the bed. Tentatively she reached out and stroked Chloe's hair. It was short, cropped close to her head. Soft to the touch, more like fur than hair.

'He would've hated to see you so down and depressed, sweetheart. He only ever wanted you to be happy.' It was good to feel her daughter press her head against Eloise's hand, accepting affection. It emboldened her. 'He would've wanted you to spread your wings. Embrace the next stage of your life. Maybe now is the time for a fresh start, somewhere new. Why don't you think about getting away from Scarborough and all these unhappy memories?'

She'd gone too far. She could tell immediately.

Chloe rolled away from her on the bed, swung her legs over the side and sat rigid on the edge of the mattress, looking away. Her voice, when she finally spoke, was cloggy with unshed tears. 'Yes, well, that might be easier if everything wasn't so up in the air.'

But Eloise persevered. 'Yes, I can see that.' Chloe was so quick to see a barred gate rather than the path beyond. 'But I'm sure you'll work something sensible out. Your dad obviously trusted the three of you to do the right thing or he wouldn't have left it up to you, and Liv, and Noah.'

Chloe still looked truculent. Eloise patted her hand. Time for a change of venue and tempo – and a much-needed glass of something cold and crisp.

'How about we go down to the bar for a quick drink before we head back up to the house? A chance for us to catch up properly without everyone else around?' The bribe of time alone with Mummy: some things never changed!

Chloe smoothed the bedspread with her fingers, before eventually, grudgingly, saying, 'Okay.'

Eloise slipped on some shoes and grabbed her bag, ready for an evening that was unlikely to be plain sailing.

Chapter 30

THEY HAD scattered like Arthur's thrown chess pieces.

Chloe had insisted on going to the hotel with Eloise... *to see her safely settled in*. Their mother's expression had clearly indicated that she had no need of such help. Of course their departure had given Noah the excuse he was looking for to slope off as well. He'd gone to buy more beer and wine – not that they needed any. He certainly didn't. He had been slurry on Friday night, his anecdotes rambling to the point of incoherence. Watching him stumble his way upstairs at the end of the evening had made Liv feel an additional layer of itching frustration with him.

'How about a kick-about in the garden?' For an awful moment Liv thought Angus was asking her. But, of course, he meant the boys. They didn't need asking twice, and in a flash they raced off in search of their trainers. As Angus hauled himself up from the sofa, he affectionately scuffed the top of Liv's head – a heavy-handed benediction. 'Why don't you go and have a lie-down for an hour or so? There's nothing doing here.'

'Thank you.' She smiled, too late for him to see it. Liv felt sad – they seemed to spend their lives heading off in opposite directions. For a second she contemplated getting up and going out into the garden with them, but a fat splatter of rain against the window dissuaded her.

A lie-down seemed too much like giving in, but a bath... A bath sounded like bliss.

For a change, there seemed to be lots of hot water. Liv scanned the bathroom shelves and selected a bottle of Radox with a centimetre of dark-green bubble bath in the bottom. That had to have been her father's. She poured it all in, sluicing out the bottle to get at the last few drops. A strong scent of pine rose from the foaming water – another jolt from the past: the reassuring fragrance creeping under the door into her darkened bedroom, as she drifted off to sleep as a child.

Liv tried to lock herself in the bathroom, only to find that the bolt, which used to provide a sanctuary from the invasions of her siblings, had been painted over. She undressed regardless. They were all out; no one was going to bother her. She eased herself into the running water, relishing the heat. A bath at this time of day – in fact at any time of day – was an indulgence. Liv was, by nature and necessity, a shower person.

But the problem with a bath was that it encouraged reflection.

And there was a lot for Liv to reflect on.

Their mother, for a start. Having her in the house was a fresh complication, but one that, the more she thought about it, Liv welcomed. Eloise had always had an edge of impatience about her, an edge that had been sharpened, not dulled, by age. It was a characteristic they shared, indeed prided themselves on. Strong women – like mother, like daughter. Or at least like one daughter.

In the current circumstances, Eloise's 'cut the crap' attitude might come in useful. Something was needed to drag them all out of the morass they seemed to have sunk into. Perhaps her presence would shake Chloe out of her slump, and rein in Noah's randomness. Perhaps? That Chloe was already monopolising their mother was no great surprise. Old habits died hard. Liv would need to break them up at some point, in order to engineer an audience alone with Eloise. She needed to establish whether Noah's take on their mother's intentions, and expectations, was accurate.

That was the problem: if the division of their father's estate had, as she'd expected, been simply a matter of arithmetic, Liv would have been fine. She was a good administrator – thorough, accurate, scrupulously honest – but it was obviously far more complicated than that. What they each wanted, and thought was fair, was so complex and nuanced that she worried they might never arrive at a solution.

Take Chloe wanting to keep The View, for utterly sentimental reasons. It made no sense. Surely Chloe must know that. As always, she was hanging on to the certainty of the past, because she was frightened of the future. The problem was that Chloe had no idea what sort of future she wanted. She'd never been able to make up her own mind, about anything.

Liv turned off the hot tap and lay back in the water.

At least Chloe wasn't motivated by greed, unlike their brother. Noah plainly wanted to get as much as he could from the estate – which shouldn't come as a surprise, given his fluid relationship with money. Noah could be generous, but he was also profligate, always preferring the indulgence over the necessity. Josie had been a stabilising influence on him, but her common sense was a counterbalance, not a cure. She had not, it would seem, managed to fundamentally change Noah's easy-come, easy-go attitude. He would never be sensible or steady. Perhaps it was his job that gave him a taste for the high life. A job that was, in itself, frivolous and self-indulgent – especially for a man with a family.

Liv's own thoughts on what to do with their inheritance were a congealed mess. She couldn't deny that the money would come in useful. It would, for example, cover the boys' education for years to come. And she had high hopes for Freddie and Arthur; not medicine necessarily, but certainly – with luck and hard work – professional lives filled with value and purpose. Such careers tended not to come cheap. But in truth it was less the actual legacy and more the principles at play that were troubling her. Their father had obviously been trying to teach them something with his will; and Liv, ever the diligent student, wanted to correctly decipher and fulfil his last-ever lesson. If his objective had been to get them to behave at their best, then that's what she needed to steer her siblings to do.

The problem was Liv wasn't sure what was for the best. She felt horribly conflicted about Megan and uncertain as to what their mother expected, or deserved. The whole thing was riddled with emotion and irrationality.

But somehow they were going to have to come up with an acceptable solution, and she needed them to do so by the close of play tomorrow at the latest. Because whatever happened, Liv couldn't tolerate this going on beyond the weekend. She simply couldn't. She hadn't the time or the mental energy for it.

Enough! She needed to concentrate on herself – if only for a few minutes.

She stretched out in the hot, pine-scented water and took an inventory. A sight-check first, looking for signs of oedema. There was some around her lower abdomen, in her finger joints and her ankles, but it was minor. It was certainly not something anyone else would notice, unless they were looking for it. Crucially, Angus hadn't registered anything – not yet. The thought saddened her. He obviously took her body so much for granted that he didn't actually see it any more. They still made love, every now and again, in the slivers of time that existed between life and kids and work, in the dark; but they no longer pawed over each other, no longer knew each other's flesh intimately, tenderly, precisely. It was unsurprising. It was what happened to most couples, she imagined. She gathered up a handful of bubbles and draped them across her midriff like a cloth. Besides, Angus not noticing the changes in her was what she needed. It bought her time.

Time to think.

Time to decide.

Because although there were very few outward physical signs as yet, she could feel the changes taking place deep inside her physiology. Cells were dividing and multiplying, an unstoppable process governed by a biological imperative that, as she knew only too well, was no respecter of personal choice or desire. And that mitosis was creating other appreciable side-effects, aside from the slight oedema. The fatigue was getting worse and the dizzy spells that occasionally struck her were becoming increasingly unpleasant, but most frustrating of all was the lack of clarity in her thinking. It was this weakness that was Liv's real concern. Now was not the time to be fuzzy and wrong-headed – there was too much riding on her decisions, at home and at work. The unbalanced feeling that had so unsettled her when she'd been down by the sea with Noah returned. She closed her eyes and tried to practise what she so often preached to her patients at times of stress and physical upheaval. A slow, deep breath in, for the count of five, a slow breath out, for five. Inhaling from her stomach, focusing on her own steady breathing instead of the furore in her mind. In, out. In, out.

'Oh, sorry!'

Liv sat up, sending a small tidal wave over the taps. Megan stood in the doorway, a stack of towels clutched to her chest.

'I didn't realise anyone was in here.'

Liv felt ridiculous, sitting in her stolen-bubbles bath, with her arms coyly covering her breasts, like she had been caught doing something illicit. She started defending herself. 'I thought it was a good time to have a bath – before the evening rush.'

Megan then did something really weird. Instead of hastily retreating and leaving Liv in peace, she stood in the doorway, making conversation, as if the situation wasn't totally awkward. And this from a woman who had spent the past twenty-four hours studiously avoiding even the simplest of verbal exchanges. 'I can imagine you don't normally get much time to yourself.'

Liv checked to see the bubbles were still providing adequate coverage. 'No.' Brevity – that might make her leave.

Megan shifted the towels slightly. 'But Angus is good with the kids, isn't he? He seems to enjoy spending time with them.'

'Yes, he is.' What the hell did she want? 'But they are half his, after all!'

Megan studied Liv, as if trying to compute her comment, but she still didn't move.

Liv had had enough. 'Megan, if you don't mind.'

Megan tilted her head slightly, like a pigeon. 'No, of course not. I'll leave you to finish your bath.' But instead of retreating, she came into the bathroom. 'I'll just put these away.' And to Liv's consternation, she proceeded to cross over to the linen cupboard in the corner and start putting the towels away. It seemed to take an inordinately long time. 'I've left those bank details you wanted in your room. Sorry it took me so long to dig them out.'

'Thank you,' Liv responded. Megan was such an odd person and she seemed to have grown odder in the wake of Jonathan's death. Perhaps it was simply the impact of grief, but Liv had her suspicions that Megan's weird, almost catatonic state might be medically as much as emotionally induced.

Was she ever going to leave?

Seemingly not, because after she'd put the last towel in the cupboard, Megan turned round. 'I know how difficult this is for you, Liv. How uncomfortable. Even more so, now your mother is here. I suppose I should leave, let you sort it out as a family.' Liv said nothing. 'I have thought about it. Leaving. But I don't know where else to be, at the moment. This is my home.' She corrected herself, 'Was my home. With Jonathan. I can't leave it. Not yet. Not until he does.'

Liv was confused. 'I understand,' she said, though she didn't, not fully. Or perhaps the more honest answer was that she didn't want to understand Megan – didn't have the requisite energy to. Besides, Noah had a point: why was she trying so hard to accommodate Megan's emotions and rights along with everyone else's? It was too much. Megan was nothing to Liv. She certainly wasn't family. And the comment about Dad not having *left* yet, Liv didn't know what to make of that. The queasiness rolled through her again. Most of all she just wanted Megan herself to leave – at least the bathroom, if not the house. To encourage her, Liv made Megan a promise that she alone could not guarantee to keep. 'We'll get something sorted tomorrow, Megan. I'm sure we will. It doesn't have to be complicated.' If only that was true. 'Then we can all move on with our lives.'

Megan nodded, but it was a small, hesitant nod. At least she seemed to wake up enough to realise how inappropriate it was for them to be having this exchange in such circumstances. 'Well. Yes. I'll leave you to recharge.'

As soon as the door closed, Liv got out of the bath – what little tranquillity she'd been able to achieve now shattered. She quickly swaddled herself in one of Megan's freshly laundered towels. As she bent down to pull out the plug, she lost her bearings and stumbled. Her right kneecap cracked against the bath. For an awful moment she thought she was going to faint. The see-sawing feeling in her head drove her backwards. She landed heavily on the toilet lid, where she sat, hugging herself, waiting for the nausea to subside. It did, slowly, draining away like the bath water.

Her options were stark.

Keep the baby growing inside her or have an abortion.

The pressure to decide was exhausting. The lack of someone to share her struggle debilitating. But who could she tell, without opening the floodgates of other people's emotions and opinions? It was her body, her life, her decision, and yet the loneliness of the position she found herself in was crushing.

Her confidant on anything that really mattered in life was usually Angus. He was her sounding board and her support; the person who loved her most in the world and the one who spoke the most sense, but this... No, she couldn't tell him this, because she knew what he would say, what he would want, what he would convince her of, with the sheer power of his love for his family, and his delight at the thought of extending it.

Liv rocked forward, folding her stomach to her spine. From the moment she said she was pregnant, he would begin dreaming. A baby girl. That's what his heart would reach for. He would say it wouldn't matter what sex their next child was, but that wouldn't be true. Big, bluff Angus had always wanted a little girl in his life. And here, growing inside her, could be that daughter.

She couldn't tell him she was pregnant, set free all that hope and longing, then rob him of the reality.

If he knew she was considering terminating this pregnancy – if she went ahead and had an abortion – it would kill something in their relationship. It would, she was absolutely certain, fundamentally change how Angus loved her, and she couldn't endure that.

But equally she couldn't envision having this child.

She was thirty-seven. Her last two pregnancies had not been straightforward. She had two small children already. She had a career that consumed her. Many, many people who relied upon her. She was bone-tired. Her dad was dead.

She simply couldn't do any more.

Couldn't face being responsible for anyone else.

She sat up and rubbed her forehead, trying to knead away the fog. She needed to get it together. This messy, self-pitying indecision was not her. She would not let herself play the victim. This pregnancy wasn't a punishment; it was just bad luck. She had choices.

She stood up. Dropped the towel. Got dressed quickly. Dragged a brush through her hair and set her shoulders.

She needed to deal with her current overload like she tackled everything else, which was by focusing on one task at a time, before moving on to the next challenge. The priority was obviously agreeing their father's legacy. She could tough out another twenty-four hours, as long as they reached a resolution by the end of it.

With the will resolved, she would be able to go home. Go back to work. Regain control of her emotions and her actions.

And then, and only then, would she decide.

Chapter 31

Noah was killing time playing Hide-and-Seek with the boys until Chloe and his mother deigned to show their faces back at the house. Given that they were a sibling down, any further conversation about the will had been suspended. They weren't *quorate*, apparently. Where the fuck did Liv pick up these words?

Their mother's arrival was a surprise, and not a wholly welcome one. Noah had never been able to read Eloise – not as a child, or now as an adult. It was a mug's game trying to guess what her attitude to their weird weekend get-together was. Trying to establish her thoughts on the conditions contained within the will was also difficult. Eloise and Megan being put in the same boat by their father – that couldn't have gone down well. Maybe Chloe would have got the low-down, after their jolly to the hotel together. Noah made a mental note to scope out his little sister about their mother's intentions later that evening.

'Six, five, four, three, two, one. Coming, ready or not!' Noah hollered. Then he sat on the arm of the chair, took a swig of his beer and carried on half-watching the football.

After a minute or so Liv asked, 'Aren't you going to, you know... *go seek*?'

She smelt of soap and warmth – she'd just come down from having a bath. It was comforting. Noah lingered, breathing in the scent. Their conversation in the café had reminded him that Liv was a human being, with her own worries and concerns, as well as his insufferable big sister. 'I'll go in a minute. But I know where they'll be hiding. And besides, I think it's good for them to practise keeping quiet for longer than thirty seconds.'

Liv either didn't notice or chose to ignore the dig. 'Do you remember how you used to cheat when we played as kids? You'd keep changing your hiding place. It drove me mad.'

'I remember. That was half the fun of it. It's a good house for Hide-and-Seek.'

'It is.'

They sat in companionable silence for a few moments. Their time down at the beach had obviously stirred up some happy memories in both of them. Noah finally, reluctantly, pushed himself upright. 'I suppose I should go and find them.' Liv nodded. 'Now where could Arthur be, I wonder?' he shouted.

Liv's wistful smile was worth the effort of leaving the drowsy warmth of the front room.

Arthur was hiding behind the door in the dining-room. He was happy to be found quickly. At three and a half, he had very little patience with anything that involved being still or quiet. 'Now, are you gonna help me find Freddie?' Noah asked. Arthur, grudge finally forgotten, nodded and raced off, glad to be moving again.

They had a scout around the ground floor, just to spin out the game a little longer – and to let Arthur practise his knee-slides across the hall – then they headed upstairs. Noah knew that Freddie's favoured hiding spots were the gap at the side of the linen cupboard in the bathroom and under the beds. But this time he was in none of the usual places. Noah and Arthur came back downstairs and did another sweep, but they still couldn't find Freddie. By now Arthur was bored. Liv took him off Noah's hands by offering him a biscuit.

Noah thought for a few seconds, then realised there was one room he hadn't looked in. His dad's room. He hesitated. Surely it was unlikely that shy, obedient Freddie had ventured into his grandpa's room? But – as Noah himself had reassured his nephew – Jonathan was no longer in the house, so there was no reason not to.

On entering the room, Noah was shaken. He'd foolishly imagined it returned to its old use as a study, but when he stepped inside, it was still very much his father's last resting place. It was an unsettling thought, made only slightly more palatable by the sight of Freddie's feet sticking out from underneath the bed, the underside of his socks grey with dust. Glad of the distraction, Noah pretended not to have seen his nephew. He made a circuit of the room, checking behind the curtains and in the corners, muttering, 'I wonder where he could be?' before crouching down, grabbing a foot and yelling, 'Found you!'

Freddie screamed with mock terror and wriggled further underneath the bed, forcing Noah to lie down on the carpet. From his prone position he could see Freddie pressed against the wall, curled up in a ball, his eyes screwed shut. The old '*If I can't see you, you can't see me*' gambit. Noah grabbed again and snared Freddie. This time he allowed himself to be hauled out. He emerged from beneath the bed with what looked like a small box clutched in his hands.

They sat on the carpet together. Noah waited for a moment, then asked, casually, 'What have you got there, Fredster?'

'I found it under Grandpa's bed. I think it's treasure.' Freddie held the box tightly, obviously wary that his uncle was going to take it off him – which was precisely what Noah found himself wanting to do.

'May I see?'

Freddie chewed his bottom lip, politeness and self-interest at war. He was so obviously Liv's child. His compromise was to hold the box out for Noah to look at.

'Have you looked inside?' Noah was conscious of his heart rate increasing.

Freddie shook his head and drew the box back into the safety of his lap. He traced his grubby fingers across the pattern on the top.

Noah was very careful about what he said next, aware that he needed to strike a tone of adult authority rather than his usual uncle chumminess.

'You know that we shouldn't really be in Grandpa's room touching his things, don't you, Freddie?' This was mean. Freddie looked away. 'It's okay. I know you were just playing, and it was a great place to hide – it took me ages to find to you – but we'd better clear out now, before anyone finds us in here. We wouldn't want to upset Megan, would we?'

Freddie shook his head. The tips of his ears had turned bright pink with shame. Noah felt shabby, but he absorbed the feeling. Freddie got to his feet, still clutching the box to his chest.

Noah kept his voice neutral, but firm. 'Put it back where you found it, eh, Freddie? Even if it is treasure, it's not yours, is it?' He walked towards the door, deliberately keeping his back to the boy.

Freddie was obviously thinking. Noah gave him one more nudge. 'Someone hid that box away, to keep it a secret. And you know that a secret worth hiding is worth keeping.' He heard Freddie sigh, then the whisper of wood on carpet as his nephew slid the box back underneath the bed. 'Good lad.'

They left the room and Noah pulled the door shut. When he looked at Freddie, he was relieved to see that his nephew was empty-handed, the secret box returned to its hiding place for someone else to find.

Chapter 32

THEY WERE eating late, to allow time for Arthur and Freddie to be fed and put to bed. The boys were cranky after the excitement of their trip to the beach and Grandma's surprise appearance. Noah didn't offer to read them their bedtime story – he felt he had compensated enough. What he really wanted to do was go back into his father's room and retrieve the box Freddie had found, but with all the human traffic in the house, that was proving to be quite tricky. Noah was worried that Freddie would renege on their deal and try to reclaim his find. The thought of it sitting under the bed nibbled away at him, an itch he couldn't scratch. Who hides a box underneath a bed unless there's something in it worth hiding? His father? Megan? There was a moment when Liv and Angus were bathing the boys – one threat neutralised – and Megan was in the kitchen preparing dinner, when he'd been about slip into the study, but on cue, the front door had opened and his mum and Chloe clattered in. At that point Noah resigned himself to waiting until everyone was in bed, before he could retrieve Freddie's find and discover whether it really did contain any 'treasure'.

The box now beyond reach – for the time being – Noah turned his attention to another more pressing issue for which he needed privacy.

The air was sharp with frost as he walked up the drive. The exertion made his chest feel tight. Noah tried Josie's mobile. Her bright, breezy recorded promise to *get back to him as soon as possible* sounded like a taunt.

He looked at the house, windows blazing. He could see Megan and Liv in the kitchen, sorting out the evening meal. From this distance it looked as if they were working in synchronised harmony – which just went to prove how deceptive appearances could be. In the sitting room the only person visible was Angus. He was standing by the fire, a glass of wine in his hand, studying the picture on the chimney breast, totally at home. The painting was some modern-art abstract splodge-thing his father had bought with Megan on a trip to Barcelona, or perhaps it had been Bilbao. Noah hated it, on principle. It represented Megan's influence on his father's interests and tastes. Of his mother and Chloe there was no sign, though they could easily be in the room with Angus, sitting out of sight, heads together, plotting. They had taken their time at The Crown. Noah wondered what they had talked about. From a distance, the house glowed. To an unsuspecting passer-by it might look like the type of home to envy. Big, spacious, cosy – a proper family home.

Noah couldn't wait to see the *For Sale* sign go up.

He returned his phone to his pocket, watched Megan carry a dish out of the kitchen, and Angus, perhaps summoned by a shout from Liv, walk out of view.

Meal time.

Still he delayed.

Josie used to love coming to Scarborough. She said it felt like going on holiday. She once confessed – after they'd been going out for quite a while – that she'd expected Scarborough to be like Blackpool, all *Kiss Me Quick* hats, sticks of rock and donkeys. She'd been surprised to find it wilder, in parts truly beautiful, more finely balanced between tackiness and splendour. She had loved The View as well. It was Josie who had made him appreciate its location, its size, its solidity. She'd enjoyed pointing out how the house was an apt metaphor for his childhood: comfortable, insulated from reality, generous. As the high-rise, flat-dwelling daughter of a single mum, Josie had been amused that Noah had had such an Enid Blyton childhood.

Seeing things through her eyes – he missed her perspective.

He missed her.

He slid his phone out and checked it again. No message.

He couldn't see anyone in the rooms at the front of the house any more; they must all be at dinner. His presence was required. With a heavy heart, he walked down the icy path back into the heaving, oppressive bosom of his family.

Chapter 33

NOAH STROLLED into the dining-room at the last possible second, when all the food was dished out, the wine poured and Liv was in the middle of bashing out a text, informing him that *dinner was served and they weren't waiting for him.* His muttered, 'I was on a call' wasn't much of an apology.

With everyone seated, they fell on their food. There was very little conversation, just the grating of cutlery across crockery and a lot of swallowing. Angus was the only one to have the good manners to comment on the meal. His 'This is lovely, thank you, Megan' failed to draw any similar acknowledgement from the rest of them.

The meal, which had taken Megan two hours to prepare, cook and serve, took them five minutes to demolish – or, in Eloise's case, pick at. She left more than she ate. Megan felt the intended slight.

Bellies full, they moved on to more wine, with Noah leading the charge again, drinking with the same gusto as the boys had guzzled their squash.

Megan thought about starting to clear away, but decided to stay put when the talk turned to Jonathan. Or, more accurately, what Jonathan had been like as a father. Chloe started it, with a story about an ill-fated trip to Flamingo Land one summer. Traffic jams, Chloe being sick in the car and having to wear a selection of Noah and Liv's borrowed clothes – the shorts apparently kept falling down, showing her knickers; arguments about which rides to go on; an ice-cream and wasp sting incident, topped off with them never even seeing the flamingoes. It was one of *those* anecdotes, family folklore with clearly assigned roles: Jonathan cast as intrepid, Eloise – long-suffering, Liv – impatient, Noah – reckless, Chloe – cute and klutzy. They each added to the tale, contradictions and details, embroidering more emotion onto the day, until they were satisfied that it presented them as comically, and as colourfully, as possible.

The next half-hour was a cascade of such reminiscences.

Jonathan's varying reactions to their school reports and parents' evenings. His teaching them all to drive, with very different degrees of success and patience. His grilling of any unsuspecting boyfriends who foolishly ventured up to the house. His very explicit career advice. His implicit views on their own parenting skills. Their stories overlapped and overtopped each other. Couldn't they hear it? The jealousy wriggling beneath their stories, the little side-swipes at each other, the pettiness behind each of their carefully crafted offerings to their father's altar. The room filled with heat and noise and effort, as Megan sipped and listened, and they drank and talked. Even Angus joined in, with his version of *Jonathan the Great,* some story about a game of golf, a hole-in-one and a startled rabbit narrowly missing death on the eighteenth tee.

The only person – other than Megan – who said very little, who by the end was saying nothing at all, was Eloise.

Watching their performances, it struck Megan how few of the anecdotes featured their mother or, if they did, how she only played a bit-part, or an unflattering role. For the first time, probably ever, it made Megan wonder what it must feel like to know that you're the sidekick, not the hero parent. By the veiled expression on Eloise's face, she suspected it was not good.

Distracted by her contemplation of Eloise's role in Jonathan's family before the divorce, Megan missed a question aimed at her. 'Sorry?'

Chloe had red wine stains on her teeth, and it made her look vulpine. 'Liv was saying that it might be nice if we all chose a special memento to remember Dad by.'

'Yes. That's a good idea.' What else could she say?

Liv swivelled round in her seat so that she was facing Megan. 'What would you choose, Megan?'

Their conversation in the bathroom must have stirred a little sympathy in Liv's soul. 'Oh, I don't know. I'd have to think about it.' There was a disappointed pause. Megan knew she'd come up short on the Coulter family participation measure, yet again.

Patience expired, Liv switched her attention to Noah. 'What about you, No?'

He upended the last of the bottle into his glass. He didn't seem to need long to think about his choice. 'Well, if no one else wants it, his laptop would be really useful. Mine's on its last legs.'

'I think Liv meant something more personal?' Chloe prompted him.

Noah looked away for a second. 'I'll take the chess set, if that's all right with everybody else.' There was a ripple of nods.

'Chloe, what about you?' Liv asked.

'I know you're going to think I'm weird, but I'd love to have his old Barbour. Being able to wear something that I associate so strongly with Dad would be nice.' She made an odd gulping noise, which they all respected with silence, except Noah, who used the hiatus to open another bottle of wine. The squeak of the cork was loud. Having composed herself sufficiently, Chloe asked, 'What would you pick, Liv?'

Liv scratched her eyebrow, considering. 'Angus and I love the picture in the lounge.' Megan felt her nails cut through the thin skin on the top of her hand. She and Jonathan had bought the painting on their first weekend away. Madrid, bright sunlit days spent sightseeing, and dark nights cloistered in a gloomy little hotel buried deep in Los Austrias. The picture had hung in her house in Darlington for months, a cherished reminder of their secret relationship. Giving it pride of place on the chimney breast in The View had been a symbolic affirmation of their legitimacy as a couple. Did Liv know that? It certainly wasn't a picture that had been in the house for years – not part of the fabric of her childhood memories. Perhaps she was just picking what she liked, what would fit into her lifestyle and her lovely big house in Cheadle. Megan was about to object, but stopped herself. If she said 'No', they would want to know why she was obstructing Liv's choice, and that would mean explaining, in front of Eloise, about the picture's significance.

They had obviously taken her silence as consent, because the conversation had moved on to who should have Jonathan's watch. 'Don't you want it, Mum?' Liv asked. The watch was inscribed with a message from Eloise – a twentieth wedding anniversary present – given at a time when it had been possible to inscribe love into metal with confidence.

'No.' Eloise was as economical with her words as she was with her emotions.

'Are you sure?' Chloe seemed hurt by the lack of sentimentality being shown by her mother.

'Quite sure.'

It was only then that Megan realised Liv was holding the watch in her hands. Where had she got it from? From Jonathan's bedside table? Their erosion of her tenure was ceaseless. 'It's a lovely watch. I'm sure all it needs is a new battery. Why don't you take it, Noah? I think Dad would've liked it to go to you.' Liv passed it across the table to him.

Noah picked it up, turned it over in his hands, put it down on the table and stared at it. Then he said very quietly, in a voice that seemed gutted of his usual energy and confidence, 'No, thanks.'

'Whyever not?' Liv asked.

'I...' For once he seemed lost for words. 'I don't wear a watch.'

Liv frowned. 'Well, you don't have to wear it. You could just keep it as a memento.'

Eloise chipped in with, 'Actually, Liv, you do have to. It's one of those mechanisms that only keeps working if you wear it.'

But Noah was having none of it. He pushed it away from him across the tablecloth. 'Well, in that case it should go to someone who will wear it.'

'Noah!'

He cut Liv off. 'For God's sake, Liv. I said, "I don't want it." Angus can have it. Or keep it for the boys. Or you wear it! Do what you want with it.' There was pain as well as anger in his voice.

To Megan, it seemed as good a juncture as any to go and fetch dessert.

Chapter 34

SHE WAS like a bloody dog with a bone. He didn't want the watch. Why did Liv have to keep banging on about it? Noah took another slug of wine. The thought of slipping the chunky gold-link bracelet onto his own wrist and snapping shut the clasp actually made him feel sick.

Why?

Because Noah wasn't without imagination. He knew how many lonely hours his father had spent sitting by the window, staring at the sea and the sky; how little he'd slept; how the pain he'd had to endure day in, day out had warped time, making it drag and creak; how long the last few months must have been at the end. He knew how often his father must have sat looking at the second hand crawl around the face of the watch as it measured out the last dregs of his life.

The watch had marked out every agonising, slow minute of his father's illness and death.

So, no. On reflection. Noah did not want his father's watch.

He felt, rather than heard, his phone buzz as Megan brought in the cheesecake.

Josie. A WhatsApp.

Making sure his screen was angled away from his mother, Noah clicked on it. It was a photo of Lily, in her ballet tutu, grinning. The message read: **She did fab. Loved every minute of it. Even tolerated me trying to get her hair tied back. If you want to call before she goes to bed, that's ok.**

Noah was away from the table in a second. He grabbed his jacket on the way out, banging the front door shut behind him.

He listened to the dial tone, aware of a breathlessness that this time had more to do with anxiety than with his walk up the drive. Josie's phone rang, and rang. His call went to voicemail. *Damn, damn, damn, damn!* It was only then that he thought to check the time. 8.51 p.m. He looked at the picture of Lily again. Time sent: 6.43 p.m. The fucking signal in the house! More than two hours late. Lily would be in bed, fast asleep by now. Josie would be fuming. He still had to try.

The ringtone echoed through the dark garden. *Pick up. Please, just pick up the sodding phone!*

Josie appeared in the screen, the image small. She was obviously holding her phone at arm's length, keeping her distance. 'Yes.' One short, sharp word, standing in for a thousand longer repressed words. Josie on the sofa in their home, the lamp casting a warm halo around her. A cosy domestic scene that couldn't have been staged any better – if the intention was to punch a hole in your heart. The night air around Noah seemed suddenly darker.

'Josie. I'm sorry. I only just got your message. Just this minute. You know what the phone reception is like in Dad's house.' Silence. 'I've been trying to reach you all day. You must have seen my missed calls.'

'We've been out. Lily was tired. I wanted to get her settled before I spoke to you.'

'Ah, yes. The competition.' He gabbled, 'She looked lovely. How did she get on? Did she remember her steps?'

'She was fine.'

Come on, Josie, please.

Josie reached for her glass of wine and took a sip.

Noah heard the crash of glass on wood as she put it back down, clumsily, on the side. He wanted to keep the conversation on their daughter – the light spot in their relationship. 'She wasn't scared having to perform in front of an audience?' He was desperate for Josie to relent and speak normally to him, about normal things, without this swirling undercurrent of resentment.

'No. She enjoyed it.' Long pause. He waited it out. 'She is her father's daughter – in some things.'

He swallowed the jibe, offered a compliment in return. 'It looked like you did a good job with her hair. Almost Royal Ballet standards.'

Silence again. This one loaded with pressure on him – to stop using their daughter as a buffer.

'Josie?'

'Yes.'

'Can we talk?'

'We are talking.'

'You know what I mean. Properly.'

'Well, that's quite difficult Noah, given that you're not here.' Her mouth looked tight.

'You know I had to come this weekend. I didn't have a choice.' He didn't add that she and Lily could have come as well, if she hadn't been so pissed off with him.

'The problem we have, Noah, is not this weekend – it's that you're *never* here. There's always something more important or, let's be honest, something more interesting or exciting you'd rather being doing than be with us.'

'That's not true.'

'Yes, it is. You just don't want to admit it.'

'I have to work.' That provoked her.

'And so do I, Noah, but when I'm here, I'm here. Committed. Switched on. Even when you do grace us with your presence, you're not really with us. You're always tired. Or off somewhere in your head. Or pissed.'

That was low – but true. 'I'm sorry. I know it's been a bit of a rough patch lately. And now with Dad passing.'

'Lately!' It came out in a burst of frustration. 'Sorry isn't enough, Noah. Not any more. We've had this conversation before – hundreds of times. You promise to change. You do, for a day or two, and then we're back in the same old pattern. Me looking after Lily, the house, life in general; and you dropping by, like some part-time father, wanting the good stuff with none of the responsibility.'

'Josie. I love Lily. I love you. More than anything else in the world.' He did.

'Do you, Noah? Do you really? Well, you've got a very funny way of showing it.' In her agitation she'd started leaning further and further forward – her face was so close to the camera that it blocked out the rest of the room.

How was it that every argument they had always descended into cliché, and yet it was those clichés that hurt the most. His general uselessness. Her all-round effort. His lack of staying power. Her stoicism. Perhaps because the clichés were true?

She stopped speaking, but Noah could still hear the anger in her breathing. He didn't know what to say for the best – for them, or for him.

'Has Lily missed me?' he asked, out of cowardice.

Josie took a sharp, short breath. 'No. She's been perfectly happy, because she's used to you not being here.'

'Josie, please—'

She cut him off. 'No, Noah. You need to stop with the "please" and the "sorry", and the empty promises to change. It has to stop!' She flopped back, forgetting about her phone, and dropped her head.

The image on the screen slid off-kilter and went dark. She must have dropped her phone in her lap. He was closer to Josie than he'd been in weeks. Noah waited, wishing he was there with her. When she finally picked up her phone again, her expression was more one of sadness than of anger.

'I know this is a really bad time for you, Noah, losing your dad. I know you're hurting. I know how much you loved him. I loved him, too. But shutting me out simply isn't an option. I can't live like this, not any more. It's too lonely. I understand that you need some time to sort everything out at home with Liv and Chloe – that's fine. But, Noah,' she leant forward again, peering at the camera as if trying to really see him, 'I need you to remember... *we* are your family as well. We have to matter, even with everything else that's going on.'

She held the phone even closer to her face. He saw how lovely, and how tired, she was.

'Please, Noah – while you're over there, you need to really think about whether you want a family, and what it's going to take for things to improve between us. I don't want the same thing to happen to us as happened to your mum and dad. I couldn't stand it. Not for Lily, or for me.' He started to say something, but she kept talking. 'Please, just listen for a change.' He shut up. 'I want you to think about what sort of father – and partner – what sort of man *you* want to be. Really think. If you can't do that, I don't know what we're going to do.' And with that, she hung up.

She was right – that was what was so hard to deal with. There'd been too many trips away with work, too many missed bedtimes, too much chasing other priorities, too much running around.

But even as Noah found himself agreeing with what she'd said, he began to argue with her in his head.

Josie didn't understand. He was doing it for them – to make them secure, put some money in the bank for when they needed it. That's what a man was supposed to do, wasn't it? Provide for his family. It was all right focusing on emotions and exploring what she needed in order to *feel* loved, but life didn't operate on love and caring and listening. There were practical considerations – some of them huge and pressing. It was like worrying about the mood music and the canapés while the ship headed straight for the iceberg. Josie was still blithely ignorant of what it had cost him to scrape together the deposit on the house in the first place. Oblivious to how close they had come to losing it when he was out of work and she was on maternity leave. Without his dad's help, they would never have managed. Josie's willingness to accept his assurances that it would *all be fine* was a sign that she simply didn't want to know. When it came down to it, despite all her talk of feminism and equality, the cost of their living was his responsibility.

Standing in the cold and the darkness, Noah stoked his sense of persecution and fear. He was the one in an impossible position.

He was the one mourning his father while fighting to put his family on a safe footing. The one standing outside in the cold and the darkness while she sat at home, in the warmth, with their daughter safely tucked in her bed upstairs.

He coughed. His throat was suddenly full of phlegm, but instead of swallowing it down, he spat. The sound in the still night air was disgusting.

Christ, how would they manage without him?

And, even more importantly, how would he cope without them?

Chapter 35

THEY WERE all drinking solidly. Liv's glass seemed full to the brim all evening. It was only a matter of time before something kicked off. The conversation about which items they each wanted to remember their father by nearly lit the fuse, but the simultaneous arrival of Megan's home-made cheesecake and the abrupt departure of Noah helpfully prevented a flare-up.

The cheesecake was consumed in surly silence.

Noah reappeared just as Megan was clearing the table – a pack of cards in one hand and yet another bottle of red in the other. It was going to be a long night. He proceeded to deal Liv, Chloe, Angus and himself a hand, as Megan reached awkwardly between them, removing the last of the plates and glasses.

Eloise refused to participate in the game or the clearing up.

She curled her legs up underneath her and settled back on the couch. A good vantage point. The couch was new. And although she was loath to admit it, it was a vast improvement on the uncomfortable old chesterfield that used to dominate the room. This sofa was comfortable, squishy, designed for cosy nights in, snuggled up in front of the new, sleek TV. It was disconcerting to feel fresh jealousy after all this time, and after all her efforts to expunge such emotion from her heart. Eloise idly wondered if she was sitting in Jonathan's or Megan's spot. An image of Jonathan, his left leg crossed over his right, popped into her head. She blinked and stared at the kids to dispel it. The noise level was ratcheting up, voices raised and cards slapped down. Competitive to a fault, all three of them. Another of Jonathan's legacies.

After a while their shouts and squabbling began to grate. Eloise got up and left the room quietly. None of them noticed.

The rest of the house was blessedly quiet, apart from the clink of glassware and the sound of a tap running – Megan slaving away in the kitchen? A tagine, a cheesecake, an eye for soft furnishings: the woman was a walking advert for *Homes & Gardens*. One item that had escaped her remodelling was the gloomy seascape that hung in the hall. It was a reproduction of a John Atkinson Grimshaw painting of the South Bay. Milky moonlight. The sea like a millpond. The fragile masts of the boats silhouetted against the coppery sky. A traditional, wistful evocation of life by the sea. Eloise walked over and studied it. The calmness of the scene was in stark contrast to what was going on behind her in the dining-room. She'd never really liked the picture. But there again, she'd never really looked at it before. It had come with the house – just another of the old-fashioned fixtures and fittings they'd inherited from Jonathan's mother. Jonathan had claimed to like the picture when she'd threatened to take it down. Now Eloise saw why. It had a quiet, seductive charm.

The sound of Noah celebrating a win broke the moment.

She headed upstairs. Now was as good a time as any to take a tour of her old stomping ground – see how far Megan's taste had extended.

The upstairs hallway had been decorated in a neutral off-white, and the floor had been sanded and revarnished. There was a new rug. Quite a nice one. Wool, by the look of it. A splashy Kandinsky-style pattern. There seemed to be vases of flowers on every available surface, the classic sympathy choice of white lilies and roses – the same flowers people chose for weddings. Eloise noticed that the water in the big vase on the chest on the landing was topped with an inch-thick layer of green slime. Whoever had arranged the flowers hadn't trimmed the stems properly or removed the lower leaves. So, Megan wasn't good at every domestic duty. The scent of perfume and scummy water was unpleasant. Eloise stood still and listened. All she could hear was the occasional shout from the dining-room. She opened the door to the 'master bedroom'. What a pompous phrase!

Her composure wobbled.

Their old room.

The marital bed.

But of course it wasn't. It was a new bed, for a new lover, a new life.

She told herself to get a grip. It was a room. Just a room. Everything in it was different from when she'd been its occupant. Every memory erased. She stepped inside and disliked, on principle, the oversized headboard, the understated bed linen and the contrasting voile, blind and curtain combination framing the window. It was all very feminine and tasteful, and totally lacking in personality. How apt! Eloise drew the line at opening the wardrobe, but not at stepping lightly across the carpet and nudging open the door to the en suite.

Here a male component was more in evidence. Toothbrush, razor, aftershave. But on closer inspection, Jonathan's presence was more a shadow than an imprint. The bottle of aftershave was frosted with dust and the shaving stuff looked unused.

Another wobble.

Jonathan had always liked to be clean-shaven. The only time he ever went unshaven was when he was ill. Eloise wondered whether he'd ended life with a beard, his strong features obscured by stubble. She couldn't imagine that. It would not have been Jonathan. There again, he hadn't been *her Jonathan* for years. To escape the thought, she focused on Megan's stuff. The make-up, perfume and toiletries. There was very little. In fact it was a paltry collection for a pretty woman in her thirties. It was all so banal – that's what hurt. The classic tale of the older man, his age-appropriate wife usurped by a younger woman. The shock had not been lessened by the predictability of it all. Because Eloise had, foolishly but understandably, thought herself secure in Jonathan's affections. She had simply never thought it could happen to her, or him. Infidelity. Unfaithfulness. Lies. So many lies. That was what had really shaken her: the lack of respect for the investment they had both put into their marriage.

Jonathan's lust for another woman had cut deeply.

His love for Megan had nearly broken Eloise.

It suddenly struck her that what she was doing was pathetic, and more than a little creepy. It was beneath her to be sneaking around in Megan's bedroom. She backed out of the en suite and hurried across the deep, yielding carpet. In order to rid herself of the slight sense of shame, she crossed over the landing and opened the door to Noah's old bedroom. A shaft of moonlight spilled into the room through the gap in the curtains, illuminating Arthur's bed. Freddie's remained shrouded in darkness. The sight of her grandsons' lumpy sleeping forms made Eloise feel better.

At least they had good, unsullied memories of their grandfather. For that she was grateful.

'Is everything all right?'

Eloise jumped. Megan had materialised on the landing, out of nowhere. 'Yes. I was just heading for the bathroom. While I was up here, I thought I'd check on them.' It was an unnecessarily long-winded explanation.

Disconcertingly, Megan came to stand by Eloise's side. They both looked in through the door. Arthur was sprawled out in his bed, snoring loudly, while Freddie was curled up underneath his duvet, silent. Once again Eloise bumped into a thought that she would have preferred to avoid. Megan's childlessness. Had that been her sacrifice for Jonathan, or a personal choice? With Eloise, Jonathan had been adamant that three kids were more than enough. Or was it she who had been adamant? Of course it was absolutely none of her business what Megan's maternal aspirations were, or had been, and yet she wondered. As much as Eloise's own children caused her endless irritation and anxiety, even at times – like tonight – embarrassment, she couldn't imagine life without them. They were, and always would be, flesh-and-blood evidence of her relationship with Jonathan and their one-time faith in each other.

From downstairs came another volley of words. It shook them both alert and back on guard. They moved apart. Eloise remembered to make for the bathroom – the ostensible reason she was upstairs in the first place, and Megan headed to her room. At the doorway she stopped. 'Will you tell them I've turned in for the night?'

Eloise said, 'Of course', though she was pretty sure none of her children would have noticed that Megan had gone.

Chapter 36

MEGAN CLOSED her bedroom door and listened until she heard Eloise's footsteps heading downstairs.

Wherever she turned there was a member of Jonathan's family taking up space, with their mess and their noise and their demands. They seemed to have infiltrated their way into every nook and cranny of the house. The volume and intensity of them was suffocating. As she stood with her back pressed against the door, she realised something truly shocking: in the past twenty-four hours she'd been so taken up with catering for them, avoiding them, clearing up after them, worrying about them that she'd barely thought about Jonathan.

They were even stealing her grief from her.

She went into the bathroom and stripped off, turned on the shower and stepped into the cubicle. The water scalded her pale skin, raising red patches on her breasts and thighs. She scrubbed shampoo into her hair, ridding it of the smells of cooking and subservience. When she couldn't stand the water any longer, she got out and towelled herself dry roughly, efficiently, ruthlessly.

Her heart was pounding in her chest as if she'd been sprinting. She glanced in the mirror. A woman she didn't recognise looked back at her. Mid-thirties, slim, bordering on gaunt. A woman with long dark hair and a face that was so full of shadows it was hard to see her features. Megan wondered what Jonathan had seen in her.

Jonathan.

She ached for one clear, true memory of him.

She yearned for the pain that such a memory would bring.

She turned off the harsh bathroom light and went through to the bedroom. She switched off the light in there as well. Darkness might help. She crossed the room and climbed into bed, huddling down beneath the duvet. Alone, at last, she tried to summon Jonathan – the one true love of her life, the man for whom she'd sacrificed so much.

He refused to come.

She refused to give up.

She lay still, waiting for memories of their time together to assail her.

Still he didn't come.

Still she refused to give up.

She sat up, searching for something that might help conjure him up.

Then she remembered.

She crossed over to the chest and opened the second drawer. There, lying on the top, was the robe. She ran her hand over it, feeling the slither of silk beneath her water-wizened fingertips. It was soothing to touch something so delicate after so much harshness. She shivered, the heat from her shower long gone. She lifted the robe out of the drawer and wrapped herself in it. Silk against skin. Softness over sinew. She stroked her hands up and down her arms, hugging herself.

They retreated.

He approached.

She closed her eyes and welcomed him.

It was one evening in late June. Too hot for running really, but she'd been desperate to get out of the house. A forty-minute loop was all she allowed herself out on the Filey Road – uphill out, downhill back, watching the sun sink – but it had cleared her head. She was about to dash upstairs to grab a quick shower before going to sit with Jonathan, when Lisa intercepted her in the hallway. 'There's no rush.' She smiled, glanced at the door to his room. 'He's not quite ready for you yet.'

There were times when Megan resented Lisa's presence in their lives so intensely that she wanted to scream. These bouts of sudden, irrational rage made her feel like she was going mad. It must be madness, surely, to feel aggrieved with the one person who was making life bearable – for both of them. Because there was no arguing with the fact that Lisa was a godsend. She was efficient, conscientious, discreet and, even more importantly, Jonathan liked her. But there were occasions when her attitude seemed, to Megan, to be more proprietorial than professional. It was almost as if the two of them were vying for Jonathan's attention and, on occasions, it was Lisa who was winning.

Standing in the hall, red-faced with exertion and irritation, Megan was glad that the one skill Lisa did not possess was mind-reading. 'Okay. Thank you. But I won't be long.' Without Lisa there would have been no run, no time to shower, no leaving the house at all. She should stop being so ungrateful.

Lisa smiled even more brightly. 'Honestly, there's no rush. I'm around for the next hour or so.' She disappeared into Jonathan's room, closing the door behind her.

With Lisa's words in her head, Megan took a little longer in the shower than usual. She even left the conditioner in her hair for five minutes, for *better, more glossy results* – as it said on the bottle. When she'd finished, she stepped out and, instead of getting dried in a blind rush, like normal, she stood still and studied her reflection in the mirror. Her wet hair looked almost black against her skin. It framed a face that was thinner, the cheekbones prominent. A drop of water trickled down her chest. It slid down to her left nipple, then dropped onto the floor. Her weight loss was nowhere near as dramatic as Jonathan's, but it had carved away the softness from her belly and her thighs. In another life, Megan might have been pleased at this slimmer, firmer version of herself. She was certainly slimmer and firmer than Lisa.

She reached for the jar of moisturiser on the shelf, the one that Jonathan had bought for her birthday – a lifetime ago. She had used very little of it. There hadn't seemed much point; what her skin smelt like was an irrelevance nowadays. Slowly she dabbed tiny blobs of moisturiser across her shoulders, arms, breasts. She moved on to her belly and legs, creating a dot-to-dot across her body. Then slowly she massaged the rich cream into her skin, using small circular motions. She took care to be gentle with herself, breathing in the scent of the natural oils.

When she was finished, she went through to the bedroom and sat on the bed. She smelt of lemon verbena. Downstairs she heard Lisa's footsteps cross the hall. Another irrational pulse of jealousy rippled through her. She opened the wardrobe and, on a whim, picked out her favourite dress, the blue one with the thin straps. From the chest of drawers she chose some pretty matching, rarely worn underwear, eschewing her usual cotton knickers. She brushed her hair, put on some make-up – made herself look like her 'old', younger self. When she'd finished she was pleased with the result, but suddenly self-conscious. Either Jonathan would notice her efforts and feel sorrow for what they had lost, or he wouldn't, and she would. Shaking the thought away, she stepped out onto the landing.

The house was quiet. She made her way downstairs, feeling foolish. His door was closed. For some reason she knocked. When she didn't get a response she waited, then knocked again, expecting Lisa to come and open it. But there was no response. Chiding herself for her nervousness, Megan opened the door.

The change threw her.

She stopped in the doorway, feeling confused until the delight caught up with her. The room was a flicker of candlelight. There were three big church candles she'd never seen before glowing in the fireplace, some twenty or thirty tea-lights scattered around the room and, on the mantelpiece, the wrought-iron candlesticks she and Jonathan had bought as a memento of their weekend in Devon were finally being put to use. And there was music playing; not the usual discordant jazz that Jonathan listened to, but something she recognised, something she liked – Aretha.

Jonathan was sitting by the French doors, smiling. 'Well, that was worth it, to see the look on your face. You approve, m'lady?' He bowed.

She walked over and kissed his cheek. 'It's lovely.'

'Is it not? A serious fire hazard, I grant you, but I'm sure we'll be okay for a few hours. We do have one able-bodied adult present'

– he meant her – 'and Lisa has taken the precaution of putting the fire extinguisher from the kitchen in the corner, just in case. Take a seat.' He gestured to the chair that had been set up opposite him. It was the armchair from the lounge. It occurred to Megan that it must have taken someone – Lisa – a lot of effort to drag it into position. Beside the chair was a table covered with a white cloth. On the table there was a bottle of champagne, two glasses and a plate of antipasti. Megan flushed to think she'd been snotty about Lisa, when in reality her suggestion of a long shower had been a ruse to give her time to put all this together. She would buy Lisa some flowers the next time she was in town.

'What's the occasion?' It wasn't an anniversary – she would know.

'Do we need an excuse? You look lovely, by the way. Smell good, too.'

That he had noticed made Megan want to cry. Instead she smiled and smoothed down her freshly conditioned hair self-consciously. 'Shall I?' She picked up the bottle. Jonathan hadn't been able to open a bottle, even a screw-top, for more than a year. But she always asked; the illusion of normality was important. She poured two glasses, knowing that only one would be drunk. 'Cheers.' She clinked her glass against the rim of his, as it sat on the table. He didn't pick it up. He watched her take a mouthful.

'Is it good?'

She nodded.

'Tell me.' They used to do this a lot: she would drink or eat something and describe it to him. As his swallowing and digestion problems had increased, it had begun to seem a cruel taunt and they'd stopped. But if that's what he wanted tonight, she wasn't going to argue. Sharing a pleasure, however one-sided the experience, was so much better than not sharing at all.

She sat back, crossed her legs, let her dress fall open. 'It's good. Well chilled. The perfect amount of bubbles. Dry, but not too dry.'

'With a hint of...?'

She took another sip, swished it around in her mouth like a wine connoisseur, swallowed. 'I'd say... subtle tones of sarcasm, with a hint of self-congratulation. Vintage Coulter.'

Jonathan laughed. He caught her eyeing up the olives and Parma ham. 'Go on, eat. I had mine earlier.' A protein drink. 'Please.'

She didn't make him ask twice. She speared some artichoke and cheese, aware with each salty mouthful of his loss. His appetite was still strong, just not his ability to feed it.

His gaze was unsettling. It was a long time since she'd felt Jonathan's attention on her. She made herself relax into it – aware there was a subtext, but also aware that she needed not to rush him. He wanted to have control of the situation; she understood how important that was for him. And if the past couple of years had taught her anything, it was patience. She ate a little more, wondering where Jonathan had sent Lisa to do the shopping. She finished her drink and, with a nod of encouragement from Jonathan, poured herself another. She sipped. Savoured. Sat back and met his gaze. Still he didn't say anything. Aretha gave way to Curtis. Perhaps he had just wanted them to spend some time together – pretending to be normal. She was okay with that.

Megan found herself relaxing. She let her shoulders rest back against the chair and watched the candles flicker. It was seductive. She pulled her legs up underneath her and made herself more comfortable. Another sip.

He cleared his throat. It was a painful sound, one she hadn't got used to, but she tried to let it wash over her. Finally he spoke. 'You do know how much I love you, don't you?'

What was she supposed to say? 'Yes.'

'And that I'm sorry.'

'For what?'

'Hell, Meg. Where do you want me to begin? For this.' He looked down at himself.

'The disease isn't you, Jonathan.'

'But it is, isn't it? There's no getting away from that.'

'We are tonight.'

'Yes. Sorry. We are. That's the whole point of the mood music and lighting, after all.' He smiled.

She took another sip of champagne to cover up her mixed emotions. Where was he going with this?

'I've been thinking.'

'God help us!' She tried to get him to smile, but he resisted – wanted to get back onto the serious track.

'I mean, thinking about us. Our relationship.' Megan stopped herself from making any comment. 'I have so many regrets.' She automatically assumed he was talking about Eloise and the impact of their affair. He must have seen something in her expression because he hurried on, 'Not about you. You are, without doubt, the best person ever to walk into my life.' The strain of the emotion brought on another bout of uneven breathing and swallowing.

She paid him the respect of not leaping up and fussing, but waited as he slowly got himself under control.

'I'm so sorry I left it too late.'

'For what?'

'For us to get married.'

She made herself meet his eyes. 'It doesn't matter.'

'Yes. It does. You're keeping a promise you never even got to make.'

'Jonathan. It really doesn't matter.'

He smiled then, but sadly. 'I love you for saying that, but I know you're lying. And besides, it matters to me. I should have stood next to you, in front of the kids and my friends – in front of everyone – and said, *This is the woman I love.*' He took deep breath. 'Megan, I wish you were my wife.'

She leant across and kissed him, gently. As she withdrew, Jonathan held on to her, pulling her back towards him. There was so little strength left in his arms that it felt like a faint request, but the expression on his face was anything but weak. She kissed him again, properly. Their first passionate kiss in months. It was like kissing a different person – which, of course, he was – one who felt, smelt, moved, spoke and looked totally unlike the Jonathan she had fallen in love with. When they broke apart, his eyes were alive, his breathing very erratic. She tensed, worried that he was having another pain episode, perhaps the effort of the evening had brought it on.

But she was wrong. It wasn't pain he was feeling, it was passion. 'Come to bed with me. Please.'

'Of course.' Her heart twisted.

But their moment of passion was immediately overshadowed by the logistics of his illness. She would have to ask if he needed the toilet, help him to change and get settled, sort out his meds. Be his carer, not his lover.

But even that, Jonathan had planned. 'Will you do something for me?' She nodded. 'Will you wear the robe I brought you back from Washington?' He was sending her away so that she wouldn't have to help him into bed, like she had a hundred times before.

'If that's what want.'

'Tonight, it is.'

She kissed him again and did as he asked.

Jonathan had bought the robe for her at the beginning of their relationship – when their love affair had been exhilarating and illicit. It was made of caramel-coloured silk. It was the most indulgent item of clothing Megan had ever possessed. She stepped out of her dress and wrapped its soft folds around her body. Then she sat on the bed and waited, listening to the sounds of Lisa helping Jonathan get settled, trying to hold on to the romance. The effort he had gone to, the desire to remind them both what their love used to feel like – still did feel like, beneath the mountain of worry and awfulness that was heaped on top of them – made Megan want to cry.

At last she heard Lisa shout 'Goodnight' and the definitive slam of the front door. That was her cue.

She headed downstairs.

Jonathan was waiting for her. The room had been transformed again. The only light now was from the wrought-iron candlesticks left burning on the mantelpiece. The bed had been pulled away from the wall and pushed into the middle of the room, so that it was facing towards the French doors, which were open, letting in the breeze and the smell of the sea. Jonathan was in bed. Megan climbed in beside him and put his arm around her. They took a few moments to find a position that was comfortable – too many nights apart made fitting back together a conscious act. He was naked, apart from his boxers. She rested her head against his chest and he breathed in and out. She could hear the effort, but she tried to ignore it. Neither of them said anything for a long time.

She pressed against him. Silk against skin. Skin against skin.

'Thank you,' he whispered.

Megan put her fingers to his mouth and traced his lips, showing him she loved him, but also silencing him. She didn't want thanking; she wanted loving. She raised herself up and took off the robe, but didn't discard it. It had a role to play. Gently she laid it across Jonathan's chest – a kind disguise. Then she began to stroke his chest through the silk. It slipped and slid across his skin. She moved her hand down his torso and across his hips. She felt him tense and relax, strain against and then away from her touch. His breathing caught, but this time she knew why and she didn't let it concern or stop her.

After he came, he cried. Then he slept, propped up, with Megan at his side.

She stayed with him as long as she could, watching the clouds scud across the moon, before she quietly got up, closed the French doors and climbed the stairs back to her empty bed.

Chapter 37

Liv's 'boys', all three of them, were flat out. She could hear Arthur's ruttly snoring through the wall. As a family, they only had two settings, *on* and *off*. Liv was used to unpredictable sleep patterns, due to a lifetime of shift working, but of late her brain simply wouldn't switch off, even when she begged it to. As a result she was living in a twilight world of tiredness, her senses perpetually on alert. Angus rolled over – oblivious to her wakefulness. A bottle and a half of red could do that to a man, even one as big as Angus. His generous consumption had helped to blur his awareness of her covert abstention. A full glass didn't need filling if you never drank from it.

There was a part of Liv that was disappointed Angus hadn't noticed the changes in her behaviour; that her husband and soulmate hadn't questioned her, forced the issue and discovered she was pregnant. But a far bigger part of her was relieved he hadn't – that he viewed her rattled state as a natural reaction to her father's death. It bought her time, although the weary chewing away at her dilemma was robbing her of her peace and her sanity.

Liv gave up on sleep and slid out of bed. It was cold in the room. She pulled on her dressing gown, grabbed one of Angus's jumpers and slipped it on top. There was a pair of his socks on the floor, so she put them on, wrapping herself in his layers – protection against the chill. She took her laptop and went to sit in the chair in the alcove, with the passcodes and key card that Megan had finally given her.

If she was destined to be wide awake in the dark hours of the night, she might as well put her insomnia to good use. It was time to find out if Megan really was trying to hide something.

Liv chose the joint current account as her start point, not knowing what she was expecting to find, but on the lookout for anomalies. Megan's resistance to Liv having access to the bank accounts could very well have been just her way of protesting at the vulnerable situation she found herself in. But it could be something else.

God, she was beginning to think like Noah!

The light from the screen seemed very bright in the dark room, but Liv knew it wouldn't bother Angus. He could sleep, as he liked to boast – with or without a skinful – *on a washing line*. She set to work. The current account statements told an everyday story of mundane expenses: shopping, petrol, household bills, direct debits for two credit cards. A card each. Neither of them registered particularly high balances. There was also the regular payment to the care agency that supplied Lisa. Liv noted, but not with surprise, how expensive home-care was. On the evidence of the joint account, it would be hard to make a case for Megan being a big spender. Indeed, if anything, the statements tended to highlight how curtailed her life seemed to have been. There were very few bills for restaurants, no gym memberships, no extravagant purchases, certainly not in the past year. Liv began to feel churlish for having doubted her. If this was a reflection of Megan's spending, why had she been so reluctant to give Liv access to the accounts? Liv sat back in the chair and listened to the snoring, drawing comfort from the presence of her family. A sleeping child was one of the best things in the world. A snoring husband less so. Thankfully, Angus sighed and rolled onto his side.

Liv closed down the joint current account, opened Jonathan's personal account and began scrolling through. One name in particular stood out, but it was not Megan's. On the first of every month there was a transfer of £150, to Chloe; 150 quid every month, without fail, going back months. Liv checked. No, not months – years. As she waded back through the transactions, another name cropped up that gave her reason to pause. Noah. Two lump-sum payments: £10,000 in January 2014 and another £7,000 in September 2017. What the hell had those been for? Liv racked her tired brain trying to recall what her brother had been doing around these times. Loans to tide him over when work was hard to come by? Help when he and Josie bought the house? Perhaps. She trawled through the deposit entries, but Noah had not paid any of the money back. It was interesting to note that he had opted not to mention these two very generous 'donations' when they had their cosy heart-to-heart in the café not ten hours ago. So much for coming clean about things!

The discovery that her siblings had, in their own ways, been gouging money out of her father shocked Liv. It was not so much the amounts, though the transfers constituted a sizeable chunk of change to both of them, but more that her dad had never offered Liv any similar financial support. Not a penny. Not since she'd been studying. He had supplemented her education, of course – very few people graduated in medicine without the support of their families – but from the moment Liv got her first job she had been financially independent. There had been small gifts, when she and Angus got married and when the boys were born, but nothing on this scale.

The knowledge that her siblings had been relying on her father financially angered her. That they hadn't said a word about the handouts during all their conversations about fairness, when it came to apportioning the estate, infuriated her.

They must have known she would discover these 'gifts' from her father eventually. Liv reached for her phone and did a rough tally of what she'd found. Chloe was into her dad for, give or take, £9,000, Noah for £17,000 – and that was only what she'd discovered so far! She sat back and looked at the amounts. Oddly enough, it was the handouts to Chloe that bugged Liv the most. Chloe's life was one long chain of unsatisfactory jobs and short-lived new starts. Each move must have incurred costs. The periods of rethinking, retraining, regrouping – or unemployment – had been frequent. That her father had financially supplemented it all shocked Liv. No, on reflection, that wasn't true; it wasn't really much of a surprise. Jonathan had always indulged Chloe: expected less of her, tolerated more. That's what really ticked Liv off.

She knew why he did it – the affair! There was an established family belief that Chloe had been the one most badly affected by their parents' split, because she was around for the fallout, living at home at the time, in between jobs and partners yet again. She was like a yo-yo, recoiling home at the first sign of trouble. And, let's not forget, there was an extra layer of indulgence – because

Chloe was the 'sensitive' one in the family, the one less able to cope when the shit hit the fan. The fact that she turned the fan on herself, quite often, was conveniently ignored. Liv could feel her anger raising her cortisol levels, making her heart thump, doing her no good.

Noah and Chloe obviously believed they were entitled to their father's help.

Upsettingly, their father appeared to have indulged those assumptions.

Not for the first time, it struck Liv how different she, Noah and Chloe were, despite their shared blood and upbringing. But what she rarely acknowledged, because it was too painful, was how those differences might well have been fostered and cemented by the way their father had treated them. Had the die been cast at her birth? Had she always been destined to have the most pressure and the greatest expectation piled on top of her? Had Noah and Liv been free to grow up as their natures intended, because the burden of parental expectation was already being fulfilled by her?

Why had her father pushed her, where he pulled them?

Through the wall she heard Arthur fart, mutter and roll over, self-settling, a knack learnt early. She wondered how much her own parenting was already having an impact on the way her boys viewed and valued themselves. Whether Freddie's nervousness and Arthur's robustness were less inherent predispositions than learnt behaviours. Instinctively her hand crept towards her belly. Buried deep beneath the layers of clothing, skin and muscle, another potential child waited for Liv to make, mar, or destroy its future.

She was wide awake now. Mad with her brother and sister. Mad with her father. She reasoned she might as well go looking for Megan between the lines, in the seemingly innocuous debits and deposits.

She pulled the throw off the end of the bed, wrapped it around her legs, balanced her laptop on top of her makeshift 'desk' and began trawling through the hundreds of entries in her father's accounts. Helpfully the statements went back years and included the period around the beginning of her father's affair with Megan – as dated by Noah.

It didn't take her long to find the evidence she was looking for: the debits for bars and restaurants in Darlington and Newcastle. She felt bruised and hurt by anything that might represent a gift for Megan. The payments to jewellery stores and bookshops and wine merchants all made her suspicious. There were regular orders of flowers – no way of knowing which had been for Megan, which for her mother; which had been a romantic gesture, which a distracting lie. The thought made Liv's stomach ache. The purchase of a new, additional phone was the most obvious proof of the treachery.

Liv stored her anger away – on the debit side of the column for Megan.

Her anger with her father, for his duplicity and unfairness, had nowhere to go. That she had to absorb.

Around the time of the actual marriage breakdown it got messy and expensive. The withdrawals to pay solicitor's fees starting appearing and escalating, as did the frequency of his wine deliveries. And there was increased evidence of trips to Darlington, and to Megan. The new love of his life.

Liv was exhausted, but she kept going. It was like reading a book with a predictable plot. Even though she knew where the story was heading, and that there was not going to be a happy ending, the compulsion to keep going was strong.

The next few months of statements were dominated by the new spending patterns prompted by Jonathan setting up home with Megan in The View at the same time as he severed his ties with their mother. It was an expensive period financially and, Liv had to imagine, emotionally.

After that, the spending settled down, as Megan and her father played Happy Families. In fact it became so monotonous scrolling through the 'evidence' of their cosy, settled, holiday-strewn life that Liv nearly missed the sudden appearance of a different solicitor on the payee list: Latimer & Co. Bone-tired as she was, she Googled the name. There were six solicitor firms with Latimer in the title. One of them in Darlington. That had to be the one.

Liv glanced at the time: 2.36 a.m. She should stop, but she couldn't.

She read on, scrutinising each entry. There were a number of transfers to Latimer & Co. across the winter months of 2018, the last one for more than £120,000. As she reviewed the payments, Liv allowed an understanding of what she was looking at to seep into her tired, overwhelmed brain.

Her father had bought a house.

In Darlington.

Purchase price £127,000.

Paid in full.

Liv sat back. It made no sense, but then again, with a stirring, uneasy sensation, she realised it did. Around the time his prognosis had become terminal, her father had used a proportion of the pension he would never get to draw to provide Megan with a home after he was gone.

The enormity of the gesture – its generosity and consideration – shocked and impressed her. There it was, in black and white:

proof that her father had not abandoned Megan to their mercy. Quite the contrary, he had protected her from it.

And yet she had not said a single word about it.

It was too much.

They were all liars. Megan. Noah, Chloe and, worst of all, her father. He had reached out and put his arms around them all, but not her. He had left Liv to fend for herself.

Quietly and sadly she whispered into the darkness, 'What about me, Dad?'

Chapter 38

THE HOUSE was in darkness. Everyone else presumably asleep, or at least staring at the ceiling, in polite adherence to the bedtime etiquette at The View. It used to be 'the law' when they were little... *Once you go up to bed, you must never come back downstairs, no matter what.* As a child, Noah remembered wondering whether the rule still applied if the house was on fire, but he'd never plucked up the courage to ask. Well, it was going up in metaphorical flames now, and he wasn't six any more.

He pulled on his sweats and went downstairs, keeping close to the edge of the stairs, avoiding the creaks. Force of habit. The wine from dinner and afterwards was still in his system, but instead of softening the craving, it only seemed to have increased it. After the night he'd had, he needed a proper drink – something to cauterise his mind and his emotions. What he wanted was a slug of his dad's single malt. He knew where it was hidden. But first he padded silently into the dining-room and opened the cabinet. There was a muddle of glassware inside, including the stylish Norwegian tumblers that Noah himself had given to his

father a few years back – a gift from one of his many trips abroad. He doubted they had ever been used. He and his dad had stuck to the old-fashioned, heavy-bottomed bevelled glasses that had been a wedding present. They both liked the feel of the cut-glass against their fingertips as they held their drinks up to the light like connoisseurs, before swallowing it like alcoholics. It was one of the rituals that had survived his dad's diagnosis. Booze was obviously *verboten* when you had MND, but a shared sneaky Scotch – in defiance of medical advice, Megan's wishes and, very probably, common sense – was one of life's true pleasures. And as his dad used to say with a wry smile, when you're suffering coordination and speech problems... *who the hell is gonna know you've been hitting the bottle?*

Spirits to keep your spirits up. *Cheers!*

Leaving his dad's glass on the shelf, Noah crossed silently over the hall and opened the door to his father's room. He slipped inside. In a bid to banish any irrational guilt he might be feeling about sneaking around, he switched on the lamp and went over to the window. Bold as brass. The Scotch was there, tucked in the corner, hidden behind the floor-to-ceiling curtains. The bottle of ten-year-old Talisker that Noah had smuggled into the house a few months back, swaddled like a baby inside one of his jumpers. A gift. A secret shared between father and son.

Noah unscrewed the cap and brought the bottle to his nose, breathing in the peaty sourness. He set his glass on the small table and poured himself a generous double. One measure for him, one for his dad. As he set the bottle down next to his glass, it struck him that there was barely a third left. The thought that his dad had managed a few sneaky drams on his own made Noah smile. He raised his glass to the night sky, toasting his father. The heat in his throat, then his stomach, hit the right spot. With his back to the room, he took another sip. He wasn't a philistine – the good stuff needed to be savoured, not guzzled. But it was possible to sip quickly; in fact it was probably advisable at times of stress, and his situation was very definitely on the upper end of the stress scale.

Glass empty, he put it down and refilled it.

To the task at hand.

Uncomfortably aware of the hiccup in his heart rate, Noah crossed the room and dropped down onto his hands and knees. He peered into the gloomy void beneath the bed. The box was still there, just where Freddie had left it. Noah retrieved it. He climbed unsteadily back to his feet and returned to his spot by the window.

He lifted the lid, in expectation of... treasure? A secret stash of jewellery that Megan was keeping schtum about? Letters that would reveal the true state of his father's mind in the last months and days before his death?

Nope.

The box was empty.

For fuck's sake!

He flung it across the room. He registered the first crack as it collided with the wall, but not the second as it hit the floor, because by then Noah was already reaching for another drink.

'What are you playing at, Dad?' It was the malt, and the frustration that had been building up inside him for days, talking. Noah glared at the empty chair across from him, conjuring a version of his father.

The one that took shape was surprisingly well defined. Clean-shaven, smartly dressed, relaxed. Noah was relieved.

He didn't want to resurrect Jonathan in his latter months, the invalid with shaking hands and a wavering head. This was the father Noah wanted to remember – fit in mind and body, sharp in spirit. The ghost of his father looked to be listening, which made a nice change. Noah decided it was time for some straight talking.

'Seriously, Dad, what the fuck?'

His dad leant back in his chair and crossed his legs, left over right, with ease and nonchalance.

'If your objective was to cause a fucking riot, well, I can tell you, you've succeeded. Liv has gone into overdrive, and Chloe is having kittens.'

His dad raised an eyebrow, questioning.

'Me? I'm just trying to work out what you were thinking.'

The ghost father kept his own counsel.

'Why the big secret? Why not tell us what you were planning? We are adults.'

His dad looked doubtful. He was resolutely giving nothing away. The old cat-and-mouse routine – making any victory hard-won, even a conversational one. It pissed Noah off, as it always used to.

'I get that it's some sort of test: forcing us to come together and agree something. But it seems – I don't know – a bit of an extreme way of making a point. And leaving Megan's share for us to decide, what's that about? You must have known it would cause a ruck. She's barely said two words since she found out we're the sole executors and that it's down to us to decide what she does, or doesn't, get. I can't say I blame her for being hacked off really. I know I would be, in her situation.' Noah took another hit of Scotch. Felt the warmth and the loosening of the restraints.

'Unless she's known all along what you were planning. Did she, Dad?'

The ghost raised his hand to his face and ran it along his jaw, obscuring his mouth. Noah matched his father's gesture by raising his glass to his lips again and finishing off his drink. Jonathan looked away, staring out at the night, ignoring Noah's questions. His face, in profile, was calm, untroubled.

'Dad!' Nothing. Noah ploughed on. 'If she didn't have a clue, then I don't know what we're supposed to make of that. Is it some sort of message? Because if it is, it would have been a lot simpler to bloody tell us!'

Jonathan didn't respond to his son's raised, slurred voice. Noah could hear his words sliding and colliding into each other. Maybe he wasn't making total sense. Maybe he wasn't as articulate and restrained as Liv, but that didn't mean he didn't have the same right to express himself. No one could stop him talking. Not Liv, or his father, or Josie!

'And what about Mum? Thirty-five years of marriage: doesn't that count for anything? Cos that's the real nastiness in your weird little plan, treating her as if she's on a par with Megan. Not even a mention in the will. I know you two weren't close any more. Who am I kidding? "Not close" – you couldn't stand each other by the end, could you? But she's still our mother. She still loved you, and honoured her vows to you for all those years, before you shat on your marriage from such a great height with your grubby little fling. Which apparently wasn't a fling! Which was... *true lurve.* Or so you claimed.' Frustration, coldness and fatigue mixed with Scotch, even a ten-year-old malt, were not conducive to coherence. 'And yet...' Noah refilled his glass, not spilling a drop, despite the

buzz in his head and the tremble in his hand. 'Here's the final slap in the face: there's five thousand pounds for the carer! A total fucking stranger gets more than Mum. That was very generous of you, Dad. And totally effing vindictive!' He raised his empty glass to his father again, this time in mock salute. 'This Lisa Browne woman must have been something quite special to warrant such a big chunk of change.'

Jonathan continued to stare out at the darkness, unmoved by Noah's appeals and accusations. Impervious as ever.

Noah realised it was pointless. His father was never going to answer his questions, because this wasn't a real conversation. It was a figment of his tired, alcohol-soaked imagination, and his anger. In direct response to this sober thought entering his head, the image of Jonathan faded, leaving an empty chair.

'Sod you, Dad!'

All their cosy chats, all the banter, all the joking and the joshing before he died. His father had known he was dying. They all had! Surely it had been the perfect opportunity for some home truths. But not a word about any of this. Not an ounce of trust. No honesty on either side. Just two blokes meeting up every month or so, drinking expensive Scotch, telling each other self-aggrandising tales! Cricket, work, politics – safe topics, nothing personal. No weaknesses, no failures, no fears; just a studious, complicit avoidance of anything that was difficult.

Their list of no-go topics had been long.

The affair – never mentioned, unless by an awkward slip. The fiction being that the marriage had been coming to an end anyway. That Megan simply happened to come along at the right time. That his father wasn't just another randy old bloke with an insatiable hankering for a younger model.

Then there was Megan herself – typecast as the home-maker, not the home-wrecker. A person who always had to be treated with respect and deference, while their mother was only spoken of obliquely, with a dismissive icy politeness, as if she was a vaguely remembered distant relative.

And finally – the biggest charade of them all – Jonathan's illness: only ever discussed as if it was an adversary that could be beaten by superior wit and cunning. Or, even more ludicrously, as nothing more than a minor inconvenience, with comic 'anecdote-rich' side-effects.

What a steaming pile of horse shit! It was always a performance of a conversation, based on artifice and avoidance rather than real communication. Well, it was too late to call out his father now.

Noah's throat hurt and his chest felt congested. When he tried to clear his sight by wiping his face with his sleeve, he was confused to find it wet.

He felt ill. His head hurt and he was cold and sweaty. The thought of hauling his aching body upstairs was too much. A small, soft, deep-buried part of him wanted to wail like a baby. Instead he swayed over to his father's bed, dragged back the duvet and collapsed, face-down on the mattress. As the world rocked and tilted around him, indifferent to his distress, Noah rolled onto his side, pulled the covers around him like a cocoon and waited for unconsciousness to ease his symptoms.

Chapter 39

CHLOE HAD wanted them to have a nice evening together, as a family, just like in the old days.

It hadn't panned out like that.

They had all been out of sorts. Megan had been as vague as ever, Liv totally distracted and Noah prickly. The way he kept upping and walking away from the dinner table had bordered on downright rude. Even her suggestion of them each picking a memento of their father – which she thought would be a nice trigger for some positive memories – had somehow soured the atmosphere even further. Chloe had hoped their mother's presence might change the mood, stir up some of the affection that used to bind them so tightly, but Eloise had seemed disinterested or, if not exactly disinterested, then indifferent. It was as if she had lost patience with them, and yet she'd only been in Scarborough for a few hours. Chloe was still smarting from Eloise's jibe at the hotel about the future. That had been totally uncalled for, and quite harsh, in the circumstances.

As Chloe lay in bed listening to the house creak, she was fully aware that she was drifting through life. She didn't need her mother to point it out to her. She was twenty-six years old, single, a graduate, working part time as a checkout assistant in Marks & Spencer for £10.06 an hour, living at 'home' – again (with her now dead father's mistress). She knew she had no prospects and no plan.

Her share of the inheritance would change all that, of course.

As much as she disliked herself for thinking about it, she couldn't not. There was going to be money coming her way – how much exactly she didn't know, but by the look of it, it would be a substantial enough sum to make a real difference to her life. She would be able to pay off her debts, finally, and in full this time. She would – as her mother had so tartly pointed out – be able to start over again, somewhere new, somewhere more vibrant and exciting than a small seaside town. She might retrain. Maybe do something useful for society, something worthwhile – work for a charity, perhaps. Whatever she chose, she could reboot, write a new script, give herself a starring role, for a change. With some money behind her, she would be able to do whatever she wanted.

The problem was that she had no idea what she wanted to do.

And the thought of having to decide was overwhelming.

Chloe didn't really want choices – look what had happened when she'd followed her instincts, and her heart.

Knowing it would only increase her heartache, Chloe reached for her phone, and her past. She scrolled back to a time in her life when anything had seemed possible, even probable – because of Hanna.

She and Hanna had become friends at the end of their second year at university. Chloe had always liked and admired Hanna, a lot, from afar. She was arty, independent, strong-willed – all the characteristics that Chloe admired. Becoming her friend had made Chloe braver, and better. It was Hanna who set her sights on London after graduation. Hanna who found a flat with her boyfriend, Keiron, which they could just about afford. Hanna who persuaded Chloe she had nothing to lose by giving life in the capital a try.

Tooting Bec. It was hardly the centre of the universe, but it had felt like it after three years in Huddersfield. Chloe had a job she enjoyed that paid peanuts, at an arts centre, found for her by Hanna; and another, at a cinema, that paid her a tiny bit more. With the income from both jobs, she was just about able to find her share of the rent every month. She was skint most of the time, but she was happy. She had independence and excitement and fun, and a network of late buses that led to unexpected places and brought her into contact with new people, some of whom seemed to like her, a few of whom even seemed to fancy her.

It had all been going so well – until the night in Battersea, on the pavement outside The Magic Garden, when Hanna and Keiron had another of their sudden flashy arguments.

Chloe had actually held their coats as they cut into each other with flare and passion. It had been short and nasty. Beer was downed and wine was thrown, then Keiron left, in a macho flounce, with a promise to *never come back, not even if she begged him on bended knee.* (He'd promised as much many times before, in equally florid terms.) Hanna had given Keiron the finger and gone back inside the pub to buy another round. She'd returned, eyes glittering with adrenaline, her dark hair freshly brushed, her lips reglossed, and announced to Chloe, to The Magic Garden's clientele and to half of Battersea that Keiron could *go screw himself... And he was going to have to, because she had no intention of going anywhere near him ever again!*

The rest of the night had been great fun. Laughing at Keiron *in absentia*. Decrying all men as a waste a space. Linking up with a random assortment of other feisty girls in the bars and ladies' loos of South London. They'd eventually washed up in one of the little late-night cafés on Battersea Park Road, along with the usual mix of hard-core party animals and the early-rising workmen.

They'd both ordered the meat-free breakfast. Hanna was vegetarian.

As they drank tea and waited for their fry-ups, the frantic mood faded into something more reflective. The inevitable comedown. Chloe guessed that Hanna was regretting the fight, maybe even worrying about where Keiron had got to and why he hadn't called. 'Why don't you message him?'

'He'll be crashed out round at Liam's by now. Total lightweight. Always has been.' She pulled a face, but there was no vitriol in her tone any more.

Chloe, picking up on the signs, gave Hanna the opening to talk about her relationship with Keiron that she seemed to be looking for. 'Has it always been so ... fiery between you two?

Hanna rubbed at a mark on her top, stretching the fabric across her breasts. 'Yeah. But that's what I wanted ... *want*. We fell for each other hard when we first met. Really hard. I liked that he wasn't a student. We were SO into each other. Literally couldn't get enough. I suppose it covered up the fact that we actually have bugger all in common.'

'Other than a temper.' It came out of Chloe's mouth before she could stop herself.

But Hanna was amused rather than annoyed. She smiled, a little sadly. 'Yeah, true enough. But you can't have everything in a relationship, can you? If you have passion, you're gonna fight. You have opinions, you're gonna argue.' She flicked her fingers. A habit Chloe was familiar with. It denoted that Hanna was bored of a subject or a person and it was time to move on. 'But enough about me. What about you?'

'Me?'

'Yes, you. You're a dark horse.'

'I'm so not.'

'We never see any guys, or girls, creeping out of your room at odd hours. No random boxers in the laundry basket. We wouldn't mind, you know, if you had a few – or hundreds – of overnight guests.'

'I know.'

'So?'

It felt strange to be the sole focus of Hanna's attention, for a change. She had a steady gaze, despite the volume of alcohol she'd put away. Dark-blue eyes. Long, real lashes, loaded with mascara. The sharp edge that normally surrounded her was gone. 'There's no one – at the moment.' Chloe felt naïve.

Their food arrived, which provided a welcome distraction. There was a pause as they buttered their toast, burst the tops of their fried eggs with their hash browns and shovelled forkfuls of food into their mouths – a mirrored attack on their breakfasts. But Hanna hadn't given up. 'There must have been someone who's succeeded in breaking down that famous Chloe reserve.'

The truth was that Chloe's 'relationship' history was woeful. A crush on her GSCE English teacher, some teenage groping and grappling, her virginity 'given away' to the first lad who asked for it in Freshers' Week. It had been a relief to get it over with, but the experience hadn't been anything to write home about. The thought made Chloe laugh out loud, which made her realise she was still quite drunk. The image of her younger self providing her parents with a blow-by-blow – she laughed again, nearly choking on her baked beans – account of her 'deflowering' was gloriously ridiculous.

'What's so funny?' Hanna asked, sleepy-eyed but attentive.

'My love life.'

'Why are you always so self-deprecating?'

Chloe pushed her beans around on her plate. 'I'm not always.'

'You are. At work, around the flat, when we're out. You need to go for what you want, Chloe. People don't just hand out the good stuff. Sex, jobs, money, affection… you have to ask.'

'That's your way, not mine.'

Hanna seemed about to argue, then changed her mind. 'Speaking of which, if you're not gonna eat it, can I have your sausage?'

Chloe laughed, speared it with her fork and offered it to Hanna. Instead of simply taking it, Hanna leant across the table and took a bite. Eye contact for a brief second. Teasing. The three guys at the next table leered and cheered.

By the time they left the café the sun was coming up, dusting some much-needed pink across the concrete and asphalt of Latchmere Road. They walked slowly back to the flat, crippled by their good night out and their full bellies – Hanna barefoot, her sandals swinging at her side. Chloe had the key. Hanna rarely took one out, after losing too many in the past. Another source of conflict with Keiron, when she rocked back up in the early hours and had to ring the bell.

The flat was quiet. They crept along the dark, narrow corridor that led to the bedrooms. Chloe was about to turn into her room, but Hanna stopped her with a hand on her arm and a fingertip to her lips. She pushed open the door to the room she shared with Keiron. The bed was empty. 'Told you!'

There was nothing left to do but say 'goodnight'.

But they never did.

The pause lasted long enough to become charged. That charge increased when Hanna swayed forward and kissed Chloe, slowly. Then she stopped and looked at her. 'Your choice.' She pushed the bedroom door wider open.

It wasn't a decision Chloe needed to think twice about, but she had some standards. Or at least she did at that point. 'Not in there. In mine.'

Hanna smiled, a sharp, awake smile. 'Ah... assertive all of a sudden. I like it.'

And so began the best, and the worst, time of Chloe's life.

It was the most alive, most fulfilled, most in love with someone – and with herself –that Chloe had ever felt. She and Hanna were yin and yang. Opposites that made a whole. Two souls destined to be together. A perfect–imperfect match. All the clichés, but true. Hanna filled Chloe's life, and her head, and her heart.

There was, of course, the problem of Keiron, and the sneaking and cheating and lying and pretence. And the pain. The pain of watching the love of your life being someone else's girlfriend. Because although everything changed that night in Battersea, nothing did. Hanna still slept with, argued with, made up with, ate with, laughed with, shopped with and went away with Keiron. And Chloe let her, because it soon became clear that she didn't really have a choice. If she wanted Hanna at all, she had to share.

And so she did.

And the longer she put up with it, the more it cost her. The little self-confidence she had built up by being in London seeped slowly, inexorably away, to be replaced by a perpetual state of anxiety and dependence. In her heart she knew disaster was looming on the horizon, so what she did was studiously avoid looking up. Her desperation was, in retrospect, pathetic. Even when Hanna told her that Keiron had proposed, Chloe still clung on to a sliver of hope that his declaration of undying love might force the issue – make Hanna finally pick one of them.

It did.

She chose Keiron.

And just like that, Chloe's world shattered. She lost her home and her job – she couldn't face working alongside Hanna day in, day out. She lost her purpose and, with it, she lost the plot.

She hung on in London for a few months, sofa-surfing, but it was too depressing for words, so she took a job in Leicester for a while – a favour set up for her by a friend whose futon she camped out on – but that fell through after only a few weeks, leaving her jobless, skint and another friend down.

Her life had unravelled.

Chloe had no choice but to go home.

And even then, her timing had been impeccably bad. She arrived in Scarborough, with a full suitcase and an empty heart, the week before her mother found out about Megan.

One shit storm straight into another.

It had been awful having a front row seat for the last act of her parents' marriage. Whereas before, there had only ever been the occasional sharp comment and brooding silence – a strict adherence to 'not in front of the children' – after the revelation of her father's affair there was no such restraint. Thirty-five years' worth of rage and recrimination spilled out, splashing over everything in the vicinity, including Chloe.

It had been a relief, though also another huge loss, when her mother had finally stormed out of the house for good. At least then things calmed down.

For a short period Chloe and her father had hunkered down inside The View, licking their respective wounds. It was the first time in her life that Chloe felt she had something in common with her dad. They were both in crisis, both struggling emotionally. Though they avoided discussing the gory details of their respective meltdowns – too much shame on either side – they could at least recognise and sympathise with another broken spirit. They spent their nights eating ready meals, watching anything and everything on TV, even total crap that in the past her father would have refused to have on. They got up late. They didn't clean the house. Didn't do anything constructive. They didn't respond when the outside world came calling. They sank into the mire of self-pity together – it was nice to have company. And Chloe finally saw her father as fallible, a human being who was as flawed as everyone else. It had been a strange and not altogether unhelpful comfort.

But of course their recoveries had taken very different trajectories. Within a few short weeks her father had pulled himself together. He got back into his brisk morning routine of rising at 6.30 a.m. and running, having a healthy, nutritious breakfast then heading off to work. He got on top of the house, and his life. He was back on form. But why wouldn't he be? He had emerged from his crisis *with the girl*. He had a new love and a new future ahead of him – once the difficult issue of his first wife was resolved. It was brutally impressive.

As he recovered, the intimacy and understanding of their painful emotional weeks huddled together faded. Once Megan moved in – which she did with indecent speed – their connection died completely. Chloe drifted back onto the periphery of her father's life. Supported financially, but neglected emotionally.

Over the next few years, things continued to be tough. There was a series of false starts with jobs; new friends who turned out to be unreliable; and, to top it all, there was Chloe's abject failure in terms of a finding a fulfilling, healthy relationship.

And then her father got ill.

And then he got worse.

And then she moved back to Scarborough, again. His MND gave her a purpose and a role: the self-sacrificing daughter returning home to support her terminally ill father. He needed her. Or at least that's what she told other people, and herself.

Now, Jonathan's sudden death had kicked away the last unwavering constant in her life. She was on her own – except for her mother, her sister and her brother.

There was a muffled thud, followed immediately by another. Chloe sat up in bed, clutching her knees to her chest. Noises from below in the dead of the night. Something stirring in her father's room, again. She listened. Silence.

She was losing her marbles.

Her father was gone.

It was time to quit her pathetic part-time unskilled job and move out of this house, which was no longer her family home. It was time to leave the ghosts behind.

The problem was, Chloe had no idea where to go.

Chapter 40

MEGAN WAS up first. She was glad. She wanted some time on her own before they took over. As she crossed the hall on her way to the kitchen, she noticed that the door to Jonathan's room was slightly ajar. Out of habit, she went in to check. Even before she stepped inside she knew someone was there. Presence and absence, they had markedly different qualities.

The door caught on the carpet, as it always did.

Her shock at seeing Noah sprawled on Jonathan's bed was visceral. How could he? The lack of respect was deplorable. Noah didn't stir. From his deep breathing, Megan could tell he was fast asleep. She walked over and looked down at him. He was lying on his side, fully clothed under the covers, his stubbly face slack. This close, she could smell the booze on his breath. She studied him.

She hated to admit it, but Noah looked a lot like his father. They had the same colouring, the same thick thatch of hair, the same strong jawline and nose. For the first time, she noticed some grey hairs mixed in with the brown at Noah's temple. She searched for more signs of ageing, wishing his face was less handsome, less familiar. She wanted the nastiness that she knew lurked inside Noah to have sullied his looks, but even comatose and reeking of Scotch, he was handsome. The desire to shake him roughly awake faded. Noah's sleep was not peaceful, she could see his eyes flickering beneath his lids. She wondered what he was dreaming about. Suddenly his body tensed and jerked and his fists clenched. She knew the feeling, that sense of dropping off the edge of a cliff, the awful whoosh of free fall, the desperate grasping for anything to hold on to. Instinctively she reached out and laid a hand on his shoulder, anchoring him. He took a few short breaths, hovered on the cusp of waking, then slipped under again.

Megan rarely touched Jonathan's children, nor they her. Jonathan's death hadn't changed that. Even their hugs of sympathy immediately after his death had contained a hesitation, a stiffness. It was as if the three of them had made a pact to hold themselves apart from her. It was an effective snub from a family that was naturally very tactile. Hugs, kisses, back-slaps, they were forever touching each other, but not her. Even the children seemed to have picked up on it. They always wriggled away from her attempts at physical affection. Yet here she was comforting an unconscious Noah. His breathing deepened and he began to snore. She took the blanket from the back of the armchair and draped it over him. She would leave him to sleep.

It was as she turned to walk away that she saw the box. It was lying in two pieces on the floor against the skirting board. She picked up the base and the lid. One of the hinges was bent and the lid had a deep crack in it – damage caused by being thrown and hitting the wall? She ran her fingers across the broken pieces, feeling a mix of dismay and disbelief. Was nothing sacred?

Holding the remnants of the box in her hands, she returned to Noah's bedside, not caring to make her footsteps light this time. She looked down at him wallowing in his self-pity, insensible to the offence he had caused – was causing – every time he opened his mouth and made one of his wisecrack comments. She flung the pieces of box at his head. They hit him and bounced onto the floor.

He stirred, muttered, flapped a hand across his face, but didn't wake.

She turned away, her mind made up.

They had forfeited the right to know anything!

Let them stew in their speculation and spite.

On her way out Megan made sure to slam the door shut as loudly as she could.

Chapter 41

ELOISE REWARDED herself for surviving the previous night's *festivities* with a lie-in. Reclining in her hotel bed, on a mountain of pillows, all she could see was the slate-grey sky and the occasional smudge of a high-flying seagull. Her view was soothing in a blank, boring kind of way.

It had taken time to get used to, but Eloise now enjoyed sleeping alone. She revelled in having the full expanse of a double bed to herself, apart from the occasions when she chose to share it, of course. So many things that had seemed difficult, or nigh-on impossible, in the immediate aftermath of her marriage break-up now seemed normal. Solus decision-making, choosing what to do with her own, hard-earnt money, risk-taking, developing new friendships, finding new lovers, DIY! – all of it had proved possible, much of it enjoyable. Her new life was both fuller and more unpredictable than her old one. She liked it that way.

After staring at the sky for twenty minutes, Eloise got up and showered. She dressed casually, but with care. Appearances mattered this weekend, at least to Eloise. Small advantages, and

She moved towards Eloise, forcing her to retreat. They stared at each other: no more than a foot apart. Megan – taking short, shallow breaths; Eloise – breathing slowly, steadily, maintaining her composure.

'I'm sorry,' Eloise said. She was, and she wasn't. Maybe coming back hadn't been such a good idea. It had certainly muddied the waters. Megan was now a real person, not a fiction that could be fashioned into whatever shape Eloise chose. 'I didn't mean to intrude. I just thought you might need some help.'

'I really don't need your help.' Megan's voice was quiet, but her resolve was very clear.

'Okay,' Eloise demurred.

The flicker was still there, pulsing beneath Megan's pale skin. Eloise saw it and recognised it for what it was – grief. Jonathan had been Megan's for so little time, and what time they had shared had been so damaged by his illness. Losing him must hurt, deeply.

Megan stood her ground. 'I'd appreciate it if you, and everyone else, stayed out of this room until I clear it.' She stretched out her hand, obviously intending to close the door; Eloise was in the way. 'If you don't mind, I want to get on.'

They were standing very close. Eloise held her position for a second, then she relented and stepped back out into the hall, ceding territory and ownership to Megan.

The door was shut firmly in her face.

Chapter 42

MEGAN TRIED to breathe, but Eloise's perfume clogged up her throat. She crossed the room and threw open the French doors, letting in the bright, cold air. So, it had come to this – fighting over the last remnants of Jonathan's life. It was a fight she knew she was going to lose. She couldn't hold them at bay much longer, not now Eloise was in the house.

When she'd seen Eloise sneaking around upstairs the previous night, Megan had been depressed not to feel anger. She had every right to be livid, or at least shocked, but she hadn't felt either emotion. What she'd felt – when she saw Jonathan's ex-wife standing on the landing, in the moonlight – was acceptance. The sight of Eloise looking in on her sleeping grandsons, her hand resting elegantly on her door handle of her son's old room, had seemed perfectly natural. Eloise was where she was supposed to be: in her home, with her family. Because even now, after all this time, and despite everything that had happened, Megan couldn't shake the belief that Eloise was still the rightful inhabitant of The View.

It was she who was the interloper.

Megan rested her head against the door frame.

The awful suspicion that Jonathan had come to think that way as well only added to her distress.

It was a bright, cold April day – more like winter than spring. Jonathan had been sitting by the windows in his study when she'd got back from work. Not that the seasons had the same relevance any more for Jonathan.

What immediately struck her as odd was that he was doing nothing. The absence of his laptop or a book was unusual. Even his phone was nowhere to be seen. She felt a ripple of ill ease. Was this the beginning of the next stage? She swallowed down her concerns. She was getting used to ingesting sorrow. The printouts of the candidates' CVs lay on the desk in the same neat pile. She reminded herself to say PA, not carer. Patience and sensitivity were attributes she still struggled with. She had little hope that Jonathan had looked through them.

'What are you doing?' She dumped her bags on the floor.

'Just looking at the view.'

'It is beautiful out there today, isn't it?' Not that he had been 'out there' for days. There were so many pitfalls that she kept stumbling into.

He agreed and continued looking out across the garden. There was a stillness about him that was different – perhaps it was the new drugs making him feel zoned out – but when she pulled up a seat opposite him, he seemed alert enough.

They watched the sea breathing in and out down below in the bay. It was hypnotic. She felt her eyes grow heavy.

'Meg. You know how much I love you, don't you?'

'I do.' She smiled, brightly.

'And that if things were different, there isn't anyone else in the world I'd want to spend the rest of my life with.'

'I'm not sure anyone else would have you!' She smiled even more brightly, trying to lift the mood, but his expression didn't lighten.

'Good, because it's important you know that, before I say what I'm about to say.' Her stomach contracted. He stared at her, unblinking. 'I'm sorry, but I don't think I can do this any more. It's killing me.'

'Jonathan, please—' She wanted him to stop, because she couldn't bear the responsibility of trying to convince him things weren't as bad as they were, and that the future wasn't as bleak as it undoubtedly was going to be.

He interrupted her. 'No. Please, I need you to hear me out.' Megan sat back, forced to concede his right to express the darkness they both usually tried so hard to suppress. 'I've had plenty of time on my hands lately to reflect on what's coming down the line for me. That's the odd thing about this,' he gestured at his failing body, 'I seem to have too much time – though in reality that's precisely what I haven't got.' He shrugged. Even this movement was affected by the weakness on his left side. 'I honestly think I've got my head around the dying bit.' He smiled, crookedly. 'It's a lottery, isn't it? How and when you "go". I just so happen to have drawn a particularly crappy route to the Grim Reaper. I can accept that – most of the time. Why not me, eh? No. What's really killing me is not the MND; it's watching *you* watching *me* deteriorate.'

He shook his head, pre-empting her objections. 'I know how impossible I am to live with. I'm withdrawn. Down. Let's be honest, I'm a complete pain in the arse a lot of the time. I don't want to be, I truly don't, but it's hard to focus on anything other than what's happening to me. Other people's lives, their everyday worries and concerns, just don't seem that relevant or interesting to me any more. Even yours.' He was staring at her, checking that his words were hitting their target. 'And I know I get angry about the small stuff – you might even say unreasonably so. But that's because there's no point being angry about the big stuff, is there?'

He lifted his hand, a gesture to stop her interrupting. It shook, as it did all the time now. 'With every day that passes, I get more and more frustrated. And as much as I try to be better – to be less of a total misery – I can't. I fail every single day, and that failure makes me feel worse. That's why I hide away in here. I truly can't bear you seeing me like this. It's utterly pointless, for both of us.'

She couldn't let him go on. She had to challenge him, despite the truth in what he was saying, because if she didn't challenge him, where did that leave them? 'It's not like that all the time. You have bad days and better days. I understand that. We're coping.'

'But it's not enough, is it, Meg? It's not a life! Not one I want to lead anyway. It's certainly not the life I want you to have to endure.' There was anger in his voice. It was the first real passion she'd heard from him for months.

'It's enough for me,' she lied, willing him to stop.

He didn't; there was a zeal about him that, but for the topic of conversation, would have been reassuring – a sign there was still some fire in his belly. 'It shouldn't have to be. I honestly believe it's worse for you than for me. I have something to fight, something to blame; you...' he swallowed and regrouped, 'you have to sit, and watch, and be patient and kind and considerate, all the time, like some sodding handmaid.'

She felt the tears in her nose and attempted to control her distress, lowering her head trying to block him out, but he was relentless.

'Meg, please, look at me. I need us to honest with each other. What is the point of you being shackled to me, like this, until the bitter end?' The look on his face was frightening her. 'I should never have gone anywhere near you. Never.'

'Jonathan, please,' she pleaded.

'I'm sorry,' he said, but that didn't stop him talking. He seemed to be gripped by an awful compulsion to keep going. 'I don't mean I regret falling in love with you. I've never regretted that. Or I have, but only because that's what landed us – you – in this nightmare. But the truth is... if I hadn't acted on my feelings, we would never have got together. You could have been happily married now, or at least living with someone fit and well. Maybe you'd have had a child.' Megan couldn't believe he was being so cruel. 'There's no getting away from the fact that, without me, you would have had a normal life, and you could have been happy.'

She wanted to argue with him, tell him she was happy, that she had no regrets, but she couldn't. It was too obvious a lie. He was right. She had no life. She worked at a job she was hanging on to by her fingertips. She looked after him. That was it. She had virtually no emotional support. Her family was too far away to help, and Jonathan's family was no use. Her friends were well-meaning, but had their own responsibilities, freedoms and social lives – ways of living that were now totally impossible for her and Jonathan. She was living a life that consisted of nothing but worry and responsibility, and an endless charade of cheerfulness.

And he was right. She was childless, and would forever remain so. So yes, she was unhappy – who in their right mind wouldn't be? Jonathan's voice brought Megan back to the present. He stared at her. Calm. Focused. Resolute. 'I want you to leave.'

'What?'

'I want you to go.'

'Jonathan!' She brought her hands up to her face, a defence against his implacable insistence.

But he ploughed on. 'Please, Megan. If you love me, and if you have any respect left for me, I need you to listen to what I have to say, and I want you to promise that you'll think about it. I've thought about it – a lot.' He coughed and gathered himself for the *coup de grâce*. 'I don't want you to watch me die. It will only make it worse for me – harder for me. If you leave I can be selfish, get there in my own time, concentrate on it, do it as well, or as badly, as I'm able to, without the pressure of performing for you. We – I – can hire people to help out. Professionals. There seem to be plenty of them out there.' He gestured at the pile of CVs. 'I don't want it to fall on Chloe; that would be unfair, she shouldn't be the one to inherit the problem. And Liv will see the sense in what I'm suggesting. She may even be able to provide some advice. It's workable. I should be able to stay at home for a while. Then maybe a hospice, at the end, if needs must.'

He had gone mad, and that madness was making him cruel. 'So I just up and leave you! That's your solution, is it? I abandon you to die on your own.'

'I won't be on my own. I'll have people who know what they're doing looking after me.'

'Oh, well, that's all right then! Complete strangers. That's going to work just fine, isn't it? You'll hate it. You hate the physio coming, and that's only twice a week. How do you think you're going to feel, relying on a parade of different people – for everything? It's ludicrous to even suggest it.'

'Don't, Meg. I have thought this through. It's what I want.'

He really meant it! 'Oh, good. I'm glad it's a solution that works for you.' Jonathan looked at her impassively, and she had a sudden urge to shake him. 'It's ridiculous. Totally wrong-headed.'

He refused to concede that she was right. He just stared at her, eerily calm.

Megan resorted to a different tack. 'Out of curiosity, Jonathan, where am I supposed to go, in this grand plan of yours?'

'Back to Darlington, back to your life before me.' He really seemed to think it was an option.

'So you have a time-machine now, do you, Jonathan? What are you gonna do? Spin the dial and send me back to the spring of 2013 – five seconds before I walked into that training session. Make sure we never meet? Send me on a new trajectory into some sort of parallel life?'

He absorbed her anger – stoically. 'No, I know I can't do that. I truly wish I could. But you *can* go home.'

Suddenly she was no longer sad, she was furious. 'Home! This is my home! This is my life. Our life! You have to stop with this crap, Jonathan. Right now! You're depressed. I get it. It's bad. I get that. But *this*... I'm not listening to any more of *this*!'

Jonathan opened his mouth to say something else, but she cut him off.

'You can't control this, Jonathan. I can't begin to imagine how dreadful that must be. I really can't. And I can understand you wanting to have some say in how it all ... ends, but the one thing you can't control is other people's feelings – especially my feelings. And it's arrogant of you to try. This might be what you *think* you want – though I doubt even that – but what about what I want? Have you factored what I want into your ridiculous scheme?' She was vibrating with pent-up emotion. Anger at him, at their situation, at the cruelty of life. She stood up. 'So no, Jonathan. I won't think about your plan. I won't leave. No matter how sad and ill and depressed you get.' She gulped, trying to control her shaking voice, wanting it to sound as firm as her intentions. 'No matter how hard this gets, Jonathan, I will never leave you.'

She stood up and walked away from him, paused and turned back. 'I refuse to listen to any more of this rubbish. We love each other. That's it. You don't get to decide the fate of our relationship. I do. And I choose us.'

She had refused to listen to him that day, in this very room, with the same cold air blowing in from the sea, just as she had refused to listen every other time Jonathan tried to bring the subject up. The minute he broached her going back to Darlington – and he did so repeatedly over the next few weeks – she walked away.

It had been relief when he finally gave up.

As she stood by the window, staring at the waves in the bay, Megan wondered whether she had been right to close him down. Perhaps she should have encouraged him to talk through his warped but meticulously thought-through solution to their predicament, let him express and expunge his burden of guilt. Had she added to his distress in the last few months of his life by dismissing out of hand his version of saving her? Had it been her fault that he had confided more in Lisa than he had in her? Had she left him no choice? Very probably. She should at least have listened. Heard him out. Shouldn't she?

And there had been another consequence of her refusal to listen.

Her deafness had left her ignorant, weakened, ill prepared for what was happening now.

She was cornered. Trapped by the very secret that was supposed to be her salvation.

Was it time to retreat or come out fighting?

She had no idea.

It took Megan a few moments to register that the burring noise she could hear was her phone. Someone actually wanted to talk to her.

'Hello.'

'Hello.'

'Are you all right?'

'No.' It was such a relief to be honest.

'Do you want me to come to the house?'

'Can you?'

'Yes. When?'

'Could you come now?'

'If you want me to.'

'I do.'

'Okay. I will.'

'Thank you.'

Chapter 43

THEY WERE back together, sitting around the dining-room table, waiting for their mother, none of them looking good. The mood was simultaneously tense and flat. Liv was familiar with the atmosphere. She'd walked into enough family rooms in hospitals to update relatives on the fate of their loved ones to recognise exhausted expectation when she saw it. The difference was that this time she was one of the relatives.

Noah and Chloe started talking about some film they'd both seen. Liv tuned them out.

The cliché would have it that knowledge was power, but to Liv it felt more like pressure. The house in Darlington was a bomb ticking away quietly but insistently beneath their feet, and only she could hear it. Should she detonate it? She didn't know. She tilted her head left to right, trying to loosen the tightness in her neck. Her head was too heavy because her brain was too full. She knew, of course, that was nonsense. The whole situation was making her lose her grip, but she was still struggling to come to terms with the perversity of her father's actions.

One parent who was an enigma because he was dead. Another for whom being enigmatic seemed almost a style choice. A brother who was selfish. And a sister who was as good as useless. Liv suddenly, profoundly, wished she'd been born into a different family.

On cue, the door opened and their mother finally put in an appearance. Liv had wanted to speak to her privately, but it was too late for that now. It was too late for many things now.

Eloise drew up a chair. 'Oh, you didn't wait for me, did you? There was no need. Please.' She actually waved her hand to indicate they should proceed – like royalty.

'Okay.' Liv set her shoulders and looked down at her folder. With its pages of meticulous notes and carefully filed letters and statements, it was testament to the many hours of effort she'd put in. She was, after all, the only one actually doing the work of an executor. In front of Chloe there was a dirty glass and a half-eaten bagel. In front of Noah a mug of coffee and a blister pack of paracetamol. As Liv reached for the file, it occurred to her that she could tell them virtually *anything*, in terms of what Jonathan's estate was really worth. Add a house in Darlington. Take one away. They would never know. As much as Noah was very interested in getting his hands on his inheritance, Liv was confident he'd done little more than glance at the paperwork she'd given him. Likewise Chloe. They were both so sodding lazy, and dishonest.

'As I told you yesterday, the biggest unknown is the size of Dad's pension fund. We obviously know he cashed in one of his annuities to cover Mum's settlement.' There was a crackle in the atmosphere, but no one said anything. They would all, Liv had no doubt, love to know what their mother had received, but none of them had the balls to ask. Eloise glanced at her watch, then out at the garden, but declined to enlighten them. Liv carried on. 'The pension company is being incredibly stringent about security, so we may not know for another week or so what the total value of the fund is.' Although she, of course, knew it would be at down by at least £127,000. The cost of purchasing a nice two-bedroom cottage or, at a pinch, a three-bedroom new-build in the North-East.

At this point Noah actually yawned. Did he do it to provoke her? Or was he unaware of his impact on others?

Liv carried on. 'Last night I couldn't sleep' – Noah wasn't the only one who was tired – 'so I used the time to go through Dad's various bank accounts.' She let that hang. Waited, for one beat, two, three, four. Nothing from Noah or Chloe, not even a downward glance or a flushed cheek. So much for being upfront. She tried to keep her tone level. 'As I've mentioned before, there was the escalating cost of his care in the last year of his life.'

There was a humph from Noah. He was obviously still hanging on to his petty resentment at Lisa's legacy. It seemed hypocritical for him to be aggrieved by his father's generosity, when he had been such a substantial beneficiary of it. Liv tried to push the thought to aside.

'But totalled up – allowing for any debts that need to be covered, such as his credit-card bill, household bills, et cetera… I reckon there's going to be a cash lump sum of about fifty thousand pounds left.' She went on, 'If we estimate six hundred and fifty thousand pounds for the house, plus whatever is in his pension – I'd say, at a conservative estimate, maybe another hundred and fifty thousand pounds – we're looking at about eight hundred and fifty thousand pounds.' Noah kept his expression neutral. 'We'll need to reserve a proportion for professional fees – the solicitor and suchlike, including the cost of the house sale. And,' why not rub a little salt into Noah's wound, 'there's the five thousand pounds for Lisa, but should leave us with somewhere in the region of eight hundred and thirty thousands pounds to share out.'

It was a lot.

There was silence as they each contemplated such an inheritance.

It was Eloise who broke into their thoughts. 'So have you worked out how you're going to split it?' Their collective mumble summed up their progress nicely. Namely, they were no further forward than they had been on day one. 'Well?' She looked from one to the other.

Noah had told Liv to be more direct – no irony there – well, here went nothing. 'We don't know what to do about you, and Megan,' Liv said.

Eloise's unconcerned expression didn't waver. If she was offended by being put in the same category as Megan, she glossed over it well.

'Because your father saw fit not to leave any specific instructions?' At least her mother cut to the chase.

'Exactly.'

'Well,' Eloise picked some lint off the sleeve of her jumper, 'I'm assuming that you plan to divide the bulk of the estate three ways?' Chloe shuffled in her seat, Noah nodded and Liv sat perfectly still. Their mother smiled. 'Well, why not do that? Each of you take your *cut*.' Chloe winced. 'Then you can decide, individually, whether you feel you should share a proportion of what you inherit with anyone else.' It was such a typical Eloise answer, seemingly simple, but in reality nuanced and complex.

'Are you saying you're not expecting anything from the estate?' Liv had had enough of her mother's elegant avoidance.

Eloise didn't so much as blink. 'Liv, I long since gave up expecting anything from your father.'

'But that doesn't seem fair.' Liv now knew, with absolute certainty, that it wasn't.

'Oh, you're trying to be fair, are you?'

'Yes. I think it's important, even if no one else does.' Liv was as startled as the others to hear the vehemence in her own voice, though, if anyone had asked her, she would no longer have been able to articulate who or what she was fighting for.

Their mother assumed an amused expression. 'Well, good luck with that.' She sat back in her chair and folded her arms. A clear signal that she was washing her hands of the issue – just like she used to do if they ever came to her to resolve an argument when they were kids.

Noah visibly brightened. 'So that's agreed then. We divide the money equally, in three, and see Mum right between us.' He looked relieved.

'What about Megan?' Chloe asked.

'Like Mum said, that's up to each of us.' Noah bristled.

'And I can guess what you'll give her,' Liv said.

'Oh, can you now, Sis?'

There it was again, that nasty edge to his tone. Liv was ashamed of him. Such naked avarice made her uncomfortable, and angry. 'I'm guessing you intend to give her absolutely nothing.'

'Indeed I do!'

'Whatever we may think of Megan's relationship with Dad, she did look after him through it all. She bore the brunt of his care. Was here every day and every night as he got sicker, when we weren't.'

Liv ignored Chloe's plaintive 'I was here.'

'We may not like the woman, but we do have to do right by her.' Liv wanted to see just how brutal Noah was prepared to be.

'You do what you want, Liv. Keep on polishing that big old halo of yours. Me, I can live with not giving away our legacy to Dad's mistress.'

And with that pronouncement, Noah made up Liv's mind. Megan could keep her house. Could keep it secret, if she chose to. Her father had been wrong to trust in their kindness and their ability to put the needs of others before their own. His experiment had been cruel. And it had failed.

'Are you going to bother with a donation to the MND charity? Didn't he stipulate that they should get it all, if you couldn't agree?' Eloise added a few more drops of oil to their already-stormy waters.

Noah was swift to respond, no doubt wanting to keep his decisions close to his chest, where they could be as self-serving as he saw fit. 'We can donate separately.'

Liv fought back. She was sick of Noah getting his own way. 'Mum's right. We should make a donation. And we should do it from the estate, so that the bequest is in Dad's name.'

'Does that really matter?'

'For God's sake, Noah. Yes, it does! Dad obviously wanted to leave some money to help people suffering from the same awful illness as him. That has to be part of his legacy.'

Finally Noah reacted with something that looked like shame. He flushed, a deep, unsightly crimson, which sat oddly on top of his sallow complexion. It made him look quite ill. But when he opened his mouth, it was not contrition that emerged, but spite. 'Oh, stop, can't you? Just for one sodding minute, stop!

Why do you always have to be the noble one, Liv? We all know Dad thought the sun shone out of your arse – that you were his golden girl. Me and Chloe have always been the "also-rans". But Dad's not here any more, is he, Liv? He's dead. No amount of cash to some charity is going to change that. Give your share away, if you want to. Be the saint. But some of us mere mortals need that money!'

Liv was sick of it all.

Sick of Noah.

Sick of Chloe's passivity and their mother's aloof indifference.

Sick of the responsibility.

Sick of the secrets and unfairness.

She felt her self-control slipping. It was a horrible feeling, yet at the same time it was exhilarating. This was what happened when you pushed someone who was at the end of their tether too far. 'How dare you? If it wasn't for me, we'd be nowhere. I've spent hours liaising with the solicitor, and the pension company, pulling everything together. Hours and hours of work. Me! Me and my head-girl tendencies and my full-time, full-on job, and my two kids, and my house, and my husband, who I never see; and my family, who seem to think that I'm a robot with no troubles of my own!'

'What do you want, Liv?' Noah taunted. 'A round of applause for being so wonderful? Is our lovely, self-righteous big sister feeling undervalued? Oh, I do apologise.' Slowly, mockingly, he put his hands together and began to clap.

Liv was incensed. 'At least I stand on my own two feet like an adult. Unlike you!'

'Meaning?' Noah snapped.

'What was the seventeen grand for, Noah?'

That shut his mouth.

Chloe seemed finally to wake up. 'What seventeen grand?'

Liv rounded on her sister. She didn't get to slide out from under this, either. 'Oh! I'm sorry, didn't you know?' Sarcasm was not simply Noah's preserve. 'You weren't the only one Dad was doling out cash to. He gave – or should I say "loaned" – Noah seventeen thousand pounds. Which, as far as I can tell, he never paid back. Not a single penny of it.'

Noah glared at Liv. 'You petty, mean-spirited bitch!'

'Petty! Petty! You call thirty thousand pounds between the two of you petty!'

Chloe lowered her head and whispered, 'Please', but neither of them heard her.

Liv no longer cared. 'I've always known Chloe leant on Dad. She's the baby of the family, after all. Always has been. Always will be. But I thought you had a bit more self-respect!'

'At least he liked me!' Noah yelled.

There was a beat.

A point of no return.

Noah ploughed straight on through it. 'We had fun together, even towards the end. I knew how to cheer Dad up. I brought some joy into his life. All you did was bang on about his physio and his diet, and this new therapy, and that new drug, which he simply *had to* chase up his consultant about. Pointless! It was all pointless. He was dying!'

'It wasn't pointless.' Liv heard the crack in her own voice. 'It helped. I was trying to make life as comfortable as possible for him.'

'He didn't want you to be his doctor, Liv! He wanted you to be his daughter.'

'How would you know? You were never here.' Now they were getting into it. It was weirdly cathartic, letting go of so much unspoken resentment.

'At least when I was here, we had a good time together.'

'Oh, and that makes all the difference when you're dying, does it? Having a jolly time!'

They had both somehow risen to their feet and were facing each other across the table. Noah swayed. 'Do you know what, Liv? Yes. I think it did make a difference – more than all your nagging and bullying. Dad felt like you expected him to fight and somehow beat it. Do you know that? You added to the pressure. Made him feel like he was failing as his condition got worse.'

'Did he say that to you?' She hated to think that what Noah was saying might be true. That although her father had respected her, he had never really liked her. That he had, in truth, preferred his irresponsible son and his softer, altogether more agreeable younger daughter.

'Not in so many words, but it's true. That's the way you make us all feel. Like we're not good enough, that we're not trying hard enough, that we're not meeting your very high expectations. MND isn't like that. It's a fucking bastard of a disease. It gets you and it eats you up, and there's not a sodding thing you can do about it!' He was shaking and sweating, and Liv hated every word that was coming out of his mouth... because deep down she feared there was some truth in what he was shouting.

She finally let go. 'I loved him,' she screamed in her brother's face.

'Not as much as me,' Noah roared back.

Chapter 44

MEGAN HEARD a gentle tap at the door. 'May I come in?' It was nice to have someone ask. She opened the door.

Lisa took in the chaos of Jonathan's room at a glance, but made no comment. She stayed on the threshold. 'I rang the bell, but no one heard. I let myself in. I hope that's all right.' Megan nodded. Lisa came into the room. 'How's it been?'

'Not good.'

'No, evidently not.' They could both hear raised voices coming from the dining-room. Lisa closed the door on them. 'Oh!'

Megan followed Lisa's gaze to the side-table. She'd spotted the broken pieces of the box.

'What happened?'

'Noah.'

Lisa's face betrayed shock. 'Deliberate?'

Megan said, 'I don't know, not for sure. But I can't see how it can have been an accident. I found him in here this morning. Asleep in Jonathan's bed. The box was on the floor. Smashed.'

'Grief comes out in different ways.'

In Noah's case, that seemed to be in the form of a wild, unfocused anger with spurts of energy, then sudden collapses. But Megan was in no mood for empathy, given that so little had been shown to her. She picked up the lid of the box, ran her fingers across the cracked top. The next thing she knew, Lisa's arms were around her. It was the first proper hug she'd had in months. Strong, firm. The physical shock and pleasure of it were overwhelming. She swayed slightly, but Lisa held on, keeping her upright. Only when Megan said, 'Thank you' did Lisa let go.

'Can I help?' She gestured at the mess.

'Not with this, no. But I would like to talk to you.'

'Of course.'

They shoved aside some of the clutter and pulled the chairs over to the window, drawing as close to the outside – and as far away from their spiteful voices – as possible. Without asking permission, Lisa closed the doors to the garden. Megan realised she was right to. The room was freezing. But once they were settled, Megan found she didn't know where to begin. It was as if, after weeks of repressed thought and speech, she had lost the capacity to express herself.

'So, they know about the house?' Lisa asked.

'I'm not sure. The keys weren't in the box. But Liv has access to the bank accounts now, so it's only a matter of time.'

Lisa nodded. Megan wasn't surprised Lisa knew about the house in Darlington. She knew everything. She seemed to have helped Jonathan plan most of it. Christ, she'd probably bought the box. Megan's feelings about her ricocheted uncomfortably: jealousy, resentment, reliance, affection. It was so hard to know what to feel about somebody who knew so much – had seen and done so much – but said so little. Megan put the broken pieces of the box aside. 'You knew what Jonathan was planning all along, didn't you?'

Lisa kept her chin up and her eyes on Megan. There wasn't so much as a glimmer of discomfort. 'Not at first. No. But by the end, yes, I knew most of it.'

Megan felt jealousy pinch at her heart. 'It hurts that he trusted you more than me!'

'That's not true.'

'Oh, but it is!'

'It isn't, Megan. It wasn't a case of him *wanting* to confide in me – he *had to*. And it didn't happen overnight. I had to earn his trust.'

'But you did.'

'Yes, I did.'

'He should have confided in me.'

Lisa thought for a moment. 'Would it help if I told you that most people who know they are dying don't share their innermost thoughts and wishes with the people they love the most. They simply can't. It's too hard. Too fraught with emotion. It's much easier to plan your death with a stranger.'

Megan shifted her gaze to the view beyond the window, unable to look at Lisa sitting in the chair opposite her. She couldn't stop imagining all the conversations that must have gone on between Lisa and Jonathan in this very room. Intimate, important, private conversations that she'd been excluded from – had excluded herself from.

Lisa shifted her position, but kept her thoughts to herself.

Megan tried again to get some answers, or at least an explanation, from the only person who seemed to have been privy to Jonathan's thoughts. 'What I don't understand is why he made it so complicated?'

Lisa folded her hands in her lap. She chose her words carefully. 'Jonathan carried a lot of guilt with him, especially in terms of his relationship with you. He believed he'd been selfish. Which, I suppose, he had – knowing what he knew when he met you.'

Megan felt Lisa's eyes on her. She held up her hand, warding off Lisa's meaning. She knew what Lisa was referring to; had for the past two years.

Jonathan had known he was ill when they met.

Whether he knew it was MND, whether he was aware that his condition was life-limiting, Megan wasn't sure, but she was sure he'd known enough to have made different decisions. He could have chosen a different path, one that led away, not towards, her.

Seeing her reaction, Lisa had the good sense not to pursue it, but she wasn't done defending him. 'He was determined to try and make things right by you. He may not have gone about it the way you or I would have done, but his motivation was to make amends. I'm sure of it.' She obviously sensed that Megan was not convinced, because she went on, 'You know how little time he had for superstition, or religion, but he told me that when he saw your house had come back on the market, he just knew he had buy it. It was the only time I ever heard him talk about Fate.'

'And so a year and a half ago he bought me my old house, thinking it was the ticket for me to go back in time and simply pick up where I'd left off!' Megan heard the hurt in her own voice.

Her anger seemed to glance off Lisa. 'No. At the time I don't think he thought any further than wanting the house to be there for you… after he'd gone. Signed, sealed, delivered. A decision taken out of the hands of his executors.' Lisa didn't say 'children', because they weren't. 'But when his symptoms worsened, he obviously started seeing it as a potential route out for you.'

Jesus, was there nothing she hadn't known?

'When you refused to discuss leaving, he gave me the keys and the deeds and the letter, and made me promise to give them to you after his death.'

Megan felt a fresh burst of anger at Jonathan. 'But it was an escape route I couldn't possibly have taken, even if I'd let him tell me about it.'

'Yes. That was the flaw in his plan.'

'I couldn't leave him.'

'I know.'

'I hated it when he talked about dying.'

'I know.'

'That's why I wouldn't listen. It felt too much like giving up.'

'I do understand.' Lisa spoke softly, gently, but that only served to provoke Megan.

Her anger stirred and stretched its cramped limbs. 'You knew all this, you saw me struggling to communicate with him, to understand what he was thinking, and feeling. You knew about it all, but you didn't say anything!'

Lisa's gaze remained steady. 'Jonathan was my patient. He placed his trust in me. I had to respect that trust. It was one of the very few things I could offer him at the end.'

There had been so many closed doors, so many conversations that had ended when Megan entered the room. She should have challenged them both. But she hadn't. Lisa looked at her, kindly but unflinchingly.

Lisa went on. 'And besides, I thought you'd made your choice… to get through it by living each day at a time, not thinking about the future. I felt I should respect that as well. I tried my best to respect you both.'

Was she speaking the truth? Was Lisa just a well-intentioned, professional carer who had made Jonathan's last few months bearable, or had she been his confidante – someone who had listened, advised and influenced? The answer was… she had been both.

They were silent for a while.

There was another loud smatter of shouting from across the hall. Unfinished business.

Lisa glanced at the door and the argument beyond, then back at Megan. 'What do you want to deal with first? This…' she indicated the half-cleared room, 'or them?'

Megan didn't need to give it much thought. 'Them.'

Lisa stood up. 'Are you sure you don't want me to help finish up in here?'

Megan shook her head.

Lisa had done enough.

Chapter 45

MEGAN WALKED into the dining-room without knocking.

Liv and Noah were facing each other across the table, swaying like punch-drunk boxers. Chloe sat silently by, ringside, her face drawn, tears in her eyes. Eloise was poised at the end of the table like a dress shop mannequin. At the sight of all four of them, Megan felt a powerful mix of anger and pity. Their inability to take a step back and, in doing so, see each other was so depressing. Someone had to put an end to it.

'For God's sake, stop it!'

Liv and Noah seemed to emerge from the blurry depths of their anger slowly. They looked at her for a few seconds as if they didn't recognise her. Liv was the first to recover. 'Megan. Sorry. Did we disturb you?'

They hadn't a clue! Noah rocked forward. He was a very odd colour, like putty.

'Sit down.' They both hesitated, unused to being told what to do, especially by her. 'I said, "Sit down".' Possibly more out of shock than compliance, they did.

Megan pulled up a chair – finally taking her seat at the table. Chloe wiped her face on the sleeve of her jumper. Megan noticed that it came away covered in mascara and make-up. One last check on Noah. He was still a dreadful colour, but the anger in his eyes had dimmed. Liv sat bolt upright, two spots of colour on her cheeks. Only Eloise looked composed.

Finally she had their attention.

'This weekend has been awful – for all of us. All the wrangling and arguing and suspicion.' None of them reacted. Megan no longer cared; she was way past the point of needing a response from them to determine what she was going to do. If only she'd realised that sooner. 'I won't have any more of it. Not here. If you want to keep squabbling over Jonathan's legacy, you need to do it somewhere else. This house is still my home, for the time being, and I will not have it taken over by your nastiness.' They said nothing. 'You seem to be forgetting that it's your family home as well. It shouldn't be reduced to being merely the backdrop to your disagreements. It's bad for the boys, it's bad for you, and I can't stand another second of it.'

Liv blushed and Noah finally had the good grace to look down.

'Your father would have been so upset – no, he would have been appalled – by how it's been this weekend. All Jonathan ever wanted was for the three of you to get along.' There was no use pretending that Jonathan had hoped she and Eloise would ever be friends, or that the kids would accept her – they had both known that was never going to happen. 'He used to be so pleased if any of you mentioned spending time with each other, even that you'd spoken to one another. All he ever wanted was for you to be happy, for you to feel loved by him and each other. He never lost his sense of guilt at the damage our being together caused to his relationship with you all.' Megan strengthened her voice. 'But for God's sake, you're adults, not children. Life's complicated. You all know that. You need to get over whatever resentments or bitterness you still hold about our being together. It's gone on long enough. Your father and I loved each other. Nothing you can say, or do, will ever change that. And I, for one, am done apologising to the three of you.' She took a breath. 'But maybe I do owe you an explanation.'

Liv looked up. The other two kept their heads down. Megan was undeterred. It was her turn to have her say.

'Your father and I didn't have long together before he got ill. And that was hard. It wasn't the caring for him, though that was difficult. No, what was worst was watching him shrink away from me while he was still there right next to me. And, I confess, I got it wrong sometimes. A lot of the time. I wasn't there for Jonathan in the way he wanted me to be. And perhaps I didn't reach out to each of you as much as I probably should have. The painful truth is I didn't want to deal with the reality of the situation, and now it's too late to change that. All I can do is deal with the future, in a way he would have approved of.'

At this point Noah looked up, interested in her views at last. Megan took a shallow breath and went on, 'I know my relationship with your father – in life and in death – was, and still is, a problem for you all. The not knowing where I fit in. Let's be honest, that's always been an issue, hasn't it? Never his wife. Not his widow. I know I'm just "the other woman" to you.' She didn't look at Eloise, but that didn't mean Megan didn't feel her presence at the head of the table. Sod her! Megan raised her chin. 'But I've realised something over the past few days. I have the power to put an end to this purgatory.' She had their attention now. 'Do what you want with this house, his money, his possessions. I don't care. I don't want, or need, anything from his estate.' She could have sworn that, even at this late stage, after all her efforts to keep and make the peace, Noah's lips twitched into a fleeting self-satisfied smile. How little he knew. 'Jonathan planned what he wanted to happen very carefully. His death, his will, your role as his executors. But it might surprise you to know that he didn't leave me out of his plans completely. In fact he was thinking about me from the very beginning.' She glanced around the room. They all looked puzzled – except Liv, who met Megan's gaze and gave a small but very definite shake of her head. Permission to keep a secret. Megan banked it.

She went on, feeling more composed and relaxed than she had done in weeks. 'I already have my inheritance from your father. So there's no need to *give* me anything else. It's yours. All of it: the house, the savings. You can do whatever you want with it. If that helps you to finally reach a decision, then I'm relieved. I want us to be able to lay him to rest without this atmosphere of mistrust. And we can only do that when this' – she waved her hand at the large file of documents in front of Liv – 'is sorted out. Then we can get on with the funeral, you can put the house up for sale and, I promise, as soon as I'm able, I'll move out. After that, we can go our separate ways.' She drew breath. 'Which, I'm sure, is what we all want.'

She stood up, mustering as much dignity as she could, and headed for the door. On her way out she paused by Noah's side, looked down at him and said, 'And the next time you want to know something, can I suggest it might be better, and much less disrespectful, just to ask. Though there's still no guarantee you'll get the answer you're looking for.' And with that, she walked out.

Chapter 46

ELOISE FOUND herself wanting to clap. It was such a bravura performance. The mouse that roared. The look on each of their faces was priceless. 'Megan!' Eloise hurried out of the room after her.

Megan stopped at the bottom of the stairs. 'Yes?'

'That was really quite... impressive.'

She rejected the compliment, turned and began climbing the stairs.

Eloise felt a strong urge to stop her. 'I don't suppose you fancy getting out of here for an hour or so. Leave them to it? I don't know about you, but I could do with some fresh air.'

Megan stopped for a few seconds, her back to Eloise, before she said, 'Yes. Why not?'

Chapter 47

THE SIBLINGS did not speak.

They listened to Megan and their mother talking in the hall. Heard footsteps up and down the stairs. Then the rattle of the front door. The sound of a car engine starting up and fading away up the drive.

The silence in the room was heavy.

Chloe looked from Liv to Noah, expecting one of them to break the impasse. Neither of them did. She waited. Still nothing, but the odd look in Liv's eyes and the drumming of Noah's fingers on the table told her it wasn't over.

Noah coughed.

That was the trigger.

Liv pushed her chair back away from the table. It made an awful scraping sound. 'I'm done with this.'

'What do you mean?' Chloe asked.

Liv's voice was steady, but flat – blanched of any emotion. 'It seems we've finally fulfilled Dad's wishes, after a fashion. We're agreed on a three-way split. So be it. I'm fine with that. And I'm happy for you two to do as you want, with regards to the charity donation. Do whatever you want. It's all absolutely fine with me.' She stood up. She looked anything but fine.

Chloe glanced nervously at the fat file of paperwork that squatted on the table. A mountain of work. 'But, Liv, there's still lots to sort out.'

Liv nodded. 'Yes, there is.' She put her hand on top of the file and shoved it, hard, in Noah's direction. It hit his arm and skidded onto the floor, spilling sheets across the polished floorboards. 'But I'll not be the one doing it.'

'What?' Chloe could feel the panic rising in her chest.

'You've both made it very clear that you find my approach' – she paused – 'or is it just me, *overbearing, bossy, insufferable.* Well, you don't have to suffer me any more. The will named all three of us as executors. It's your turn now.'

And with that, she walked out.

Chapter 48

ELOISE SET off driving aimlessly. Where to? One thing was certain: they needed to get out of Scarborough. On a whim, she headed through the town and out onto the A171. Very quickly the neatness of suburbia gave way to the wildness of the moors: wide open skies, a lot of blackened heather and a few weather-beaten sheep. The scenery had resonance. Megan sat beside her in the passenger seat, her head turned, looking at the view. Neither of them said anything and the longer the silence endured, the more seductive it became.

Eloise realised it was the first time she'd ever been alone with Megan.

They shared so much, but none of it overlapped, except Jonathan.

It was oddly soothing to drive and not speak. After the cacophony of noise over the past two days, Megan's silence made a welcome change. Eloise concentrated on the twists, dips and hidden hairpin bends in the road. It wasn't too much of a stretch to see the road as a metaphor. Thank God she was driving. She wouldn't have wanted to put her trust in someone else on a route this twisty.

As they climbed up towards Fylingdales, Megan said, 'I forget how beautiful it is up here.' It was more an observation than a conversation starter, but that didn't stop Eloise responding.

'Yes. Me, too. It's amazing how you can live somewhere for years and never properly appreciate it.'

'Do you miss Scarborough?' Megan asked. Eloise couldn't detect anything other than a simple enquiry.

'No. Not any more.' Eloise checked herself. 'If I'm honest, not ever. I always found it a little claustrophobic.' They swung down and up another dip. Eloise relished the brief sense of flying as they crested the hill. Surprisingly Megan seemed untroubled by the speed. 'It's a nice place, but there's no denying it has an "end of the road" feel about it.'

Megan didn't respond for a few seconds. 'Why did you and Jonathan choose to live there then?'

'He never told you?' Eloise pondered why he hadn't, and assumed he'd decided it all sounded much too comfortable and bourgeois for an academic whose specialist field was underachieving, working-class white boys.

'No.'

'He inherited the house from his mother. As an only child, it all came to Jonathan after she died.'

'When was this?'

'A long time ago. The house stood empty for a couple of years after her death. Jonathan refused to sell it or even rent it out, but it didn't make sense for us to move in. He'd not been teaching for very long, and I hadn't even settled on what I wanted to do. Then I fell pregnant with Liv, and Jonathan got it into his head that

used to walk along to the refreshment hut near the archway for ice creams. They would eat them sitting on the wall looking at the padlocks.

At some point, many years previously, someone must have attached the first lock to the railing leading down the slipway. For what purpose, no one knew. But that was part of the fun: guessing at the motivation of people choosing a padlock and bringing it with them to the seaside, to click into place, alongside the hundreds of others. Some of the padlocks were etched with messages, many were not, the meaning of the gesture known only to whoever had stood with the salty wind in their face, adding their token of emotion to the collection. The kids used to like looking through them, picking out their favourites, reading the inscriptions. Noah would always work his way along the railing, trying as many locks as he could, seeing if he could pull one free. He never succeeded.

One day, after they'd finished eating their ice creams, Jonathan had called the children over. He'd come with them for the day, for a change. He reached into his rucksack and produced three padlocks. The kids had gone wild, clustering around him in their eagerness to see. They were not bog-standard brass padlocks, but three very old locks, each a different weight, size and colour. All complete with keys. They were oddly beautiful, in their own way. Eloise never did find out where he got them. It was a lovely thought – which quickly descended into something far less lovely. Because, instead of letting the kids run off and add their locks to the railing, Jonathan couldn't resist turning the occasion into yet another 'learning opportunity'. He began to bang on about how padlocks were *known to have been used in Roman times by merchants travelling across Asia, to protect their goods from marauders.* His history lesson was cut short when an argument broke out between Noah and Liv as to which of them should have the biggest padlock. The dispute was settled with a game of rock, paper, scissors, at Eloise's suggestion. Liv won and gloated, while Noah loudly and furiously declared that his lock was the best anyway. At which point even Jonathan conceded it might be sensible just to let them attach their padlocks and be done.

Eloise remembered how each of them had picked a space as far away from their siblings as possible, before clicking their padlock onto the railing. They kept their wishes and their hopes to themselves. Locks locked, Eloise decided it was time to head home.

As they walked back around the bay, Liv asked her father to look after her key for her, which he duly did, placing the heavy scroll-topped key inside his wallet for safe-keeping until they got home. Eloise wondered whether Liv still had it. She wouldn't be surprised. Without asking permission, Noah hurled his key into the sea. A sudden exuberance, which was followed by instant, denied regret. Behaviour that, in hindsight, was typical Noah. Chloe held her key in her chubby little hand all the way back to the car. Only to find, when they got home, that she'd lost it. There followed a sustained bout of sobbing, at which point Eloise poured herself and Jonathan two very large glasses of red wine.

The locks were still there, gathering rust and significance. Row upon row of indecipherable gestures of love, regret and remembrance. Eloise stopped and ran her hand across the padlocks, enjoying the metallic clicking noise they made. Megan stood and watched, asking nothing.

Nostalgia bout over, Eloise turned around. 'Shall we double back to the café? Get a drink?' The response from Megan was a non-committal shrug.

It was fuggy with warmth in the café, so much so that Eloise had to strip off her coat on entering. Where everyone had come from was a mystery. Megan declined food and went off in search of a table. Eloise ordered for them both, coffee and sandwiches. Her appetite, if not Megan's, was still healthy. The young girl behind the counter said she'd bring their food over to them when it was ready. In the Ladies, Eloise washed the metallic taint of the rusty padlocks off her hands.

Megan had found a table in one of the back rooms. The other customers all seemed to be elderly couples. Eloise and Megan stood out, by virtue of their age and gender. Two friends, out for a spot of late lunch and a catch-up? Hardly.

Eloise sat down. She was unsettled. A stroll down memory lane had not been her motivation for their little jaunt. Curiosity, that was the real reason. Megan in the flesh. On her own. Eloise's nemesis. The focus of so much hatred and bile, and not only hers. The person who was now positioning herself as Megan the Magnanimous – waiving her rights to any of the inheritance, in a bid to draw the family together. She was such a conundrum of a woman.

What Megan's motivation was, for agreeing to come along on this little trip, Eloise couldn't begin to fathom, other than an understandable desire to put as much distance between herself and Jonathan's squabbling children as possible.

The café windows were steamed up. The sea view obscured. There was nowhere to look, other than at each other. Eloise served up the first question. 'I wonder how they're getting on back at the house?'

Megan refused to return. 'I really don't care. Not any more.'

'No. I gathered that.'

Already their conversation was teetering on the brink.

It was Megan's turn to set up the next point. She attempted an ace. 'Why did you come this weekend?'

At last, a proper question. Eloise went for a short return. 'They invited me.' Megan pulled a face, seemingly doubting Eloise's motivations. Correctly. Another sign of life? 'And because I was curious – to see the house again.'

'Just the house?'

'No.' If Megan wanted to go *there*, Eloise wasn't going to stop her. 'I suppose I thought it was time you and I met in person.'

Megan nodded. They looked at each other, eyeball-to-eyeball, raw inspection, no niceties. Only the arrival of the young girl with the food stopped it becoming some sort of juvenile staring competition. 'Thank you.' The girl unloaded a cafetière, mugs, cream and milk, and two plates of what looked like very nice sandwiches.

'I said I wasn't hungry.' Megan seemed to be surviving on grief and thin air. Was that proof of true love, or just the signalling of it?

'I know – but I am.' Eloise bit into a sandwich and poured herself a drink.

'I don't know what you want from me?' There it was again: the sharpness that gave the lie to Megan's pretence of calmness.

'An apology would be nice. The kids may not deserve one, but I think I do!' It came out before Eloise could stop herself. She hated how petulant she sounded.

'Okay.' Megan brushed her hand against her cheek. 'I'm sorry.'

Eloise couldn't read her tone. 'For...'

'For falling for Jonathan. For breaking up your marriage. For making you leave your home. For causing all that heartache.'

The woman at the next table actually leant forward, shameless and fascinated. Her husband was far more interested in his crab sandwich. Eloise was glad to hear the apology out loud, but felt deeply unsatisfied by it. The words were too pat, too slight, too abrupt. But if not now, when? It was time for Megan to offer up some answers as well as some contrition.

'Why on earth did you get involved with him in the first place? You must have known he was married. I can't see Jonathan being the type to slip his wedding ring on and off at every opportunity. Though what do I know? I was stupid enough to believe he would never cheat on me.' Megan looked about to say something, but it was Eloise's turn to control the game. 'He was old enough to be your father, for God's sake! Go on, tell me: what was it that made a middle-aged married academic with a bit of a paunch so irresistible?'

'Do you really want to know, or are you just shouting at me to make yourself feel better?' Megan asked.

The cheeky bitch! 'No. I really want to know.'

Megan went very still. She looked past Eloise at the steamed-up window, composing her answer carefully. 'It was his voice that first attracted me to him; that, and his passion for his subject.'

Eloise felt vaguely nauseous. 'That's everything you need in a TV evangelist, not a... lover.' The word was like a hairball in her mouth, distasteful, liable to make her gag.

Megan was not distracted by her barbed comment. 'I loved the way he talked about all sorts of things. And he listened.' He hadn't, at least not to her. Eloise must have snorted, because a flash of defiance flared in Megan's eyes. 'Do you really want me to tell you? Or not?'

Eloise found herself nodding. She wanted the story that had for so long been denied her.

'I met him at a conference. He was one of the speakers, and he ran one of the workshops I attended.' Of course it would have been one of his many 'slightly maverick, academic hotshot performances' that had hooked her. 'We started emailing each other. Professional stuff, mostly.' *Mostly*. Jonathan in his bloody study, flirting his way into her knickers. 'Then one day a few weeks later he wrote and told me he had a trip to Newcastle coming up. We arranged to meet for a drink.'

'Who suggested that?' Eloise couldn't stop herself.

'I don't remember.'

'Don't patronise me!

At the adjacent table the husband was now finishing off his wife's neglected lunch. She was far too distracted to eat.

'Okay. He did.'

'And it went from there?'

'Yes.'

'And at no point did you think to stop it?'

'Of course we did.'

'But you didn't.

'No. Obviously we didn't, or you and I wouldn't be here now, would we?'

Eloise felt the venomous buzz of jealousy creep through her veins. She recognised it immediately, the same fiery concoction of anger and hurt that had pumped through her body after she'd first found out about Jonathan's betrayal. She refused to let it infect her again. Instead she took a deep breath and poured herself some more coffee. She took another bite of her sandwich. Chewed. Swallowed. Took another bite. Hell, she might even order a slice of cake – the red velvet had looked tempting. Anything to regain control of the situation and the conversation.

'These are really good. You should try one.' The negative emotions stirred up by Megan percolated their way slowly through Eloise's system. She let them. The breakdown of her marriage had strengthened her, made her far more emotionally resilient. It had forced her to take ownership of her own happiness and well-being. And she had done that, very successfully. Jonathan's death must not be allowed to undo all the effort she had put into rebuilding herself. She would not let it. Within a few minutes she was back in control, nothing but blood and caffeine flowing through her heart.

Not so Megan. When Eloise really looked at her, she saw that she was truly heartbroken.

Again Eloise was surprised to feel a spurt of sympathy for her old rival. Losing Jonathan when he was still the love of her life must have been so hard for Megan to bear. Nursing him through his illness, awful. Doing it largely on your own, frightening. And watching him die – that didn't bear thinking about. No, Eloise no longer envied Megan. She was doomed to grieve for months, if not years, to come. Eloise was not.

She dabbed at her mouth with her napkin and flashed a broad smile at the nosy woman at the next table, who looked flustered and announced, to her silent husband, that *it really was time they made a move* – as if he'd been the one dallying. Eloise decided that if she really was committed to ridding her system fully of her anger with Megan, then it was best to do it all at once.

'I used to hate you, you know.'

Mrs Nosy Parker hesitated and pretended to struggle with the zip of her red puffer jacket, snared by this last tasty morsel.

Megan blinked. '"Hate" is a strong word.'

'You did have an affair with my husband. You did get him to lie to my face for months. And, in the end, you did win. He chose you over me. I think that's valid grounds for at least a little animosity.' Megan looked down. 'But being back at the house reminded me of something I'd rather too conveniently forgotten.'

'What? Just how much you detest me?' Megan asked.

'No. Well, yes, at first. But then I realised something.'

'What?'

'I remembered that I wanted to leave long before you came on the scene.' It was true. Megan had undoubtedly been the catalyst, but if Eloise and Jonathan had been stronger, perhaps they would have survived. Other couples did. They used the momentum of an affair to make changes, to purify their relationship of old habits and pretences. Eloise had not had the stomach, or the emotional generosity, for that. Perhaps she should be grateful. Without Megan, she would not have escaped from Scarborough and the house, and her escalating sense of isolation and purposelessness. Nor would she have 'avoided' Jonathan's awful demise. 'The truth is… I'm happier now than I was when I was with Jonathan. I think that's what lets you off the hook. If I'd been miserable, it would be different. But, in the long run, I think you did me a favour. You and Jonathan getting together forced the issue. I had to leave to regain my self-worth and, once I'd gone, I realised I was okay on my own. In fact I was better than okay. I was good.'

Megan finally took a sip of her coffee and absent-mindedly picked at a sandwich. The woman really was going to waste away if she didn't start eating something. The coffee was cold – Eloise couldn't bear to watch Megan drink it. She asked one of the waitresses to bring a fresh pot. They sat in silence until it arrived, digesting their conversation.

Disappointed perhaps by the tame denouement, the nosy woman and her husband finally shuffled away. It was Megan who broke the silence. 'Do you think it was a punishment?'

'What?'

'His illness?'

Christ, she really had had the stuffing knocked out of her. 'No, of course not! It was just shitty bad luck. For him – and for you. If I'm being generous, which for some reason I feel inclined to be – possibly to offset the rather appalling behaviour of my children – you seem to have coped with it far better than I would have done.' Eloise poured them both a fresh cup. 'I wouldn't have had the patience. I think motherhood used up what reserves of self-sacrifice I had.' The fresh coffee was good, hot and strong. 'I can't imagine Jonathan was a very good patient. He must have been very frustrated by it all.'

Loyal to the bitter end, and beyond, Megan refused to criticise him. 'He struggled, but who wouldn't?'

Out of cowardice, Eloise asked no more. She had no desire to wrest Jonathan's illness from Megan – that horror was hers alone. 'Well, I'm glad he was with someone who loved him… at the end.'

Megan accepted Eloise's acknowledgement with a small nod.

They seemed to have reached an impasse: enough said for them to feel they had moved on; nothing left to be said that would change anything.

'Do you want to head back to the house?' Eloise asked.

Megan pulled her hair over her shoulder and held on to it. 'Not especially.'

'Me neither. A slice of cake?'

For the first time ever, they smiled at each other.

And so, by mutual consent, they stayed exactly where

they were, sipping their coffee and eating cake, watching the condensation trickle down the windows – just like a couple of old friends out for a spot of late lunch and a catch-up.

Chapter 49

NOAH KNEW there was no point calling Josie, but he did anyway, his phone pressed tight to his ear to cut out the wind. From his spot at the top of the drive he saw a light come on in the upper floor of the house. Freddie and Arthur having an early bath? Sand to be washed out of every crevice after another fun day on the beach with their doting dad. Thank God they hadn't been around to witness the day's histrionics. His heart ached for Lily and his own home. Josie's ultimatum rang through his head as the dial tone sounded: *Get the will settled with Liv and Chloe, sort yourself out, decide what you really want – then we'll talk.*

Well, at least the first objective had been achieved – not that he was going to get to tell Josie that, as it was obvious she had no intention of answering his call.

It had been a bruising day, with he and Liv going at it. The thought made him feel unsteady, and vaguely ashamed. But he was confident she would come round. She always did. Always had in the past. He'd wait for her to cool down, then he'd apologise.

That would do the trick. It normally did. But the look on her face when they'd been screaming at each other haunted him. He'd never seen Liv like that before. Raw, mad as hell and unnervingly, brutally honest. It was almost like he was seeing her properly for the first time.

His head throbbed and he was cold. He pressed 'end' on his call to Josie.

He walked up to the main road. Scanned the passing cars for his mother's BMW. What the hell was she doing out with Megan all this time, while her children were tearing themselves apart?

What he needed to focus on was the fact that the deal had been done, rather than on the collateral damage to his relationship with his sister. The money mattered. It guaranteed Josie and Lily some security, and he owed them that – especially if he wasn't going to be around in the long term. At least one black cloud had lifted, but that did not do much to lessen the intensity of the storm. An urge to cry suddenly swept through Noah. He rode it, waiting for the self-pity to wash through him. He knew he needed to pull himself together. Stop being so pathetic.

Her dialled Josie again. The long snake of red tail-lights wound along the coast road as the dial tone reverberated inside his head. She was ignoring him. He let it ring until her voicemail kicked in. He cleared his throat. His breath plumed white in the frosty air.

'Hi. We've put it to bed – finally. We're seeing the solicitor in the morning at ten. I'll head home afterwards. I'll ring you when I'm on my way.' Long pause. Did she want him back? Should he be going back? He didn't know. He felt compelled to say more, though he didn't know what *more* he could bear to say. 'Josie,

I've given a lot of thought to what you said, about us – about me – needing to make some changes. I know I'm on borrowed time.' He ended the call.

His *I love you. I'm sorry* was said to the wind.

Chapter 50

No one else seemed to register that the boys were feral with hunger. There was no evening meal prepared, Megan having clocked off from domestic duties after her declaration of independence. Chloe went out and bought everyone fish and chips. When she came back, Megan and their mother had finally returned. Megan declined her fish supper, saying she'd already eaten, and disappeared upstairs without explanation. They ate standing around in the kitchen. All of them avoiding each other's eyes. Chloe looked at her mother for answers.

'Where did you go?'

'We went for a drive, to Sandsend.' Eloise was picking at her fish, with a cake fork of all things, not eating any.

Chloe couldn't imagine Megan and her mother sitting side-by-side in the car, chatting. 'Why Sandsend?'

'The café down on the sea front does very good coffee.' Liv flicked their mother a glance, which prompted a little more. 'There was nothing else she, or I, could add to your discussions, so it seemed sensible to get out of your hair for a few hours. And it seems to have worked.'

'What did you talk about?' Chloe toyed with her scraps.

'This and that.'

'It just seems odd, the two of you going off like that – together.' Noah chipped in – ever the one to go to the heart of the matter, without subtlety or sensitivity.

Eloise stabbed her dainty little fork into the belly of her fish. 'Okay, we talked about your father. Is that what you want to hear?'

All three of them looked down at their plates.

'It's not so strange, if you think about it. We both knew your father – quite well.' Eloise looked around the room. She seemed to be enjoying their discomfort. 'What it may surprise you to hear is that we found some common ground, aside from being left out of his will.'

Chloe winced at her mother's inappropriate attempt at humour.

'What sort of "common ground"?' Noah couldn't keep the distrust out of his voice, or maybe he didn't try.

Eloise turned towards him, her gaze steady, her words clear. 'I really thought you might have learnt by now, Noah – some things are private.' No one said anything. All of them felt too fragile to put up any defence. 'Evidently not.' She pushed her plate away and folded her arms. 'As the two women he chose to have a relationship with, Megan and I share a unique insight into your father. We spoke about that, and other things. Like jealousy and guilt, and blame and honesty. Oh, and cake! For a small café, it really does have a surprisingly good selection of pastries. None of which – apart from the cake news – is any of your business.' She reached for the kitchen roll, tore off a square and dabbed her mouth. 'Thank you for supper, Chloe.' She'd barely touched her food. 'It was very... filling, but I have a long drive ahead of me, so I think I'll be making tracks. As I said, I don't feel there's anything else I can usefully do here, so I shall leave it in your capable hands. I hope everything goes well at the solicitor's tomorrow. You'll keep me posted on how it goes, I assume?' She directed this at Liv, but it was Chloe who nodded.

She summoned the boys and crouched down. Big hugs were exchanged, then Eloise worked her way around the room, offering a kiss on the cheek to each adult. Circuit completed, she headed for the door. 'I'll see myself out.'

There was a beat. They waited for her to have the final word.

'Please say "goodbye" and "good luck" to Megan for me.' That was it.

They heard her heels clip across the floorboards in the hall, and a pause – perhaps for one last glance around – then the opening and closing of the front door.

Chapter 51

LIV WAS so worn out that she pulled off her jeans and sweater without thinking, totally forgetting Angus was sitting up in bed. Thankfully he seemed absorbed in his book. She was relieved to get away with it. 'Do you want to read for a bit?'

He snapped the book shut. 'No. You're tired. Let's settle.' He turned off the light.

She rolled away from him, onto her side, hoping to fall asleep quickly. God, she *so* needed to sleep. The bed creaked. She felt him shuffle across the mattress and press himself against her. A solid, reassuring presence. He stroked her back gently with his big hands. She could feel his breath on her skin. His breathing was steady, deep, slower than hers, a good rhythm to try and match. The house was quiet. All of them in bed early, wanting to get through the night and the following day's meeting, then leave.

As she began to relax she heard him whisper, 'Liv?'

'Yes.' She didn't lift her head from the pillow.

'Are you all right?'

'Yeah.'

'I know it's been really difficult today, but at least it's sorted now.' Angus was always a 'glass half-full' kind of person.

'Yes.' She tried to inject some enthusiasm into her voice.

'You still seem very tense.'

'I'm fine. I'm just tired.'

There was a pause and she heard him hold on to his breath and his thoughts for a few seconds longer as he decided on his next move – which was to raise himself up on his elbow and lean over her. 'Liv, you're always tired. But this is different. I've never seen you struggle as much as you are at the moment. I'm worried about you.'

She rolled over, forcing him to back off, but also giving him the respect of showing him her face, or at least her profile. The darkness helped. In the dark, nuances were harder to detect, along with lies. 'It's just this whole thing has been so stressful. I knew Dad was dying, but it was still a shock. I thought he'd be around for a little longer. Then his bloody will complicated what was already going to be a tough situation. On top of work. And the kids. It's been a lot to handle. I really am worn out.'

'Um.' Angus usually accepted her reassurances, because, well... because usually she was telling him the truth. Maybe he could sense that she was holding out on him. They were not a couple who talked through every last thing, but still... a pregnancy – she shied away from the word 'baby' – was hardly a small detail.

She stirred herself to try and convince him, or at least give him a credible explanation for her lack of energy and her low mood. 'Being here has stirred up lots of memories.'

'And?'

She shuffled around, trying to get comfortable. 'I suppose it depresses me to realise that we haven't have grown up much. Me and Noah and Chloe. We're still fighting like we used to when we were kids, still vying for attention, even though neither of our parents is watching any more. It's pathetic really. We're all as bad as each other.'

'Oh, I couldn't possibly agree with that. You've behaved just fine. Better than fine. You, my lovely wife, have been awesome.'

She was glad Angus hadn't been in the room to see her screaming at Noah. Glad he couldn't see the veins of resentment that now ran through her soul about all the money her dad had given to her brother and sister, but not to her. Glad he didn't know how deep her sense of unfairness was at the way her father had treated her, compared to everyone else. She sensed Angus reach out to put his hand on her stomach, and only just managed to roll onto her side in time. As compensation, she stroked her fingertips down his cheek.

'Ah, thank you for the vote of confidence, my dear, but I'm afraid your opinion is somewhat invalidated by your lack of impartiality.' He interlaced his fingers with hers. It felt good to be listened to, in the dark, with the covers forming a warm cocoon around them. 'We haven't even talked about losing Dad, not really – only his money and who gets it.' It was true. That was shameful. 'When Chloe gets all weepy and panicky, I feel irritated. And Noah' – she felt fresh fury and frustration with her brother – 'I know there's something going on. I don't know whether he and Josie are having a rough patch, or if he's got problems with his job or debts that he's covering up, but he simply won't talk to me. And he's drinking too much. You must have noticed. The slurring, the stumbling around. I know he likes a drink, but I've not seen him this bad for ages. I've had enough, Angus. It's awful to say it, but I can't do it any more.' She heard the wobble in her voice. 'And I'm not going to.'

'Hey,' he squeezed her fingers, 'I get it. I understand. But you have to remember that it's not your job to fix them. They rely on you too much, as it is.' He paused. 'We all do.' He kissed her. 'But that's what happens when you're Superwoman.' He closed his eyes and kissed her again – kept them closed after the kiss ended. She was relieved; mindless comfort was all she wanted, all she could cope with. They lay, face-to-face, not talking, until he fell asleep and she slipped out of his embrace.

Chapter 52

IT WAS nearly over.

The house was dark and quiet, all of them in bed.

The solicitor in the morning.

Then they would be done.

Eloise had left hours ago. Megan had heard the front door slam and watched her car pull away up the drive – washing her hands of them, and the will, with a spray of shingle and the blink of an indicator light. It seemed like a small gesture of solidarity – a judgement on Jonathan's children and their behaviour. Having an ally, of sorts, after all this time was a strange feeling. The irony that it had turned out to be Eloise was not lost on Megan. Jonathan would have been dumbfounded. The thought raised the ghost of a smile. In the café Eloise had, in her own haughty way, exonerated Megan of at least a portion of her guilt. Megan hadn't seen that coming, or expected it to matter so much. But as she stood by the window, she realised it did. Eloise was the only person Megan had ever knowingly hurt. To hear her say that she was glad Megan had been with

Jonathan at the end was a curious comfort – even though it wasn't true.

It was cold in the bedroom, the heating had clicked off and the window was still ajar, but Megan couldn't rouse herself to get up and close it. Something about the coldness in the room made her think of cleanliness… her mind made the jump to godliness. Sunday school teaching really did sow its seeds deep down in the cracks. Jonathan had been an avowed atheist – religion being far too irrational and too marked with mankind's fingerprints for him. He believed that when you were gone, you were gone.

So had she.

The moonlight rippled across the ceiling like water. She closed her eyes and listened to the waves. She knew that she would forever associate the sound of the sea with Jonathan's death.

He had been dead when she entered the room.

Still.

Silent.

Gone.

She'd felt a flush of intense heat at the sight of him. She remembered feeling confused, thinking grief should surely be cold! Lisa had stood behind her, waiting for a reaction, a word, a sign that Megan had grasped he was dead. Her emotions began to push their way through the thick blanket of shock – not sadness or grief, but something red-hot and sharp: jealousy.

'Why didn't you wake me?'

Lisa's voice was disembodied, calm. 'I'm sorry. There wasn't time. It was very quick. I think it was his heart.'

'His heart?' What right had Lisa to talk about his heart?

'A cardiac attack, I think. It has to have been something like that, for it to be so sudden.'

Megan's sense of injustice was so huge that it engulfed every other emotion. 'You were with him?'

'Yes.' Lisa paused. 'He asked me to sit with him, like he does sometimes when he can't sleep. We chatted for a bit, then he dozed off. I was about to leave. He woke up and said he felt unwell. He obviously had some pain. I was about to offer him something to ease it, then come and fetch you, but there wasn't time. He went quiet, curled up on his side. It was over in a matter of moments.'

'What do you mean, he curled up?'

'Just that. He sort of contracted.'

Megan couldn't breathe.

'I held his hand. Then he was gone. He didn't struggle. Not for long.'

Megan felt the phrase lodge like a splinter in her brain, knowing that it would be embedded there for ever. 'Did he say anything?'

'No.' The cold air coming in through the open windows smelt of the sea. 'There wasn't time.'

It was over.

He was gone.

Lisa had held his hand as he died. Hers was the last face Jonathan saw. Megan fought the thought. 'This doesn't make sense. He was okay when I left him.' He had been. There had been no indication, nothing at all, that it was going to be different from any other night. That's why she'd gone up to bed. But there was no arguing with Lisa because there he was, Jonathan, lying on his side. A body, not a person.

'Megan.' Lisa made a move towards her, but Megan shifted away sharply. That didn't deter Lisa from trying to offer comfort, but this time without the physical overture. 'It sometimes happens this way. I know it's a dreadful shock. But, for Jonathan, it's over now. Quickly. Better that way than—'

'Don't. Just don't!' Megan felt the heat inside her intensify. 'I don't want you to say another word.'

Lisa took a step back, in deference to her anger and her grief. 'Of course. I understand. I'll leave you with him. I'll be outside if you need me.' And with that, she finally left.

Megan remembered edging around the room and sitting down on the chair beside the bed, at last taking up her rightful position.

He had gone without her.

She had not been there at the end, to hold him and absorb his fear.

She had not told him that she loved him. Nor he her.

Megan opened her eyes. The moonlight shimmered across the ceiling.

At least he had not been alone.

Lisa had been there, for his last breath, his last touch, his last moment... and for that Megan was grateful, and deeply, intensely jealous.

The sound of the waves filled the room.

She had not been with Jonathan at the very end.

And for that there was no absolution.

But perhaps, with time, there might be acceptance.

Chapter 53

Ten days since their last meeting and the Coulter family was back at Greenwood's – all of them punctual this time, ready and waiting in the conference room, sitting in the same seats as last time. Rachel Hewson smiled briefly as she took her place at the head of the table. One weekend together to unravel the knot of Jonathan's last will and testament. It was quite impressive really. Three siblings, an ex-wife, a new partner, the threat of it all going to charity, a generous bequest to a virtual stranger, a somewhat ghoulish instruction preventing burial until there was agreement... it was only natural that she was more invested in the outcome than normal.

After the handshakes and greetings, it was time to get down to business. Rachel looked at Olivia Coulter, expecting her to lead proceedings, but surprisingly it was Chloe, the younger sister, who spoke. She began somewhat hesitantly, but no one chipped in; they let her speak without interruption. Rachel was impressed, and intrigued. Family dynamics were so often ossified by time and precedence, it was refreshing to witness an example of change.

'Thank you for making the time to see us today.' Chloe Coulter glanced down at the sheet of paper in front of her, pulling it closer for support. 'As you know, we've spent the weekend discussing Dad's will. Unsurprisingly, it threw us slightly – its contents and the circumstances in which it was written. But we have, as he instructed, arrived at an agreement that we are all happy with.' She glanced around the table and each of them gave their silent assent. 'Firstly, we have a message from our mother' – Chloe seemed to be overcome by an awareness she was dealing with something legally significant and sat up straighter – 'Eloise Coulter. She has told us she wants nothing from the estate, on the grounds that she received a substantial settlement after her divorce from our father in 2015. She is happy to confirm this in writing, and by signing anything that you need her to. Her one request,' at this point Chloe touched her mouth – nervously Rachel thought, 'which we all agreed to, was to have the picture of Scarborough that used to hang in the hall at the house. I hope it's okay, but she's actually taken it already.'

Rachel was not about to nit-pick over a picture, though the solicitor in her wondered what it might be worth. She really needed to do less death and divorce work. She refocused on her note-taking.

'As to the rest of the estate… this is what we've unanimously agreed.' Chloe picked up the piece of paper. 'To sell the house and all the contents, with the exception of certain personal mementoes that each person would like to take, in memory of Dad. We've provided a list of what those items are.' Liv passed a copy to Rachel, which she glanced at, but didn't read. 'And that the proceeds from the sale of the house, and its contents and any and all remaining financial assets belonging to our father, after the payment of any debts, should then be shared equally between the following: Olivia Redpath, Noah Coulter and myself, Chloe Coulter.'

Rachel Hewson gave Chloe an encouraging nod to let her know that she had expressed herself clearly and correctly.

Chloe went on, 'Despite our mother declining a share, we want to give her nine thousand pounds out of the estate. We think it's only right that she gets something.' Chloe flushed, then stuttered on. 'That's three thousand pounds from each of us.'

Megan didn't move a muscle.

Chloe got back on track by looking down at her notes. 'And we want to donate another three thousand pounds to the MND charity, in Dad's name.'

Rachel nodded, making sure her views on their decision weren't showing in her demeanour, her expression or her tone of voice. But she obviously wasn't in full poker face mode, because she heard herself saying, 'So you're doing everything in threes.' It was not the time for levity.

Chloe blinked. No one else said anything.

Rachel scrambled back onto safer ground swiftly, but clumsily. 'And you do remember the bequest to Lisa Browne for five thousand pounds.' That didn't fit in quite so neatly. 'I presume you are happy for that to be paid?'

There was a pause and a ping-pong of glances around the table. Chloe nodded. 'Yes, we are okay with that. Aren't we?' Her question met with no dissent.

Rachel waited. Surely that couldn't be it.

Megan sat unflinching. No one looked at her, but it was palpable that they were all, including Rachel, thinking about her, or at least about her omission – so far.

'With regards to Megan,' Chloe swallowed, audibly, 'she has also waived her interest in the estate.'

Rachel looked up sharply, no longer caring whether or not she appeared totally impartial.

'I have.' Megan's voice was clear.

Chloe went on, 'Megan is to remain in the house until it's sold or until she's ready to move out – up to a maximum period of three months. The executors will take over all the running costs of the house from now, going forward. When Megan does move out, she can take those items that belong to her, plus any electrical goods or furniture that would be useful in her next home, in agreement with the executors. The joint current account that she shared with our father will be closed, and the remaining balance will be transferred to Megan to assist with the move to her next property.'

Rachel felt the need to say something. But all she came up with was, 'Okay.' So they had cut Megan out of Jonathan's legacy, and Megan was accepting it. Families. Not for the first time, Rachel was glad she didn't have one.

Chloe folded her notes in half and sat back, obviously mightily relieved to have finished.

They all looked at Rachel. The baton of responsibility was being handed back to her. 'Well. Okay then.' She laid down her pen. 'I think that more or less covers all the main points. It's certainly enough for us to be getting on with.' She moved on to the usual platitudes. 'I hope that, having arrived at a decision, you all feel better able to move on.'

Liv finally spoke. 'Yes. It's good to get it sorted.' There was another ripple of small nods that came to a stop with Megan.

Chloe added, 'We're getting arrangements for the funeral

under way. I assume that we're okay to proceed with it now? We're hoping to be able lay him to rest before Christmas.'

'Good, good. But as I said when we last met, that stipulation from your father wasn't ever legally binding. I'll have a look at this list of items from the house, but I'm sure it'll be fine. It is your family home, after all. As long as you're in agreement, it's up to you to disperse any personal items as you see fit.'

Noah Coulter, released by the conclusion of the business in hand, started shuffling around, flipping his phone over on the table. 'So that's it then, is it? You process any paperwork, we chase the pension company, we get a final balance and we're good to go.'

'Well, yes. Given that I now have clear instructions, there's very little to do from a legal viewpoint, except to write it all up and send you each a copy of the documentation to sign. And even that is for reference more than anything else. I just want to be sure that we have everything recorded correctly, given the slightly unusual approach your father took with regard to his will.'

'And will the wrapping up of the estate take long?' It was Noah, the son, agitating again.

'Not necessarily. Not now there's a clear plan. There's probate to get through. Though that can normally be completed in a few months. Then there's the house sale. That's obviously in the lap of the gods. Greenwood's would, of course, be more than happy to help with the sale of the property, should you wish us to get involved.' There was an awkward pause. Touting for business – Rachel was almost ashamed of herself, but not quite. 'The distribution of funds will only occur when we have a final balance. But we will try to expedite everything as soon as possible.'

There was a noticeable easing of the atmosphere in the room. They obviously thought they were done.

Chapter 54

It was nearly over.

A few clear and coherent sentences from Chloe, who seemed, surprisingly, to have been nominated as the chief spokesperson, a patch of blessed silent acquiescence from Liv and Noah and that was it. The arguments settled, the division of the estate agreed, the future sealed, the past sorted. Ms Hewson made precise notes in her neat handwriting, her expression set to neutral, though Megan noticed her eyes flick over to her more than once, sympathy lurking beneath her professional demeanour. Megan gave her nothing in return. She had no use for the sympathy of strangers. Ms Hewson read back the key points of the agreement, checking that she had their unanimous consent – she had – then promised to enact their wishes as swiftly as possible. With a restrained flourish, she set aside her notepad and recapped her pen.

As denouements went, it was an anticlimactic one.

It was at an end.

Or perhaps not.

'If you could just bear with me for a few moments.' Ms Hewson stood up and excused herself, saying that she had one last piece of paperwork to give them. In her absence the silence held. She was back almost immediately, clutching some envelopes. She sat down. They all looked at her. She seemed suddenly self-conscious. 'I have one last task to fulfil, at the behest of your father. Jonathan instructed me to give you these, once you had arrived at your decision.' She passed an envelope to Chloe, Noah and Liv in turn. Megan felt a shiver of sadness on seeing Jonathan's wavery handwriting. The notes must have been written near the end of his life. The disease stole many things from him, including his elegant handwriting.

'Should we open them now?' Chloe seemed to be getting used to acting as the family envoy.

Ms Hewson remained professionally, politely indifferent. 'That's completely up to you.'

They glanced at each other. Noah took the decision. He stopped spinning his envelope round on the surface of the table and picked it up. By the time he'd started ripping it open, his sisters had joined in. The room was filled with the rustle of tearing paper. Ms Hewson looked at her hands. Megan watched them, her focus flicking from face-to-face, trying to work out from their reactions the content of the letters – her fatigue with Jonathan's grand plan only deepened by this last act.

Whatever Jonathan's last message to them was, it was obviously short. Chloe lost her composure and starting sniffing. Liv and Noah looked up from their sheets of paper at each other briefly and back again at their letters, with expressions of confusion.

'What does yours say?' Noah broke the impasse, as direct as ever.

Liv suddenly smiled, a soft, sad smile that transformed her face. 'Just that he loved me.' She slid her letter across the table to Noah.

'Same here.' Chloe laid hers on the table as well.

Megan saw that each missive was extremely short – a date, their name and one line of writing. *I love you. Goodbye, Dad x.*

'Is this it?' Noah's voice struck a discordant note. His frustration yet again drowning out the quieter emotions of the others.

Ms Hewson nodded. 'His instruction was simply to give you these, once you'd arrived at a settlement.'

Megan couldn't take her eyes off the loopy, shaky letters; the words looked as if they might slide off the page if you lifted up the paper. Despite their brevity, each letter must have taken him hours to write. One last huge effort at communication with his offspring. An effort appreciated by Chloe and Liv, but obviously not by Noah. What more did he want? A flash of anger ripped through her.

'What else were you expecting, Noah? Is "this" not enough, for you? Confirmation that your father loved you. Loved all of you. Equally.'

As Megan was speaking, Liv drew all three letters towards her and lined them up. Laid out thus, it was even more obvious the pains Jonathan had taken to write each one. But there was something about the alertness in Liv's body that seemed to signal more than just an emotional response to her father's last message. 'Ms Hewson, when did Dad give you these?' Liv asked.

Ms Hewson replied, 'Your father didn't pass them to me himself. Miss Browne brought them into the office.'

'But when? What date did she deliver them?'

The letters were all dated 12th November.

Ms Hewson tugged the front of her blouse straight, pointlessly – she already looked immaculately neat. 'I'd have to check my calendar to be absolutely certain... but I think it was the week before he died.'

Liv had everyone's attention now. 'And you didn't think it odd that the week before he died, he gave you letters to give out in the event of his death?'

Ms Hewson looked calm, but there was a slight increase in volume when she answered Liv. 'No. I knew your father's diagnosis was terminal. When Ms Browne brought the letters, I assumed that his health had, sadly, deteriorated further. It seemed – it still seems – wholly consistent with what I knew of his character and his wishes.'

'But prescient, no?'

'A little, perhaps.' Another tug of her shirt.

Noah chipped in. 'Liv, what are you getting at?'

'I'm thinking it's a bit of a coincidence that Dad wrote these letters and gave them to the solicitor's just four days before he died.'

Chloe looked aghast. 'You're saying that he knew!'

'Yes.' Liv's brain seemed to be going into overdrive, her expression reflecting an avalanche of thoughts. 'Chloe, you said it yourself. He'd been better than he had been in months. The meds were helping. His breathing was fairly stable. It certainly was, the last time I saw him.' Liv suddenly looked at Megan and a pulse of energy ripped through the room. 'What do you make of it, Megan? When you went to bed that night, did you have any inkling it would be his last?' When Megan didn't respond, Liv asked again. 'Well, did you?'

Megan knew her silence was damning, but she was choking on her own rush of thoughts and emotions. At last she managed a quiet but firm, 'No.'

They all stared at her, waiting for more. She forced herself to speak.

'No. He was obviously still very poorly, but no, I had no idea I was about to lose him. If I had, I would never have gone to bed.' And slept through his death, leaving Lisa to be there for Jonathan at the very end. A fact that no one else in the room was aware of.

'Are you saying he put all this in place,' Noah waved his hand around the room, 'the will, that mad Statement of Wishes thing, these letters, then – when it was all sorted – topped himself?' Noah asked.

Ms Hewson's polite 'Please, this is all speculation' went unheard.

Liv had momentum now. 'Actually it's not just possible – it's likely. Think about what Dad was like about having control of things, of his life, of us.' There was a pause as they did exactly that.

'He wouldn't,' Chloe said.

'He would,' Liv replied. 'And who could blame him, given what he was facing? It was only going to get worse, and it was already bad. I know he hated the thought of how he was going to end up. We talked about it once, soon after he was first diagnosed. The dependency, the lack of control horrified him.'

'How?' Noah asked.

'What do you mean, "how"?'

'If he did kill himself, how did he do it?' Noah's voice was flat, parched of emotion.

'How the hell would I know?' Liv flared.

'Whoa. I'm not accusing you of anything. I was just asking.'

'Stop it!' Megan's instruction landed hard in the middle of their speculation. They looked at her. She summoned up all the courage she could muster. 'Have you learnt nothing from this weekend?' She looked at each of them in turn. 'What difference does it make? He's gone. He provided for all of us. He played his part, right up until the end. One of his very last acts was to write to each of you, telling you how much he loved you. Why not be satisfied with that? Why not leave him in peace? Don't you think he deserves that?'

There was the longest pause – during which Megan waited for the accusations and the venom to start up all over again, but they didn't.

It was Chloe who finally spoke, calmly and kindly. 'What do you really think happened that night, Megan?'

Megan would always wonder, but she now realised she no longer needed to know for certain. 'I don't know.' The room stilled as they listened to her. 'Maybe he simply decided he'd had enough. I can understand that. Having lived through his illness with him, I think everyone, at the end, has the right to choose what's bearable and what isn't for themselves. Whether he just gave up that night and let death come and get him, or whether he did something more... I don't know. And, honestly, I no longer care. I think he did his best, by us all, and I don't think we can ask for any more than that.'

Chapter 55

MEGAN LET herself into the house. She stood in the hall looking around. All evidence of their 'invasion' had disappeared: the coats and shoes and bags. The radiator ticked erratically. Now what?

Tea.

She went into the kitchen, filled the kettle – too full for a single mug – flicked it on, then stood waiting. The doorbell rang before the water had finished boiling. Two tentative blasts. She had no idea who might be calling.

It was Noah. That threw her. 'Oh, hi. Did you forget something?'

He stayed on the front step. 'No.' There was a pause. 'I know the last thing you probably want is another conversation, especially after these past few days, but I was wondering if you could spare me a few minutes. I'm honestly not here to cause trouble.'

Twenty-four hours earlier she would have shut the door in his face, but they had moved on. It was all settled now. She could afford him the courtesy of hearing him out – she supposed. 'Okay. I was just making a drink, would you like one?'

'Thank you.' He stepped into the hall, unzipped his jacket. As he hung it on the hook, he glanced into Jonathan's room. The hospital bed was still there, stripped and ready, awaiting collection back to the depot to be cleaned and delivered to someone else. Megan would be glad when it was gone. Another step completed in the dismantling of the past. Noah paid her the courtesy of not mentioning it, embarrassed, hopefully, by the memory of his drunken collapse in his father's room on Saturday night.

They settled in the lounge. Noah waited for Megan to sit down before he lowered himself into a chair, polite all of a sudden; but once seated, he seemed hesitant to begin speaking.

'What is it you want to talk about, Noah?'

He put his mug down, on a coaster, not on the table. 'Firstly, I want to apologise for some of my behaviour this past weekend. At times I know I was rude, disrespectful. Saying that I've been upset isn't much of an excuse.' He must have seen a hardening in her expression because he hurried on, 'Is *no* excuse. Anyway I want you to know, I'm sorry if I upset you.'

Megan nodded her acceptance. She felt she owed him nothing more. There was another awkward pause.

'And I wanted to ask you some questions, if you don't mind, about Dad. About his illness.'

She had assumed it was going to be a conversation about something in the house that he wanted – correction, *something else* he wanted. She hoped he wasn't going to start unpicking Jonathan's death or his legacy. She couldn't bear that. 'I suppose that's okay.'

'I appreciate it's a bit rich. Asking now. After everything. I know I avoided it when he was first diagnosed and when he was ill.'

She nodded, feeling disinclined to offer him more, until she knew his motivation for asking, and where he was going with his questions.

Noah seemed to be in some sort of compulsive confessional mode, because he added, without prompting, 'We used to talk about other stuff when we were together. I convinced myself that was what Dad wanted. Distraction. Tales from St Elsewhere. But, in truth, it was because I found it very difficult to talk to him about what was happening.'

Megan took pity on him, a little. 'You weren't the only one. We were all in denial a lot of the time. It felt like the only bearable way to deal with what was going on.' They were quiet for a while. She thought about her comment and felt compelled to revise it, based on the evidence of how much Jonathan had, obviously, thought about his demise in the last year of his life. 'To be fair to your father, I know – now – that he thought about the impact of his illness on other people a lot. Certainly a lot more than I realised, or gave him credit for.' That was enough. Noah had no right to know how much shame and guilt she felt for frustrating Jonathan's numerous attempts to talk about his impending death. She took a drink of her tea. Noah mirrored her. 'So – what do you want to know?'

Noah pulled at the neck of his sweatshirt. 'Can you tell me a little bit about it was like living with him? What I mean is... living with someone with MND.'

It was such a personal question. And although she had absolutely no obligation to protect the feelings of a fully grown man – who in the past forty-eight hours had said, and done, some truly hurtful things – she still edited herself. 'He was brave. Rarely complained about the symptoms, the pain, the sheer grinding hard work of it. What he struggled with more was having to be helped. You know your dad: he prided himself on being self-sufficient. He hated having to rely on me, and Lisa,' after a tiny pause she added, 'and Chloe for things. Towards the end, the indignity of it got him down. It made him angry – not at me, but at it.'

Both of them went quiet, thinking about the circumstances of Jonathan's death, but neither of them spoke of it. A pact had been made to accept his demise as 'fitting'. It seemed that Noah was going to observe it. He looked distressed. Part of Megan felt some sympathy. They had all, in their own ways, avoided the realities of Jonathan's illness.

'Did the drugs help?'

'At the beginning, yes. They made a huge difference. Reduced the tremors, gave him back most of the function in his hands, but over time they worked less and less well. The dose can only be increased to a certain level – but they enabled us to have a more normal existence for at least a couple of years than we would have done without them.'

Noah nodded. 'So you'd say he had three reasonable years after his initial diagnosis before he... really deteriorated.' She winced at his wording and he noticed. 'Sorry. That was clumsy.'

Megan studied him and felt confused. It made her disinclined to say anything more. 'Noah, what is this about?'

He looked out of the window – a buying-time tactic if ever there was one. 'I feel guilty. I should have got involved more. Found out more about what he was going through – what you were going through.'

What could she say to that, other than shout in his face, '*Yes, you should!*' Which, of course, she didn't. They sat in silence, each with their own regrets.

Noah seemed to gather himself up. 'I know he wasn't the easiest man in the world to live with.' How dare he assume that, but he went on, 'I can only imagine how tough it must have been for you, coping with him, and the illness.'

There was a pause. If he was expecting her to describe what it had really been like, he was going to have a long wait. The time for shared confidences was long gone. Indeed, the chances that she would *ever* have confided in any of Jonathan's children had always been nil. And their behaviour over the will had only served to underscore that lack of respect. The affection she had once hoped for was never going to manifest itself, Megan knew that now.

Noah ploughed on. 'Well, what I'm trying to say is "Thank you". Thank you for being there for him, for caring for him right up until the end.' He made a weird shrugging move as if trying to shift a weight that wouldn't budge. He stopped talking and there was an awful yawning pause. It went on and on.

Megan desperately wanted him to leave, but he didn't move. She stood up to prompt him. He looked at her and finally seemed to remember that he was on her territory – and it was still hers, for another month or two.

'Noah, if you don't mind, I have things I have to get on with.'

'Oh, yes. Quite. I understand.'

They walked through to the hall together. As she opened the front door to see him out, he delivered one last, bizarre little speech. 'I wish you well, Megan, in whatever you do. And like I said, *Thank you.* My dad was lucky to have you in his life.' With that odd, far-too-late endorsement ringing in her ears, Megan shut the door on him.

Chapter 56

THREE WEEKS later they made their way down to the beach in single file, each of them carrying a portion of Jonathan's ashes. It was like an extended, out-of-whack version of the three kings in the Nativity – though, it was hardly the festive celebration they had planned. The kids were skittish. To them, the trip was an adventure. They ran in and out of the procession, weaving the adults together, the light of their torches like fireflies. Uncle No's promise of a bonfire on the beach had ramped up their excitement to nuclear levels. They sought out kindling from the bushes as they walked along the path, returning with good 'burning sticks' for the adults to carry. Soon Angus and Noah's arms were full.

The adults weren't speaking much, not because of any lingering ill will or resentment, but because the occasion seemed to demand solemnity, not jollity. But once they got down onto the empty beach the mood lifted. Under the darkening sky they lined up the identical cardboard tubes of Jonathan's ashes on the sand. The 'boys' helped Noah scoop out a hollow for the bonfire, while the 'girls' went down to the shoreline in search of some flat stones to line the edge of the fire pit. The spaces between the adults were filled with the shouts of the kids and the regular shush of the incoming tide. It was like being suspended in time and place. When it was time to light the fire, they instinctively gathered in a circle around Noah, creating a natural windbreak as he knelt and began striking matches. It suddenly mattered very much that their joint efforts hadn't been in vain and that the dark and cold, which were now pressing against their backs, were pushed back by light and heat.

By the twentieth match there was silence; even Freddie and Arthur were quiet, holding on to Liv, their little faces white in the light of Chloe's phone. Another match flared, Noah hunched low again, his head almost buried in the mound of twigs and sticks as he edged the small orange flame into the heart of the kindling. It glowed briefly, then died. Freddie sniffed, close to tears. Noah looked up and smiled. 'Hey, Buddy. Fire takes patience. Like Grandpa used to say, "If at first you don't succeed, try, try..."' He waited for the kids to finish the saying.

In unison they chorused, 'Try again.'

Angus came to the rescue. He knelt down and unzipped his jacket, then, to the amazement of the boys, took hold of the seam and ripped it.

Freddie was horrified and transfixed. 'Daddy!'

Angus proceeded to pull some of the wadding out of the lining. When he had enough, he passed a tuft to each of his boys. 'Give this to Uncle No.' Armed with the expensive innards of Angus's coat, Noah got the fire going at the next attempt. As the glow spread and more and more branches caught, they all cheered.

Jonathan's funeral, the previous week, had gone well. Megan's father and sister had been there to support her. Having Sarah by her side had been a comfort. It had felt like having backup, which had made getting through the day bearable. There had been a big turnout. A surprising number of Jonathan's former work colleagues travelled long distances to pay their respects, and a lot of old family friends and neighbours came. The non-religious service was, most people agreed, perfectly pitched. The children, and the adults, were impeccably behaved and the wake was well catered and not too boozy.

It had been, everyone agreed, a fitting send-off.

But it had been a performance that had somehow missed the essence of the man.

They had all come away from it feeling strangely dissatisfied.

It was Chloe who'd suggested they get together to scatter his ashes. She'd asked Megan first, cautiously, expecting her to say 'No.' But Megan – who had been swaddling a set of wrought-iron candlesticks in layers of bubble wrap at the time, sorting out her possessions, readying herself for moving out – had agreed, saying they should have a proper send-off with all of them there, so that they could to say 'goodbye' to Jonathan, and each other, one last time.

There was heat and light from the fire now. It brought them closer together.

Chloe picked up the containers and passed them around.

They all stared at the flames.

Eloise passed her container on to Megan. 'I don't need to say goodbye to him. We said our goodbyes a long time ago.'

Megan didn't argue with her. She had learnt some interesting things about herself and her place in the Coulter family over the past month, foremost of which was that status had to be claimed and owned. She was not Jonathan's widow; but he had been hers, at the end. Hers and no one else's. Megan smiled and touched the sleeve of Eloise's coat by way of acknowledgement. The fire burnt bright and fierce, heating their faces and their hands, while shivers coursed up and down their backs. Around them the darkness thickened, making the open spaces of the wide bay seem limitless. The children had quietened and calmed. They stood close to their parents, as if frightened that to stray would be dangerous. Lily was leaning against Josie, her thumb in her mouth, her eyes screwed shut, whether because of the smoke from the fire or because she was tired was difficult to tell.

Noah, Liv and Chloe were all clutching their share of their father.

It was time.

The agreed plan had been to scatter Jonathan's ashes on the waves, let the sea carry his remains wherever, a Viking burial of sorts, but the thought of leaving the bright circle of the fire and venturing into the darkness down to the shoreline made Megan feel nervous. The notion of throwing him into the cold sea was too brutal. Chloe met Megan's eyes, questioning, wanting it over with, but deferring to her nonetheless.

'He preferred the warmth to the cold.' Megan's voice was surprisingly steady. The waves whispered in the background. No, the sea was too vast and lonely. She unscrewed the lid of the first tube, punched through the perforated top and held the container out over the flames. As she tilted it, she thought of all the things she regretted not saying to Jonathan, all the conversations she'd redirected or stopped, all the times she'd be about to say something, but hadn't. Now was the time to put that right and speak her heart.

But nothing came out of her mouth, or the tube. There was a moment when they all looked at her. She shook the tube. Still nothing. In the end she had to resort to squeezing and banging the container, trying to loosen the contents.

'He's hanging on till the bitter end!' Noah's attempt at humour was ill judged and yet perfectly timed.

Megan laughed.

The moment for words had passed.

Jonathan was gone.

This was dust.

One last strike of her hand and the ashes began to pour out. The others set to work on their tubes – Freddie helping Liv, Arthur helping Chloe, and Lily helping Noah. Together they sprinkled their lover/father-in-law/dad/grandpa onto the flames like icing sugar on a cake. For a few seconds the flames flared and crackled, burning bright white, then they died back down. It was a fitting, brief, fierce exit.

Chapter 57

FOUR MONTHS LATER

THE ROOM was small and shabbily furnished, but nice enough. It faced out onto the front garden. There was a view, during daylight hours, of the flower beds, which were currently full of blousy, bright daffodils and of a high green hedge that blocked out some, but not all, of the noise from the road. Lisa was glad to be working on the ground floor. She preferred it to working with the residents who lived in the rooms on the long corridors on the upper levels of the home. Not because she resented the extra legwork, she was used to hard work, but because she believed that everyone – even the poor souls lost in the fragile, crumbling labyrinths of dementia – needed to be close to the natural world.

Lisa had been at this particular care home for a couple of months now. She'd started to build connections with most of the residents on her section and was beginning to get a good sense of their wishes, and their fears.

After her stint with Jonathan, she'd treated herself to a break. A week up in Scotland just before Christmas. The trip had been a luxury, and a rarity, but she'd needed it. Jonathan Coulter's death had left her feeling restless. That was unusual. Normally she went from one job to the next, untroubled, unaffected. Caring was her vocation. She couldn't imagine doing anything else – didn't want to do anything else – but this time it felt different. As she wandered around Edinburgh, with its glitter of Christmas lights, she finally worked out what was troubling her.

It wasn't Jonathan's passing.

His death had been one of the most meticulously planned and well-executed ends she'd had the privilege of being involved with. There could be no regret about that. No, it was more personal. As she sat outside one of the pavement cafés, wrapped up against the cold in her pure-wool coat, her neck swathed in the luxury of a cashmere scarf – items she'd treated herself to, in anticipation of the money Jonathan had so kindly, and so unexpectedly, left to her – she realised what she was feeling was grief.

It was an emotion she had little personal experience of. She had, of course, witnessed plenty of it – it was unavoidable in her line of work – but she rarely *felt* the deaths of her charges personally. Indeed, her emotions at the end of each placement or stint in a home were normally positive: a quiet sense of pride in a job well done, the satisfaction of knowing she had made a difference. But there was no denying that her low mood and heightened emotions after leaving the Coulter household were the result of the sorrow she was feeling at the loss of a friend.

Friendship.

It was not a common component in her life.

As she raised a glass of red wine to Jonathan on the last night of her holiday, Lisa made a pact to protect herself better in the future. Her job was a delicate balance: caring without getting too involved, having compassion whilst never losing clarity, helping without interfering. With Jonathan, she had let that balance tilt.

Because?

As she sipped her wine, she thought about why her time with Jonathan had been so affecting. It was because he had been a different kind of client. He had had intelligence and humour, and charm. And also, more importantly, he had recognised some of those qualities in her. That was unusual. As a carer, Lisa was normally invisible. A hired help – relied on, and sometimes appreciated, but rarely recognised as a person in her own right. Jonathan had 'seen' Lisa from the very first meeting. He'd been combative, provocative and testing. And she'd risen to his challenge, enjoying the push and shove of their conversation that day. By the end of the hour, she'd known he was going to offer her the job.

What she hadn't known was that it was going to be a very special seven months for both of them.

Jonathan had not been an easy person to work for, but he had been interesting and interested. That they'd forged a true friendship, despite the ignominies of his illness, had been truly remarkable. Often the people Lisa cared for could only get through the indignities of their failing bodies by absenting themselves. When they had to be washed or forced to exercise, or spoon-fed their medicines like children, their eyes would go blank and she would know they were mentally removing themselves. They would stare at a point beyond her head and cease talking for the duration of the intervention. At such times she, their carer, and they, her patient, would both collude in pretending that none of it was happening – which meant that for long periods of time it was as if Lisa herself didn't really exist, and that the work she did didn't matter.

Jonathan had been different. He'd been clear-sighted and coolly direct about his needs and his infirmities. She'd discovered this very early on, when he'd bitten her head off whenever she resorted to any indirect or imprecise language. He couldn't bear any coyness. 'I'm not one of your old ladies, Lisa. Do me the courtesy of treating me like an adult, please, or this is going to end in tears… and they won't be mine.'

After only a very short period of time, that directness between them had segued into banter and gallows humour. He'd pushed her, and she'd responded in kind, and before long they'd discovered a shared willingness to call a spade a shovel. There'd been a joy and a release in that for both of them. Very little was off-limits. It had made caring for Jonathan a pleasure for her, and less of an indignity for him – or at least she hoped it had.

He waited three weeks into her employment before bringing up the subject of death. He started, as was usual, by asking about other people's passing; but unlike many of the people she'd cared for, Jonathan hadn't been fishing for reassuring anecdotes about 'good ends', he'd wanted the truth, and the detail. And so she'd given it to him, to the best of her ability. Not totally unvarnished – that would have been too cruel – but as honestly as she could.

That had been the first time he'd taken hold of her hand, as if comforting Lisa as much as himself, as she spoke.

There had followed a quiet couple of days, which worried her, but then when she went back in one morning Jonathan seemed much better, excited almost. No, not almost, he had been genuinely buzzing. He was conspiratorial, promising he would 'tell her everything' when Megan had gone to work. The minute the front door banged shut, he shouted for her. On entering the room, he asked her to shut the door. She obliged – wondering what was coming.

She instinctively started tidying around his room, much to his annoyance. 'Oh, for God's sake, Lisa, leave it. I want to talk to you.'

She hadn't complied. It was best not to let Jonathan have everything he wanted immediately. With the clothes folded and his next lot of meds lined up ready, she came and sat in the chair opposite him. In the weak sunlight he looked both profoundly unwell and, at the same time, very alive.

'What?'

'Oh, it's like that now, is it? I remember the days when you were all meek and mild. Familiarity obviously does breed contempt!'

She said nothing, letting him have his moment. That's when he had told her about his 'grand plan'. It was all very impressive. Meticulous. Convoluted. Very Jonathan. His pride when he was talking about it was obvious. He explained, at length, his joy at seeing that Megan's house was back on the market at the beginning of the year, courtesy of Zoopla, and the hoops the solicitor had had to jump through to make the purchase legally watertight. As he spoke, Lisa glimpsed the man Jonathan must have been before he fell ill.

And at no point in their conversation had Lisa been in any doubt about his motivations.

Love.

And guilt.

But as Jonathan laid it all out in front of her, expecting her admiration and approval, Lisa had spotted the major flaw in his carefully thought-through plan. 'Have you told Megan what you're planning?'

He'd fallen silent then.

'Well?' she'd pushed.

'I've tried.' He looked away. 'But she refuses to talk about the future and what'll happen after I'm gone.'

Lisa nodded. She sympathised with Jonathan's compulsion to try and control what was happening, *and* she understood Megan's refusal to accept how ill he was. They were both in denial. It was a natural, logical reaction to the nightmare they were trapped in. But conditions like MND were brutal, efficient levellers. Everyone, irrespective of how intelligent, educated, well off or powerful they were, had to accept the fate they'd been dealt – no matter how unfair it might seem.

Jonathan leant forward. Coughed, cleared his throat. Coughed again. She waited. 'That's why I need your help, Lisa. I need someone I can trust.'

'And that person is me, is it?' Lisa asked.

'Yes, it is.'

She'd been touched, surprised and a little fearful. It was stepping over any number of professional boundaries to get so involved in Jonathan's life and death. But was that not what caring was: doing what the patient needed? Nevertheless she resisted him, out of principle and good practice. 'You need to try to talk to her again.'

But he was adamant. 'No. It's too cruel. Megan doesn't want to think about my death. She wants us to have these last few months together. Be happy for what little time we have left, if we can. I have to respect her wishes.' He straightened himself in his chair, as much as he could. 'But it doesn't change the fact that

I'm going to die, and sooner rather than later.' He studied Lisa intently, checking she understood his meaning. 'What I need is someone to be here for Megan at the end, and once I'm gone. I want you to make sure she understands that she has a future.' Lisa said nothing. 'Well?' He was so impatient.

'Just a minute. I'm thinking.'

Jonathan shuffled, trying to find a comfort that now forever eluded him. 'Lisa. Please. This is something I can't do without your help.' He conjured up a crooked smile. 'You wouldn't deny the last wishes of a dying man, would you?'

And, in the end, she hadn't.

But as she sat in Edinburgh, wrapped in her beautiful warm coat and scarf, Lisa vowed never to get so close to a patient ever again. She was there to help the dying, she had a gift for it, but it was not her place to get enmeshed with the living.

Hence her signing on with the temp agency as soon as she returned from holiday.

And it was exactly what she needed: high-volume, high-turnover work – still valuable, perhaps even more so – but there was blessedly little opportunity for emotional attachments to develop.

This evening her charge was Margie. Ninety-four years old, bed-bound for the past three months. Ready, waiting, wanting. Margie was on 'death watch'. Hence the one-to-one care. Lisa had volunteered for another night shift with her, much to the relief of the other staff, thereby fulfilling a promise made to Margie when she'd been lucid. They'd sat together a lot over the past month, talking occasionally, but more often just watching the birds in the garden. Lisa had met Margie's son and grandsons. Bumped into her daughter once in the corridor. Shared a hug and some words of comfort. She'd encouraged them to 'say their goodbyes while Margie was still "present"'. Too much was made of 'deathbed farewells', in Lisa's view. Death wasn't a performance that needed an audience. In reality, many of Lisa's charges waited until their loved ones left the room before finally breathing their last.

She instinctively pulled the covers up around Margie, but it was a reflex action. She no longer needed keeping warm. The old lady's breathing creaked and juddered as Lisa sat at her bedside, calmly, quietly – a benign participant. She waved the drugs nurse away when she did her rounds, saying Margie had no need of anything; nature was taking its course, drugs would only prolong the process.

The corridor outside grew quiet. It was a big home with only a skeleton night crew. Once the day staff left for the evening, Lisa was confident they would not be disturbed.

She left the light off. She watched the colours in the room fade to grey as Margie's breathing started to catch; when it became laboured, Lisa took hold of the old lady's small, frail, thin-skinned hand and helped her to let go.

Chapter 58

AT ELOISE'S prompting, Lorna went up to her room at about 10.30 p.m., *exhausted* after a day of sightseeing and a long, lazy evening of eating and drinking in the hotel's elegant mirrored dining-room. It was amazing how tiring having a good time could be. They'd splashed out and booked separate rooms for the trip, at Eloise's insistence. To hell with the cost, this was her treat or, to be more accurate, Jonathan's treat. As much as Eloise got on with Lorna – they'd been friends since university – she was glad finally to be on her own. There was an ulterior motive for their jolly nice city break to Venice, besides shopping and sauntering and pretending to be young and carefree. Eloise slipped on her jacket and wove a path through the clumps of couples in the bar. On the steps of the hotel she paused, taking in the softness of the air. It was a gloriously warm night for April.

The idea of a Venice jaunt had come to her as she drove back from Scarborough after they'd scattered Jonathan's ashes. A sudden clear, simple solution to what she was going to do with the money the children had given her from their inheritance.

She'd chosen a different hotel of course, a nicer, much more expensive one, in the beating heart of the old city. A proper 'establishment', with a marble-topped bar and an internal courtyard, *perfect for an early evening cocktail*; multiple airy reception rooms and two liveried doormen, one of whom had just held open the heavy mullioned glass door and tipped his hat at her. This was what Jonathan's money was buying: the trappings of elegance and old world charm. Eloise hoped he would have approved. She thought he might – though he would have been surprised by her choice of holiday destination. She turned left and began strolling through the narrow streets, joining the tourists and locals promenading between the pools of yellow light cast by the street lamps.

Out of respect to her late husband, she had not invited Alex along on the trip. He'd been disappointed and had sulked, quite badly. She'd been secretly pleased by his show of pique. If he missed her while she was away, so much the better. Theirs was a fairly new relationship. Their joy and delight in each other was fresh and exciting, but it was still good to hold something back. The slow reveal was half the fun, after all.

In truth, it had never been an option to travel with her new lover.

Venice was a city that would always belong to Jonathan.

Eloise checked the street name on her phone and turned down one of the paths that took her deeper into the back streets, away from the shops and bars, into the realm of overflowing dustbins and graffiti – the still-vibrant, but far seedier side of Venice. At one point she came to a dead end, had to double-check the directions and retrace her steps. This was not, after all, an aimless wander. Then suddenly there it was, the restaurant they'd eaten at all those years ago. It was still a going concern, although at this late hour it was closed and shuttered. Its survival pleased Eloise: *proof of life.* She knew she was being sentimental, but that was the purpose of the trip – for her to make her peace with her past.

She walked past the restaurant slowly. It looked the same, from what little she could remember. A local neighbourhood trattoria. No frills, good food, cheap, or at least as cheap as it got in Venice. She recalled that they ate outside, at one of the few tables crammed onto the narrow strip of paving in front of the restaurant. They'd been on a tight budget, so she guessed they'd had the *prix fixe* menu and the second least-expensive bottle of red on the list. What they talked about she couldn't remember, but that they had talked, and talked, and talked, she was fairly confident.

After their meal Jonathan had casually suggested a stroll.

Perhaps they held hands, perhaps not, she couldn't remember, but she did have a clear memory of the darkness and the sense of being the only couple on earth. That had been a good feeling, one she now didn't regret – the certainty of being loved.

She walked on beyond the restaurant, deeper into the darkness. Two men approached, appraised and passed her with a '*Buona notte*'. She smiled, but didn't reply. The slap of the water told her she was close.

The bench was still there.

She sat on it, facing the inky water of the canal. Thirty-five years of marriage began on this spot. A lifetime of experiences, arguments and compromises. A home. Three children. Three grandchildren. Not a failure. Just not a complete success. She looked at the crumbling beauty in front of her and let herself love Jonathan again, without recrimination. It was a relief finally to be able to think of him without bitterness. Him and her, before him and Megan. Two separate relationships. One replacing another, but the second not obliterating the first. Because it hadn't. Jonathan had loved her first. Loved her properly, fully, wholeheartedly. And she, for many years, had loved him.

She reached into her bag and took out the small gold-edged ring box. He had chosen well. A simple, classic diamond solitaire. The facets caught the light from the street lamp. The diamond shone as bright as new – as if Jonathan had just bought it, after haggling at length with a jeweller on the Rio Terà Cazza, bids and counterbids being scribbled on the back of a receipt. Jonathan had shown her the receipt when they'd returned to their hotel room – proud of his negotiating skills. The ring glittered. She returned it to its box. She placed the box on the bench, stood up and walked away, leaving the ring on the exact spot where he'd proposed, for someone else to find and do with it whatever they wanted.

Chapter 59

CHLOE WAS working a twelve-to-eight shift.

She adjusted her chair; if you didn't, you paid for it with backache. She tidied up the pile of food order leaflets and threw away the shreds of receipt paper that Lynne had ripped off and left scattered around the till when she put in a new roll. Lynne was an untidy bugger. Branded fleece on, to keep out the chill from the fridges, Chloe was good to go.

She smiled. This new, more organised version of herself was still taking some getting used to. But although she was a different creature, she was a definite improvement on the previous model. Chloe Mark II had been born out of the events of the awful weekend just after her father died. It was a weekend that had changed the dynamic within the family, for ever, and for good.

At the time, of course, it hadn't felt good; it had felt terrifying. Things had been said that should have been left unsaid. Tempers had been lost. Feelings trampled on. They had all behaved badly in one way or another, especially towards Megan.

After the huge argument between Chloe and Noah, Liv had refused to have everything more to do with the execution of the will or the sale of the house. Chloe had initially assumed that her sister was acting out of anger and fatigue, and that – after she'd calmed down – Liv would take up the reins once again, driving the whole thing through with her usual ruthless efficiency. But Liv had been as good as her shouted words and refused to get involved, at all, with the thousands of decisions and actions required to dissolve and distribute their father's estate. At first Chloe had been confused, then the panic had set in. Because – surprise, surprise – Noah had proved to be of very little practical use.

It had all fallen to Chloe.

The revelation was that it had all been doable – with a lot of help from the ever-patient Ms Hewson. The mounds of paperwork, getting her head around the money-laundering rules and regulations, the complexities of structural surveys, the chasing of estate agents, the liaising with the banks. They had found a buyer for The View very quickly, which had delighted Noah, but only served to ramp up the pressure.

But Chloe had managed it all. And without Liv breathing down her neck, it had been surprisingly okay. Scary, but okay. And with each email and call that Chloe had made, she'd grown in confidence, to the point where she was no longer pretending to be competent – she *was* competent.

The queue of two people, who had been watching her preparations, shuffled impatiently. Let them wait – all of one minute. When she was good and ready, she smiled and started bipping and scanning, on polite autopilot.

The discovery of the house purchase in Darlington had been a shock, of course. But even that, Chloe believed she'd handled well. Or at least with a maturity that would have been beyond her only a few months earlier.

She'd slept on it for a couple of nights and only then called Liv. It had been an awkward and surprisingly short conversation. Liv had confirmed that she already knew about the property, and that she personally believed Megan was morally and legally entitled to the house. Liv then lobbed her bomb, telling Chloe she was happy to leave the decision on whether to tell their brother about it up to her. At the time it had felt like a cop-out, but in hindsight, Chloe recognised their conversation as the pivotal moment when her relationship with both her siblings changed.

She had solved the problem of Megan's secret legacy by sharing it with Liv and keeping it from Noah.

Chloe's reasons for keeping quiet about the house were many.

Top of the list was a desire to respect her father's wishes. He had bought the property for Megan, therefore it was only right she should have it. Chloe's decision also held within it her ill ease about how been cruel they had been to Megan, not only in the wake of her father's death, but for years. She agreed with Liv: the house in Darlington went some way to rebalancing the scales. And, she reasoned, Noah knowing about it would only cause more upset and aggro, and they had had enough of that. But above all, it was the romance of the gesture that Chloe responded to. The thought of her father going to such lengths to buy back the home Megan had given up, in order to be with him, reflected the type of world Chloe wanted to inhabit. It spoke of love, and she still wanted to believe in love.

As the months passed and the pain of her father's death softened and became more malleable, Chloe was surprised at how frequently she thought of Megan. She often wondered how she was getting on. Chloe had no idea. Once Megan had moved out of The View, they had had very little contact; and what contact they did have had been through Greenwood's. Megan had literally vanished out of their lives – just as they had always thought they wanted her to. Chloe had texted her a couple of times asking how things were going, but she'd had no response. She didn't blame her; indeed, on some level Chloe admired Megan. She had stayed while Jonathan needed her. Left when he was gone. Megan proved it was possible: leaving somewhere you loved, even with grief weighing you down.

There was another lull in customers. Chloe let her mind roam.

As always, she found herself back in the rat-run of dilemmas about her own future. The key difference was that now she had money – a considerable amount of money – plenty to change her life beyond all recognition, and some hard-earnt but very valuable self-belief.

She could give notice on her rented flat – though she liked the view across the bay and the high ceilings, they reminded her of home. She still missed living in The View. She often strolled past the top of the drive, just to check on the comings and goings. There was always at least one workman's van outside: different trades, different days. The sound of drilling and hammering could be clearly heard from the road. The new family wasn't moving in until the house had been renovated. Chloe didn't like to imagine walls coming down and windows being taken out, but that was their prerogative as the new owners. Breathing life into an old house. It was what people did.

She could be gone in a month. She could move to whatever city she chose. Rent or buy somewhere nice. Put down roots. Or travel, anywhere in the world. Or bite the bullet and retrain for a new career. Alternatively she could do something worthwhile – volunteer for something she cared passionately about.

She could be anything she wanted to be.

Do whatever she wanted to do.

But whatever she did, she was going to have to do it alone.

'Well, good morning, my dear. How are you, this fine spring day?' It was Harold, resplendent in his lightweight suit. He carefully lifted his pack of ham, his small, white sliced loaf and his two tins of soup – one oxtail, one vegetable – onto the conveyor belt. His hands were cramped with arthritis. She was relieved to see him. He'd not been into the store for a few days, and that was unlike him.

'Good afternoon, Mr Webster. We've missed you this past week.'

He was struggling to unfurl his ancient string bag. Chloe knew better than to insult him by offering to help. The girl behind Mr Webster – blonde crop, sportswear, beautiful, in every other day for her lunch – indicated that she was in no rush. At last he got his bag untangled. 'I've just been a little under the weather. But I'm A-okay now.'

'I'm pleased to hear it. Are you enjoying the sunshine?' Chloe asked.

'I am indeed. Makes all the difference, doesn't it, my dear?'

'It does.' Chloe smiled. The girl behind Mr Webster smiled – at Chloe.

She scanned his goods. He carefully put them into his shopping bag, taking his time. He paid in cash – as always. She counted out his change into his shaking blue-veined hand. Wallet stowed in his trouser pocket, bag shouldered, he tipped his hat at her.

'Goodbye, Chloe. I'll be seeing you soon.' He walked away slowly, leaning heavily on his stick.

A veggie wrap, a packet of nuts and seeds and a bottle of water. A health junkie. It showed. She never bought crisps.

'Does he come in often?'

'Mr Webster. Yeah. Most days.'

'Bit like me then?' The girl smiled. Blue eyes. No, or very little, make-up. She didn't need it.

Chloe smiled back. The atmosphere shifted. Chloe was almost sure of it. She took a risk. 'Not at all like you in other ways!' She felt herself flush. 'I'm Chloe.'

'So I gather.' They looked at each for a long second. 'I'm Natasha. Tash to my friends.'

Chloe risked a glance. 'Nice to meet you, Tash.'

The girl laughed, a short, loud, carefree bark of a laugh. 'Likewise.' She picked up her lunch. 'Same time tomorrow then?' A raised eyebrow.

'I'll be here.'

She sashayed away. Chloe watched her, heart rattling. At the end of the row of tills, Tash stopped and glanced back.

Perhaps there was a reason to stay after all.

Chapter 60

IT WAS 8.45 a.m. by the time Liv handed over her last patient. Home time. She'd been feeling much better of late, her symptoms less onerous – or perhaps she'd just got used to living with them.

She opened her locker, collected her bag and fished out her phone. There were two new messages. The first was from Angus, checking what time she'd be home and reminding her that the plumber was coming to fit the new shower in the downstairs bathroom – he did at least sign off with an emoji heart. The second message was from Chloe, wishing her well on her last day. Liv's relationship with Chloe was so much better than it had been. It was still delicate and tentative – they had a lot of old baggage to unpack – but since Chloe had stepped up and Liv had stepped back, they had begun to communicate. Not only was there more respect, there was more affection.

She retrieved her jacket. Her locker looked shockingly empty.

A flash of sadness ripped through Liv. This was the last time she would finish a shift for quite a while, the last time she would lead a team, make life-and-death decisions, be the professional she'd striven so long and hard to become.

Letting go of the things that used to define you was scary.

Colette's voice startled her. 'Where are you sneaking off to?'

'Home.'

'Hell, no. You need to come with me.' Colette tugged her by the arm back onto the ward and there, at the central station, were her colleagues bearing gifts, with daft grins on their faces.

Lou, the senior sister, had obviously been nominated to give the speech. 'As you all know, Dr Coulter is leaving us today. "Rat and sinking ship" comes to mind, but I've been warned by senior management to be more positive about her dumping us in the shit while she swans off on maternity leave, so I'll do my best.' She mock-cleared her throat. 'We couldn't let her skulk away without saying something... nice, heartfelt and obviously very short, given we have a waiting room full of people, and I believe the patient in bay six is still anxiously anticipating his enema.' There was a ripple of laughter. 'Anyway, we all wanted to say congratulations, and good luck. We're going to miss you – something rotten. You've been an absolute pain... sorry, pleasure to work with – most of the time! Particularly in Resus.'

Liv had a reputation for high standards, bordering on intolerance, which she was proud of; and which was, she believed, justified by the number of crash patients she'd saved over the years.

'But I'm getting off track. We hope everything goes well. We'd toast your departure if we could, but you know the rules about drinks on the unit as well as anyone else. So, cheers.' They all raised imaginary glasses to her. 'Oh, and we also thought we should warn you: young Dr Amit here says he should be doing his stint on Maternity around your due date, so if you want to avoid him popping up at the business end with a pair of forceps, you might want to think about having this baby over at St Mary's!'

As they hugged her and her seven-month bump, Liv was overcome by affection for her colleagues, and by the realisation that this would be the last time she'd see many of them for at least eight months. Possibly longer. But she and Angus had agreed: this time she was taking her maternity leave – in full. No going back to work only weeks after the birth; no expressing milk like a cow, sitting on the side of the bath crying; no nanny turning up at 6.30 a.m.; no blur of too much to do, and far too little time and energy to do any of it well. No endless anxiety that she was in danger of killing a patient or her child, or herself, through tiredness. Because this time she was having her baby like a sensible person.

The thought was a huge relief.

The memory that she had, however briefly, contemplated sacrificing their child for her career now horrified her. The insane period around the time of her dad's death seemed a lifetime ago. She was not that woman any more.

The breakthrough had come the night they'd gathered on the beach, not as they stood together near the heat and the light, but as they'd walked back up to The View in the darkness.

Once the 'ceremony' of scattering the ashes into the flames had been completed, the kids had collapsed with tiredness. Angus somehow managed to hoist Freddie *and* Arthur onto his back for the long hike back up to the house – it was a good job he had broad shoulders. Noah carried Lily. She was already fast asleep, her thumb wedged in her mouth. But despite their respective burdens, Angus and Noah were still far quicker up the twisty path than Liv. She soon fell to the back of the group, her feet leaden, her head down. At one point she stopped completely and watched the wavering light of their phones flickering through the trees. She had no momentum. The stress, the arguments, the showdown with Noah, it had all taken it out of her. They forged ahead without looking back. It was tempting to let them go.

Another child.

It wasn't possible.

She couldn't do it.

Not again.

It was too much.

'Liv?' Her mother appeared at her side. 'Come here, sit down for minute.' There was a bench, perfectly positioned to take in the view of the old town and the castle headland. Liv allowed her mother to take her hand and lead her over to it. The lights on the sea front curved elegantly around the bay. 'Do you want to talk about it?'

She considered her mother's offer seriously, as she did most things. 'Who says there's an "it"?'

Eloise turned to face her. 'Liv! As you know, all too well, there's always an "it" when you have a family. Is it you and Noah? Are you still at loggerheads? He's stubborn. You're stubborn. You'll get sick of being mad with each other, eventually.'

'No. It's not that.' Liv didn't have the energy to be worrying about the state of her relationship with her brother. That was the least of her concerns. She stared at the lights. She had a husband and two children who mattered more to her than anything in the world, but they were already too much. How could she possibly cope with the burden of another child at her age? A child conceived in error, for God's sake.

'Talk to me!' Eloise insisted.

Liv caved in. 'I'm pregnant. Angus doesn't know. I can't keep it.'

Eloise simply said, 'Oh!'

Out at sea a solitary trawler bobbed and blinked in the darkness.

'Can't? Or don't want to?' Eloise asked.

It was a good question. 'Can't,' she said. It was what she believed. Liv made her decisions logically and carefully – and working full time, at a demanding, stressful, 'ridiculous hours' career whilst trying to raise not two but three children, just wasn't possible.

'Because?' Her mother was being deliberately obtuse. She must know why?

'My job.'

'So you're saying your career takes precedence over having another child... at the moment? It's perfectly okay if that's true – but I just want to check.'

'What do you mean, "at the moment"?'

'Liv. You're pregnant... now. You have your career and the huge responsibilities that come with that job... now.' She paused. 'But "now" is not for ever. What I'm saying is: you have choices. You could keep working as you are and have another baby later on, or not, if you decide not to. Or you could take some maternity leave and have this baby now, then find a different job, or even go back to the same, job later on. It's a question of timing – and working out what's right for you.' The trawler disappeared over the horizon. 'I think that might be part of the problem. You deciding what you want.'

Liv felt a wave of exasperation with her mother. She lived a life wholly determined by her personal desires. Did she not see the difference? Liv was trapped in a web of responsibilities and obligations. What she wanted barely mattered.

Her mother squeezed her hand. 'Liv. Ever since you were a child you've always done what's been asked of you. And done it amazingly well. But pleasing other people is a dangerous substitute for making your own decisions. And,' she smiled, 'it's a bit of a cop-out.' Liv tried to pull her hand away, but Eloise held on to it. 'My advice, for what it is worth, is to stop thinking about what you need to do and work out what you *want* to do.' She stood and pulled Liv to her feet. 'But for now, I suggest we get back up to the house. If we don't, Angus will be sending out a search party.'

They walked onwards and upwards.

Eloise kept hold of Liv's hand all the way.

By the time they'd reached the top of the climb, Liv had made her decision.

A little girl.

A sister for the boys.

She couldn't wait.

Work would.

It was time for her to focus on her own family.

At least for a little while.

Chapter 61

NOAH GOT an Uber back from the airport. As it neared home, the sensation that his insides were peeling away became almost unbearable. His last few conversations with Josie had been incredibly strained. The demands and denials that used to characterise their exchanges had been replaced by a profound, stultifying wariness of each other. This is what happened when even the commitment to argue ran out. Lily had tried to fill the gap, but it was obvious she was aware of the tension. Their daughter's increasingly desperate attempts to get her parents to speak to each other had been shaming. Perhaps that was why they had ended up beached on hollow topics, such as the leaky guttering at the back of the house and what Lily was going to wear for World Book Day. Noah knew Josie was waiting for him to get home for the real showdown. And given that he was arriving home mid-morning on a weekday, and Lily would be at school, there was every chance that the final act of their relationship was about to be played out.

He was so tired he almost welcomed it.

They had to have one last fight. Josie had to accuse him outright of the infidelity she suspected him of, and that he had not dissuaded her from believing in. He had to fudge his answers yet again, infuriate her, escalate it so quickly and horribly that she threw him out. It had to be her who made the decision. That way, there could be no going back.

The knowledge that he would not be unpacking his bag, crawling into their bed, sleeping – oh my God, sleep – then waking up when Lily got home and rocketed into their bedroom, battering him with cuddles and questions, hurt. But Noah was too far in; he had undermined Josie's trust in him so much, set her so far down the path of wanting him gone. He had to tough it out and get over the line.

He climbed out of the car and it drove away. He walked through their gate up to their front door. Waited. Josie did not come and open up. The days of her waiting by the window, holding Lily in her arms, were long gone. Noah dug his keys out of his bag and opened the door, to be greeted by the familiar sight of their too-narrow, chipped-paint hallway.

Home.

He didn't shout her name. Couldn't – he didn't trust himself. He headed into the kitchen at the back. It was the nicest room in the house: big, warm, as much living room as kitchen. Josie was standing with her back to the garden, resting against the sink, looking straight at him, her arms crossed.

'Hi.' To his surprise, his voice did work.

'Hello.' She didn't move.

He walked into the room and dropped his bag. They stood facing each other. Josie's expression softened and she put her hand out. 'You look tired. Come and sit down, Noah.' He knew he shouldn't, but he let her take his hand and guide him to the sofa. She gently pushed him into it and fetched him a glass of water. He took a couple of gulps.

She pulled up a chair and sat opposite him. His courage failed. He couldn't do it. But he had to. He didn't get the chance.

Josie's eyes didn't leave his face. 'This has got to stop, Noah. All the pretending. I know what's going on.'

'I don't—'

She cut him off. 'Yes, you do. I know why you've been behaving so oddly. Why you keep running away from us.' She took a shallow breath. 'I know you're ill and you're frightened.' She sounded brave, but her eyes said otherwise.

It was like a ship tilting; everything seemed to slide and crash to one side. 'How?'

'Megan wrote to me.'

'Megan?' The deck tilted again.

'Yes. She found out, from Eloise, that things weren't good between us.'

It didn't make sense. Megan was out of their lives now. Why would she get involved? And how come his mother and Megan were talking? He thought none of them had had any contact with her since she moved out. 'But I don't understand.' The jet lag, the shock and the already-screwed bits of his brain were all conspiring against him.

'She and your mum must have kept in touch.' Josie rested her hand on his leg. Her touch undid him. 'It doesn't matter how Megan knew. That's not important.'

He looked at her slim fingers and ached to touch her, but he didn't.

Josie's voice firmed up. 'Noah! Listen to me. Eloise must have talked to her about how you've been behaving. Something must have clicked. Megan remembered a conversation she apparently had with you that weekend, at the house, when you went over to sort out your dad's will.'

It came back to Noah in sudden startling clarity: sitting in the lounge in The View, in the winter sun, talking about his father's death. He hadn't sworn Megan to secrecy. He hadn't thought he needed to because, at the time, he didn't realise he was revealing his crappy hand.

With a telepathy developed over nearly ten years of living together, Josie answered his unspoken question. 'She wrote to me about what you talked about that day. She said that, out of nowhere, you started asking about your dad's illness and death. Not general questions – things any grieving son might feel the need to know – but really personal stuff about what his first symptoms were, how quickly things deteriorated, how they coped as a couple. Very intense questions. Megan said it felt like what she told you really mattered, but in a way that, at the time, she didn't grasp. What surprised her the most' – at this point Josie increased the gentle pressure on his leg – 'was how keen you were, suddenly, to know what it had been like for her having to look after your dad. She said it was the first time anyone in the family had ever bothered to ask how hard it had been for her to watch Jonathan get ill and die. She put two and two together.'

It was his last chance. He tried, but it was a feeble attempt to keep his plan on track. 'And came up with twelve—'

'No, she came up with four,' Josie interrupted him, taking control. 'Noah,' she pinned him with her eyes, 'have you inherited MND from your dad?'

There was a moment when they were suspended in time,

before their futures switched tracks and crashed, then he said simply, 'Yes.' Jesus, it was such a relief.

As if they were one, they breathed out together.

Neither of them said anything. They didn't fall into each other's arms or cry or shout or even move. They just sat opposite each other, with the truth irretrievably there, slap-bang in front of them. It eventually fell to Josie to pick it up and start dealing with it. 'How long have you known?'

'Known? For definite? Four months.' He'd had it confirmed by a neurologist, privately, a month after their dad's funeral. That had been a doozy of a late Christmas present. 'Suspected?' He tried to convey how deeply sorry he was in his tone of voice. 'About seven or eight months, maybe a little longer.'

'So you're in the early stages.' He nodded. 'Symptoms?' she asked.

'Tiredness. Some pain in my joints. My hips and my right arm are the worst.' Josie's expression was unbearable. 'But nothing I haven't experienced after a heavy night out.' So it began – the joking and minimising. Neither of them laughed.

Josie bit her lip. 'Oh, Noah. All this time! Why on earth didn't you tell me?'

'I'm sorry. I thought it was for the best. I was trying to keep it away from you and Lily.'

'For the best!' Josie's voice rose an octave. 'Abandoning us. Running away. Letting me think... all sorts. What exactly was the plan, Noah?'

He couldn't look at her. He focused on the cracked floor tile in front of the cooker. 'At first it was just that I didn't know how to break it to you, but as things went downhill for Dad and I saw the impact on him, I came to the conclusion you'd be better off without me, once I'd sorted out the inheritance. So I decided to fuck us up.' He stopped, shocked by his own brutality. 'My plan was to make you so fed up with me, so pissed off, you'd think that me leaving was better than me staying.'

'And what was that supposed to achieve, other than hurting and confusing me, and Lily?' she pushed.

He sighed, defeated. 'It would put some distance between us. I'd move out and we'd split up. I was trying to get it all sorted before it became obvious I was ill and you were tied to me until the bitter end.'

'Like you think Megan was?'

He nodded. It sounded stupid, said out loud, but was it really that ludicrous to try and protect the people you loved most?

Josie suddenly changed the dynamic in the room by getting up and going over to the dresser. She opened a drawer, came back with a copy of an email in her hand.

'I want you to listen to something. And, Noah, I mean really listen. This is what Megan wrote:

> I've thought long and hard about whether to write to you or not. I very nearly didn't. I don't really know you, and you don't know me. I have no idea what your marriage to Noah is like, or what sort of husband he is. No one knows what someone else's relationship amounts to, not really. But, given the circumstances, I think my experience might be relevant – whether it's helpful is up to you to decide.
>
> What I've learnt, having lived with, and lost, Jonathan, is that any relationship worth hanging on to is a partnership. It's two individuals with separate identities, likes, dislikes, views, emotions, opinions, who forge a bond that ties them together,

for better and for worse. It's a couple. Two people. Not one. You don't meld into each other, like the books and films would have us believe. That's romantic crap. Love is a choice, an active decision you have to make every single day – every moment of every day. When someone falls ill and their illness becomes terminal, that choice becomes a promise.

Josie's voice wavered, but she took a breath and read on strongly, clearly, filling the kitchen with Megan's words:

I still don't know what I would have done if I'd known Jonathan was going to get ill when I met him – was, in fact, already ill. But I know I chose to love him.

It was my choice to start a relationship with him, when I knew he was married. My choice not to back off, when it all came out. My choice to want him enough to stick it out and face the wrath of his family, until Eloise walked away. And, when he fell ill, I still had choices to make, though they were obviously far harder.

I think you have the right to decide what happens in your relationship with Noah, however impossible those choices may seem.

Josie took a breath to pace herself. She looked up at Noah, double-checking he was listening. He met her steady gaze, feeling anything but steady. She read the last few lines slowly:

If Noah has MND, I am truly sorry. If he hasn't, then I'm glad, but I'm still sorry, because your relationship sounds like it is under threat either way. Whichever it is, I wish you luck. I really do. I won't contact you again. Please forgive me for intruding, but I felt I had to. Megan.

Josie laid the sheets of paper on the floor. 'So you see, Noah, Megan did make her own choices. She wanted to be there for your dad because she loved him. And I love you. And I think you need to respect and trust me enough to make up my own mind about how we deal with this.'

Only then did they embrace, fiercely and firmly.

Noah cried. Josie did not.

Eventually she pulled away from him. 'Go up and get some sleep. I'll be here. I'm not going anywhere. I'll wake you in time for us to go and pick up Lily together. She's been *so* looking forward to you coming home.'

Noah wiped his face on his sleeve.

Josie kissed him, softly, on the lips and smiled. 'And so have I.'

Chapter 62

SUNLIGHT, SHOWERS and an enamel rainbow.

Jonathan had been right after all.

Time travel was possible.

The little front garden was in need of attention, the previous owners had obviously had very little interest in gardening. Only the lilac by the gate seemed to be thriving. It was smothered in a canopy of heavy, pure-white blossoms. As Megan ducked beneath the loaded branches, a burst of perfume descended on her. A benediction, welcoming her home. She walked up the eight steps to the blockwork path slowly, taking in her surroundings. Someone had painted the door an insipid light blue. It used to be a shiny dark red. She was going to have so many decisions to make about what to keep and what to change.

She slid the key into the lock. Turned it.

Heard her heartbeat thud in her ears.

Anticipation. An unfamiliar but welcome emotion.

The door opened onto the sitting room. No hallway, no preamble – just straight into the heart of the house. The room was empty, stripped bare of all but small reminders of its most recent inhabitants: a scatter of fingermarks on the switch plate, a dent behind the front door where the handle had dinged against the plaster, holes in the walls where their pictures had hung. Megan made a quick mental note of all these small injuries to the fabric of the house. The beginning of a list of things she would need to put right.

She dropped her bag at the foot of the stairs, walked into the middle of the room and turned 360 degrees, taking in every little detail. She hadn't realised how small the house was before, but anywhere would seem cramped after the high ceilings and large rooms of The View.

But it would do.

It had suited her before.

It would again.

She took another slow rotation, like a ballerina in a jewellery box, but without the tutu and the tinkling music. As she did so, she caught sight of the woman in the mirror above the fireplace. There was nothing fragile and glittery about her. She was in her mid-thirties. Her hair was caught up in a loose bun at the nape of her neck. She had pale skin. Good cheekbones. Dark-blue eyes. The woman in the mirror lifted her chin and looked straight at Megan. Her stare was steady and resolute.

Jonathan had sent her back to a new beginning.

What happened next was down to her.

Step one: she would wait for 'the man with the van' to arrive. He was bringing her stuff from the storage unit. There wasn't a lot – a few sticks of furniture, her kitchenware, her bedding and some other bits and pieces. She'd taken very little from The View. Why take what was never hers? In truth, she could barely remember what she'd packed away during those bleak few weeks over Christmas. By that point all she'd wanted to do was get away from the house.

It had snowed the day she moved out, which seemed fitting.

Sarah had insisted that Megan come and stay with them for a while – be around a loving family, for a change. It had been the right decision. Those quiet, sad months of the new year had allowed her to grieve, to start to recover and to plan. She would for ever be grateful to her sister for that much-needed period of support and respite.

But now it was time to put her plan into action.

Over the next few days she would clean the house from top to bottom, get the Internet sorted, stock her fridge, maybe even find time to dig some dandelions out of the handkerchief of a lawn and put in some new plants – a signal to the neighbours that the house was owned once again, cared for once again. She wondered how many of them she would still know, how many would recognise her? She would need to have an explanation ready for her return to the house after all these years – a heavily edited version.

Then, in a fortnight's time, she would begin work. Supply teaching at a large comprehensive with a poor Ofsted rating, on the outskirts of Middlesbrough. Tough area. Tough kids. The thought made her heart thump – with trepidation and excitement. It would be a fire-and-brimstone baptism back into real life. But what better choice was there than a school full of disaffected kids consumed by their own issues and problems?

She had been a good teacher and mentor of just such kids before.

They used to be her forte.

They had been her path to Jonathan.

They could, perhaps, be her salvation now.

She walked through to the back room, which merged into the galley kitchen that led out onto the tiny yard. A nice, straightforward 'what you see is what you get' house. The back room looked even shabbier than the front – more gouges and marks on the walls. Purple! Who in their right mind painted an already-dark room the colour of a prune? She was going to need Polyfilla and paint, lots and lots of paint. No matter, it would give her something to do. DIY, another step to reasserting her ownership of the house.

As she drifted around, touching surfaces and walls, reacquainting herself with what was, once again, hers, the tightness that had been ever-present in her chest for the past year began to ease. For the first time in months Megan felt full of energy. She lifted the blind, opened the back door and let the fresh air flood in. She took a deep breath, another and another.

The insipid blue front door, the purple walls, whatever technicoloured horrors lay in wait for her upstairs, the dents and scratches and marks, the scruffy evidence of other people in her home – she would get rid of it all.

She would paint the whole house white.

A perfect blank canvas.

She heard the sound of a vehicle reversing: the 'man with the van' pulling up outside her new address. *Ms Megan Brooke, 16 Thorpe Road, Darlington, DL1 1AG.*

A new start in her old home.

It was time to lay claim to her legacy.

Acknowledgements

WE GET through life, if we're lucky, because people care for us. Yet so much of the caring that takes place in society goes unseen and unrecognised.

So my acknowledgements are simple.

I want to say 'thank you' to everyone who shoulders the responsibility of looking after others.

That includes all the dedicated, hard-working staff at Leeds Weekend Care Association, Henshaws, Farfield House and Wheatfelds Hospice in Leeds.

Closer to home, my admiration goes out to Linda, who knows the cost and the importance of caring; to my sister Sue, for being a great foster mum; and to my sister-in-law Liz, for having the patience of a saint when it came to getting Pritt Stick out of Alan's carpet.

I would also like to thank Christina Taylor at Morrish Solicitors in Pudsey for our very useful conversation about wills and Statements of Wishes.

Lastly, should you venture to Sandsend, there is an excellent café near the beach that serves great crab sandwiches, good coffee and a wide selection of lovely cakes, but there are, as yet, no padlocks on the railings.